Judson Lovell

And they shall drive thee from men, and thy dwelling shall be with the beasts of the field: they shall make thee to eat as oxen, and seven times shall pass over thee, until thou know that most High ruleth in the kingdom of men, and givith it to whomsoever he will.

The same hour was the thing fulfilled upon Nebuchadnezzar: and he was driven from men, and did eat grass as oxen, and his body was wet with the dew of heaven, till his hairs were grown like eagles' feathers and his nails like birds' claws.

Daniel 4:32 & 4:33

SKINNERS

A Novel

By

Judson Lovell

Cover Design
Tamera Lucas & Judson Lovell

Literary Consultants
Michelle Richards & Mikayla Blackstocks

SKINNERS

Lizard King Publications
Lincoln City, Oregon

E-mail
lizardkingpublications@yahoo.com

Mail Orders Welcome
$15.00 - First Edition
Purchaser Responsible For Own
Applicable Tax

For $15.00
I'll Cover
Shipping & Handling
USA Only
Single Edition Orders

ISBN 978-1-60458-842-2
Original WGA 629543
(Shapeshifters)

INTRODUCTION

I've always found it fascinating over the years when talking to friends on which entity they would like to become. We all fantasize at one time or another about being something else; a wizard, a fairy, an elf, a witch, a vampire or even a werewolf. I've always been partial to Lycanthropes. "An American Werewolf in London" written and directed by John Landis is still my favorite.

However, over the years, special effects has been advancing, like in the "Underworld" series. Notable films include; "Wolf", "Dog Soldiers", "Van Helsing", "Silver Bullet", "The Company of Wolves" and even the first in the modern horror genre, "The Howling" series. Yet, all of our Hounds of Hell are represented as evil. Why is that?

Clive Barker made a film called, "Nightbreed". It had a few shapeshifting characters. However, the film did not concentrate on them throughout the storyline. They were characters supporting the plot and not the plot itself.

"Ladyhawke" is unlike these other mentioned films. It is a depiction of Shapeshifters restrained by a curse. Rutger Hauer plays Captain Etienne Navarre with Michelle Pfeiffer playing Isabeau d'Anjou. They are always together, yet always apart; night and day separates them. Navarre exists in his human form during the day, as Isabeau is a hawk. During the night, Isabeau exists in her human form, as Navarre is a black wolf. Neither of them are evil... they are simply cursed.

What if the art of shapeshifting was a gift and not a curse? Would the person use the gift of transformation for good or abuse it? What if it was an "at will" gift instead of a punishment or uncontrollable urge? Why would Shapeshifters be confined to Lycanthropes? What would distinguish different types and different species of Shapeshifters? You're about to find out...

Don't Dream It... Be It!
Judson Lovell

~ I ~

"I'm not gonna let you die," Gordon says in a fatherly tone. He clutches onto Sonja's cold hand and tightly squeezes it. The low, annoying sounds of the medical equipment surrounding them is a constant distraction.

There are no windows in Sonja's private hospital room and the ceiling is lower than usual. If Gordon were to stand, he could easily reach up and touch the frosty surface. The room strangely resembles a commercial freezer in the back area of a trendy restaurant.

The walls of the room are filled with an assortment of large stuffed animals and children's toys. A hand carved rocking horse stands off in the corner, quiet and unused for some time now.

Numerous framed pictures are seen about the sparse counter space of the room. Photos of Sonja's father, Gordon's brother, holding her in his arms with mom close by. Other images are of her father and mother playing with her. The loving family looks happy together. It was nice while it lasted.

Gordon reaches over to a bedpan filled with ice cubes and stale water and dunks in a washcloth. He tenderly presses the frigid cloth against his niece's forehead, as if to sooth a breaking fever. Yet, she does not have a fever... it's something else. She's going to die and there's nothing he can do about it.

Gordon Jamison is a charming looking man with thin facial features. Although only in his late twenties, he shows slight signs of graying above his ears. His hair is short and coarse. It is unsure of Gordon's heritage, he's possibly of Jewish descent.

Gordon's six foot frame seems to tower over his five year old niece as he refreshes the cold cloth and wipes her forehead. He continues to assist in keeping her temperature very low. "I see you're wearing the nightgown I bought you," he whispers to Sonja.

Sonja's golden locks of hair appear matted under her head. Her eyes remain closed, yet fluttering. Although she remains in her therapeutic hypothermia induced coma, Sonja senses that her uncle is there for her.

An experimental IV bag hangs from a hook near the heart monitor. An extremely chilled solution drips from the clear bag and runs along the hose into Sonja's blood system. The cold intravenous fluid infusion maintains her hypothermic condition.

She lays on a cooling blanket with chambers filled with circulating cold water. The blanket keeps Sonja's core temperature at a near freezing level. A hose runs from the side of the blanket to a medical component about the size of a standard air conditioner unit. The component circulates the cold water through the hose with a low humming sound.

The nasal cannula supplying her oxygen would be a constant irritation if she were conscious. The constant low beeping sounds of her pulse echo throughout the room from the wheeled cart of medical equipment. "Mr. Jamison, visiting hours are over," a pleasant looking nurse quietly says from the slightly opened door of Sonja's vacuum sealed private room.

Gordon places the damp cloth into the bedpan and stands. The ice cubes rattle. He tenderly kisses Sonja on the forehead and smiles, "I'll see you tomorrow." Gordon turns and quietly shuffles passed the nurse, who approaches the far side of Sonja's bed.

Gordon makes his way along the sterile hallway. There is neither waiting patients on gurneys for treatment nor the expected doctors or nurses making their rounds. The special C.D.C. wing of the hospital appears to be cold and lifeless.

Gordon approaches the end of the hallway and faces a thick transparent door. On opposite sides of the door, transparent walls extend outward and appear secured to the solid walls of the hallway. Gordon reaches up along the solid wall and presses the intercom's button. He looks up toward the surveillance camera and gives a slight wave.

The transparent door clicks and pops open. Gordon steps inward and closes the door behind himself. He stands in the center of a small transparent room at the end of the hallway. An identical transparent door and see-through support walls stand directly in front of himself.

The overhead florescent lights dim. Gordon raises his arms and hands in a scarecrow manner and waits for the scanning process to begin. Ultraviolet light floods the small transparent room. Eerie shades of blue and orange beam across Gordon's shoes and slowly makes their way upward.

Gordon slowly turns in a complete circle allowing the odd lights to scan his entire body. The lights run across his shoulders and face, pause a moment then dissipate.

The overhead florescent lights flicker on as the opposite facing transparent door clicks open. Gordon steps out from the small transparent room and continues along the sterile hallway leading out into the afternoon sun.

Gordon sits at the far table of the medical research laboratory staring into the lenses of his microscope. He is focused and diligent. The large room is cluttered with beakers, odd looking electronic equipment and Bunsen burners. Mazes of tubes and wires run across the numerous work stations and stainless steel tabletops. "Hey, Gordo," a voice calls out from the main doorway. Gordon continues to study the small sample on the thin glass under his microscope, seemingly ignoring the voice from behind.

Reece Taylor bounds into the laboratory toting a newspaper under his arm. He's an average looking man, slightly shorter than his fellow student at the University. "Hey, Gordo! You awake?"

"Yeah, I'm awake."

"Did you hear the news?" Reece asks as he removes the newspaper from under his arm and slaps it down onto the metallic tabletop next to Gordon. "Malcolm was shot yesterday. By his own kind."

"What do you mean *his own kind?"* Gordon replies with annoyance in his voice. He looks up at Reece with a slight scowl. "I thought we were *all* the same kind."

"That's *not* what I meant."

"I know what you meant," Gordon says with a condescending tone. He pauses a moment as he looks down at the newspaper's headlines;

MALCOLM X - ASSASSINATED IN HARLEM

"How's Sonja doing?" Reece asks, quickly attempting to change the subject.

"As well as can be expected," Gordon replies as he spins halfway around on his wheeled stool. "The doctors can't figure it out. They keep saying she's got something mutated like Lupus, Polio and MS all rolled into one. As long as she stays in her coma, the disease won't spread."

"I've been thinking about that. Over here." Reece motions his head for Gordon to follow. Reece and Gordon approach a metallic tabletop with a large set of balancing scales. Next to the scales, an electrical component with numerous levers, switches and an attached wand.

Reece reaches over to a glass fish bowl of sorts and retrieves a pair of steel ball bearings from a collection of about one hundred. He sets each of the ball bearings onto separate platters of the scales. They are equally weighted and balanced. "I was researching the similarities of the diseases and found that density is a factor in the degenerating muscle tissue."

"I was thinking about that as well."

"I came to the conclusion that if you could manipulate the density of the muscles, you could slow, halt or even cure the disease."

"How could you do that?"

"I'll show you," Reece says as he flicks on the switch of the electronic component. He removes one of the steel ball bearings and places it onto a wooden slab similar to a kitchen's chopping block. With the absence of the ball bearing, the scales become unbalanced and drastically shifts its weight with the remaining ball bearing remaining on the platter.

Reece takes the electronic wand in hand and waves it over the ball bearing resting on the wooden slab. An electric charge bombards the metallic sphere for several seconds. He switches off the electronic component and sets down the wand. "Now, watch. This is so cool!" Reece takes the ball bearing in hand and places back onto the empty platter of the scales.

CLANK!

The identical pair of steel ball bearings have become severely altered. One platter has been raised high above the balancing scales with the other resting on the metallic tabletop. "I manipulated the density, causing a ten to one ratio."

"That's fine and dandy for a steely but what about human tissue?"

"Don't know. It could cause paralysis, blindness, kidney failure... even death. I just don't know yet. I'll need to test a human subject."

"I can't take that chance with Sonja. Use a rat or something."

"A rat doesn't have what Sonja has. I need to start with a sample of her blood. If that shows promise, I'll need her bone marrow."

"There has to be another way," Gordon says with a disappointed sigh. "Density, huh? You might be onto something, Reece..."

The university's library is quiet and still. The overhead lights have been extinguished for the night. Rows upon rows of extended tables are seen throughout the vast assortment of shelved books. Lit table lamps provide the only traces of light.

Gordon sits in the center of an extended table with mounds of opened books all around himself. He looks worn and tired. Gordon flips through the pages of an older looking book and scans through the passages.

Taking a pen in hand, he scribbles down several entries into his notebook. Gordon slides the book away from himself and pulls another opened book closer. He reads a passage and adds it to his growing collection of handwritten notes and research.

Pulling yet another opened book closer to himself, he looks upon the images filling the page. A rare tribe of Pigmies, indigenous to the depths of the South American jungle, are seen. Gordon studies the picture for a long moment.

The men of the tribe wear next to nothing. It's not that they are shameless, they live in the jungle, there's no need to wear too much. Simple leather loincloths tied at their waists with several beaded strands. Necklaces made from animal teeth and a single bone sticking out sideways from the center area of their noses.

One male Pigmy stands along the furthest edge of a makeshift teeter-totter. A large stone rests on the ground in the middle of a coarse plank creating the balancing effect. The Pigmy stands firmly on the plank which rests on the floor of the jungle. Oddly enough, the opposite end of the teeter-totter is high in the air with five male Pigmies standing upon the plank.

Gordon slides a small piece of paper inside the binding of the book and marks his place. He flips through several pages until coming across another photo. Gordon stares for a long moment at the mysterious man.

The Shaman of the tribe looks directly into the camera's lens as the photo was taken. He appears to be unafraid of his soul being taken or any other Western beliefs that have been made up. He smiles, having no fear.

Upon the Shaman's head, the ears, eyes and muzzle of a black leopard, similar to a Native American Medicine Man's wolf headdress. The skinned, black leopard's fur coat and hide drape down along the Shaman's back, protecting him from evil.

The Shaman wears a similar leather loincloth with numerous beaded strands about his waist. Through the lower center area of his nose, a more pronounced animal bone sticks out sideways.

Gordon stares at the image of the Shaman for several moments. Reading the passage below the Shaman's image, he slaps the page of the opened book in triumph; he's found what he was searching for!

"Gordo, what are you doing?" Reece asks. Gordon continues to wrap several beakers with loose newspaper pages then carefully stuffs them into a large backpack. The laboratory is in disarray. It appears Gordon has ransacked it, searching for his much needed items.

"I'm going Reece," Gordon says with an urgent tone. "I found something that might just work."

"Going where?"

"Cordillera de la Costa."

"Venezuela? You know the University isn't going to fund that. You're on a personal quest to save your niece."

"Yeah, I know. It's a classic case of Government Groping. They have funding to research the lifespan of a moth, but no money to save a life."

"Where'd you get the camera?"

"I borrowed it from the drama department," Gordon says as he maneuvers himself toward the nearest metallic tabletop. "Never know what's gonna pop up."

He carefully picks up a sixteen millimeter camera and slides it into its case. Gordon moves around several reels of film inside of the case then zips it closed.

"Have you told Sonja yet?"

"I was on my way over there now. I've got a ship to catch."

"A ship? Wouldn't it be quicker to fly?"

"Sure, but a plane costs money. I have a friend of mine who works in the galley on a cargo ship. They're leaving tonight."

"A *friend?* I thought *I* was your only friend," Reece says with a smile. Gordon nearly laughs as he closes and secures the straps of his backpack.

"You are. That's why I'm going to ask you to look in on Sonja from time to time. Talk to her. She knows when you're there, I can feel it."

"How long are you going to be gone?"

"About two months. It takes about a week or so to get there and about the same time to back. I'll have about a month to find what I'm looking for," Gordon says as he quickly glances down at his wristwatch. "Man, I gotta go!"

Gordon and Reece stand there for a moment, awkwardly looking at each other. They give each other a brotherly hug. Reece reaches down and hands Gordon his backpack. "I'll keep trying to figure it out from here."

Reece motions toward the balancing scales, the fish bowl of ball bearings, the electrical component and the wand. He believes more in science than hocus-pocus. "See ya' in a few months."

"Don't forget what I said about Sonja... talk to her."

"I will. Now, get outta here!"

Gordon flings his backpack over his shoulder and shuffles toward the door. He takes his packed, military looking duffle bag in one hand and the camera case in the other. Gordon slightly turns and glances over toward Reece. He gives him an understanding nod then turns and exits without another word.

"Sonja? Can you hear me, dear?" Gordon asks in a near whisper. He moves about the counter areas of the private room placing additional framed pictures of himself on the flat surfaces. "I'm going away for awhile. But here, I'll always be with you."

Gordon places the last of the framed pictures on top of the nightstand next to her bed. "I'll find a cure for you. You've lost so much already. Don't give up on me. I won't give up on you, hon."

Sonja's eyes flutter. Her uncle's soft and tender words of encouragement embed themselves deep into her subconscious. She won't give up. She's a Jamison, just like her uncle, strong and bull headed.

Gordon appears anxious. He knows that the taxicab is waiting for him along the curb of the University's narrow roadway. He leans downward and kisses Sonja on the forehead. "Don't give up..."

"Hey, Doug," Gordon says nearly out of breath as he climbs the gangway. His duffle bag, backpack and camera case are increasing heavy due to the steep incline. The massive cargo ship towers over the smaller vessels secured along the maze of wharfs and docks.

"I didn't think you were gonna make it," Doug shouts down from the starboard side of the ship. Dockhands have already released the securing lines and have tossed them aside. As the gangway is slowly raised from the deck of the ship, the large vessel slowly pulls away from the wharf.

"I wouldn't miss it," Gordon says with a smile as he hops on deck. The deckhands scurry about, tying off lines and securing gear. Doug, a thin and slinky looking fellow, leans down and takes Gordon's duffle bag by the shoulder strap.

"It's not much, but let me show you were you'll be staying." Doug leads Gordon along the starboard side of the vessel, through a maze of gearboxes and levers as the ship continues to slowly move out and through the harbor.

"How many other passengers are there?"

"Technically... none. *You're* not even aboard. I owe you this, from that term paper, when I was a Freshman. We're even!"

"We're even," Gordon says with a smile. "It's good to see you, too."

"Come on, this way," Doug says, as he motions Gordon through an opened hatchway. Doug and Gordon disappear into the shadows, making their way deep into the lower levels of the ship.

"Man, this trip is about as eventful as watching grass grow," Gordon thinks to himself. He strolls along a lower passageway then enters an opened hatch. Gordon has made his way into one of the many cargo holds. Stacks upon stacks of fifty pound bags of wheat, rice and barley fill inner walls of the steel hull. *"We should almost be there."*

Gordon exits the cargo hold area and enters a narrow passageway. He passes by several opened hatchways leading into pump houses and gear rooms. At the far end of the corridor, the lower ranking seamen's living quarters.

Gordon steps through the opened hatchway leading into his room. It is extremely cramped, smaller than a submarine's living quarters. He has the room to himself. Alone and in solitude. Plenty of time to think. Think about how he's going to save his niece.

"I radioed ahead for you," Doug says, as he tosses Gordon's green duffle bag to the dock. "You'll meet your guide in about an hour. She'll take you in."

"She?"

"Yeah, you got a problem with girls?"

"Not that I'm aware of. No complaints yet."

"Well yeah, to your face."

"By the way, how's your sister?" Gordon gives Doug a playful slap on the arm. Gordon steps off the gangway and pauses, taking in the sights and sounds of the harbor city.

Local men dart across the docks, tightly clutching onto the handles of their rickshaws, transporting newly arrived American tourists. The sounds of brisk Latin music fills the air, seeping out from the acoustic instruments of the street performers.

Dockhands lift and carry large bags of rice and wheat from the opened cargo holds of numerous vessels along the wharf. Chaos of arriving and departing ships floods across the wooden planks. The moist air lingers, seeping into the area from the surrounding jungle. The humidity is almost unbearable. "We have to make a quick trip to Africa and back," Doug says.

Gordon continues to absorb his surroundings. This is nothing like where he grew up in Indiana. Has he bitten off more than he can chew? Can he do this on his own? *"Am I wearing clean shorts?"* Gordon thinks to himself. He extends out his hand toward Doug, "Thanks for everything." Gordon and Doug shake hands.

"Don't thank me, yet. You still have to get back home. We'll be back around the twelfth. That gives you about a month. Don't be late..."

"I won't. See ya' later."

"Later..." Doug says with a smile. Gordon tightens the shoulder straps of his backpack, leans down and takes his duffle bag in one hand and the camera case in the other.

He curiously looks around, taking in all the surrounding activity, as if he were being consumed by quicksand. Gordon disappears among the hundreds of moving bodies filling the dock, inviting him into their world.

"We should be there by tomorrow," Elez says as she wipes her brow. She is a dark-skinned, petite woman, standing around fifty-five inches tall. She is dressed in worn cargo pants and a sweat drenched T-shirt. Her mountain boots continue to lead them further and deeper into the jungle.

"What do I call him when I get there?"

"Call him?" Elez asks.

"Yes, call him. What's his name?"

"He has many names." Elez clutches onto the reins of the pack mule as they wind their way through a dense series of tropical trees. Gordon's green duffle bag, backpack and camera case appears strapped to one side of his mule with primitive sleeping gear and food supplies hanging along the other side. The thick foliage is beginning to close in on them.

"What do you call him?"

"I call him *father*," Elez says with a subtle smile. She continues onward, clutching onto the reins of the pack mule as Gordon struggles to keep pace close behind.

The jungle is darker than usual for this time of year. Gordon realizes that their conversations have ceased for some time now. Elez has become cautious of her surroundings. The towering trees narrow, creating a maze deeper into the jungle.

A shadowy figure catches Gordon's eye several yards away from them. The figure is difficult to make out through the towering trees and the sunlight which struggles to pierce through the above canopy. The image gallops along an unseen path and is joined by another.

Gordon quickly scans in opposite directions. Beyond the shadowy tree line, three other figures appear. He and Elez are surrounded. The figures stand slightly huddled together as if they were studying their prey, waiting for the right moment to attack.

Elez halts the pack mule. She is still and quiet. Gordon is at a near panic, trembling. Through the shadows, one of the figures stares at him. Gordon cannot make out the image's facial features; however, he *can* make out an outline.

The image stands upright with broad shoulders and a tapering waist similar to a large man. Yet, there is something different. It is not a man that he sees. It's something much worse. The figure lets out a low growl.

Gordon turns toward the opposite side of the narrow path as another figure hisses. Elez slowly walks backward, never taking her eyes off of the three figures huddled together. She stands next to Gordon and tenderly places her hand on his shoulder.

One of the shadowy images growls and sniffs the air. Another figure hisses. Gordon thinks he sees a long reptilian tongue flicking through the air. Elez remains steadfast at Gordon's side. The pack mule becomes uneasy and lets out a nervous snort. Gordon glances at the mule.

Elez slowly removes her hand from Gordon's shoulder and makes her way next to the pack mule. She pats the mule on the muzzle and grabs hold of the reins. Gordon looks in all directions. The mysterious figures have all vanished.

Gordon quickens his pace, coming up alongside of Elez. She looks at his puzzled expression. Thousands of questions are running through his head. Elez smiles at him and gives him a comforting nod.

"Elez, how can you see where you're going?" Gordon asks as he strains to see through the darkness. The tropical trees surround them. The sun has set many hours ago. Gordon clutches onto his secured duffle bag giving him bearing to the pack mule.

"I don't need to see where I'm going. *He* knows the way." Elez affectionately runs her hand down and along the mule's mane. She can sense he is getting worn and tired from the weight of the load. "We're almost home," Elez whispers in the mule's ear.

Gordon takes a sigh of relief. The tree line breaks, revealing a wide and slow moving river. Along the far side of the river, towering trees span out in opposite directions with no shoreline. The wall of trees abruptly stops at the waterline with no way in or out.

The mule begins to trot along a widening pathway. The slow moving river remains to the left of the hoofed beast as the tree line of the jungle towers to the right. Elez glances over to Gordon then motions ahead.

Elez's village comes into full view with the shore of the river nearly one hundred feet away. The wooden structures are common looking, without paint, shutters or even doors. The roofs are constructed of thick layers of grass with tanned hides covering the entryways and windows.

The dwellings are elevated by solid platforms and stilts, protecting them from the swelling river during the rainy season. Stepladders allow entry into the homes, planted solidly onto the ground then leading up through the doorways.

A crackling fire is seen along what appears to be the center of the village. The smoldering ash and cinders are surrounded by a circle of stones nearly twenty feet in diameter. A villager looks up from the flames. He is crouched down with his palms resting on his knees. He wears a simple leather loincloth and sandals.

The Pigmy appears unwavered by Gordon's arrival, like he was expecting him. "That is Puya, my brother." Elez slows the mule in front of the first wooden dwelling. "It is late. You will take my home."

"Thank-you, Elez." Gordon releases his duffle bag, backpack and camera case from the mule. Elez smiles at Gordon, turns and leads the mule deeper into the village. Puya stares at Gordon a long moment then returns to his hypnotic gaze into the dwindling flames.

Gordon tosses his backpack and duffle bag onto the wooden planked floor. The large, single room is neatly kept. A kitchen area is seen off to the side with pottery and vases. A handmade lantern hangs from the direct center of the room, casting off warm glows and dancing shadows.

There is a low standing table with no chairs for dining, just simple pillows for sitting. Several chests, handmade from indigenous vines, line the adjoining wall with numerous woman's dresses hanging from makeshift hooks. Finally, Gordon focuses his attention on... the bed! It will be joyous not to sleep on the ground or suffering through the rolling waves of the ocean.

Gordon places the camera case on the floor at the foot of the bed. The frame has been constructed with thick tree branches, secured together with vines and stands about one foot off of the floor.

Gordon sits on the edge of the bed and removes his hiking boots. He is worn out from his journey. Gordon swings his legs over and plops down onto the bed. The mattress is made from dried and tightly packed leaves which is surprisingly comfortable.

Gordon turns his head and realizes that the lantern is still lit. He motions as if to rise to extinguish the small flame but finds himself overwhelmed with exhaustion. Gordon falls back onto the bed, beginning a much needed rest.

"Good afternoon," a warm and charming voice says from behind Gordon's sixteen millimeter camera. The constant *click-click-click* of the film is quite annoying. The Shaman continues looking through the lens of the camera as Gordon struggles to adjust his sights, trying to focus on the Pigmy man hovering over him.

Gordon sits on the edge of the bed as the Shaman slightly backs away, continuing to roll the film for a few more moments, then lowers the camera. Gordon studies the pleasant looking man, standing nearly sixty inches tall.

The Shaman grins at Gordon, showing off all of his natural teeth. It is difficult to determine how old he is. However, Gordon estimates the Shaman is twice his age. He has no bone sticking out of the lower, central area of his nose. He wears no necklace made of animal teeth nor shows any signs of tattoos.

The Shaman's leather loincloth has been replaced by a pair of American jeans. "Slept the morning away. Let's get you something to eat," the Shaman says in perfect English as he places the camera onto the low standing dining table. He quickly turns and pulls back the tanned hide covering the entryway. Without another word, the Shaman is out the door.

Gordon finds his footing on the ground from the stepladder. The afternoon sun is warm on his face. The soothing sounds of tropical birds fills the air. The wide and slow moving river in front of him invites him for a bath. "Gordon!" the Shaman calls out.

Gordon makes his way deeper into the village. He is surrounded with activity. The Pigmy tribe has been up since before the sun. Along the shoreline, men continue to mend fishing nets and repair long canoe style boats. Pigmy children play and splash along the river. Several women of the tribe stay close to their homes, grinding seeds and preparing meals.

The Shaman appears standing outside of the centrally located hut, the most important looking structure of the village. He holds a large leaf in his hand and motions Gordon over.

As Gordon walks through the village, he is neither welcomed nor dismissed. He is looked upon neither as a stranger nor one of them. Simply, like he's always belonged.

Gordon begins to feel slightly foolish and embarrassed. The tribe is nothing how the pictures in the university's book depicted them. They are not primitives nor savage. The men wear an assortment of American jeans and shorts. Some wear handmade sandals as others go barefoot. The T-shirts with American logos remind Gordon of back home.

A handful of the Pigmy men wear their traditional leather loincloths. However, their ensemble is not a complete success with the wearing of American Major League Baseball

Team's ball caps. There are no tattoos on their flesh nor bones through their noses. The members of the tribe look as if they were on a permanent camping trip.

The women of the tribe are covered with plain dresses, mostly one piece. The fabric is common, looking as if the garments were picked up at a secondhand store.

Gordon approaches the Shaman and smiles. The Shaman nods and hands Gordon the leaf. On its surface, a mash of seeds, beetles and berries. "Elez thinks highly of you. She has guided many Americans through the jungle. She says you did not complain once."

"It was an entertaining trip, uh..."

"Loup Garou. It's a pleasure to meet you."

"That sounds French. I'm not sure what it means, though," Gordon says, as he takes a finger full of the mash.

"Some time ago, French Missionaries came through and stayed a few years. Casting out our evil ways. Teaching us English. Wanting to clothe us. *Blah-blah-blah*. They decided not to stay when we told them we were having *them* for our first Christmas dinner." Gordon turns pale, nearly choking on his mouthful of food. "...just kidding."

"I was going to thank Elez for her hut," Gordon says before taking another mouthful of mash.

"You might wait till she's finished," Loup replies as he motions toward the near shoreline. Gordon turns from Loup and sees Elez and a male Pigmy, Loy, bathing in the river. Their clothes appear laid out on a large rock, drying in the sun.

Elez turns to see Gordon looking upon her. She smiles. Her nakedness seems natural as she continues to wash Loy's back and shoulders. "He has returned from a journey. It is customary to bath after such a trip."

Gordon continues to stare at Elez for several moments. She turns back to Loy, facing him from behind and runs a cloth down and over his lower back. Gordon sees slight redness and almost bruise marks along Loy's back, as if he had worn a heavy backpack or a harness. "Are they a couple?"

"Why do you ask, White Man?" Loup playfully asks.

"I was just, uh..." Gordon mumbles for a polite response. "I was just..."

"You were just coming with me. I have many things to show you." Loup nearly chuckles at the American's naïveness. He leads Gordon away from his hut and approaches the near tree line. Gordon turns and pauses a moment. Loy looks deep into his eyes. There is something strikingly familiar about him.

"Loup?" Gordon asks. "How do they do that?" Gordon continues filming Payu and Loy as they appear from the far tree line. Payu, in front, clutches onto a thick log, one foot in diameter resting on his shoulder. Nearly fourteen feet behind him, Loy carries the end of the log upon his shoulder.

Gordon maneuvers the sixteen millimeter camera in a panning motion. Through the lens, he sees Payu and Loy effortlessly raise the log from their shoulders and rest it onto the ground at the far end of the village. Several other male members of the tribe continues to carve and chisel away at similar logs, creating long canoe style boats. "How do they do what?"

"Carry so much weight. I mean, they probably don't even weigh a hundred pounds. How can they carry that log?" Gordon lowers his camera to his side revealing his thickening beard. He wears a leather tanned loincloth and sandals. Gordon's blending in nicely with the tribe.

Loup smiles and places his hand on Gordon's shoulder. He gives him a reassuring squeeze then slightly motions him forward. Loup shouts out towards his tribesmen in his native language. Payu, Loy and nearly a dozen other men instantly turn toward Loup. He sternly nods.

Payu walks several feet away from the log and stands facing Loup and Gordon as a soldier would stand at attention. Loy and the other Pigmies fall in line next to him. "Go," Loup commands.

"Go, what?" Gordon asks.

"Go pick them up."

"I don't understand."

"You will..." Loup says with a smile. Gordon hands Loup his camera and slowly approaches Payu. They awkwardly face each other. Gordon stands over the native nearly a foot and a half. Payu nods his head at Gordon. "*Get on with it*," he seems to be saying.

Gordon reaches around Payu, as if to give him a bear hug. He attempts to lift the smaller man; he won't budge. Gordon is puzzled. Payu seems to weigh hundreds of pounds. He can't lift him up off of the ground. Loy pats his chest. "*I'm next*," he indicates without words.

Gordon moves away from Payu and faces Loy. He reaches around him in a similar fashion and effortlessly lifts him up off of the ground. He seems to have no weight at all. Yet, he is the same height and build as Payu. The next tribesmen pats himself on the chest.

One by one, Gordon faces the Pigmies and attempts to lift them up off of the ground. He is unable to do so with several of the men. However like Loy, others appear to have no weight. Loup shouts out at them. They humbly turn and resume their efforts along the transforming log canoes. "So, what's the secret?" Gordon asks. Loup Garou simply smiles.

Gordon's sixteen millimeter camera rests on the top of a large rock. The film continues to spin around inside, capturing the ongoing ceremony. Loup's tribe has donned their ritualistic clothing. Men in their tanned, leather loincloths with the women wearing grass skirts.

Numerous men pound mallets against the leather skins of their drums. The thumping sounds echo deep into the darkness of the surrounding tropical jungle. Pigmy men, women and children chant as they dance around the roaring flames of the centrally located bonfire.

Loup sits on the lowest rung of his stepladder leading up into his dwelling. He is warmed by a small fire a few feet away from his home. Upon his head, the skinned, black leopard. Its muzzle and upper jaw stick out and above Loup's forehead. The leopard's eyes and ears are clearly seen above his head as if the animal were spitting him out.

The leopard's fur runs down along Loup's shoulders and back. Its front legs and forepaws stretch out along his arms, fastened at the wrists with thin leather straps. Loup mixes a dark, pasty substance with a smooth and rounded end of a stick inside of a wooden bowl.

Loup takes a small, flattened piece of bark and scoops up a portion of the hashish substance, the size a thumbnail. He carefully fills a small ceramic bowl, which is as round as a fifty-cent piece. The small bowl is attached to a primitive smoking device, opened at the top and sealed with clay at the bottom.

The bamboo pipe is nearly three inches in diameter and one foot long. The small bowl rests near the lower front area of the round device with a small hole carved into the back for selective ventilation. Loup rests the pipe at the American visitor's bare feet then looks up into the sky.

Gordon wears his leather loincloth and has grown out his beard. Graying facial hair runs along his lower jaw line, blending in with his sideburns and silver temples. "There, you are there," Loup says as he points into the sky.

"Which one?" Gordon curiously asks.

"That one," Loup says as he directs Gordon's attention to a very specific constellation of stars.

"I don't know that sign."

"It is the sign of the Serpent Bearer. I can sense it in you." Gordon looks high into the sky. The stars dance and sparkle in a hypnotizing way. He is fascinated by the celestial arrangement. "Here..." Loup says, as he lifts and motions Gordon the bamboo pipe toward him.

Gordon curiously takes the pipe in hand. The thumping of the tribe's drums fills his subconscious. The roaring flames of the bonfire warms his face. Elez continues to feverishly dance in wild circles. Payu, Loy and the rest of the tribe dance around in odd patterns.

"My friend," Loup says in a fatherly tone. "You will changed forever. Consider this carefully."

"If it will save my niece... I have nothing to consider." Gordon lifts the opened end of the pipe to his lips and covers his mouth as Loup takes a stick from the flames of his fire. He holds the flame over the small ceramic bowl as Gordon deeply inhales.

Gordon holds his breath for several moments, absorbing the inhaled smoke deep into his lungs. As he quickly exhales, Loup eagerly motions for Gordon to repeat this act. Gordon nods as he presses the top of the pipe against his mouth and inhales again.

Almost in unison, the dancing tribe yells out, similar to a Cherokee warrior's battle cry. The flames continue to roar. The jungle darkens. Gordon becomes lightheaded. Loup smiles at Gordon. "There are three rules you must never break."

"Rules?" Gordon sharply says, as he exhales. "*Now* you tell me about rules! Kinda *late* for that!"

"I had to assure myself. You have nothing but love for your niece. You now have the power to save her. Use it wisely."

"What are the three rules?" Gordon asks. His vision becomes blurred. Gordon feels sick to his stomach. Elez frolics toward him. She extends out her hand, inviting him to join her in dance. Gordon attempts to stand, yet he sways to the side and falls flat onto the ground.

"Elez?" Gordon cries out. "Elez!" She approaches him in the center of the large circle and kisses him on the cheek. Payu, Loy and four other Pigmy men surround him. They clutch tightly onto long bamboo poles in a circle. At the ends of each pole, a noose of sorts made of thick vines. Gordon attempts to move, to walk in opposite directions, yet is contained like a captured stray dog.

Gordon is restrained by the neck by the nooses. Each of [illegible]esmen has a firm grip on him as he attempts to turn and [illegible]roundings.

[illegible]ride, my friend," Loup shouts. "I'll see you on

Gordon tries to focus on the Shaman. Loup's face begins to distort. The black leopard pelt appears to mutate and mold into his flesh. The human and leopard skulls blend together.

Gordon panics, he is unable to free himself. Payu, Loy and the others clutch onto the bamboo poles. Gordon feels a lightening shot of pain run up and down his spine. Elez dances toward him and kisses him again on the cheek. "The first time is always the most painful," she playfully says.

"First time?" Gordon asks. "First time for what?" His vision turns dim. He feels his body changing and growing. Gordon looks down toward his forearm and the top of his hand. His flesh dissipates and mutates into what looks like scales. The scales of a lizard.

Gordon shakes his head in disbelief. He feels his chest expanding then retracting. Overwhelming pain rips through his body. His face begins to transform, taking on reptilian features.

Gordon arches his back and extends out his arms as if he were being crucified. He drops to his knees as the tribesmen clutch onto the bamboo poles, keeping the mutating creature contained.

The cool morning air of the jungle is quiet. The birds themselves seem to be still sleeping. Towering trees create dark shadows and allow little light downward through the canopy. A soft stirring sound is heard from a gathering of stout, tropical bushes at the edge of a small clearing.

Gordon begins to awake. As his eyes flutter, he realizes that he has nothing on. As Gordon becomes more aware, he sees that he is embracing Elez in his arms. Not an embrace of a night of passion but of necessity to keep warm through the night. Elez's bare body is covered with a thin layer of morning dew. She opens her eyes and smiles at him.

Gordon tenderly pushes Elez away from himself and sits up sideways, bracing his weight with his arm and hand. Scattered across the floor of the jungle, nearly twenty member's of Loup Garou's tribe begins to awake.

Payu raises up from the arms of a Pigmy woman as Loy, several yards away, picks small loose branches from his matted hair. Their uncovered bodies seem natural as they are uninhibited by their lack of clothing. One by one, they rise and begin heading toward the thick tree line.

Elez stands, reaches down then takes Gordon by the hand. In a coaxing manner, she motions her head for him to follow. Gordon gets to his feet and walks along side of Elez, heading deeper into the jungle, back to the slow moving river and the village.

"I will miss you, my friend," Loup says in a saddened tone. He and Gordon shake hands. Gordon leans forward and gives the Shaman a hug.

"I will miss you as well," Gordon says. The village is filled with activity. The tribesmen pay no heed to Gordon's departure, he's just another American leaving his mark. There are canoes to be made and fishing nets to be mended.

Elez tightens a strap along the pack mule's back. Gordon's duffle bag, backpack and camera case hang tightly to one side of the mule with rolled sleeping pads and food supplies to the other side. Gordon turns and playfully runs his fingers through the mule's mane. "Ready to go, Loy?" The mule snorts.

Elez takes the pack mule's reins in hand. Loup smiles at her then nods. She glances at Gordon then begins leading the mule along the near shoreline. Gordon takes in one last look of the Pigmy village. This was his home away from home for nearly a month.

Several children play in the river. The air is filled with giggles and splashing. They take little notice as Gordon, Elez and the pack mule reach the far end of the village, turn and disappear into the thick tree line of the jungle.

"I want you to come with me," Gordon says as he turns away from the pack mule. His duffel bag, backpack and camera case has already loaded onto the cargo ship. Gordon tenderly takes Elez by the hands. "Come with me."

"As much as I want to, I can't. My home is here."

"There are so many things I want to show you. You'll love it in Washington." Gordon's eyes are wide and eager, almost pleading.

"Gordon! Let's go!" Doug shouts from the above starboard deck. Gordon looks up along the lowered gangway. Doug waves with a smile, coaxing his friend to board the vessel as several dockhands begin unsecuring the tie lines from the extended wharf.

"Stay here with me. Father has come quite attached to you."

"I can't," Gordon reluctantly says. "I have a niece that needs me."

"I need you," Elez whispers. The gangway begins to slip away from the wooden planks of the wharf. Gordon's ship is leaving without him. Gordon frantically looks at the vessel as it begins to slowly float away from the dock.

Gordon turns and faces Elez. He looks deep into her dark, brown eyes. "I'm sorry, I can't stay. I'll be taking a piece of you with me," Gordon whispers, as he tenderly places his hand on his heart.

"...and you'll be leaving a piece of you behind," Elez says with a sorrowful smile.

"Good-bye, Elez." Gordon tenderly kisses her on the lips. Without another word, Gordon leaps unto the lowered gangway as it clears the wharf. He scampers up the wooden slats and bounds up onto the starboard deck.

Gordon stands there a moment with his back turned toward the below wharf. He slowly turns to catch one last glimpse of Elez.

Dockhands fill the wharf, carrying large bags of wheat and rice. Others maneuver wooden crates into their proper places, waiting to be loaded on the next cargo ship. There is no pack mule. There is no Elez. There was no second thought. What kind of life would they have had together? Gordon will never know.

"This place looks like Noah's Ark," Gordon says, standing at an opened hatchway. The large cargo hold of the vessel is filled to the brim with animal cages. Doug appears from the passageway and comes up from behind Gordon.

"Let me introduce you," Doug says with a forward motion of his arm. Gordon and Doug step through the hatchway as dull roars and growls fill the stale air.

The first row of cages house zebras, water buffalos, warthogs and gazelles. Hoofed creatures for the most part. A wide opened space separates the different species of animals leading into a pair of caged black rhinoceroses. "So, how was your trip into the jungle?"

"Good. Very good."

"Did you find what you were looking for?"

"Yeah, I think I did," Gordon answers with a smirk. Passed the next opened space, smaller animals are seen; sloths, aardvarks, peacocks and ostriches. A pack of hyenas nip at each other, playing a confined version of tag. Low and deep growls continue to grow louder as Gordon and Doug approach the next series of cages.

Three male lions, each in their own cage, looks up at the pair of humans from behind their steel bars. One lion yawns then returns to his nap. The second remains focused on Gordon and Doug as they pass. The third lion is disinterested in them and continues to clean his forepaws with its massive tongue.

Gordon and Doug approach the last series of cages; cheetahs, leopards, both spotted and black and even four servals. The constant thundering from the bow of the cargo ship continues to irritate the animals. A low roar echoes out from the opened hatchway leading into the next compartment. "What's in there, Doug?"

"A last minute addition." Doug leads Gordon through the hatchway and into a narrowing passage. "She's a beauty, isn't she?" Inside of the large cage, a magnificent lioness playfully bats at her three cubs; two males and one female.

"What's back there?" Gordon asks, as he points toward and through the last opened hatchway. The low thunderous noise seems to be coming from the next compartment.

"That's the propeller room. I hate to have to put her in here but we kinda ran outta space." The lioness does seem quite agitated yet, she continues to play with her cubs, trying to keep them occupied. "Come on, it's lunch time."

Doug steps out through the hatchway and begins his route through the cargo hold of animal cages. Gordon turns to follow but pauses. He is intrigued at the female cub's curiosity.

The cub reaches out through the steel bars of her cage, attempting to reach Gordon. He squats down and faces her. Gordon wiggles his nose, taunting her. She continues to reach her paw outward, attempting to snag Gordon's shirt.

The lioness growls, as she saunters from the back of the cage and approaches Gordon. He remains motionless, facing the female cub and her mother. The lioness sniffs Gordon through the bars. She seems to bat her eyes at him, there is something familiar about this human. The lioness gives the female cub a quick lick then returns to the pair of male cubs.

Gordon reaches his hand in through the steel bars and scratches the female cub behind her ears. She begins to purr as she rolls over onto her side. Gordon runs his hand down the front of her neck then scratches her belly. She playfully bites at his arm as a common house cat would, meaning him no harm, just wanting to play.

She springs up and pounces on Gordon's hand. He maneuvers himself from a squatting position and sits on the cold deck, allowing him to reach further into the cage.

Gordon waves his opened palm in small circles causing the cub to chase and follow his movements. He quickly opens and closes his palm creating a claw of sorts. She slightly backs away then pounces. She playfully nips at his flesh, not breaking the skin.

Gordon laughs out loud. The female cub playfully growls then bats her eyes. He reaches into the cage with both of his hands and rubs her soft fur behind her ears. Gordon can faintly hear her purring under the constant thundering noise of the propeller in the next compartment.

The sky is dark and ominous as rain pours down in constant sheets. Mountainous waves violently crash against the outer hull of the cargo ship. The vessel is tossed recklessly across the massive swells of the ocean. Seawater spills over the sides of the ship as deckhands scamper for their lives.

"Gordon! Gordon, we have to get off the ship! We're goin' down!" Doug yells. He struggles to remain on his feet, bracing himself along the steel walls of the passageway. Gordon topples out of his quarters and collides into Doug. They clutch onto each other, keeping themselves on their feet.

"What happened?"

"We lost the propeller! We can't get to the compartment to close it off! A few of the cages has jarred loose and are blocking the hatch!" Gordon turns and struggles to stay on his feet. He braces himself against the steel walls as he makes his way toward the hatchway. "Gordon! Where are you goin'? We have to get off the ship!"

Gordon grips onto the wheel of the closed hatchway door. He spins it, releasing the securing latches. Leaning in with his shoulder, Gordon presses his weight against the steel door. It does not move. Frantic roars echo from the cargo hold. Again, Gordon presses his weight against the door.

An odd tingling sensation races through his body. He is overcome with a surge of power and strength. Gordon feels his body mutating. His shoulders and chest begin to expand. Overwhelming pain rips through his muscles and tissue. Gordon drops to his knees.

His thighs, calves and feet expand. Gordon's increasing mass causes his jeans to tear apart at the seams and fall from his waist. His shoulders, biceps and forearms broaden.

Gordon looks down toward his flesh. Thick, coarse and black hair begins to sprout upward from his skin. From his shoulder blades down to his tailbone, silvery hair rapidly appears. The palms of his hands continue to mutate into a black and leathery surface.

Gordon's brow and lower jaw continue to expand. His nostrils widen and transform into the similar black leathery texture as his palms. The forward area of his mouth expands outward and begins taking on a curved shape as if he was sipping soup from a bowl.

Gordon attempts to stand upright but is unable to. His transforming skeletal structure and expanding muscles prevent him from doing so. His body mass has nearly doubled. The pain overwhelms him as he lets out a ferocious roar.

A foot of water covers the deck of the cargo hold as the vessel continues to violently rock back and forth. The filled animal cages have begun to flood. The lions roar. The zebras whinny. The hyenas uncontrollably cackle.

The first cage containing a pair of zebras blocks the closed hatchway. The second cage housing the massive water buffalo is jammed against the first cage. The wheel of the hatchway doors slowly spins. Then, the steel door slowly opens.

The adult male, silverback gorilla heaves against the hatchway door. The massive weight of the cages slowly slides across the deck, sloshing through the rising seawater.

The silverback powerfully presses his weight against the door, fully opening it. The large primate has retained his counterpart's consciousness. He is quite rational. Although his outer form has changed, Gordon's inner human remains.

The silverback lumbers through the hatchway, making his way passed the frightened animals. He lopes on all fours, weaving his way through the haphazard cages with the seawater continuing to rise. The silverback approaches the far hatchway with water pouring into the cargo hold from the furthest compartment.

The silverback stands nearly waist high in water as he faces the lioness's cage. She stands on her hind legs with her forepaws clinging onto the upper steel bars of the cage. The trio of cubs have dung their claws into her shoulders, hanging on for dear life. The lioness roars. She does not recognize the primate.

The silverback makes his way to the furthest area of the compartment. Seawater continues to flood inward from the missing propeller and housing. There is no repairing it. The silverback returns to the lioness's cage and releases the latch. He opens the cage door and steps aside as the lioness roars and bites at him.

The silverback rears up and pounds his chest. He reaches up and violently shakes the cage, hoping the lioness and cubs would flee. The lioness remains standing on her hind legs with her cubs drawing closer to the surface of the rising water.

The silverback clutches onto the steel bars of the cage. He roars as an odd tingling races through his body. The silver and black hair covering his shoulders dissipates and appears to dissolve back into his flesh.

The mutation reverses, causing the skeletal structure, muscles and tissue to begin to return to their human form. The silverback's facial features dissolve and give way to Gordon's jaw line and upper brow. Yet, there is no time to complete the transformation with the seawater continuing to rise.

Gordon appears freakish in shape and size. His legs have remained in his altered state, thick and hunched as did the silverback's. Gordon's waist, torso and chest appear to be human with no traces of the coarse, black hair.

His shoulders remain broad, tapering down into his massive biceps and forearms. Gordon's facial features have nearly returned. All that remains are faint remnants of a gorilla's muzzle and sharp teeth.

Gordon quickly steps into the cage and takes the female cub by the nap of the neck. She lets out a meow, crying for her mother. Gordon takes the cub in his arms and looks down at her. She sniffs him and senses there's something familiar about this strange looking human.

Gordon opens and closes his palm inches away from the cub. She bats her forepaw at the playful claw. The lioness growls as she lowers herself into the water. Gordon steps out from the cage and leads the lioness through the hatchway with her pair of male cubs clinging to her shoulders.

With the female cub in one arm, Gordon presses his shoulder and weight against the hatchway door. A flood of compressing water escapes from the propeller room into the cargo hold. With all of his might, Gordon slams the hatch closed and spins the wheel. The rising water has stopped. The vessel will not sink.

The female cub stands on her hind legs on top of Gordon's supporting arm. She places her forepaws onto his chest and licks his face. He reaches down with his free hand and rubs her wet fur.

Gordon trudges through the flooded cargo hold. The caged animals are frighten and wet. But, they'll live. As Gordon passes in front of each of the haphazard cages, the animals sense something is different about the human. He has a sense of power and respect.

The caged animals seem to even bow or lower their heads as he passes them. Not a growl or even a low roar. Gordon motions his hand toward the lioness. She understands his intentions as she wades passed the zebra cage.

The lioness bounds through the opened hatchway with her male cubs clinging to her shoulders. Gordon follows close behind with the female cub cradled in his arm. She purrs feeling happy, content and safe.

"Hey, Gordon!" Doug calls out from the passageway. "You awake?" He gives the closed hatchway a quick knock, spins the securing wheel and flings the heavy door open. Doug steps into Gordon's small living quarters and stops cold in his tracks.

The lioness lifts up her head and growls at him. She nearly takes up the entire floor of the small room. Gordon remains asleep on his narrow bunk with the pair of male cubs licking and cleaning each other at his feet.

Gordon's human features have all returned. There are no traces of the silverback. He lays on his side, facing the far wall with his arm draped over the female cub like a child would sleep with a stuffed teddy bear.

The female cub slightly stirs then nestles her muzzle against Gordon's chest. The lioness continues to stare at the opened hatchway. Ever so slowly, Doug backs away and quietly closes the heavy steel door.

Gordon stands in the center of the small transparent room with his arms extended away from his body in a scarecrow manner. He is clean shaven and wears a well thought-out shirt and tie.

The odd blue and orange lights continue to scan him for infectious or transmittable diseases as he turns in a slow circle. The ultraviolet lights fade with the overhead florescent bulbs flickering on.

The transparent door automatically clicks and pops open. Gordon gives the above surveillance camera a polite wave then steps into the quiet and sterile hallway.

"Mr. Jamison!" the voice calls out from down the hallway of the C.D.C. wing of the hospital. Gordon slows his pace as the hospital's director approaches him. "How was your trip?"

"It was fine. How's Sonja?" There is reluctance in the director's voice as he answers.

"There's nothing more we can do for her. I'm afraid we're going to have to transfer her."

"Transfer her? Isn't this the best place in the county for her?"

"When I say *transfer her*, I mean..."

"You mean *short term*! You don't want her here when she dies!"

"Mr. Jamison." The director pauses, "I'm sorry."

"You should be!" Gordon says with a growl. He turns and makes his way down the sterile hallway. Coming up to a closed door, he quietly enters.

Gordon makes his way to the side of Sonja's bed. The wheeled carts of medical equipment surrounds her with tubes, wires and hoses running in all directions. Sonja continues to breathe through her nasal cannula and remains in her therapeutic hypothermia induced coma.

Gordon glances through the frigid private room. Little has changed since his journey into the tropical jungle. The framed pictures of Sonja, her father and mother. Photos of Gordon and Sonja at a playground. The stuffed animals and children's toys with the hand carved rocking horse in the corner.

"I'm not gonna let you die," Gordon says as he takes Sonja by the hand and tenderly squeezes it. He gazes down upon her as a father would. "Sweetheart, can you hear me?" Gordon whispers. "I think I've found something that might save you..."

* * * * *

~ II ~

"So, class," Gordon says as he stands behind his cluttered desk. "What have we learned this year? Better yet, what have you learned in life?"

Professor Gordon Jamison has aged well. He wears a dark, tweed jacket, a dress shirt with no tie, jeans and cowboy boots. Gordon keeps his long, salt and pepper hair tied back in a ponytail, hanging near the middle of his back.

Gordon moves across the tile floor and maneuvers a wheeled cart with a large television set resting on top in front of the students. "This last year, we've discussed the Medicine Men of the Native Americas, Witch Doctors of Europe and Africa, Voodoo rituals of Haiti, the Caribbean which migrated to Louisiana, Wiccans and we even touched on the Black Arts."

"Professor, you left one out," Giovanni says. He is a charming looking fellow with dark, Italian features, slim yet, well built and solid. Gio is well dressed, almost too well dressed in a very expensive looking pressed shirt and tie.

"Yes I did, Mr. Mancini," Gordon says with a smile. "Jon, would you get the light?" Sitting near the classroom's door, Jon Von Dutch shuffles over to the wall and catches the light switch.

Jon has a mischievous way about him. He wears tattered jeans, cowboy boots and a T-shirt with shredded, short sleeves. Jon keeps his long, brown hair loose and about his shoulders. However, his locks of hair looks as if it were teased and blown dry for hours, perfecting the Glam Rock look.

Jon finds his seat next to Chloe. She is mousey and almost petite wearing an extremely conservative, businesslike outfit. Chloe's green eyes pierce through the lenses of her reading glasses resting on her nose. She keeps her long, dark hair about her shoulders, hiding her larger than average ears.

The large television screen comes to life. Black and white images begin as a blur then suddenly come into focus. The sixteen millimeter film has been transferred to the modern VHS format.

Gordon, as a younger man, struggles to open his eyes. He awkwardly swings his legs from the primitive cot as Loup Garou continues to film the American. "Shamanism was and is widespread. Europe, Asia, Russia, South America, Australia... Every continent has their own version of a Shaman. However, *The Tribes of Babylon* were the great ancestors, the *original* Shapeshifters or Skinners."

"It's all hocus-pocus!" Duncan blurts out from the shadows.

"Is it?" Gordon asks, as he locates the doubting student near the back of the class.

"You've been teaching about magic and voodoo. About witches and werewolves. It's all smoke and mirrors."

"Then why did you take my class?"

"I needed the credits to graduate," Duncan replies. "...and since that's tomorrow, I'm outta here!" Not even collecting his books and binders, Duncan stands, shuffles across the floor and exits the classroom, nearly slamming the door behind himself.

"Anyone else?" Gordon asks. The black and white images of Gordon's journey from so many years ago continues across the television screen. No one else chooses to leave.

"Professor," a deep, masculine voice calls out from the middle of the class. Larry Wells flips through several stacks of collected notes and term papers. He appears studious and focused like every day was a test, a life test. "In your earlier research, you were looking for a cure to save your niece. You abandoned the scientific approach and took on a more, *mystical* path. Why?" Gio leans forward at his desk, intensely listening to the professor's response.

"I found something or I should say... something found me. Traditional methods weren't helping her. I had to discover something else."

"Is that why you turned your back on Doctor Taylor?" Gio asks with a sharp tone.

"I didn't turn my back on Reece. We had a falling out. He followed science and I followed my heart."

"...and your niece?" a soft, feminine voice asks. Kaleen Turner has a twinkle in her eye with flowing red hair laying across her shoulders. Her facial features are kind, yet with a hint of a fairy or an attractive elf. Kaleen's deep red lips seem to accent her slightly freckled cheeks and nose. Sitting next to her, Tez Madon, her boyfriend.

Tez is a quiet fellow, keeping pretty much to himself. He is a thinker and a poet. Tez's faded, leather bomber jacket hangs from his chair behind his desk. He sports his signature trademark, a dark pair of sunglasses. Rain or shine. Day or night. Tez is never seen without wearing them. He is just that cool.

Gordon turns away from the students and draws his attention to the television screen. The black and white footage continues with images of Loup Garou, Elez, Payu and the Pigmy tribe continuing with their daily activities. "...and your niece, Professor?"

Gordon seems to have fallen into a deep trance. He stands there affixed on the television screen. A splice in the sixteen millimeter film causes an abrupt transition in the black and white images.

Payu, Loy and four Pigmy tribesmen surround Gordon as they clutch tightly onto the ends of their bamboo poles. Gordon struggles to look around in all directions. His movements are confined by the thick, vine nooses secured around his neck.

Gordon catches a glimpse of the Shaman. His face begins to transform. The black leopard head and pelt mutates into the human's flesh. Gordon feels an electrical charge race through his body. He looks down toward his palms to see mutating skin turning into scales. A large, forked tongue flickers from his lips. "Professor!"

Gordon quickly regains his consciousness. His students awkwardly wait for their instructor to continue. Gordon reaches up toward the VCR and presses pause. He stares at the frozen black and white image of himself from so many years ago. Gordon feels the overwhelming pain as if it were just yesterday.

A slight ruckus suddenly draws his attention toward the back of the classroom.

Reggie and Dante seem out of place. This is a University, not prison. The lifelong friends are bored and restless. They playfully shove at each other, having lost interest in the professor's home movies. Gordon gives them a fatherly scowl.

Reggie's short, blonde hair is slightly greased back. His black leather vest is covered with various insignias and patches. Reggie is clean shaven with his strong jaw line complimenting his charming facial features. He's a handsome man.

Dante is somewhat taller than Reggie. He wears a similar black leather vest with a dark T-shirt underneath. Dante is well groomed with a tight and thin goatee and mustache. At first, his matted hair looks unattended to. However, his surfer-dude dreadlocks, not yet touching his shoulders, add to his ruffian persona. "Sorry," Dante mumbles.

"I see we're about outta time," Gordon says as he looks over the heads and shoulders of his students. He can just make out the time on the hanging wall clock behind them.

Larry glances down at his expensive wristwatch. It is very advanced and modern looking with a small series of numbered buttons which controls the calculator function. The time piece has a thermometer as well. The face has the standard hour, minute and second hands with a digital readout below;

Wednesday - June 13th 68 °F

"I'm having one last *study session* on this subject at my house. Friday night," Gordon says as he makes his way across the room. He flicks on the light switch and slightly turns at the door. "You boys can think of it as *a party*," Gordon continues, motioning toward Reggie and Dante. "I'll see you all at graduation tomorrow."

Collectively, the students begin to gather up their books and binders. Not waiting for the final bell to ring, they begin to exit. "Thanks, Professor," Chloe says, as she approaches Gordon by the opened door. "It's not really something I'm into." Chloe's never been a social butterfly. "...but I'll tell Zoey about Friday."

"Alright, dear. I'll see you tomorrow then."

"You comin' to the show?" Jon asks, as he approaches Gordon.

"I wouldn't miss it!" Gordon gives Jon a fatherly pat on the shoulder as the aspiring musician exits. Kaleen gives the professor a polite nod as she and Tez follow behind Chloe. Gio passes in front of Gordon's desk and sets down a red apple. He hesitates for a moment before turning and approaches Gordon.

"I'd like to thank you for your inspiration," Gio says with an odd tone.

"I'm glad you found something useful in my class." Gordon extends out his hand for the handshake that never comes.

"That's not what I meant. I'll see you Friday." Just as Gio makes his way past Gordon, Reggie and Dante recklessly bound through the door. Gio and Dante slightly collide into each other. A scowl is exchanged between them with an underlying agenda.

"Are we still on?" Dante sarcastically asks.

"Let's go!" Gio defiantly replies.

"Hey, you should really think about this," Reggie says with a concerned tone."

"What's there to think about?" Dante smiles as he takes off his black leather vest then slips out of his T-shirt. The far end of the gymnasium's hardwood floor is covered with white and blue wrestling mats. Along opposite sides of the gym, the wooden, retractable bleachers have yet to be put away from the previous basketball game.

A mob of sorts has gathered, forming a large circle around the edges of the mat. Dante's fellow wrestlers, as well as basketball and football players, represent the university's athletic student body.

Filling in around the opposite edges of the mat are more reserved looking seniors and juniors, the studious ones. Dress shirts and ties, polo shirts and khaki pants represent the university's academic students.

Larry and Chloe stand along the edge of the mat, somewhere between the jocks and the nerds, both being able to fit in almost anywhere. Jon, Kaleen and Tez chit-chat among themselves, motioning toward the center of the wrestling mat. "Just cuz you're the champ, doesn't mean you can take'im," Reggie says.

"I'm the best wrestler in the state," Dante confidently replies, as he slips out of his black boots.

"Yeah." Reggie pauses a moment, "You're a wrestler, he's a fighter. There's a difference."

"I can take'im." Dante stretches out his arms and shoulders. The surrounding seniors and juniors slightly quiet themselves as the two gladiators face each other near the center of the mat.

Dante stands nearly six inches over Gio who has removed his dress shirt, tie and polished shoes. They glare at each other for a long moment. Exchanging an understanding nod, Dante and Gio back away and find their marks on the large blue circle of the wrestling mat. A moment of silence is followed by-

Dante and Gio lunge toward each other. The mob of students begin to cheer, coaxing them on. Dante and Gio lock arms and shoulders, pressing the sides of their heads into their opponent's. They move around in circles, first one way then the other.

Gio swiftly releases Dante and shoots for his knees. He manages to wrap around his waist as Dante spins and scoops Gio up and under his arms. Dante and Gio drop to their knees, struggling for control.

Dante flip-flops Gio over onto his back and presses down his full weight. Gio quickly maneuvers his legs upward causing Dante to lose his grip. Gio swings his arm over and around Dante's neck. Dante twists his body and slips through an opening between Gio's armpit.

Dante comes up from behind Gio and slips in a reverse headlock. Gio struggles to keep his shoulders from the mat. Dante tightens his grip as Gio moves his arm in front of himself.

Taking his straightened pointer and middle fingers, he jabs them up and into Dante's armpit. Gio has always known he couldn't beat Dante on the mat. He's a fighter, not a wrestler; there's a difference.

Feeling the sharp pain in his armpit, Dante releases his reverse headlock. Gio slams the back of his head into Dante's face, nearly breaking his nose. Gio spins and slides to his knees, facing Dante. Gio clutches his fist and delivers a powerful blow to Dante's jaw. Dante wobbles a bit as he attempts to get his bearings.

Gio springs to his feet, clutches his fists and draws a stance, as a boxer would in a ring. Dante rises to his feet and faces Gio. They circle each other a moment, each preparing for the other to strike first.

Gio delivers a series of jabs to Dante's face. Dante bobs and weaves then swings his clutched fist toward Gio. The impact sends Gio back a few steps. He regains his footing then swings his leg and foot upward, connecting into Dante's side.

Gio slams his bent elbow into Dante's jaw as Dante turns his body and heaves his knee into Gio's stomach. Gio quickly recovers with several swift blow's to Dante's face; he's just too fast! Dante realizes that he's losing the bout.

Dante roars, as he charges forward. He collides his full weight into Gio, wrapping his arms around the smaller man. Gio's arms are confined. He struggles to free himself from Dante's bear hug.

Dante squeezes Gio as he lifts him off of the mat. Dante quickly releases his embrace, slides one arm between Gio's legs and his other arm wrapped around his neck. They are now crisscrossed and chest to chest.

Dante takes a quick step forward, heaves his leg and Gio upward then powerfully slams his weight downward. Dante's body slam nearly crushes Gio against the mat. Gio's body falls limp as he struggles to catch his breath, having the wind knocked out of him. Dante tightens his grip as Gio slightly raises his hand off of the mat.

TAP - TAP!

Dante releases his grip on Gio, gets to his knee then stands over him, almost gloating. Cheers and applauds fills the gym as the supporting mob rushes Dante to congratulate him. With a nod, Reggie tosses Dante his black leather vest. Reggie smiles, seeing Dante's relieved expression, "*Whew, that was close,*" his friend seems to be saying.

"Get off me!" Gio blurts out. His fellow linguists, biology and chemistry students have reached down to help him to him feet. He bats away all assistance. Gio stands and shoves his way through the crowd. He pauses and looks back, glaring at Dante.

The swarming juniors and seniors continue to congratulate Dante with pats on the back and cheers. Reggie and Dante lead the mob toward the far double doors, as Gio disappears into the locker room.

Gordon shakes his head with disappointment. He remains seated at the upper most corner of the wooden bleachers. Gordon has been undetected throughout the fight. Sadness fills his heart. There's still so much for the young men to learn.

"Goooood-morning, Cougars!" Tez enthusiastically says into the suspended microphone. He sits in his wheeled chair facing the medium sized control board of the university's radio station.

Off to the right of Tez, a pair of slow spinning turntables. To his left, a small stack of newly arrived compact disk players, quite modern for the era. The shelves behind Tez are mostly filled with recorded albums with only a few dozen compact disk cases. He reaches up and adjusts his dark sunglasses on the bridge of his nose before flipping open a compact disk case.

Tez slides the disk into the player and cues up the next song. "That's about it for me, Cats. I gotta get to graduation in a few hours. Gonna leave you with one of our own. Here's *The Dutch Brothers* with "Livin' Large". Thanks for tuning in for the last three years. I start a *real* gig Monday. Can you believe it? A radio station that's actually gonna pay me! One-o-one point three, K-R-W-L. I'll miss you all! This is the Taz Man signin' off! Rock on, Cats!" Tez flicks off the *on-air* feed to his microphone as he flips on the compact disk player.

A thundering drum solo fills the cramped studio of the university's radio station. Tez mimics the percussionist as if he were actually playing the drums himself. He waves his hands in the air as the deep tom-toms continue with the addition of the double-bass drum.

A screaming guitar solo begins, followed by the constant thumping of a bass guitar. The drums, bass guitar and lead guitar blend into each other as the introduction of the song concludes. Rafael Von Dutch belts out the lead vocals of the upbeat rock and roll tune with his brother, Jon, providing back-up.

Kaleen is amused at Tez's antics and frolicking about the university's radio station. She stands in the opened doorway, leaning against the side door jamb.

Tez continues to dance around the small room, unaware of Kaleen's presence, as if he has his eyes closed or were dancing in darkness. The thunderous drums continue as the lead guitar slides into a solo.

Tez spins around and suddenly collects Kaleen in his arms. He tenderly kisses her on the lips. "Your *White Diamonds* gave you away." Tez buries his face under Kaleen's neck, deeply inhaling her perfume. He nibbles at her ear. "Come on. One last time."

"Tez!" Kaleen giggles.

"What are they gonna do? Expel us? We graduate in a few hours." With a twinkle in her eye, Kaleen closes the studio door. Tez takes her in his arms and lowers her to the floor. They embrace each other and passionately kiss, as they disappear below the central control board.

"How's my tie?" Larry nervously asks, as he fidgets underneath his traditional black graduation gown. Wearing a similar gown and cap, Chloe reaches up and slightly adjusts Larry's full Windsor.

"You look great." Chloe smiles and brushes off a few loose hairs from Larry's shoulder, as he glances down at his wristwatch.

"We'd better get going." Larry wraps his arm around Chloe's shoulder, giving her a brotherly hug. They turn and find themselves near the end of an extended line of graduating seniors.

The university's historical looking buildings stand in the background of the large, opened common ground. The countless rows of folding chairs appear occupied with friends and family, waiting for the graduation ceremony to begin.

Numerous members of the administration, as well as, professors and alumni sit patiently in their matching caps and gowns along the stage, waiting for the graduating class to find their seats. Gordon stands at the edge of the stage. His gown is accented with a sash hanging from around his neck and insignias along his sleeves indicating his numerous teaching levels and degrees.

Among the nearly one thousand graduating seniors, Tez and Kaleen appear walking hand in hand. Behind his dark sunglasses, Tez doesn't seem to be bothered by his cap's tassel dangling in front of his face. A few hundred students down, Reggie and Dante continue to playfully roughhouse with their gowns fluttering behind themselves.

Giovanni keeps to himself, as he continues to walk along the line of students heading for their forward seating along the front of the stage. His gown is slightly different that the other seniors around him. Gio's graduating at the top of his doctorial class.

Near the end of the line of students, Jon waves toward his brother. Rafe waves back, as he is seen along the rows upon rows of family and friends. Due to his size, one would think that Rafe was the older brother.

Rafe stands several inches over Jon and has slightly broader shoulders. The brother's hair style is similar, thick and dark, wavy and hangs just below the shoulders; Rafe is a poster child for *Whisky a Go-Go* on the Sunset Strip. He wears tattered jeans, cowboy boots and a T-shirt with a world renown rock and roll band logo.

Rafe snaps a quick picture of Jon as he files into the last row of graduating students. The seniors stand forward, facing the stage and their instructors.

Wearing an immaculate cap and gown, the Dean of Students finds her mark behind the centrally located podium. She smiles at her graduating class as she slightly motions her hand for them to sit. With low murmurs and laughter, the seniors find their seats, filling the first several rows of folded chairs.

Family and friends find their seats as they occupy the last several rows of chairs. The Dean of Students takes a deep breath before beginning her speech. Just as she is about to begin, a low rumbling is heard. The sound grows louder and seems to be multiplying; every head turns.

Pa and Ma, with her arms wrapped around his waist from behind, lead the convoy of over one hundred bikers along the narrow, two lane paved road throughout the campus grounds.

The motorcycles vary from age and style, even a few three wheeled choppers are represented. People become nervous as the ruffians circle their cycles around the large outer area of the graduation ceremony.

Black leather vests with various patches and insignias, faded, worn jeans and black boots seem to be the uniform of the gang. On the back of the leather jackets and vests, a large circular emblem with the gold lettering;

Crystal Cove
Crusaders

Pa, Reggie's father, revs his motorcycle's engine before cutting off the motor and presses down on the kickstand.

Pa and Ma lead the hordes of bikers along the rear areas of the seated family and friends. The people are unnerved, feeling the on looking eyes behind them. The bikers are polite and cordial, even giving the well dressed families a nod or two.

The Dean of Students pauses a moment, looking over the facing graduating seniors. Then, she looks over the heads and shoulders of the seated family and friends. Finally, she glances across the family of bikers standing along the rear wings of the assembly. "Welcome to the graduating class of nineteen eighty-five..."

The monotonous renditions of days gone by have bored the audience."*Come on, get on with it,"* they seem to be thinking.

The Dean of Students continues to call off the graduating senior's names. They each, one by one, file out from their folding chairs and make their way up onto the stage. "Annette Coleman..."

Annette smiles, wearing her graduating cap and gown. She makes her way up onto the stage and strikes a pose as her mother takes a snapshot from the seated crowd. Annette shakes the Dean's hand, receives her diploma then flips her cap's tassel to the side. "Reginald Collins..."

Ma and Pa are nearly in tears, clapping and cheering. The gathering of bikers dance and wave their arms wildly through the air. Reggie is the first one, ever, of their *family* to graduate.

Reggie makes his way across the stage and shakes the Dean's hand. She respectfully hands him his diploma and nods. Reggie turns toward the graduating seniors and gives them a devilish smile.

Reggie tightly clutches onto the Dean's hand and pulls her across his body. He presses his weight down and forward. Taking his left arm, Reggie supports the Dean along her back and shoulders. He dips her in a ballroom dance fashion. Reggie plants a long, wet kiss across the Dean's lips. Reggie quickly lifts the surprised Dean upward then faces the crowd in triumph.

As Reggie makes his way off of the stage, he takes his cap and tosses it high into the air. Without a second thought, he pulls his black graduation gown up and over his head revealing his worn blue jeans, black boots and black leather vest with numerous insignias and patches.

"She's for you," Ma says, as she gives her son a motherly hug. Pa gives his son a playful slug in the arm then motions him toward his graduation gift; a new three wheeled motorcycle.

The family of bikers cheer as Reggie climbs on his trike and starts it with its electrical ignition. The chrome exhaust pipes roar as Reggie revs the engine several times. Having already removed his graduation cap and gown, Dante appears across the campus grounds. He steers his older motorcycle alongside of Reggie and taps on the breaks. "Lets ride!"

"Lets ride!" Reggie says with a grin. Pa raises his hand in the air and spins his forefinger in wild circles. The family of bikers fan out, making their way to the row of parked motorcycles along the edge of the narrow, paved two lane road.

Ma climbs on behind Pa as he revs his cycle's engine. He casually looks in both directions then speeds along the campus grounds. Reggie on his new trike and Dante on his broken-in cycle, follows directly behind, as the rest of the family of bikers falls into formation.

The air is filled with thunderous exhaust pipes as the motorcycles, choppers and trikes make their way through the campus grounds. As the last group of bikers slow then turn along the narrow road heading out onto the main street, they pass behind an outdoor amphitheater.

The large, triangular roof extends and hangs over the elevated stage below. The spectator's area of the outdoor venue has been influenced by Roman architecture with curved rows of concrete seating along an inclined slope of the campus grounds. Smaller than a coliseum but just as impressive.

Jon sits on the edge of the main stage with his legs dangling over the side. Slightly resting on his lap, he continues to tune his custom, double-neck guitar. The necks of the glossy black guitar are not parallel to each other but span out in opposite directions as the top portion of an "X" would.

The left neck of the rhythm and lead guitar is strung with six strings with the right neck only having four, thicker strings for a bass guitar.

Jon reaches up with his right hand and slowly turns one of the pegheads. With his left hand, he moves his fingers across the slightly modified and sensitive frets of the guitar's neck. The low sounds of the musical chord seep out from the towering speakers standing along opposite corners of the stage.

Off to the side and slightly behind Jon, three standard electric guitars are seen, upright in their chrome stands. One in particular stands out. The body's design of the six string guitar is covered with an odd print of black and white sections similar to the fragments of a broken window pane. Jon is suddenly distracted by the crashing sounds of a dropped cymbal. "Sorry, Jon," Zoey apologetically says.

Zoey looks strikingly familiar. A mirrored image of Chloe, yet not. Her green eyes sparkle from within the dark eye liner and thick lashes. Deep red lipstick accents her playful smile.

Zoey keeps her long, brown hair tied into two identical ponytails, high upon her head revealing her larger than average ears. Unlike Chloe's snappy business suit, Zoey's attire is dark and almost Gothic.

She sports thick, heavy black boots with black nylons up to her thighs. Zoey's short, plaid shirt barely covers her lower areas. She has a tight fitting black T-shirt, curved and low cut and finally, a thin, black choker with small chrome studs around her neck.

Zoey lifts the dropped cymbal from the stage floor and hands it over to Rafe, who remains behind his lime green, double-bass drum set. He takes the large cymbal in hand and secures it on top of the last vacant chrome stand.

Rafe sits on his worn-in, padded stool and surveys his set. A deep snare drum, two bass drums, two mounted tom-toms, two floor tom-toms, a hi-hat and various cymbals. "You need anything else, Rafe?" Zoey eagerly asks.

"Naw, I'm good," Rafe replies, nearly dismissing her. Zoey stands there for a few moments, waiting for Rafe to change his mind, sending her on another errand or task... which never comes.

Taking a pair of worn drumsticks in hand, Rafe begins to tap at the drumheads, making sure they are in tune to his satisfaction. Taking a small chrome drum key, Rafe slowly turns one of the mounted tom-tom's lugs as he taps on the drumhead.

Zoey makes her way off the side of the stage and finds a seat directly in front of the outdoor amphitheater. The concrete is hard and cold. Jon continues to fiddle with his double neck guitar along the edge of the stage with Rafe's thumping drum set off to the back of the stage. Rafe's tuning session suddenly stops. "Hey, Leslie!" Rafe calls out.

"Hey, Rafe. How's it goin'?" Leslie asks with a less than enthusiastic tone.

"Just gettin' ready for t'night. You comin'?"

"Naw, I don't think so. My mom's planning a big graduation party for me." Leslie is an attractive young woman with an athletic build, flawless skin and little need for makeup. She stands at ground level facing the lifeless footlights of the stage. Leslie tosses Rafe a casual nod then focuses her attention to her prey; Jon Von Dutch.

From the first row of the concrete seating, Zoey can see the disappointment in Rafe's face. He's had a thing for Leslie since he was a Freshman. It's so unfair, he has one more year to go at the University. He should be graduating with his brother. "Yeah, I'll see ya' t'night!" Rafe declares, as he angrily slams his drumsticks into the hanging stickbag along the last floor tom-tom.

"Hey! Be ready to play and don't be late!" Jon nearly commands.

"Don't worry. I won't," Rafe replies under his breath. As he steps off the rear side stage, he looks back and over his shoulder. Leslie is giving Jon the full court press.

"I'll see you tonight, Rafe," Zoey eagerly calls out as she quickly stands and waves in Rafe's direction. However, he's gone without even a good-bye. Zoey turns and begins making her way up through the concrete rows of seats, higher and higher. She is disgusted as she can still hear Leslie's flirtatious giggles and obnoxious laughter echoing from the stage.

"There you are, honey," Leslie's father announces. He is a sharp looking businessman wearing a well thought-out suit and tie. He's taller than most men, nearly standing a foot higher than his daughter.

"He's the one I was telling you about," Leslie whispers into her father's ear. Rick turns and extends out his hand toward Jon.

"Rick. Rick Stanton."

"Jon. Just Jon." Rick and Jon shake hands.

"That's a very interesting guitar you have there," Rick says as he motions toward Jon's upward "X" shaped, double-neck guitar.

"It's my prototype. Once I got it all together, I didn't have to make many modifications." Jon pauses a moment, noticing Rick's interest in the three standard electric guitars resting in their chromes racks off to the side of the stage. "Do you play?"

"...a little," Rick says with a smile. Rick slides out of his suit jacket, slightly folds it and rests it on the edge of the stage next to the lifeless footlights. Loosening his tie, Rick effortlessly heaves himself up onto the stage.

Jon plucks at his thick strings of his bass guitar as Rick takes one of Jon's standard electric guitars in hand. Rick swings over the shoulder strap and rests the guitar in front of himself.

Leslie turns from the foot of the stage and finds her concrete seat along the front row, almost exactly where Zoey had been. Rick strums along the strings of the electric guitar. First, a chord then a short riff. Rick smiles as Jon gets to his feet. They stand slightly facing each other yet, side to side. Rick strums a chord. "Oh, Dad! Not *that* song!"

Jon smiles, for he knows this song. It was one of the first tunes he learned when he first picked up an old, broken-in acoustic guitar; *Dueling Banjos*. "Hold on a sec," Jon says as he loosens the cross strap of his double-neck guitar then rests it on a custom chrome rack.

Jon swiftly takes his favorite, oddly printed black and white guitar in hand, swings it into place then taps his boot onto one of many foot pedals. The electric guitar comes to life. Jon answers Rick's invitation with a strum, along the six strings of his guitar.

Just beyond the last, top concrete row of curved seats, Kaleen and Tez appear. The couple pause a moment along the upper plateau of the outdoor amphitheater, listening to Rick and Jon's guitar banter, back and forth at the edge of the stage below.

Rick politely answers with a strum along his standard electric guitar. Jon answers back with an equal chord. Rick begins to pick out the introduction to the song with Jon answering every note. Back and forth between the two musicians.

Rick and Jon pause for a brief moment and smile. This electrical version sounds quite different than the traditional acoustic guitar and banjo.

Rick and Jon nod at each other. "H*ere we go,"* they seem to be thinking. Rick begins the upbeat tune with his fingers effortlessly flying across the guitar strings. Jon keeps up, answering every note of Rick's lead-in. The pair of electric guitars echoes each other for several moments until both combine, continuing the fast tempo, hillbilly melody.

Tez and Kaleen dance with each other, kicking up their heels and swinging each other around by their bent elbows. They skip a beat, spin then take each other by their other bent elbows, continuing to dance to the dueling electric guitars.

Rick's fingers are at a near blur with his left hand moving up and down the guitar's neck as his right hand plucks away at the strings. Jon continues the harmonic interlude, yet is beginning to fall slightly behind. Rick suddenly strays from the melody and freestyles a solo.

Jon quickly follows Rick's lead and answers with a screaming riff. Rick and Jon duel it out. Back and forth, riff versus riff, solo to solo. Both of Jon's hand are flying up and down the neck of his guitar as Rick answers. Almost in unison, they look at each other.

Rick and Jon pick up exactly where they had left off of the backwater tune, playing together in harmony. Tez and

Kaleen laugh as they clasp hands and spin each other in a wild circle.

The musicians race to the finish, their fingers flying. Jon slams a final chord and lets it resonate. Rick slides his fingers across the guitar strings, ending the hillbilly tune with a magnificent solo. Tez bows to Kaleen as she curtseys to him. "A little, huh?" Jon sarcastically asks.

"Yeah... a little," Ricks replies as he carefully places the electric guitar back into its chrome stand. "It's been a pleasure, Jon."

"You too, Rick." The musicians smile at each other as they shake hands. Rick leans down and collects his suit jacket. He bounds off the stage as Leslie approaches him.

"What time's your flight, dad?"

"I think I'm gonna stick around for the show."

"I was right, wasn't I?"

"Yes, honey. You were right." Rick and Leslie begin walking along the front row of concrete seats. "I'm surprised you're not going tonight. Looks like *he's* your number one fan."

"I've seen him play. We were gonna met up after."

"I'm sure you are," Rick says with a fatherly tone. "Do you need a ride to your party?"

"Naw, mom's sending a car." Rick leans in and gives his daughter a brief hug as Leslie kisses her father on the cheek.

"Are we still on for the Fourth?"

"Fireworks in L.A.? I wouldn't miss it. Love you."

"Love you, too." Rick turns and tosses Jon a nod over his shoulder. Jon gives a slight wave back then returns to his double neck, custom guitar, fine tuning it for the upcoming concert.

The outdoor amphitheater is filled to capacity. Night has fallen over the University with tall lampposts surrounding the outer areas of the inclined seating, casting down soft light throughout. Reggie, Dante and the family of bikers consumes the upper plateau, playfully shoving each other and spilling their bottles of beer.

Among the gathered assembly of concertgoers, Tez and Kaleen find their seats near the front center. Tez, as always, sports his dark framed sunglasses.

A few rows back and over, Larry and Zoey continue their friendly chit-chat. Quite a contrast, Larry in his Cardigan sweater and Zoey in her vampiric attire. Gordon makes his way through the crowds and files in alongside of Larry.

Appearing along the furthest, upper row of concrete seats, Gio steps out of the shadows. He keeps to himself, slightly annoyed at Reggie and Dante's boisterous activities several yards away. Throughout the eager faces of students and graduated seniors, there is no trace of Chloe. Maybe she's at Leslie's party as well.

The lights from the lampposts dim. The soft footlights along the edge of the forward facing stage begin to glow. The air is filled with cheers and whistles. The towering speakers on opposite sides of the stage remain silent. The middle and back stage area appears void of all movement. Then, the thundering sounds of a double-bass drum cuts through the darkness.

Rafe pounds his drumsticks along the heads of his pair of deep floor tom-toms; *Everybody Wants Some*. The rhythm is similar to the war dance of Native Americans, repetitious and hypnotic.

Soft, green glowing lights slowly comes up from under Rafe, illuminating his drum set as well as himself. He continues his monstrous drum solo, caught up in his own world. Resting on his head, a wireless one ear headset. A thin arm wraps down from the padded earpiece and leads to a microphone in front of his mouth.

Jon bounds into view, finding his mark along the right side of the stage with his double-neck, black glossy "X" guitar hanging in front of himself. Standing directly above a series of soft orange footlights, Jon faces a microphone stand and a row of foot pedals below.

The elder of the Von Dutch Brothers seems quite irritated, rushed and unorganized. Rafe has started the concert without him! Stretching out his hands, Jon fumbles along the opposite set of frets, the lead-in for the guitar, as well as, the intro for the bass.

Rafe continues his rhythmatic pattern, faster and faster. His arms and feet are a blur. Jon continues to struggle to catch up with the loud and thundering introduction. He takes a few quick steps away from his orange colored lights, leans over and yells toward Rafe. "Hey, slow down! You're playin' it too fast!"

Rafe ignores his older brother's scolding as he ends the introduction of the popular cover tune and kicks into the actual song. Rafe, on lead vocals, belts out the lyrics, as he continues to play along on his drum set.

Jon returns to his mark along the right side of the stage and provides occasional backup vocals. Playing lead guitar, bass guitar, as well as, lead vocals is just too much for one musician to pull off. As the rock and roll song continues, Jon focuses on the constant bass line with his right hand as well and screaming guitar riffs with his left.

Reggie, Dante and their family of bikers dance along the upper plateau area with the rest of the filled outdoor amphitheater consumed with partying bodies. The carnival feeling fills the air as the thundering drums and lead vocals concludes the song.

Cheers and applauds ring out with arms waving wildly through the air. "What's your problem, Rafe?" Jon shouts out across the stage.

"You said be ready to play! Now shut-up and play!" Jon and Rafe scowl at each other for a moment.

"...alright," Jon says, as he turns and finds his mark directly in front of the crowd. The tips of his cowboy boots hang over the edge of the stage as Jon slams into a screaming guitar solo. Using both of his hands, his fingers fly across the neck of the guitar.

The *eruption* fills the amphitheater. There is no pattern nor beat to keep up with. Rafe sits on his padded stool, waiting for the right moment to jump in. Among the crowds, Kaleen laughs. Tez is wildly mimicking Jon's musical efforts on stage. His air guitar performance is quite amusing.

Jon slams against the strings of his guitar, holding and resonating the last chord. The moment of silence is interrupted with cheers and applauds. Just as Jon catches his breath, Rafe tears into another drum solo and introduction. This time, Jon's ready for him.

Rafe thunders his drumsticks across the pair of deep floor tom-toms, adds a snare then a cymbal or two. The double-bass drums pound, shaking the stage. Rafe's musical efforts sounds like the exhaust pipes of a large motorcycle. No more Dean of Students, no more lectures, no more professors and sadly, no more being *hot for teacher;* it's party time!

Playing in harmony with the percussion, Jon kicks in playing the constant bass line with his right and then adding guitar riffs with his left.

The crowd is at a near frenzy, jumping up and down, dancing wildly around. Reggie, Dante and the bikers have formed a moshpit of sorts, slamming into each other and bouncing off each other's bodies.

Larry and Zoey dance along the concrete rows of seats as Kaleen and Tez dance with each other a few rows away. Back in the upper areas, fading in and out of the shadows, Gio continues to listen to the concert.

He keeps to himself as he leans against a lamppost, his arms crossed in front of himself. Gio shows little enthusiasm for the show. However, his expensive shoe does tap in tune with the music.

"Rafe. Jon. Just Jon," the casual, yet well dressed businessman announces as he approaches Jon who's packing up his double-neck guitar. "Rick. Rick Stanton. Omega Records." Rick reaches into his suit jacket pocket and retrieves a business card.

In the near distance, the sounds of a hundred roaring motorcycle engines. Reggie and Dante lead the convoy of departing taillights, along the narrow, two lane roadway through the campus then out onto the main street.

Rafe inches his way around the remaining sections of his drum set. The cymbal stands and cymbals have been disassembled and lay in a stack. The pair of deep floor tom-toms lay next to each other along the supporting back wall of the amphitheater.

Zoey gathers up Rafe's padded stool and the large drumstick bag. She glances over toward Rafe who continues to unfasten the pair of mounted tom-toms from the double-bass drum. She looks for approval or an acknowledgement of gratitude... which never comes.

Taking the padded stool and drumstick bag, Zoey disappears from the side of the stage and vanishes into the darkness behind the amphitheater.

The inclined rows of concrete seats have been evacuated with the surrounding lampposts beaming brightly downward. Rafe's shadow moves across the tower of speakers as he approaches Rick and Jon near center stage. Jon carefully examines the business card. "I'd like you boys to come down to L.A. next week. We'll throw a couple tracks down and see what happens."

"You didn't say..." Rafe begins.

"You didn't ask," Rick says with a playful smile. "Call the office. I'll set everything up. It's been a pleasure, Jon."

"Thank-you! Thank-you!" Jon manages to blurt out. The record executive and the aspiring Rock God shake hands. Rick turns and heads toward the side of the stage. He pauses and glances over his shoulder.

"You boys should consider changing your name. *The Dutch Brothers* is too... VH-1. You need something catchier. See ya' next week." Rick bounds off the side of the stage and heads off across the campus grounds.

Rafael Von Dutch, the drummer, seems to have been left out of this conversation. He's been left out of this life altering decision.

~ III ~

"I heard you were accepted for a full four year scholarship," Gordon says, continuing to stand in the opened doorway of the dorm room.

"Yeah. I think *you* had something to do with that." Larry says, as he removes a stack of law books from his immaculate bookshelf. He leans over and places the thick books into an opened box on his bare, twin sized bed. The mattress sinks downward due to the weight of the numerous boxes already filled with packed law books.

The single occupant dorm room has been stripped. No accolades or framed pictures hang from the walls. The stacks of packed boxes stands off in the corner. Larry's opened closet is filled with empty hangers. "We'll keep in touch, though," Larry says as he turns from his bookshelf. Gordon has vanished from the doorway.

Larry creeps his way across his quiet dorm room and peers his head around the corner of the opened doorway. Gordon continues to walk along the brightly lit hallway, weaving his way around cluttered boxes, passing by soon-to-be departing graduates.

Just as Gordon turns the far corner of the hallway, he gives Larry a slight wave of his hand. "I expect you promptly at eight tomorrow." With that, Gordon disappears from sight. Larry smiles to himself as he reenters his dorm room and returns to his packing.

Zoey stands in the opened doorway of her double occupant dorm room. There is still so much to do. The nearside of the dorm room is dark and dreary.

Posters of ominous, evil looking clowns and scarecrows cover the darkly painted walls. Resting on a dresser top, a deck of tarot cards and a table lamp with a cobweb design. Secured along the back of the dresser, a horizontal mirror stretches out its full length.

Zoey's bedspread has an astrological print, revealing the twelve Zodiac signs and a dark colored, complimenting star speckled pillowcase. A stack of broken down boxes lays in the center of the room, separating the very different choices of décor.

Chloe's living space is on the opposite side of the room, bright and frilly. "*Yuk,*" Zoey thinks to herself. "*How can she stand so much... happiness?*" The room has an odd feeling about it, as if it were severed directly down the center.

Directly across from Zoey's bed, an identical twin bed with a light colored bedspread with dozens of butterflies. Across from the cobweb table lamp and deck of tarot cards, a horizontal mirror secured to the back of the dresser. Atop the dresser, a table lamp with a farm style design and a wooden music box.

From the opened doorway looking inward, the dorm room looks as if an invisible partition were in place. Dark and light. Night and day. Even the single window along the far, middle wall seems to be segregated. Black drapes hang from the left side of the curtain rod with the right side having thick and bright fabric.

Below the window and standing in front of the oddly colored drapes, a single nightstand. Resting on the top, a single stereo and compact disk system with a matching pair of speakers to opposite sides. This piece of furniture appears to be the only shared item throughout the room.

The left hand side of the nightstand is covered with haphazardly placed compact disk cases, disorderly and unorganized. The right hand side is neat and tidy with the compact disks alphabetically filed between the side of the stereo and the speaker.

Resting on top of the stereo system, the only object shared by the two opposing styles of décor. The photo appears charred around the edges and rests inside a common glass frame.

The image is that of a family. A happy family posing with the colorful and lively amusement park in the background. An athletic looking mother, a strikingly handsome father and a raven haired young girl with piercing green eyes and over average ears.

Zoey reluctantly inches her way across the room and steps onto the collection of broken down, cardboard boxes. She plops down onto the edge of her bed and fiddles with several compact disk cases. Finding the musical group she is searching for, Zoey slides the glimmering, flat sphere into the player.

Zoey leans over and takes a cardboard box in hand and reshapes it. She opens the top drawer of the nightstand and begins to retrieve her vast collection of black stockings and undergarments. "*It'll be good to get out of here,*" she thinks to herself as the melodic rock and roll ballad fills the dorm room.

Zoey has managed to survive four years at the University. Not by her choice, Chloe insisted upon it. They found themselves drifting further and further apart as the time slipped away.

Chloe would find herself in the company of aspiring doctors and soon to be lawyers, expanding her future career options. Zoey, well she could entertain herself watching the wind blow through the leaves along the campus grounds.

Over the years, fellow students found Zoey quite odd. Sometimes, they'd say, she'd talk to herself and answer. Sometimes, she'd talk with her dead parents. Even sometimes, *she talks to angels*. But, her fellow students really knew that was just all in her head.

The gymnasium is dark and quiet. Only a few scattered, overhead florescent bulbs provide sparse light. The opposite facing, wooden bleachers have been retracted against the walls, allowing the summer janitorial staff complete access to refinish the basketball court.

Below the opposite ends of the basketball hoops, the thick white and blue mats have been rolled up and await for next year's horde of wrestlers.

Gio stands quietly at center court. He absorbs the stillness and is refreshed by the dark shadows that surround him. Yet, the constant ringing in his ear is a distraction. Not that of the thundering drums or screaming guitar of the Dutch Brothers concert. He hears the sounds of defeat. "*I had him!*" Gio angrily thinks to himself. "*Next time, Dante. Next time!*"

Suddenly, laughter echoes out from the dimly lit locker-room. Gio turns to see Tez and Kaleen scampering out onto the edge of the basketball court. Tez seems quite at home in the darkness as he takes Kaleen by the hand. He leads her across the smooth wooden floor. "Hey, Gio," Tez says with a smile.

"Had to get one more in before you left, huh?" Gio inquisitively asks.

"We had a list at the beginning of the year," Kaleen replies with a seductive giggle. "We have one more stop."

"Well, I'll let you lovebirds get to it." Gio begins making his way toward the far closed double doors.

"You goin' to Gordon's t'morrow night?" Tez calls out. Standing along the end of the rolled up white and blue wrestling mats, Gio turns.

"Yeah, I was thinking about popping in for awhile. Sounds fun." Gio turns and disappears through the shadows of the double swinging doors. Kaleen playfully tugs at Tez's arm.

"Do you have the list," she whispers.

"Don't need the list. I know where the last stop is," Tez replies, as he nibbles on Kaleen's ear. "The Dean of Students' office..."

"Good-evening, ladies and gentlemen. The Zoo will be closing in thirty minutes." The feminine voice is pleasant and courteous, seeping out from well placed speakers hanging from lit lampposts. "Before leaving, please feel free to stop by our gift shop. Again, The Zoo will be closing in thirty minutes. Thank-you for coming and drive safely."

Gordon continues to lean over the handrailing, gazing into the simulated, natural environment of the lion pits. An occasional family passes behind him as they make their way to the exiting gates. The lampposts light the way, leading to and from the various exhibits, pens, cages and other manmade containment areas for the vast assortment of wild creatures.

A lioness casually strolls out from her cavern followed by a male. The large cats seem to know each other, more than fellow felines, more like family or even from the same liter. They approach a second male who remains laying on a boulder, slightly hanging its forepaws over the edge.

The male lions nip and playfully claw at each other as the lioness approaches the edge of the deep ravine, separating their containment area from the elevated handrailing. The lioness strolls back and forth, never taking her eyes off of the staring human. She seems to know Gordon, possibly remembering an adventure they had shared. A boat trip across the sea.

The pair of males are less sentimental of their rescue from so many years ago. They continue to paw at each other along the boulder as the lioness circles herself several times then lays down. She stretches out her paws and lets out a low roar. Gordon has departed, having vanished into the shadows.

"I graduated yesterday," Zoey says in a somber tone. She stands with her head lowered, almost as if she were praying. Zoey's dark and Gothic attire seems to compliment the pair of weathered headstones she continues to stare down it.

Zoey is surrounded by rows upon rows of gravesites and headstones. Some with freshly arrived bouquets of flowers with others having framed pictures atop their flat stone surfaces.

She appears to be the only person around, standing in solitude. Zoey carefully plans her next words as she continues to stare at the pair of worn headstones;

Jonathan Michael Richards

Samantha Kay Richards

Zoey slightly smiles to herself, remembering a time when she was younger, a time when they were all together and happy. Small gatherings of fallen leaves covers the upward faces of the pair of headstones, concealing the days of birth. But one thing is for certain, both her mother and father died on the same day.

"I don't see much of Chloe anymore." Zoey pauses. "I guess she's into her own thing now." Her tone changes, becoming slightly enthusiastic. "Oh, did I tell you? I start a new job next week, in Olympia. So, I'll be moving away." Zoey takes a deep breath. "Sorry, I won't be able to visit you as much. I'll try and get back for Thanksgiving."

"Zoey, let's go! It's gettin' late!" Reggie calls out from the narrow roadway winding through the cemetery. Reggie sits on the forward seat of his trike with Dante straddling his motorcycle a few feet away. Ma, Pa and the rest of the family of bikers are nowhere to be seen.

The late afternoon air is chilly with a few stray rain clouds floating across the sky. The boys don't seem to mind the coolness of the season. Their black leather vests, scattered with various patches and insignias are enough cover for them.

"I miss you..." Zoey whispers with a tear in her eye. She kisses her fingertips, leans down and tenderly presses her opened hand on her mother and father's headstones. Zoey quickly turns and darts toward Reggie. Dante flips up the kickstand of his motorcycle with the heel of his boot then slams down on the kick start.

Reggie flicks on the electric start of his trike as Zoey approaches and hops on the back. Dante revs his engine before heading out along the narrow pathway. "You okay?" Reggie asks over his shoulder.

"Yeah, I'm fine," she says with an unconvincing smile. "Let's get to the party!"

An odd mist fills the air with majestic trees lining opposite sides of the one lane dirt road cutting deep into the woods. Dark clouds roll across the sky with the full moon attempting to pierce through, bathing the treetops with its lunar glow.

A doe timidly creeps out from the tree line. She pauses, looking both ways along the dirt road. There, in the distance, a pair of headlights approaches. The doe scampers across the road and disappears into the opposite tree line. "Are you alright?" Jon asks his brother.

Jon sits in the forward passenger's seat of their custom, 1975 Dodge van. Rafe sits behind the wheel, steering along the dark back road of the forest. The rear cargo area of the van is crammed with Rafe's drum set and Jon's numerous guitar cases, as well as, microphone stands and rolls of cable. Directly behind Jon's seat are several filled bags of groceries. "Why do you ask?'" Rafe finally answers.

"You've been quiet all afternoon."

"I'm just concerned about you."

"Concerned about *me*?" Jon asks. This is a switch, his younger brother is worried about him. "Why wouldn't I be okay?"

"How's your breathing? You breathing okay?"

"Yeah, why wouldn't I be?"

"Well, you had your head so far up Rick's ass yesterday, I wasn't sure if you had enough air!"

"Gimmie a break!"

"No, really! *Thank-you! Thank-you! Thank-you*! You were worse than Oliver. *Oh, please, sir. May I have some more*!"

"Look, Rafe. Tez played our stuff on the University's radio station but we've had no *real* air time. This could be my shot!" Oops...

"Yeah, that's what I thought."

"I meant *our shot*."

"No, you didn't!" Rafe disgustingly shakes his head as he continues to look forward. Up ahead, passed the headlights, a break in the tree line appears.

"Rafe, com'on. You have one year of school left."

"And?"

"You'd dropout?"

"To keep *The Dutch Brothers* together? Yeah, that's what *brothers* do."

"*The Dutch Brothers*. I've been thinking about that, too."

"What, changing our name?" Rafe answers with a hostile tone.

"Something a little more catchy. *Sons of Darkness, Children of the Night* or how 'bout *The Hounds of Hell?* Rick said..."

"I don't care what Rick said!" Rafe pounds on the breaks, nearly rips his keys out of the ignition and flings open the driver's side door. "Don't forget the chips!"

Rafe slams the door and storms away from their van. He mockingly waves his hand behind himself, motioning to the extended side of their van. "Guess we better change that, too!" Words are painted along the upper rear panels of the van in bright green and orange colors;

♫ ♪♫ The Dutch Brothers ♫ ♪♫

Jon slides the side door of the van open and reaches inside. He collects the filled bags of groceries and slides the side door closed. Making his way around the front of the van, he follows far behind Rafe.

Reggie's trike and Dante's motorcycle stands off to the side of a black, two seated sports car. A few yards away, a mock, wood-paneled station wagon. Parked closer to the rustic farmhouse, Gordon's red and white VW microbus.

The plain unpainted home appears at the top of a slight incline of the terrain with its flat wooden planks covering the one and a half story structure with a complimenting wraparound porch.

A handrailing constructed of tree branches leads the route up along the walkway, heading up to a series of steps and the front door. Shadows are seen dancing across the windows of what appears to be the living room.

As Rafe steps up onto the porch, he hears laughter under the constant rock and roll music from past decades.

Gordon's property remains undeveloped. A clearing is seen through the darkness, stretching out to the vast tree line. About twenty yards away, a tall structure peeks out of the shadows. The old style, two-story barn is similar to the farmhouse, unpainted with flat wooden planks. For now, there is no movement nor light from inside.

"Glad you could make it!" Gordon cheerfully says as Rafe makes his way into the kitchen. However, there's something *off* with the drummer. "You two fightin' again?"

"Nope," Rafe says, as he pops open a beer. "Jon's right. He's *always* right. So, there's nothing to fight about."

"Hey, Rafe," Zoey says, with a twinkle in her eye. She bounces into the kitchen, dancing around Rafe. She takes his hands and coaxes him to dance along with her. Rafe tries to amuse her for a moment but his heart's just not into it.

"Not right now, Zoey. Maybe later."

"Hey, Jon," Gordon says, with a nod. Jon enters the kitchen and places the filled bags of groceries onto the rustic dining room table. Without a single word, Jon takes one of the bags, turns and heads toward the rock and roll music seeping out from the living room.

"You two fightin' again?" Zoey asks. Rafe and Gordon exchange an odd look, "*Didn't you just ask that?* Rafe starts to laugh at himself as he takes Zoey by the hand.

"C'mon! *I'm* not gonna be the party-pooper!" Rafe says, as he nearly drags Zoey out of the kitchen. Gordon shakes his head as he reaches into the older model refrigerator and retrieves a beer for himself.

"*This* is going to be an interesting night." Gordon shuts the fridge door with his hip, takes up a bag of groceries and follows behind.

"So, Professor. When are we gonna fire this thing up?" Dante eagerly asks. The centerpiece of the rustic living room is an oddly constructed coffee table, standing knee high, seven feet long and three feet wide. The flat and weather worn planks appear broken and jagged along the opposite ends. The wood appears to have been part of a sailing vessel's outer hull. At one end of the surface of the planks, a faded word is made out;

DEMETER

Resting in the center of the table, a tall, lavender hookah. Four separate hoses branch out from the main body of the glass smoking device. A singular bowl stems out near the base of the pipe with the four, glass mouthpieces at the ends of the hoses, laying on the wooden planks. "We're not going to start until everybody's here." The students look about the living room.

Gordon stands in the opened walkway joining the kitchen and living room. To his right, a wooden staircase and banister leads up to the second floor of the farmhouse.

Tez and Kaleen dance with each other off in the corner, keeping to themselves for now. Jon and Rafe stand at opposites sides of the living room, giving each other their distance.

Larry and Zoey sit next to each other along the tan loveseat directly across from Reggie and Dante seated on the couch. Larry slides his hand into an opened bag and gathers a handful of potato chips. "I don't think Chloe's going to make it tonight," Zoey says as a matter of fact.

The gathering of friends gives each other weird looks. "*Duh!*" they must be thinking to themselves. "*Of course Chloe's not going to show as long as Zoey's here.*" An odd feeling fills the room as if someone had mentioned a death in the family or another horrific event.

In an attempt to lighten the mood, Gordon makes his way across the room and approaches his outdated stereo system. He removes an eight-track tape and replaces it with another.

Upbeat, rock and roll music from the late 1960's fills the air. Tez and Kaleen continue dancing with each other off in the corner as a pair of headlights, beams into the living room from outside. Reggie and Dante glance at each other, each with a mischievous grin.

Footsteps from the second floor catches Gordon's attention as he turns and looks up the wooden staircase. A woman's wet pair of feet begin to descend. There appears to be no nail polish along her toenails. Her shins and calves are smooth and clean shaven.

The bottom edge of her damp, dark multi-colored dress flutters behind her as she makes her way to the middle of the staircase. Larry stops munching on his chips, he has become aware of the stunning sandy blonde woman.

Sonja wears a loosely buttoned white blouse with the tails tied at her waist. She appears damp, almost wet as if she had forgotten the basics of towel usage. Leaving a trail of wet footprints down the wooden staircase, Sonja approaches Gordon. "You're outta hot water."

Sonja suddenly shakes her thick sandy blonde hair as if she were a large feline beast retreating from a lake or a pond. The water splatters the near wall, sprinkles across Gordon and as well as Reggie and Dante on seated on the couch. Reggie and Dante don't seem to mind the intrusion too much. "*Oh yeah, she'll fit right in,*" Reggie thinks to himself.

Tez seems to take little notice of Sonja. He and Kaleen continues to dance to the constant rock and roll music in the background. Kaleen has his full attention.

"This is my niece, Sonja. She's staying with me for a few days," Gordon says. Larry nearly trips over the corner of the large coffee table as he makes his way toward her. Jon and Rafe are amused with Larry's boyish antics, it's like he's never seen an attractive woman before.

"I'm Larry Wells. It's a pleasure to meet you." Larry can feel his palm sweating as he extends out his hand toward Sonja. As they politely shake hands, Sonja can feel his thumping heartbeat through his fingertips. They exchange an immediate, animal attraction. As the front door suddenly opens, every head turns.

"Alright," Dante announces. "Jon and Rafe brought the chips. Who brought the dip?" Standing in the doorway with a half-rack of beer, Gio gives Dante a scowl.

"Glad you could make it," Gordon interrupts. "Over here." Gordon motions Gio toward the kitchen. Dante and Gio exchange hostile stares as Gio places the beer onto the kitchen counter. "I'm not gonna to have a problem with you two, am I?" Gordon asks in a whisper.

"Not at all. I'm here for the party," Gio replies with a smirk. He pops open a beer as Gordon manages to stuff the rest of the half-rack into the fridge. Gordon makes his way from the kitchen and stands in the entryway leading into the living room.

"Well, now that you're all here, I guess we can get started." Gordon pauses a moment then turns toward Sonja. "Larry, I'm going to need my niece for a few minutes." Larry and Sonja remain standing at the foot of the staircase. As Sonja turns away from him, he looks like a forgotten puppy, lost out in the cold.

"Hey, Rafe! While you're up." Zoey says as she holds up her empty beer can. Rafe gives Zoey a friendly nod, heads across the living room floor and joins Gordon and Sonja in the kitchen.

Gordon reaches into the opened freezer and retrieves a folded block of tinfoil, the size of a standard deck of playing cards. As he closes the freezer, the opens the lower fridge for Rafe.

"Thanks," Rafe says as he takes three beers in hand. "What's that?" he asks, motioning to the folded block of tinfoil.

"Oh this?" Gordon pauses a moment then answers with a mischievous smile, "This is party favors..."

"Is everybody in?" Gordon asks, standing at the far end of the wooden planked coffee table. "*Is every-body in? The ceremony's about to begin.*" Gordon has shed his clothing and wears a leather loincloth.

Still unsure of the upcoming events, the gathering of students remain clothed as they surround the edges of the coffee table. The loveseat and couch has been moved closer with a few additional chairs as well. The lights have been dimmed. At a lower volume now, the rock and roll music from decades gone by, continues in the background.

Gordon carefully holds the end of a lit stick, the size of an average drinking straw. He holds the flame above the bowl of the lavender hookah. Inside the bowl, a portion of the dark, pasty substance from the opened block of tinfoil.

Sitting in the center of the couch, Reggie and Dante hold onto the ends of two of the hookah's hoses with the glass mouthpieces hanging from their lips.

To their right, seated in the loveseat, Larry and Zoey hold onto the other pair of hoses, waiting for the dark and pasty substance to burn. "I will teach you to retain your consciousness while you are in your alter," Gordon says in monotone. "You will be able to act and function as you are right now, but not. "

Gordon lights the bowl. Reggie, Dante, Larry and Zoey deeply inhales and holds the warm smoke in their lungs. They look upon each other with wild eyes. "*What will happen to us?*" they all must be thinking.

The foursome exhales, as Gordon motions to them. Again, Larry, Zoey, Reggie and Dante inhales the thick smoke from the smoldering dark substance. "Remember, *you* do not choose your alter. *Your alter* chooses you."

For the third time, Larry, Zoey, Reggie and Dante exhale. They hand their glass mouthpieces to the person next to them. Jon, Rafe, Tez and Kaleen take the hoses and place the glass mouthpieces between their lips.

As he had done with the previous group, Gordon lights the replenished bowl with the lit stick. They deeply inhale and hold in the warm smoke. "The *stars* will dictate what you will become," Gordon says in monotone. "For a few of us, there are no limitations."

Gio stands behind the couch, carefully watching, taking precise mental notes. Sonja wanders freely about the living room, assisting Gordon as needed. If one of them loses control either physically or mentally, she will be there. She knows what they will be going through. She's been there herself.

Tez, Kaleen, Jon and Rafe exhale for the third time. "Hey, you're up!" Dante says with an insistent tone. Gio and Dante exchange an odd look. Was that a polite invitation? Is it time to bury the hatchet or was that a command? Jon raises up from the couch and hands Gio the hose.

Rafe bolts up from the couch and joins Jon in an air-guitar rendition of the outdated song playing in the background. Tez and Kaleen rise from the loveseat and begin twirling with each other as Gio sits in the center of the couch clutching onto the glass mouthpiece.

Gordon sits next to him, watching the eager young man. "You're not going to smoke?" Gio curiously asks.

"There's no need. Once you've stepped through the doorway, there's no need to return." Gordon hands the flickering stick to Gio. He takes it and lowers the flame to the replenished bowl filled with the black and pasty substance. Gio deeply inhales, harder and longer than the rest of the group. He is determined to learn Gordon's secrets.

The living room is a free-for-all. Clothing has been discarded as half naked bodies freely dance around the room. No longer regimented by politely taking turns, the students fire up the replenished bowl of the hookah and smoke at will.

The dark and pasty substance, once the shape of a standard deck of playing cards, is now the size of a thumbnail. Standing in the archway of the kitchen, Gordon scans the living room.

Off in the corner, Tez and Kaleen dance with each other in a tight and loving embrace. Jon and Rafe sit at opposite ends of the loveseat as they continue to mimic the rock and roll instruments of the music playing in the background. They appear to be getting along, again.

Sitting in the center of the couch, Reggie and Dante take random hits of the hookah, as they continue their playful game of thumb-wrestling.

Gio and Zoey sit in the additional chairs facing Reggie and Dante and likewise, freely smoking from the remaining pair of hoses and glass mouthpieces.

Gio is attempting to explain to Zoey about the metaphysical similarities of quantum relationships of scientific disorders and their parallel complications of coexistence. "*What?*" Zoey rattles in her head. "*Shut-up and smoke that thing!*"

"I'm surprised that Gordon hasn't mentioned you before," Larry says in his best, charming tone.

"Why would he?" Sonja asks, playing off Larry's obvious one-liner. As Larry and Sonja walk along Gordon's property, they dip in and out of the shadows with the full moon hanging high in the sky.

The student's parked vehicles appears off in the distance, accompanied by Gio's recently arrived 1965, black Mustang. "People let you know what they want you to know. No more... no less."

"I guess so," Larry responds with a less than enthusiastic tone. "So, what do you do when you're not visiting the Professor?"

"I work with the W.W.F.." Larry gives Sonja an odd look. "No, the *other* one! I'm on the road a lot working with animals. I rarely have a place of my own in The City so I crash here when I'm in town."

"I'm glad you did." An awkward moment follows. Sonja stops dead in her tracks. Taking a few steps forward, Larry realizes that Sonja is no longer at his side. He turns back. Sonja looks at him with an odd and devilish smile.

"Are you going to make the first move or am I?"

"I, ah..." Larry mumbles. He's never met a woman so forthcoming.

"Look, I don't have much time and would like to make the most of it while I'm here." With that, Sonja lunges forward and plants a long, wet kiss on Larry's lips.

"There you two are," Kaleen says, as she leads Tez across the wraparound porch of Gordon's house. Kaleen and Tez face outward, toward the darkness as Larry and Sonja slightly pull away from each other.

"The Professor says it's time to get started. Man, I thought we already had!" Tez says as he and Kaleen step off the side stairs of the porch.

Jon and Rafe bound out from the side door of Gordon's house. Rafe dives, tucks and rolls, completing a somersault in the dirt with Jon lopping close behind.

Reggie and Dante playfully shove and push at each other as they exit through the front door. They join the gathering of migrating students, across Gordon's property, through the darkness and toward the two-story barn in the shadows. "Would you do me a favor, Gio?" Zoey asks in a concerned tone.

"Sure, anything."

"Keep an eye on me. I'm kinda new at all this."

"New at what? Smoking? Drinking or going to a party out in the middle of nowhere with your half naked Professor?"

"Yes!"

"No worries," Gio replies with a brotherly tone. "I'll keep an eye on you."

"Ladies and gentlemen, boys and girls. *Welcome!*" Gordon announces, as he flings open the large, wooden double doors of the lower level of the barn.

Gordon leads them inward with lit lanterns on opposite sides of the central aisle. Toward the right and left sides of the lower area of the barn, twelve concrete foundation and wooden planked stalls; six on each side of the barn. The wooden gates appear slightly ajar with no animal occupants. "Hey, Professor!" Jon shouts out. "What's the pool for?"

"Just in case," Gordon softly replies.

"In case of what?" Zoey asks. Gordon turns and pulls the barn's double doors closed. With an old style plank lever, he locks and secures the doors. Gordon turns and faces the students.

"Now, I want you all to pick a stall."

"You're not gonna get *weird* on us are ya'?" Larry asks.

"As weird as you wanna be, Larry," Gordon says with a smile. As a flight attendant would point out the emergency exits on an airplane, Gordon points out the various directions of the opposite facing stalls. "Hurry now. You're all about outta time!"

"I'll be here when you wake up," Sonja calmly says as she leads Larry into one of the middle stalls.

"Wake up from what?"

"You're rebirth." Sonja says, as she kisses Larry on the cheek. She slightly shoves Larry into the stall covered with hay along the dirt floor.

"No!" Gordon says in a commanding voice. "Those two stalls are for you two." Gordon motions toward Tez and Kaleen.

The pair of opposite facing stalls at the far end of the barn are directly adjacent to an extended pool.

The large storage areas where bales of hay once were kept, have now been replaced by a concrete pool. The calm and clear water spans out from the barn's inner wall to its opposite inner wall; forty feet long, fourteen feet wide and over five feet deep.

"Holy crap, Professor!" Jon exclaims. "This is the best ride I've ever been on!" Jon is beginning to feel the effects of the smoked black and pasty substance. He looks down at his upper hand as wild and coarse hair begins to sprout up and outward from his flesh. *"...am I hallucinating?"* Jon thinks to himself.

"You all will be reborn," Gordon calls out in a commanding voice. He stands in the center of the aisle of the barn, watching the various mutations that were once his students. "But remember. There are three rules you must never break!"

"Three rules?" Larry manages to painfully say. "*Now* you tell us!" He appears sprawled out across loose piles of hay of his stall. Larry's body size has nearly doubled. His human flesh has been replaced by orange and black, stripped fur.

Larry's stomach and lower areas are covered with white fur with sporadic orange and black stripes. His upper and lower extremities has mutated into large paws.

"Wow, dude," Reggie mumbles. You're lookin' really strange, man." Reggie looks at his lifelong friend through the vertical bars of the adjoining stalls, almost like prison cells.

Dante's lower extremities have begun to morph and enlarge. His dreadlocks have molded down along the middle of his shoulder blades and the middle of his back.

Reggie feels his arms extending outward. His armpits fan out with his fingertips melting together. Reggie feels his hips and knees uncontrollably binding into each other. "Are you two doing okay back here?" Sonja asks Tez and Kaleen.

Sonja stands in the middle of the central aisle of the last two stalls of the barn, carefully watching the ongoing transformations. To her left, Tez had lost all of his body hair. He wallows across the hay floor with his dark sunglasses off to the side of a pile of horse manure.

His upper extremities continue to mutate, being sucked into his ribs, the sides of his stomach and his hips. Tez's thighs, knees and ankles morph into each other creating a singular stem down along his waist.

Kaleen flip-flops across her bed of hay. She retains her consciousness, for the most part. Her upper extremities seems to be unaffected by her transformation. From the waist up, she continues to be Kaleen. From the waist down, that's another story.

Kaleen's big toes mold into each other. Her flesh along her inner claves and thighs mutate, creating one singular lower extremity. The same as Tez, however drastically different.

Gio appears stronger than the other students, both physically and mentally. Finally, after all the years of endless studying, the torturous hours of his father's lecturing and the monotonous months of Gordon's classroom notes has paid off.

Gio has retained his human awareness although halfway through his transformation. He stands upright, over six feet tall. Gio is covered from head to tail with soft, black fur. His forepaws move and act as if he were still human, opening and closing his paws, extending then retracting his claws.

Gio's consciousness forces his new exterior, a full grown black panther, to walk ahead, upright on its hind legs as a human would. Its thick black tail slightly wags behind as he passes Gordon.

The professor is impressed. It took him nearly a month to perfect the hesitation in transformation; retaining his human abilities and motor skills yet, with the outer appearance of one of his many alters.

As Gio walks along the central aisle of the barn, his mutation resumes. The black panther falls down on all fours and playfully circles Gordon several times. "You want to be out in the night, don't you?" The panther lets out a growl of approval.

Gordon faces the closed barn doors, reaches up and lifts the wooden securing plank. He presses his palms against the doors and flings them open. The black panther leaps forward and dashes out into the darkness. Gordon hears low thumping behind himself. The sounds of galloping animals.

The large cheetah bounds passed Gordon and disappears through the opened barn doors, as if it'd been captive all its life and *unchained* for the first time. The cheetah is quickly followed by a full grown wolf. The wolf slows its pace and springs on Gordon, not as an attack but as a playful gesture.

The large wolf stands on its hind legs, licking at Gordon's face. The canine's thick tail wags back and forth as Gordon reaches up and scratches it behind the ears. "You'd better get going, Jon. You're brother will be tough to keep up with." The wolf lets out a bark, falls to all fours then races after the cheetah.

Gordon turns away from the opened barn doors and looks the full length of the barn. At the opposite end, Sonja remains at the side of the concrete pool. "How are they doing?" Gordon asks in a fatherly tone.

"Kaleen is being very helpful. Tez is coming along nicely." Several splashes are heard from the pool, like a pair of aquatic creatures playing a game a tag.

From the shadows of one of the stalls, a majestic North American condor flies outward. The bird of prey flaps its wings several times before soaring out of the opened barn doors. "Aw, com'on! You've gotta be kidding!" Dante shouts out in protest. He remains hidden in the shadows of his stall, almost embarrassed to reveal himself.

Gordon slowly walks along the central aisle of the barn, glancing into each of the emptying stalls. He pauses a moment, looking into the third stall in from the opened barn doors.

Zoey appears crouched down, almost in a fetal position, in the far corner of the stall. She trembles with her fists tightly clutched. Zoey is confused and is becoming more disoriented. Due to her preexisting mental condition, she is uncertain what she is seeing is real or simply a bad series of hallucinations.

Gordon stands over Zoey a moment then kneels down. They are eye to eye. She doubts her consciousness. This really can't be happening.

The hulking primitive creature in front of her has broad shoulders with dark, coarse hair. The transforming beast strongly resembles a large primate with a silverback. Yet, the creature continues to morph.

Its facial features are not that of a gorilla but smooth and scaly. Its head narrows with its face becoming a muzzle of sorts. The Komodo flicks its forked tongue at Zoey.

Atop this odd creature's head, a small pair of antlers sprouts upward, no larger than a male antelope's. Zoey timidly extends out her hand, as if to take hold of the creature. No human limbs are seen. Instead, the beast's retracted claws tenderly reach outward and rests on Zoey's shoulder. The paw is that of a large jungle cat.

As Zoey reaches out to touch the mutating creature, she sees that she has begun to transform herself. Her shoulder down to her elbow, her forearm to her wrist, is now covered with soft black and white fur.

She turns over what was once her hand and sees no fingers, no human digits. Zoey's palm has transformed into several lower pads as her fingertips now appear to be claws.

Zoey continues to stare at her mutating limb, it is becoming more difficult to look downward over her expanding muzzle covered with soft white fur. A roar echoes out from another stall, startling Zoey. The morphing creature in front of her seems to smile under its reptilian facial features. It stands and lopes out of the stall.

Zoey's thoughts race through her head. She becomes more confused and disoriented. Zoey's arms have completed their transformation into thick forearms of a type of bear. She falls forward, landing on her paws. Her vision blurs. Zoey becomes dizzy as she begins to blackout...

"Has anybody seen my watch?"

"Where are my clothes?"

"What time is it?"

"Daytime..."

"Hey, Tez! Get your knee outta my back!"

"Sorry, Dante."

"Chloe? Is that you?"

"Yeah..."

"Glad you could make it. Better late than never."

"Why am I naked?"

"Professor, put that thing away! You might hurt someone!"

"Hey, guys! I found my watch... it's Monday!"

"Monday!?"

"What happened to the last three days?"

* * * * *

~ IV ~

"Tell me, Shaman. What *is* the secret?" Gio crouches down with an empty syringe between his thumb and fingers. He is dressed in a green T-shirt, cargo pants and hiking boots.

Resting on the ground next to him, an opened black medical bag with countless bottles of serums, medications and syringes. Gathered in separate clear containers, plants, herbs and other raw materials, similar to the ones collected by the Shaman and a young American so many years ago.

"I sense you have released the creature inside of you," Loup Garou manages to say as the injected drugs begin taking full effect. Loup sits on the ground with his back tightly pressed against a thick tropical tree.

Loup's ankles are bound with vines with his arms outstretched behind himself, restrained at the wrists with primitive rope. "Yes, I have," Gio answers with a sneer. "But I want more. I want the *secret* that you showed a man many decades ago."

"Oh, yes. I remember him. The Serpent Bearer. I liked him very much. He was special." Loup fades in and out of consciousness.

"I want to be special, too."

"No, you want to be the darkness."

"Within the darkness, there is light. Show me the light." Gio pauses a moment. He reaches up and takes a hold of Loup's hair. The Shaman's head is lowered, he can barely focus or keep a thought. Gio lifts Loup's head and draws in closer. "*What* is the secret, Shaman?"

"You are *who* you are. You are *what* you are. *That* is the secret." A low growl catches Gio's attention.

The surrounding trees are dark and eerie. Among the shadows of night, unclear images are seen, waiting for the moment to attack. A moment to rescue their elder.

A half-man-half-leopard steps forward and growls at Gio. The creature is magnificent, able to utilize its outer transformed shape yet, retaining its inner human consciousness.

The beast is joined by another creature, a reptilian being with a large narrow head and a forked tongue. Although the beasts have lost the ability to speak, they appear to be communicating with grunts, hisses and head movements.

Gio quickly turns in the opposite direction as three additional creatures step out of the shadows. The beasts appear to be in a suspended state of transformation.

The upright feline seems to have feminine qualities with the one of males covered in orange, black and white striped fur. The other male has the features of a hoofed animal, similar to a small horse or a mule. The tan furred feline steps forward, pressing her paws onto the jungle floor.

Gio slightly spins and strikes a catlike stance. He extends out his hand as if he were wearing a baseball glove. Gio's fingers quickly morph and mutate. In a matter of moments, his hand has transformed into the paw of a black panther.

Over the years, Gio has honed and nearly perfected his ability to control his alter. He reaches down toward Loup's throat and extends out his razor sharp claws. Gio lets out a low and commanding growl. He knows he can take them. He knows he can take them all!

The surrounding creatures pay heed and slowly back away. However, the opposing feline is reserved. She direly wants to rescue her father. Gio wraps his extended claws around Loup's throat. The feline roars as she steps back.

Gio slowly rises as he retracts his claws. He extends out his paw for the surrounding beasts to see. Gio has complete control of his mutating limb as it quickly transforms back to into human fingers.

Gio reaches down and gathers up his black medical bag. Walking slightly backward, he begins to make his way toward the tropical tree line.

Having returned to her human form, Elez rushes to her father and begins to untie his wrists. Payu and Loy appear from the shadows and approach Loup. They crouch down and untie his ankles. As Loup begins to regain his senses, he seems uninhibited by the naked bodies aiding in his rescue.

Gio steps out from the tropical tree line, just beyond the edge of the Shaman's village. The primitive dwellings have changed very little over the many years. The common wooden structures remain unpainted without shutters or even doors. The buildings stand elevated by stilts and platforms, providing some safety from the seasonal rains and rising river.

Gio approaches the opened area between the village and shoreline. Looking over his shoulder, he sees Elez and Payu holding up Loup. The Shaman is still groggy from the injected drugs. In their human form, the rest of the Pigmy villagers appear from the shadows.

He sets down his medical bag and turns to face them. Gio extends out his hands in a gesture as if he is unarmed and defenseless. This is their chance to attack the dark one. Yet, not one being moves.

Gio retrieves his medical bag and approaches the waterline of the river. Along the shore, scattered canoes are faintly made out through the shadows. He lifts his medical and places it on top of the narrow bow of an expensive looking speedboat.

The vessel is sleek and streamlined with a third of its forward keel resting on the shoreline. Gio reaches up toward the chrome handrailing and shoves the speedboat deeper into the water of the slow moving river.

Gio effortlessly leaps upward and plants his feet onto the bow. As the speedboat slides from the shoreline, he turns toward the village. Loup has almost fully recovered from the injected drugs. He stands along the shoreline watching Gio and the speedboat slip away.

Gio swings himself about and lands on the lower deck. He tosses his black medical bag to a set of cushioned seats along the stern. Taking the nautical steering wheel in hand, he fires up the electrical ignition.

Elez and Payu approach Loup from behind. They exchange odd looks with each other. Why would their Shaman allow this human to leave? Elez looks at her father. Why would he allow this human to even live? Loup smiles and tenderly places his hand on her bare shoulder. He gives her an understanding smile. It'll all work out the way life wants it to.

The early morning sun crests over the horizon. It's only been a few hours since Gio has left Loup Garou and the Pigmy village. He throttles down the speedboat and maneuvers it through the wide opening of the slow moving river. The sleek and expensive looking vessel appears quite out of place.

The riverside community is cluttered with haphazard docks with a variety of secured vessels; hand carved canoes, decrepit rowboats, motorized fishing boats and a few older model speedboats.

The shoreline and docks are scattered with local villagers, very unlike Loup's Pigmy tribe. These inhabitants are tall, dark skinned and fully clothed. Gio slows the speedboat along a dock near the center of the waterfront community. He reaches down toward the cushioned seat of the boat and collects his black medical bag.

Gio leaps from the speedboat and lands on the rickety planks of the dock. A local villager quickly approaches and ties of the bow line of the vessel as Gio opens his medical bag and reaches deep inside. "Thanks for the boat," Gio says in a condescending tone.

"Will there be anything else, sir?" the Native asks.

"No! Here, this should cover it." Gio tosses the villager a tightly rolled stack of one hundred dollar bills. The man gazes at the money in his hand. It's more than he would make his entire life. He looks up only to see Gio departing from the edge of the wooden dock. There is not a thank-you nor words of gratitude.

Gio makes his way through the wide central walkway of the village. On opposite sides of him, primitive booths with local vendors barking out their trade. He seems to be the only American around. This is not the type of place printed on a travel agency brochure.

Gio simply dismisses the local vendors as he continues along his route through the bamboo structures and dwellings. He appears to have walked completely through the village and now faces a wide and extended clearing.

The twin engine, private jet quietly sits at the end of the makeshift runway. Gio seems to quicken his pace toward the plane as the side door behind the cockpit slowly opens. As he approaches the steps of the lowered door, Gio looks up and glances at the fuselage of one of his company's jets;

MANCINI PHARMACEUTICALS, INC.

Gio bounds up the lowered steps and disappears inside. The door begins to rise behind him as the pair of twin engines begin to hum and windup.

"Call the office," Gio says in a commanding voice. He leans his head inward through the opened hatchway of the cockpit. "I want the lab setup and ready when I arrive." The pilot nods as he continues to flip knobs and turn switches. The private jet begins to roll along the makeshift runway.

Gio turns and closes the door of the cockpit. The interior of the jet is quite unlike most private planes with a central walkway separating laboratory style tables and work stations. Among the medical equipment there appears microscopes, computers, Bunsen burners, scales and beakers.

Placing his medical bag down on a smooth work area, Gio fastens his seatbelt and slightly looks out of one of the side windows.

The private jet rolls to a halt along the far end of the primitive runway. It slowly turns and pauses. The pilot eases back on the controls, winding up the twin engines. The jet moves forward, picking up speed until finally lifting off the ground and begins heading back toward civilization.

"I figured you'd eventually end up here," Gordon says with a cheerful tone. The retired professor extends out his hand and greets Larry. Gordon has aged well. His long silver hair appears tied back in a single ponytail and hangs along the middle of his back. He is clean shaved and sports a casual dress jacket and jeans.

Larry has matured into a strikingly handsome man with his facial features more refined than in his University days. He wears a suit, tie and dress shirt and is very professional looking. Gordon and Larry shake hands. "What's it been? Three years now?" Larry asks.

"Four, I think. It was right before you started working for the D.A.'s office."

"Right..." Larry and Gordon give each other the one-two look over followed by an awkward silence. "I see *she's* back in town."

"Yeah, it's been about ten years if I figured right," Gordon says, as he turns away from Larry. The ambitious attorney seems unsettled and cautious as he too, slowly turns. Gordon and Larry lean against the upper handrailing of the massive lion pit near the center of the city's zoo.

The deep and wide ravine separates the human visitors and the *natural environment* of the captive felines. A large engraved sign stands a few feet away from Gordon and Larry;

THE CITY ZOO
PROUDLY PRESENTS
KEIKO & JAAKKO
CO-SPONSERED BY
THE JAMISON FOUNDATION

The living area is nearly half an acre, filled with slopes, boulders, tropical trees and a cave entrance leading inward toward the pens and cages. A magnificent lioness strolls along the inner perimeter of the containment, casually looking about. She is covered with golden and tan fur, beautifully kept and shiny. Then, something catches her attention.

The lioness pads her way toward the edge of the ravine. She curiously sniffs the air. Larry looks directly at her, deep into her big brown eyes. The lioness lets out a low and curious roar as she takes her forepaw and bats it in Gordon's direction. "How is she doing... *really?*" Larry asks.

"Better than I had expected," Gordon replies in a fatherly tone. "It seems the disease is in a complete dormant state. As long as she remains in her altered form, she's fine."

"When was the last time you saw *her*?"

"A few years ago for his birthday."

"*His?*"

"Yeah, *his.* You didn't know?

"Know what, Gordon?" A large shadow appears from inside one of the cave entrances. Larry turns and looks beyond the ravine, passed the on-looking lioness and through a series of tropical trees. A ten year old, male tigon emerges from the cave's entrance and leaps up onto a boulder.

The tigon has both characteristics of his tiger father and lioness mother. The large feline is covered with golden, tan fur with slight hints of orange. From the tip of his tail to the bridge of his wide muzzle, faded tiger stripes are seen. The lioness turns and lets out a motherly growl.

The tigon leaps from the boulder and strolls over to his mother at the edge of the ravine. She licks the tigon behind his fluffy ear then nudges her muzzle under the side of his neck. "Is he?"

"Yes, he's *very human*," Gordon interrupts.

"What about the disease?"

"It seems he inherited more of his father's genes than his mother's. So far, there are no traces of what Sonja has."

"What does she call him?"

"She shortened it to Jay. He's a great kid." Gordon slightly waves toward the tigon named Jaakko. He licks his chops and lets out a familiar roar.

However, the lioness is not too friendly toward Larry. It is true that she recognizes him but remembers him differently. She is resentful and holds onto her hostilities. She angrily roars at the attorney and flexes the sharp claws of her forepaw.

"I didn't find out about Jay till he was three," Gordon says, with a disappointed tone. Larry senses that she has hurt

Gordon somehow. "I saw them on some public television show documenting endangered species or something. That's how *I* found out."

Gordon and Larry continue to look into the pit. The tigon begins to stroll along side of his mother, back and forth along the edge of the ravine. "You broke *one* of the three rules, Larry. She was probably embarrassed."

"What about Elez? *You* broke that rule, too."

"That was different."

"*How* was that different? I heard the way you talked about her in class. Not *all* of us were asleep."

"I don't recall Elez and I ever being *together* in our alters. You and Sonja were.

"But why didn't she tell *me*? I would've understood. I would've even..."

"*Even what*, Larry? Marry her?"

"...why didn't she tell me?"

"That's something you'll have to ask her yourself." Gordon gives Larry a slight punch in the arm. "I gotta get goin'. Still planning on coming to the reunion next month?"

"Is Sonja coming?" Larry eagerly asks. Gordon laughs.

"You're not listening, boy! Ask her yourself. See ya'." Gordon casually waves, as he turns and begins making his way through the sparse families and couples occupying the maze of walkways throughout The Zoo.

Larry continues to lean on the handrailing, gazing forward at the lioness. She stands and begins pacing back and forth along the edge of the ravine, never taking her eyes off the human. Her tail wildly swings behind her, whipping from side to side.

The tigon is just slightly interested in Larry. Still, there is something vaguely familiar about him. Although the human's blood runs through his veins, they have never met, in either form.

RING - RING - RING.

Larry reaches inside of his suit jacket and retrieves his cell phone. "Hello?" Larry listens to the feminine voice for several moments before answering. "Yeah, Chloe. I was on my way back now. I'll be there in about an hour."

Larry flips his cell phone closed and slides in back into his inside pocket. He stands there, staring at the lioness as she continues pacing along the edge of the ravine.

The tigon flops over onto his side then begins playfully rolling around, as if he were a domesticated kitten, scratching his back on the living room floor. Larry is amused at the hybrid feline. "*I wonder what he's really like,*" he mumbles in his head.

"Alright, class. Here we are," the elementary school teacher calls out to her students. Larry is instantly overrun with children out on one of their school fieldtrips.

The plainly dressed teacher rounds up the students as they face the handrailing and gawk at the lioness and tigon. Several of the children's parents, acting a chaperones, hang back behind the group, keeping an eye on them.

"Class, this is Keiko and Jaakko. Keiko's home is right here at our zoo but after she gave birth to her cub, she began to travel around the country. Jaakko is extremely rare. He's the only known tigon in captivity able to reproduce." The school teacher pauses. "*When* he gets older."

"*Really?* Larry thinks to himself. The students are becoming loud and obnoxious. Well, obnoxious to Larry. He quickly dismisses himself from the horde of students, making his way from the handrailing of the lion pit.

As he strolls along the winding walkway of The Zoo, he hears the lioness roaring. They are not the sounds of anger but the growling tones of animosity and disappointment.

Larry fiddles with his steering wheel as his late model sports car rolls along the wide street. The late afternoon sun continues to dip across the horizon, casting amber shades throughout the accumulating rain clouds.

A soft jazz-like tune seeps out from the well placed speakers of his automobile. The song fades out and is followed by a brief radio station identification from the disk jockey. For a brief moment, all Larry can hear in the spinning of his tires against the pavement.

The unseen disk jockey cues up the next song and begins to play it. Larry begins to fidget. The song strikes a chord in his subconscious.

As the music fills the interior of his automobile, he remembers a glorious week spent with a beautiful woman. He remembers how they met, at a weird, weekend party hosted by his professor. They oddly awoke three days later, naked in the forest and for the week after, were never separated. Then, the woman with golden locks of hair simply vanished.

A whirlwind of thoughts race through Larry's head. After all this time, she's back and she has a son. "*I have a son*," Larry thinks. "*Do I have a son? Do we keep up this masquerade or do I talk to her? What do I say to him?*"

Larry can't take anymore. He quickly reaches across and changes the radio station. Loud and boisterous rock and roll music thunders out of the speakers. He needs a distraction, any distraction. Anything to keep his mind off of her.

"Judge Duarte called this afternoon. The Gomez arraignment is set for Monday morning at nine," Chloe says, remaining seated behind her desk. "You'll have the whole weekend to go over the case file."

The last ten years has been kind to the green eyed beauty. Chloe's professional looking raven hair is tied up on a bun atop her head revealing her larger than average ears.

Chloe's dark framed glasses rest on the bridge of her nose and seem to compliment her dark colored, woman's business suit. She hands Larry a thick case file as he shuffles passed the front of her desk. "Any other messages?"

"No, just Judge Duarte," Chloe replies before flipping through a growing stack of paperwork on the corner of her desk.

Chloe's office area is bright and well lit. A large picture window takes up nearly the entire wall space behind her. The wall directly across from Chloe's desk is filled with rows upon rows of law books. In front of the bookcase, a pair of matching, leather bound chairs for clients, fellow attorneys or even a judge or two.

To Chloe's right, the doorway leads out into the vast corridors of municipal court building. Larry glances through the case file for several moments. Chloe can see that he's not that interested in the documents. "Larry, is something wrong?"

"No, not at all. I just ran into an old friend today."

"You wanna talk about it?"

"No, not really," Larry says, tossing Chloe a casual nod. With the case file in hand, Larry passes the leather bound chairs and bookcase and heads for the closed door leading into his office. A brass plaque hangs from the door;

Lawrence Wells
Assistant District Attorney

Larry's office has a warm feeling about it yet, somehow rustic as well. The opposite facing walls are filled, floor to ceiling, with shelves of thick law books. Framed accolades, certificates and degrees hang along the wall next to the backside of the closed office door.

Larry makes his way passed a matching pair of leather bound chairs facing the front of his desk. He tosses the case file onto the cushion of his high-backed chair then rounds the corner of the desk.

The large picture window fills three quarters of the wall. Larry stares out through the glass, taking in the well maintained grounds of the judicial campus. Across the way, the court house, justice hall then the capitol building.

Larry removes the case file from his chair and slides it across his desk. He plops down in his high-backed chair and unenthusiastically looks about his quiet office.

He slightly leans back and opens the narrow desk drawer directly in the center and below the desk top. The extended drawer is unlike the rest of his office. It's filled with loose pens, papers and is generally cluttered.

Larry pulls the drawer out further and reaches his hand inward as far as it will go. He rummages around for a few moments until grasping onto what he was searching for.

Larry retrieves a strand of pictures, three in all. The kind of photos that can be obtained by one of those picture booths, commonly found in a shopping center or a mall. The edge of the top photo appears frayed or torn. One of the photos is missing. Larry smiles as he stares at the three photos taken a decade ago.

In the first photo of the strand, Larry and Sonja appear cheek to cheek, as they stick their tongues out at the camera lens.

Larry and Sonja have turned and face each other. They give each other a loving kiss on the lips, as the second photo was taken.

Larry and Sonja look into the camera lens for the third photo. No goofy facial expressions. No kiss. They pose as if they were taking a high school senior yearbook photo. Yet, they look like a caring couple, almost serious... almost in love.

David Kessler sits in an odd flower print chair attempting to read his paperback book. While he was in the hospital recovering from his viciously inflicted multiple injuries, nurse Alex Price began reading, "A Connecticut Yankee in King Arthur's Court", to him. He feels kind of obligated to finish it.

David is a handsome man in his early twenties with dark, slightly curly hair and stunning eyes. His gray T-shirt with *NYU* printed in large red letters across his chest reminds him of home in America. This trip through Northern Europe, then ending up in London, hadn't quite turned out the way he had planned.

Alex's flat is quaint and well lived in. A bay window looks out to one of the countless side streets of London. A white fireplace and hearth are at the center of the far wall with matching shelves on opposite sides, filled with books and framed pictures.

Across the room, directly adjacent to the flameless fireplace, the door of the flat remains slightly opened, leading out into the hallway and common area of the apartment building.

Next to David and his flowery chair, a plastic figurine of Mickey Mouse stands atop an eight cornered end table. Next to the end table, a brown older style couch with several throw pillows and a folded quilt.

David fiddles with the pages of the paperback book, trying to refocus, just trying to kill some time before Alex returns from her swing shift at the hospital. "Jesus Christ!"

David slides out of the chair and drops to his knees as the book falls to the floor. He clutches his fists along his forehead. David is covered with sweat as horrific pain shoots through his body. "What!? What!?" David screams out.

Violently trembling, David manages to get to his feet. "I'm burning up! Jesus!" He is overcome by intense pain. David reaches up to the collar of his T-shirt and tears it off of his body. He reaches down, feverishly unbuttons his jeans and painfully slides out of them.

David stands naked in the center of the flat and feels the painful transformation beginning. He raises his right hand and stares at it. The top of his hand expands up and outward. Yellowish colored claws have begun to take the place of his fingernails. His hand grows larger and larger.

Black, coarse hair begins to mutate along his upper arms and shoulder blades. A thick trail of the black hair runs down his spine from the back of his neck to his tailbone. His right hand continues to transform and mutate.

A new and more powerful series of spasms race through his body. "Help me! Somebody help me, please! Jack!" David drops to his knees in the center of the flat covered with sweat.

Both of David's hands are in full transformation, taking on the characteristics of a massive wolf. Black fur, claws and pads below. The arches and ankles of his feet mutate and expand with a low painful crunching sound.

David falls forward, bracing himself with his mutating claws. Down on all fours, the horrific pain continues to consume his body. David's shape and appearance is quickly expanding. "I didn't mean to call you meatloaf, Jack!" David says with a painful growl.

A low crunching sound, as if bones were being grounded up, runs up and down David's spine. His back is covered with black fur. David's spine raises upward and becomes more ridged and defined.

David's facial features continue to mutate sprouting coarse fur along his sideburns. His teeth have become yellowish and jagged. The pain is unbearable.

Awkwardly, David flips over onto his back. He horrifically looks upon himself, as he struggles like a turtle flipped over onto his shell. His ankles and feet continues to transform taking on claw-like features.

David's ribcage and chest has greatly expanded, nearly tripled in size. His upper arms, chest and head are now completely covered with black fur. With his wolfish claw, David reaches up and stares directly into the camera-

"That's not how it really happens," Tez says in a low voice.

"What are you talking about?" Dana whispers.

"That's *not* how people change. That's *not* how they act."

"Right, Tez. How does it happen then?"

"After the movie..." Tez whispers as he reaches over and grabs a handful of popcorn. Tez and Dana sit near the center of the historical looking movie theater. They are surrounded by fellow moviegoers who are all still in love with one of their favorite comedic-horror films of the early 1980's.

Tez remains true to his retro University years. Faded jeans, leather bomber jacket, thick hair hanging about his shoulders and of course his trademark, dark framed sunglasses. He's still that cool.

Dana is quite different than the girls Tez dated while attending the University; *girls*. There was only one truelove for Tez. The fiery redhead that took his breath away. Dana, his casual love interest, will do for now. That's just it, his current relationship has nothing to do with love. Tez takes another handful of popcorn as the ongoing film continues to fill the forward screen-

The camera pans in and holds on a tight shot of the plastic Mickey Mouse figurine. David's facial features continue to mutate and transform. His nose expands outward taking the characteristics of a muzzle. David's eyes burn with flaming yellow colors.

David's ears mutate upward, forming into points. His muzzle continues to expand, becoming more defined into canine features. The beast lets out a low roar and are the first sounds of a howl. The transformation is complete.

The massive werewolf stands on all fours in the center of Alex's flat. The creature growls, as it slowly flexes its newly acquired structure and form. Then, the gigantic creature moves forward and slips out through the opened door, out into the hallway and common area. Out into the night.

"Are you sure about this, Tez?" Dana asks, as she sets the parking brake of her late model sports coupe.

"Yeah, come on. It'll be fun," Tez replies, as he flings open the passenger's side door. Dana and Tez find each other around the front of her car. Well placed lampposts line the outer perimeter of the park which has been closed for hours. Operating time is from dawn till dusk.

Holding hands, Tez and Dana make their way from the vacant parking areas, across a stretch of grass and approach the upper edge of a retaining concrete seawall. The west boarder of the park overlooks The Sound with distance lights of waterfront homes to the north and south.

It'll be a few days before the moon is full as it effortlessly hangs above the cloudless sky, bathing across the smooth water of The Sound. Tez and Dana maneuver themselves around small clusters of driftwood and waterlogged fallen timber.

Dana and Tez face the shoreline, as he takes in the serine landscape. He feels the cool evening air, the light breeze flowing through the trees of the park and the soothing water of The Sound which eventually leads to the ocean.

Tez smiles as he gives Dana a kiss on the cheek. He lifts his foot and grabs hold of the heel of his cowboy boot. Tossing it aside, he removes his other boot then quickly takes off his shirt. "Are we going for a swim?" Dana playfully asks.

"I want to show you something." Tez unbuttons his jeans and slides out of them, standing naked along the shoreline.

"I've *seen* that something before," Dana says with a smile. Tez gives Dana a smirk as he removes his dark sunglasses, tosses them to his pile of clothes then scampers into the water. He wades deeper and deeper. Ankles, knees, thighs then stops with the water splashing around his waist.

Tez dunks himself several times, drenching his limbs, torso and head. He turns and faces Dana who remains on the shoreline watching the silly man. "You're gonna love this, Dana. This is such a *cool change.*"

Tez slowly raises his arms up and out of the water and slowly moves them in a windmill fashion. He stretches his arms upward, over his head like he was stretching before Yoga class. Tez begins to take rhythmatic breaths and holds as still as he can.

He slowly and purposely lowers his arms to his sides. The soothing rays of moonlight beam down on his back and flicker across the surface of the water as the transformation begins.

As if a large vat of hot wax were being poured him, Tez's body becomes smooth and mutates for a split second into an hourglass shape. There are no defined features. No upper extremities, no shoulders, no neck, not even a head. Just an obelisk of flesh standing in the water of The Sound.

The alien-like creature begins to expand upward and nearly doubles in size. What should be Tez's neck, face and the top of his head mutates into a narrowing cone. The pale neck area expands to the circumference of the rest of the lower areas of the transforming creature.

Where Tez's elbows had been moments earlier, the pale flesh transforms into growing triangular extremities. The limbs flatten as they continue to expand and lengthen taking on the characteristics of flippers.

The warm blooded, aquatic creature has nearly completed its transformation. A large dorsal fin protrudes from the middle of its smooth, pale gray back.

Below the surface of the water, its legs have molded together and taper downward. The last remnants of Tez's human form are his feet, mutated together at the ankles. Due to the lack of support provided by his human legs, the pale gray mammal topples over and splashes into the water. The transforming creature disappears from the surface as Dana frantically inches her way toward the shoreline. "Tez!?"

The moonlight blankets The Sound. There is no breaking surf along the shoreline. No lapping waves. Just an eerie silence. Dana creeps closer to the water as she scans the surface. There is no sign of Tez or the creature he has become. "Tez..." Dana whispers in a pleading voice.

Suddenly, a dolphin explodes from below the surface of the water. He seems to be suspended in thin air for a long moment before plunging back into The Sound. The waves of splashing seawater soaks Dana.

Tez has completed his transformation into his alter. Although his outer appearance has changed, he retains his inner human consciousness.

The dolphin leaps in and out of the water several dozen yards away from Dana with the rays of the moonlight dancing across his majestic and sleek body.

He swims in a wide circle then darts toward her. The dolphin raises his coned head out of the water and clicks his mouth, inviting Dana to join him. She giggles as she strips out of her blouse and jeans.

Dana dives into the water and swims for several yards, resurfaces then pulls her hair way from her damp face. Dana turns in a slow circle, searching for the dolphin. The pale gray creature appears swimming along the surface, heading directly toward her.

The dolphin raises his head out of the water mere inches away from Dana. She tenderly clasps her palms on opposite sides of the dolphin's beak. He happily clicks his mouth several times.

The dolphin slightly slides away from Dana and begins floating alongside of her. She reaches out and runs her palm along the smooth surface of his back then up along his dorsal fin. She laughs out loud. This is just too weird!

The dolphin begins to swim further out into The Sound. Dana's hands slips away from his flipper as she is forced to tread water. The dolphin takes a sharp corner and swims back toward Dana. He playfully quacks several times as he carefully nudges her in the ribs with his beak.

Dana tenderly takes hold of the dolphin's dorsal fin and flipper. He seems to be nodding his head in approval as he begins to skim across the surface of the water. Dana hangs onto the dolphin like she was clutching onto an inner-tube being pulled by a speedboat.

The dolphin and Dana swim in haphazard circles throughout The Sound. He begins a swooping motion, repeatedly rising upward then plunging below the surface, taking Dana along for the ride.

The dolphin carries Dana deeper into the water. As she gently clings onto him, their smooth bodies press closer together. Dana releases his dorsal fin and flipper then floats, effortlessly moving her hands and feet to sustain her position. The dolphin swims around her, clicking his mouth, making sure he knows where she's located.

Dana begins to swim toward the surface as the dolphin appears from below. He tenderly swims alongside of Dana, offering her a fin. She takes hold of his dorsal fin and is carried quickly to the surface. She seems to embrace him as they break the surface.

The dolphin abruptly turns and swims away. Dana continues to tread water as she sees his dorsal fin cutting along the water. Around and around the dolphin swims until diving deep below. Dana watches as the dolphin explodes from below the surface of the water, appears suspended in flight and silhouettes the nearly full moon.

~ V ~

"Hurry up! You're gonna be late," Reggie blurts out toward the tree line. The once ruffian university student, leans slightly back on the aged seat of his trike. His black leather vest with various insignias and patches has faded somewhat over the years.

Reggie has matured very well over the years. He is no longer the young whippersnapper, full of obnoxious energy. Reggie's blonde curly hair hangs loosely along his shoulders with his tightly trimmed beard and mustache well kempt and maintained.

"C'mon, man. Do I really have'ta wear this crap?" Dante shouts out from beyond the trees. "I felt stupid wearing it the *first* time around."

"You know it's what they expect. You were the Champ!" Reggie swings his leg over and straddles the seat of his trike. The three wheeled motorcycle looks worn and weathered. Yet, still fully functional.

Reggie has only made a few modifications to the trike over the years. A type of an emergency break or lever, down along the left side of the engine, close to the left rear fender and wheel. A gearbox rests directly in the center of the rear fenders and behind the rear passenger's seat.

A light weight, titanium chain sticks out of the end of the gearbox and dangles a few links. Attached to the end of the chain, a four pronged anchor commonly used on a fishing vessel. "Dante, let's go!" Reggie flicks on the electrical starter and revs the trike's engine as Dante reluctantly appears from the tree line.

Dante tosses his small backpack directly at Reggie's head. His best friend laughs, as he takes the filled backpack with Dante's usual clothes and hangs it over the handlebars.

Dante is shirtless, revealing his broad shoulders, flexing biceps, a ripped abdomen and a tapering waist. His dreadlocks hang down to the middle of his back and are loosely secured in several spots forming a single, matted ponytail. Dante continues to sport his tightly trimmed mustache and goatee.

Resting on the bridge of his nose, an oversized pair of dark sunglasses. No ordinary pair of shades. The red, yellow and orange flames appear across his eyebrows and cheekbones, swooping out and upward passed his temples then peeking to fiery tips above the top of his head.

Drooping across the back of his neck, over his shoulders and loosely covering his chest, a red, yellow and orange boa made of large feathers.

About Dante's waist, a gaudy, gold colored buckle of sorts. The face is over a foot across, eight inches from top to bottom and is etched;

N W W
Champion

The hideous buckle is secured around Dante's waist by a red, white and blue elastic belt nearly six inches wide. As he makes his way closer to Reggie, his spandex pants seems to shimmer, capturing the afternoon sun. The stretchy material is fundamentally black with red, yellow and orange flames shooting up from his knees and thighs. "You look great!"

"I look like Elton John!" Dante growls. He approaches the trike and swings over his heavy, bright yellow, knee-high wrestling boot with red laces. Dante plops down on the passenger's seat as Reggie sets the trike in gear and accelerates. "How's the knee?" Reggie asks.

"I'll let you know," Dante answers, with an unsure tone. Leaving billowing dust in their wake, Reggie and Dante speed off, disappearing beyond a lull in the landscape.

Rolling hills surround the lush valley below. To the far end, clusters of trees boarder the vast forest, stretching out for miles. Along the near end of the valley, a single lane dirt road. Traveling at a moderate speed, Reggie and Dante appear riding the trike, closer to the main event.

A large circle has been formed in the center of the valley. Along one side, expensive automobiles, coupes and limousines, all parked inward.

Extremely well dressed men stand along the inner edge of the circle, staying close to their vehicles in case of a quick getaway. Attractive women, wearing out of place evening dresses and high heels, cling to their escorts, laughing at their senseless jokes and silly one-liners. Filling the opposite side of the makeshift arena, Reggie's family members of bikers.

The row of motorcycles and handful of trikes are parked in a similar manner, as the four wheeled vehicles, completing the circle. The number of bikers have dwindled over the years. Over half of them has returned to *normal society.*

The remaining motorcycle enthusiasts still don their black leather vests with scattered insignias and patches. However, there is no sign of Ma and Pa. Leadership of the family has been handed down to Reggie.

A group of the bikers sidestep, creating a space for Reggie to park along the circle. Roaring cheers and applause fills the air as Reggie revs up his trike several times then kills the engine.

He's acting it up, playing the part of Dante's manager and promoter. Reggie springs off his trike and bounds toward the center of the arena, waving his hands in the air and whooping it up.

Across the way, a driver approaches the rear passenger door of a sleek, white limousine. A well dressed man, known only as Blake, steps out of the vehicle. He adjusts his sunglasses as he approaches Reggie in the center of the circle. "Good to see you again, Reggie. How's your boy?"

"Oh, he's fine. How's your last guy healing up?"

"Four broken ribs and a concussion. How'd you be?"

"Yeah, I see your point," Reggie says with a smirk. "Same odds as last time?"

"Well, since Dante's beaten my last three contenders, I think we need to up the stakes."

"I don't know, Blake. I haven't even seen your new guy yet."

"You sound worried, Reggie," Blake says, as he lowers his sunglasses. "Don't think Dante can take'im sight unseen?"

"Fine, but four to one odds," Reggie says as he pulls out a thick roll of one hundred dollar bills from the front pocket of his jeans. "Five grand."

"How much of that is mine?"

"Not much. I have a large family to feed," Reggie mockingly says as he motions his head toward his fellow bikers circled behind him in the distance.

"Deal!" Blake says as he and Reggie shake hands. Blake raises his left hand and raises a finger, then two, then three, then four indicating the wager and the odds. A few moments later, the front passenger's door of his white limousine opens.

Blake's assistant approaches with a briefcase in hand. He lifts the case and opens it. Inside, rows upon rows of stacked one hundred dollar bills. "Four to one, Reggie," Blake says with a smirk.

Reggie tosses his bankroll inside the briefcase as a lanky biker, Shelby, approaches from behind. Blake's assistant and Shelby stare at each other. They are assigned to keep each other honest and the briefcase in sight.

Blake turns and begins heading toward the front of his limousine. "By the way, how's his knee?" he loudly asks over his shoulder. A seductively dressed woman takes up alongside of Blake as he looks directly through the windshield of his limousine. With a snap of his fingers, the opposite rear passenger's door open.

A heavy black pair of boots are seen first, followed by a pair of massive hands, pulling the towering man out from the vehicle. Tork emerges from the limousine, standing nearly seven feet tall.

The professional fighter wears a pair of light colored baggy pants, commonly found in a karate dojo. Tork is shirtless, showing off his massive arms and shoulders. He's a monster of a man.

Dante and Tork approach and face each other near the center of the assembled circle. Blake's assistant and Shelby stand inward from the circle, hovering over the filled briefcase.

Reggie has rejoined his family of bikers as a stillness falls across the valley. Tork looks down toward Dante. "You didn't have to get all dressed up for me."

"All part of the show, man."

"I'll try not to hurt you... too much."

"You can try..." Dante says with a smirk. He turns and makes his way toward Reggie. Dante quickly takes off his flaming sunglasses and boa then hands them to Reggie. "He's bigger than I thought he'd be."

"Remember what they say. *The bigger they are the harder...*"

"Yeah-yeah-yeah!" Dante interrupts with an irritated tone. "Hold my belt!" he nearly commands. Dante hands Reggie his red, white and blue championship belt. The large buckle glimmers in the afternoon sun.

Dante slowly makes his way back toward the center of the circle. He and Tork begin to circle each other, studying their opponent. Blake and the well-dressed men as well as Reggie and the family of bikers, are still and silent; just waiting for the battle to begin.

Tork strikes first. He swings his powerful fist toward Dante who easily evades the attack. The well dressed men and bikers cheer and wave their hands in the air. Reggie and Blake remain composed, giving each other a subtle nod.

Tork swings several times as Dante bobs and weaves out of the way. The smaller man is slightly unnerved. He can hear the low swooshing sounds of the towering man's fists as they fly dangerously close to his head.

Dante clutches his fists and slams them into Tork's stomach several times. He steps back and simply smiles at the smaller man. There was no effect. Tork delivers a right hook then a left jab, missing both times.

Dante slams his fists into Tork's ribcage then delivers several blows to his kidneys. Again, there is no effect. Tork backs away several feet then swoops his right foot toward Dante's left leg. Dante instantly pulls it away, avoiding the blow. He's is obviously skittish of his left knee.

Dante begins to bounce from side to side, making himself a more difficult target. Tork lumbers forward with his fists clutched. All he needs is to land one good punch. Tork swings and misses.

SWOOSH!

Dante sees an opening and delivers several blows to Tork's jaw. The towering man smiles with the faintest traces of blood lining his teeth. That stung no more than a mosquito bite. By the look in Reggie's eye, he's becoming nervous.

Tork spits out a mouthful of blood and steps forward as Dante continues to bounce from side to side. Dante jabs and connects with Tork's jaw. Again and again. It's apparent the former pro-wrestler has learned to fight over the years. But, will it be enough?

SWOOSH-SWOOSH KA-WHAP!

Tork connects with Dante's face, sending him painfully to the ground. Dante crawls around on all fours, trying to regain his bearings. Cheers and thunderous applause fills the air from the well dressed side of the inner circle. Blake smiles.

Tork lunges downward and picks up Dante by his matted ponytail. He dangles the littler man in the air. Dante's arms and legs flop about as a helpless ragdoll. Dante attempts to strike out, but due to his haphazard position, he pathetically fails.

Tork roars as he arches his back and flexes his massive chest. He effortlessly tosses Dante aside. Dante flies through the air and lands with a thud on the valley floor. He staggers as he manages to get to his feet.

Tork looks at Dante. The man is beaten, he just doesn't know it yet. Looking over Dante's shoulder, Tork sees Blake giving him *the look.* Tork nods as he begins to move toward Dante, preparing to deliver the final assault.

Dante feels an overwhelming burning sensation in his legs. His thighs expand with his calves slightly thinning. Due to Dante's primarily dark colored spandex and the ongoing, chaotic situation, the transformation of his lower extremities are unnoticed.

Like his fellow Skinners, Dante has learned to control his inner creature, able to tap into his alter's strength and power. As he feels the completion of his lower transformation, Dante looks up to see Tork charging toward him.

Remembering his wrestling moves from years gone by, Dante shoots for Tork's legs. Dante wraps his arms around Tork's knees then spins his body. Tork is top-heavy, causing him to fall to the side.

Dante quickly releases Tork and shimmies up along his back. He grasps onto Tork's arm and twists it painfully behind his head. Sliding his arm under Tork's armpit then across his throat, Dante grabs onto his other wrist, tightening the sleeper hold.

Tork manages to get to his feet. With his free arm, he attempts to reach for Dante, trying to remove this insect from his back. With his vision becoming blurry, Tork staggers to the side. He's drawing dangerously close to unconsciousness. Then, Tork takes a knee.

Tork flip-flops across the dirt with Dante hanging on for dear life. The former pro-wrestler and the gigantic fighter looks like a cowboy riding a vicious bull at the state fair rodeo. Tork's movements become sluggish as he reaches out toward Blake. The shady businessman shakes his head. He knows it's all over.

Blake looks across the central clearing and gives his assistant a nod. Without even waiting for the bout to end, Blake rounds his limousine and slips inside the rear passenger's door. His assistant reluctantly hands Reggie the briefcase. "Dante, you can stop now!" Reggie shouts. "You won!"

Dante tightens his grasp around Tork's throat as the large man falls completely limp. He slightly twists as if to snap Tork's head from his neck. Dante pauses a long moment then takes a sigh of relief.

He releases Tork and shoves him to the ground. Tork moans as he struggles to breathe as the inner circle of vehicles quickly depletes. The convoy of luxury cars and limousines race along the narrow dirt road, quickly approaching the main highway. Only one vehicle remains.

Four large, well dressed men approach Tork and stand on opposite sides of him. They struggle as they pick him up under his arms and drags him toward the vehicle. The four men shove Tork into the backseat of Blake's white limousine like fitting a large foot into a small shoe.

Dante brushes off the dust from his spandex pants as he watches the last luxury car speed away. He sits back sideways on the seat of Reggie's trike as he unlaces his yellow knee-high boots. "How's the knee?" Reggie asks.

"My knee is fine but I trashed my boots." Dante sets the first boot onto the trike's seat, then examines the other. The supporting back seam has been busted apart with the sole inside appearing to have deep gouges and cuts.

"You shifted!?" Reggie asks in a hostile tone. His loud and abrupt question is unnoticed by his fellow bikers for they already know Reggie and Dante's secret. "You didn't think you could bet'im on your own?"

Dante takes his pair of shredded boots and begins tying them together by the laces. He raises up from the trike's seat and glances around the valley. Under his primarily black spandex, his thighs remain enlarged. The red, yellow and orange flames run down his legs, until the fabric ends just below his knees.

Dark colored and thick, coarse hair sticks out from the lower edge of the spandex pants similar but not identical to horse's hair. Where his feet once were, Dante has adopted a pair of dark hooves, each about the size of a normal sized man's hand, completely spanning out his fingers. His lowers extremities remains in their bighorn appearance.

Dante loops the laces of his damaged boots around the back of his neck and swings his hoof over the trike's seat. "Careful of the chrome!" Reggie playfully barks before switching on the electrical ignition.

"Like you could tell it was scratched." Dante lifts his hand and presses his palm to his reddening eye. He's *really* going to feel this in the morning. "I need a drink..."

Gordon looks out of the back living room window of his shoreline home. He takes a sip of his tea as he continues to gaze passed his back porch and deck, across the waters of The Sound and beyond the late afternoon fog. He can clearly see The Space Needle from where he lives.

His property spans out along the shoreline, about a half mile in both directions. Gordon's island home is well secluded, far enough away from any onlookers or unwanted visitors.

The back living room has a warm and welcoming feeling throughout it. A matching couch, loveseat and easy chair are centered around the familiar coffee table constructed from the outer planks of a historical sailing vessel. Next to the easy chair, an end table with a lamp, a small personal address book and an older style rotary telephone.

The hearth and fireplace rests along the far wall with a stack of cut and split wood along the stone floor, just waiting to be burned.

A full sized, mounted moose head with a full rack of antlers hangs above the hearth filled with scattered framed pictures. Gordon really doesn't care for the taxidermist's efforts but kept it anyway. It came with the house.

Several of the images filling the pictures are of him, Sonja and a young blonde haired boy, Jay; a camping trip, a coastal train ride, a day at an amusement park.

At the center of the hearth, a larger framed picture is seen. Gordon, his brother, his brother's wife and baby Sonja, direct from the delivery room.

Slightly tilted upward, resting against the framed picture, a shot of Larry and Sonja posing inside of a photo booth commonly found in a shopping center or a mall.

The bottom edge of the photo appears frayed. Larry and Sonja appear happy in the photo with their heads slightly pressed together, looking into the lens as their images were captured.

Hanging from the wall between the moose head and entryway leading into the kitchen, a magnificent framed marquee poster is seen. The captured image is familiar; it's Dante!

He strikes an attacking pose with a snarl on his face. He's in his full, pro-wrestler costume. Flaming boa and gaudy sunglasses, yellow knee-high boots with red laces, black spandex pants with flames and his red, white and blue championship belt. Yep, back in the day, *Dante's Inferno* was a sight to see.

Symmetrically placed on the opposite side of the hearth from Dante's marquee, a additional framed poster is seen on the wall; an enlarged cover of *Rolling Stone* magazine. Among one of the many text articles featured inside;

The Zøø Crüe
Too Much... Too Late?

The candid photo is of the band members, mostly roaring and snarling at the photographer as the shot was taken. Jon wears a wolf's head and fur along his shoulders, arms and back. Dangling in front of himself, his custom, black glossy "X" double-neck guitar.

Rafe simply poses with his back slightly turned toward Jon. He has his arms crossed with a pair of worn drumsticks in his hand. Rafe looks like he's covered in a thin layer of baby oil. His countless cheetah tattoos glisten.

To the left of Jon and Rafe, Mark roars. His zebra mohawk nearly sticks out of the top of the magazine's cover. His black and white zebra striped guitar matches his black and white zebra spandex pants.

Clutching onto his giraffe designed bass guitar, T-Bone stands to the right of Jon and Rafe. T-Bone is an enormous man with a bulging chest and powerful looking arms. Atop T-Bone's head, a full set of Texas longhorn antlers. Hanging from the center of his nose, a large gold ring.

Directly below the framed poster of the rock and roll band, three guitars appear to be resting in their chrome stands. T-Bone's autographed, first edition, giraffe printed guitar, Jon's autographed, first edition, peacock printed guitar and Mark's first edition signed zebra printed guitar. Resting on a small pedestal, a pair of Rafe's signed drumsticks.

Gordon takes a glance at his wristwatch before taking another sip of his tea. He makes his way from the living room window and plops down in his easy chair. A few images catch his attention from the television directly across from the couch.

Gordon has transferred the sixteen millimeter footage from film to a VHS format years ago. There on the television screen, Elez, Loup Garou, Payu and Loy are preparing for the ceremony. Payu and Loy clutch onto long bamboo poles with types of nooses at the far ends.

Elez tenderly runs her palms along Gordon's back and shoulders as she moves him into place. Payu and Loy carefully loop their nooses around Gordon's throat and cinch in the slack.

Elez moves around Gordon and lovingly faces him. She gently holds his face with both of her hands as she draws him closer. Elez closes her eyes as she kisses Gordon on the lips. The image freezes.

Gordon sits in his easy chair with the remote control in his hand. He smiles to himself with his thumb on the pause button. Gordon remembers that day as if it were just yesterday. The warmth of the ceremonial bonfire, the constricting nooses around his neck and the soft lips of the Native girl.

"Thanks for calling. I'm not home right now. Just leave a message and I'll get back to you," Chloe's recorded voice says in a somewhat chipper tone.

BEEEEP.

"Hey, Chloe. It's Gordon," he says, sitting back in his easy chair. Gordon has progressed from his afternoon cup of tea to a stout glass of whiskey on the rocks. "Just callin' to see if you're still planning on going to the show next month. I sent you a ticket. Look for it in the mail." Gordon takes a sip of his drink. "Well, talk to you later."

Gordon runs his finger down the page of his personal address book. He doesn't have to look far. Chloe and Zoey's names are one after the other.

RING-RING.

RING-RING.

"Madam Zoey's. Can I help you?" Zoey says as she politely answers the phone.

"Zoey, it's Gordon."

"Hey, Professor! I got your ticket in the mail."

"So, you're goin'?"

"Sure, wouldn't miss it!" Zoey says with a giggle in her voice. A large, red piece of cloth is wrapped around her head with the tied ends dangling along her back. Zoey's piercing green eyes and raven hair seems to compliment her campy outfit.

Zoey's shoulders and the upper area of her chest and back are bare with her white, frilly blouse hanging loosely along her upper arms. A wide, leather-like sash covers her midriff with an additional red piece of cloth wrapped around her waist like a sarong. Her full length, multicolored dress and her black, high heeled boots completes her fortune teller's costume.

JINGLE - JINGLE - JINGLE.

The single, Christmas-like bell ornament announces as the front door of Zoey's shop opens. "I gotta go. See ya' next month." She quickly hangs up the phone and slides it out of sight. Zoey smiles at the four college aged women as they enter the eerie and dark room.

Zoey quickly sits behind a round table with an odd colored cloth covering its surface. She is alone at the head of the table with several inviting chairs around it. In the center of the table, a soft glowing crystal ball rests on a small wooden stand.

The walls are covered with odd colored tapestries, concealing the aging paint and the cracks in the plaster. Along one of the draped walls, a rustic dresser with dimly lit table lamps which provide the only light throughout the room.

Resting on top of the dresser in the direct center, a wooden chest, the size of a breadbox. Hidden inside of the chest, a full set of Tarot cards.

Directly across from the dresser, a freestanding room divider conceals a work desk, a rickety chair and a third generation laptop computer. For now, the computer screen is dark and lifeless. "Welcome. I am Madam Zoey. What is your pleasure?" Zoey asks in a low voice, attempting to be mysterious and haunting. "Palm reading? Tarot cards? Would you like to *gaze* into the crystal ball and *see* your future?"

"You would already *know* why we're here if you could see the future," Renee says with a smirk.

"*Ah, The Skeptic,*" Zoey thinks to herself, there's one in every crowd. "Please, make yourself comfortable," Zoey says as she opens her arms, inviting the four women closer. Renee finds her seat directly next to Zoey. A better vantage point to catch any deceptions or parlor tricks.

Brenda takes a chair next to Renee and finds herself diagonally across from Zoey. Abby, the birthday girl, sits next to Brenda as Jill slides in on the opposite side of Zoey. If the shadowed ceiling had eyes, the women sit at the five points of a mystical star. "Do we pay you now?" Jill timidly asks.

"If we don't *see* nothin'... we don't *pay* nothin'," Brenda announces. Zoey chuckles in her head. The young women's characteristics are just spewing from them and they don't even know it; The Leader, The Bubble Head, The Non-Believer and then The Follower.

"*This'll be easier than I thought,*" Zoey thinks as she continues to study each of them. "Well, I can see you are all intelligent and educated women. So, none of my *common* talents will impress you."

Renee, Brenda, Abby and Jill exchange looks. By their facial expressions, this is going to be a total waste of time. Zoey extends out her palms. "Everyone, hold hands and close your eyes."

The young women obey the medium, taking each other by the hand. Zoey takes a hold Renee and Jill's hands, completing the circle. The four women close their eyes as Zoey takes a final look at each of them. Zoey takes a deep breath then closes her eyes as well.

Zoey's head begins to slowly sway from side to side. The dim glow of the crystal ball softly illuminates the five women's faces. Renee looks across at Abby. Jill looks across at Brenda. Zoey falls deeper into her self-induced trance with a low humming sound creeping out from the depths of her throat. "I see a football stadium," Zoey finally manages to say.

"*Well, duh!*" Renee thinks. *"Our college team is one of the best in the country."*

"I see a shiny lighter and a dull flame," Zoey continues in a low and mysterious voice.

"*I can't believe we're doing this*," Jill thinks.

"*I hope my hair looks alright*," Abby thinks.

"I see..."

"I see you're full of crap!" Renee blurts out as she opens her eyes. "Let's go girls!" Renee stands from her chair. Zoey tightens her eyelids as she lowers her head. Ever so slightly, she squeezes Renee and Jill's hands. The circle remains unbroken.

As if an uncontrollable spirit has clutched onto her shoulders, Zoey is forced back into her chair. The four women struggle to release their hands from each other. However, they are unable to. They become frightened as Zoey continues her self-induced trance, now with her hands beginning to tremble.

Suddenly, Zoey's eyes burst open as she abruptly stands. The circle of hands has yet to be broken. "Brenda, you slut!" Zoey declares staring directly at her. "You had sex with Paul in the announcer's booth right after The Football Championship!"

"You had sex with Paul?" Abby squeaks. "While *we* were going out?"

"Oh, The Debutant has room to talk," Zoey sarcastically says. "Abby here is more concerned with which one of you is going to get her the most expensive birthday present." Zoey turns her head and stares at Abby. "By the way, Happy Birthday!" she growls.

"*Please leave me outta this*," Jill rattles in her head.

"I don't think so, Jillian," Zoey states as if she had actually heard Jill's thoughts. "The shiny lighter and the dull flame belongs to you." Jill's three friends curiously look across the table at her.

"Jill?" Brenda asks.

"Jillian here is a closet smoker. She started by taking her mother's pack and lighter, a Zippo, from under her mother's mattress. She snuck out to the garage and puffed away. One or two at a time so her mother wouldn't notice the missing cigarettes too much."

"Jill, you smoke?" Renee asks. Zoey feels a sudden surge of energy run up her arm from Jill's hand.

"Oh, I see," Zoey says in a saddened tone. "You still have the lighter. It's in your purse." Zoey pauses a moment. "It's the only thing you have left of you mother." Zoey gives Jill a tender smile. "I know *that* feeling..."

Zoey takes a deep breath and briefly closes her eyes. As she opens them, she releases her grasp. The invisible force keeping their hands glued together has vanished.

A deathly stillness falls across the dimly lit room. The bewildered women exchange confused looks. How did this strange woman know of these things? How did she even know all of their names?

Jill is the first to raise from the table. She takes her purse in hand and opens it. Zoey smiles as she sees a pack of cigarettes and a shiny Zippo lighter. Jill reaches into her wallet and retrieves a thin stack of bills. Without counting it, she hands the payment to Zoey.

There are no words exchanged. There is no thank-you nor good-byes. Remaining at the round table, Zoey sees Jill exiting the front door of the side street parlor. Jill reaches into her purse, takes out a cigarette and lights it with her mother's lighter.

Brenda and Abby head for the opened front door, tossing Zoey a glance over their shoulders. Renee is the last to raise up from the table. She gives Zoey a casual nod as she walks across the cracked tile floor. "Congratulations, Renee."

"For what?" Renee asks. Brenda and Abby turn around, eager to hear what the fortune teller has to say.

"It's a boy," Zoey says with a devilish smile. "You're about fourteen weeks along." Zoey pauses a moment. Brenda and Abby curiously look Renee up and down. She's concealing her pregnancy very well. "So, Tommy's asked to you to marry him. What'cha gonna say?"

"I think you already know that, don't you?" Renee smiles and steps out onto the sidewalk. "Good-night," she says over her shoulder.

Zoey makes her way from around the table and approaches the front door. She closes and locks it then flips over the *CLOSED* sign. Looking through the pane glass windows, Zoey sees the four friends scampering up the sidewalk. They bubble with random chatter, reliving their weird mysterious experience. Zoey smiles. "Yeah, I'm *that* good."

Gordon takes a sip of his whiskey as he looks out the picture window of the back living room. The fog has lifted, clearly revealing several fishing boats trolling across The Sound. Beyond the vessels, the city lights stream across the opposite shore, accented by the illuminated tower, left behind from a World Fair.

He returns to the easy chair and retrieves his address book from the cushion. A nighttime television news anchor babbles in the background as Gordon flips through the pages, pausing on a handwritten entry;

Giovanni Mancini

Mancini Pharmaceuticals, INC.

"I don't *even* have to call him," Gordon mumbles to himself. "I *know* he's gonna show up." He rattles the melting ice in his stout glass and flips through the pages. Coming to the end of the address book, Gordon picks up the receiver of the phone and begins dialing the number.

"Slick Rick! Talk to me, baby!" Rick Stanton nearly shouts into his cell phone as he tightly covers his other ear with his free hand. In the background, thundering drums, a screaming guitar solo, a rhythm guitar riff and a pounding bass guitar.

He slightly presses his back against the pale green, concrete wall. The surface is smooth and runs in opposite directions like a long underground corridor of a prison.

Rick's attire seems out-of-place from his usual sleek business suit and polished Italian shoes. He has donned a black top hat and a bright red jacket with long tails. His white, frilly shirt, gold cummerbund, black pants and knee-high black boots completes his ringmaster costume. Rick even has a bullwhip hanging from his hip.

"Hey, Rick," Gordon says in an elevated voice. "I just wanted to say thanks again for the tickets."

"Sure thing, Gordon. Jon can't talk right now, they're finishing their encore."

"Right! Tell the boys I called. See ya' next month."

"C-ya!" Rick flips his cell phone closed and slides it into his pocket. He turns along the pale green wall and approaches a wide opening. As he passes through, Rick is bombarded by the continuing musical encore.

Rick makes his way through a small army of roadies and technicians, keeping their distance backstage. Three hulking roadies stand at the top of the steps which leads up from the main floor to up alongside the stage.

The steps are crammed with adoring female fans all seductively dressed in a variety of costumes. For the most part, in high-heeled shoes, black fishnet stockings and similar, short skirts. A bunny, a dairy cow, a zebra, a bumblebee and an assortment of wild felines. Hanging from each of their necks, a lanyard with an attached V.I.P pass.

Rick slightly pulls back the side curtains and is flooded with the stage footlights. He smiles to himself, seeing the mass of bodies filling the sports arena. It's not the seventy-five thousand fans he'd hoped for. But, it'll do.

The screaming fans occupying the forward festival seating area directly below the foot of the stage, are an interesting looking bunch. They too are dressed in a wide variety of costumes, like the band's concert was one gigantic Halloween party.

There are no ghoulish creatures to be seen. There are no vampires, witches, goblins, fairies or ghosts. The represented costumes are of an animalistic nature. Lions, tigers, wolves, zebras, cheetahs, giraffes, elephants, an assortment of primates and longhorn bulls.

The ocean of fans scream and wave their hands wildly through the air. Among the thousands of concertgoers, additional costumes appear, although not at prevalent as the crowd, at the foot of the stage.

The festival seating is a massive wave of body motion. The enthusiastic costumed fans sing and dance as the thunderous music continues. Ladies and gentlemen... *The Zøø Crüe*!

T-Bone is positioned at right stage pounding on his cordless, bass guitar. The four stringed instrument is covered with giraffe spots. A haphazard pattern of dark brown patches boarded with white resembling a cracked, dried out riverbed.

He is a hulking man looking more as if he were a bodybuilder than a musician. Broad shoulders, pumped up chest and rippling biceps and forearms. His damp, long black hair flows freely along his sweat drenched shoulders and back.

T-Bone's costume of choice is a longhorn bull. A large, gold ring dangles through the lower, center of his nose. Yet, the gold ring is not in the way of his lips. He is easily able to provide back-up vocals into his microphone headset. T-Bone wears a simulated pair of fur pants, looking more as if he were the mythological Pan.

A pair of extended horns is carefully mounted to his head, secured in place by a clear plastic strap running along the fronts of his ears and fastened under his chin.

Mohawk Mark bounces back and forth at left stage, filling in guitar riffs as the encore continues. His cordless, flashy black and white zebra pattern, single neck guitar provides the band's solos. It appears that Jon has been replaced in the capacity of lead guitarist.

Mark is a lanky looking fellow, the kind of wannabe musicians you would find prowling along The Sunset Strip. He sports a shredded, white T-shirt and a pair of zebra striped spandex pants.

The sides of his head have been shaved, accenting his impressive mohawk when he's not wearing his concert headgear.

Similar to T-Bone's costume, a clear plastic strap is secured under his chin, runs up along the side of his jaws and is fastened to his headpiece. Mark belts out needed back-up vocals into his microphone headset, unhindered by his costumed headgear.

The largely exaggerated black hair is coarse, protruding out and over his forehead, peaking upward at the top of his head then runs down the length of his back. The head ornament resembles a mane of a zebra. Directly behind him, a full sized, glossy black and white striped grand piano similar to the hide of a zebra.

Continuing his lengthy guitar solo, Mark darts across the stage, thrashing his head. Along the surface of the stage, yellow circular trampolines have been strategically placed.

The trampolines are level with the surface of the stage. Only the concertgoers in the upper seating can see them. They are invisible to the festival seating area.

Mark nearly skips across the stage, weaving his way around the yellow trampolines. He slightly turns and approaches the outer perimeter of a massive, lime green, double-bass drum set.

Rafael Von Dutch sits on his padded stool behind the wall of mounted tom-toms, an extended chandelier assembly of cymbals, a deep snare drum between his legs and three floor tom-toms to his left. The lime green drum set is colossal.

Rafe plays along with Mark's guitar solo and T-Bone's thundering bass line for several moments. He is shirtless and wears a black, loose fitting pair of shorts, the kind a college basketball player would wear.

Mark concludes his screaming guitar solo allowing Rafe to begin his drum interlude. The double-bass sounds like a constant thunderstorm, rattling the domed ceiling. The cymbals splash and sizzle, slicing through the air. Rafe's legs and arms are a mere blur. However, distinctive skin patterns are seen across his bare flesh.

From around Rafe's wrists, all the way up and completely around his arms up to his shoulders, tattooed cheetah spots are seen. The inked, black spots also appear along his torso, upper chest, the back of his neck and shoulder blades. The detailed art is a work in progress.

Rafe has no need for costumes like his fellow band mates. He has taken his secret alter form to another level. Rafe occasionally wears a pair of costume cheetah ears upon his head. However, only during sold-out concerts.

Rafe winds up the conclusion of his drum solo with Mark and T-Bone bouncing along stage on opposites sides of the towering drum set. The pair of forward musicians, in unison, slow the tempo and hold the last screaming chord of the song. Rafe's drumsticks pound across the surrounding cymbals as the double-bass roars.

The barrage of stage lights explode sending the screaming fans into a frenzy. Mark tosses his guitar to a roadie standing off stage. He darts toward the glossy black and white striped grand piano. Remaining standing with his fingers hovering over the piano's keys, he looks up toward Rafe.

The drummer smiles and nods. In sync, Rafe and Mark begin the introduction of another encore song. Their band's rendition of another musician's most popular song, slightly more upbeat and with more of a rock and roll edge.

Along the shadows of right stage, T-Bone joins in, thumping his fingers along the four strings of his bass guitar. Suddenly, the stage lights come up, flooding the stage with orange, green, red and blue colors.

Jon Von Dutch stands in all his glory, stretching out his arms with his back arched and looking up toward the hanging stage lights.

He his draped with a black wolf's fur. The forepaws are fastened to his wrists, run up his arms and completely covers his shoulders and back. His black spandex pants glimmers as the footlights of the stage quickly change colors.

Jon lowers his head, he gazes upon the ocean of costumed fans. As the lights continue to intensify, the remaining portion of his costume is made out. A black wolf's head rests on top of his own, resembling what a Native American would wear on a hunting party. Under the wolf's head, his microphone headset remains in place.

A thick guitar strap crosses his bare chest with a cordless, single neck guitar hanging from behind, slightly covering a section of his black, wolf's fur. The six string instrument is primarily bright green with colorful blue spots resembling the feathers of a peacock. The guitar is rarely used and is mostly for show. However, tonight is different-

Rafe pounds his drumsticks across his cymbals-

T-Bone runs his fingers along the four strings of his bass guitar-

Mark's fingers move across the keys of the black and white stripped grand piano, continuing the repetitious musical introduction-

Jon whips around his guitar and strums a slight chord across the strings. This is the cue for the rest of the band that the musical introduction is over and that he's ready to begin singing. Jon belts out the lyrics into the microphone of his headset-

"*I saw a werewolf with a Chinese menu in his hand,*
walking through the streets of SoHo in the rain.
He was looking for the place called Lee Ho Fooks,
gonna get a big dish of beef chow mein."

The crowds sing out the lyrics and accompanies Jon-

"*Ah-wooooo, Werewolves of London.*
Ah-woooooooo.
Ah-wooooo, Werewolves of London.
Ah-woooooooo."

Jon belts out the second verse of the cover song with an imitation pair of canine teeth peeking out from inside his parted lips. The backdrop of the stage changes and becomes similar to a television set during a weatherman's forecast.

The screen explodes with images of a dark and ominous lightning storm. A thick bank of clouds rolls across the large screen with bursts of lightning bolts-

"Ah-wooooo, Werewolves of London.
Ah-woooooooo.
Ah-wooooo, Werewolves of London.
Ah-woooooooo."

Jon races across the stage. He springs into the air, glides through the air for just a moment then lands in the center of a yellow trampoline. Jon bounces and flies upward toward the grand piano. Due to his momentum, he slides across the glossy black and white striped surface. Jon quickly turns to face the raging audience and kicks into a guitar solo.

From the weatherman type green-screen covering the backstage wall, powerful images of thunderclouds and lightning strikes continues in front of a full moon rising. Remaining on top of the glossy black and white grand piano, Jon concludes his screaming guitar solo. The crowds sing out the lyrics and accompanies Jon-

"Ah-wooooo, Werewolves of London.
Ah-woooooooo.
Ah-wooooo, Werewolves of London.
Ah-woooooooo."

The band's sound is much different than their earlier endeavors. They no longer sound similar to another pair of brothers who had formed a rock and roll band in the mid 1970's. The Dutch Brothers have conformed. They have sold-out if you ask some fans.

No longer do they have the powerful backbone of the double-bass drum and the front man playing lead and bass with his custom "X" guitar. The band sounds preassembled and manufactured, like the *poison* that had once ran through their musical veins has been replaced with pop-rocks.

As The Zøø Crüe continues to play their encore for the crowd, Rick can see that the upper, nosebleed seats are empty. Even before the band concludes their last song, the middle seats of the sports arena are beginning to clear out. The once dedicated fans have lost their interest.

"Jon!" Rick loudly says, as he stands halfway inside the opened door of the roomy backstage dressing room. He is unnoticed for several moments as the ongoing, after show party continues to rage on.

Rafe, Mark and T-Bone are swarmed with the seductively dressed female fans. A bunny, a dairy cow, a zebra, a bumblebee and an assortment of wild felines. Jon removes his set of imitation canine teeth before taking a sip of his scotch and water.

The large, brightly lit dressing room is filled with an assortment of bottles of whiskey, scotch, tequila, bottles of beer and champagne. The mood is carefree as loud thundering music, from another rock band, fills the air from the expensive stereo system. "Jon! Can I talk to you for a sec?" Rick shouts out over the music.

Rick backs away from the opened door and presses his back along the pale, green wall. Jon steps out into the extended corridor and closes the door behind himself. The sounds of laughter and music continues to seep outward from the ongoing party inside. "Yeah, Rick. What's goin' on?"

"Great show tonight." Rick says, in a somewhat un-enthusiastic tone.

"But?"

"But, ticket sales are down *another* fifteen percent."

"We're playin' our guts out!"

"That's not enough anymore," Rick sternly says. "I remember this young, cocky kid that used to play a mean double necked guitar, lead *and* bass at the same time. What happened to the edge you used to have?"

"There are at least *six* other guys that can do that now. *Better* than I ever could. That's nothin' special anymore."

"But, you were the *first* one."

"Just cuz I was the first, doesn't make me the best."

"You don't *have* to be the best, only the first. No one remembers the best. There are a lot of bests. Best baseball player, best football player, best car, best pair of shoes. But, you'll *always* remember your *first.*"

"Yeah..." Jon replies with a whisper.

"You better come up with something, Jon. Something *special*. Something *first."* Rick pauses a moment. "...or Omega Records will be forced to drop the band. There's nothing I can do about that." Rick pushes himself away from the smooth, pale green wall and pats Jon on the shoulder. "Enjoy the rest of the party."

Rick begins to make his way along the corridor, heading toward the far exit doors. As Jon turns to rejoin the party, Rick slows his pace and points his finger. "Oh, yeah. One more thing."

"Yeah, Rick," Jon says, as if he were being scolded. Rick slowly begins making his way back toward Jon.

"Leslie wanted to know if you were going to take the kids for a few weeks when you get back."

"I was planning on takin'em for a month or so if she doesn't mind."

"I don't think she'll mind. It's been a long tour. She could use some space."

"Did you make sure she got last month's check?"

"Don't I always? See ya' in Omaha..."

"C-ya'," Jon says with a wave of his hand. Rick shuffles his way along the extended walls and disappears around the far corner. Jon stands there for a moment looking blankly across the pale green surface. "*Something special. Something first..."*

Jon takes his hands and briskly runs his fingers through his damp hair, attempting to be presentable. He steps forward and takes hold of the dressing room's door knob. Just as he flings the door open, he is bombarded with spraying champagne bottles.

Rafe, Mark and T-Bone explode from the dressing room and surround Jon. They quickly circle him as they continue to shake up their champagne bottles and spray him. Jon is drenched! "Oh, you guys are gonna get it!"

The trio of musicians laugh, as the turn tail and vanish back into the dressing room. Jon bolts from his puddle of champagne and charges after them.

The loud, thundering music is joined by playful screams from the accompanying ladies. From inside the dressing room, a grand chase is heard. Bottles crash, chairs are tipped over and laughter fills the air. Such is the life of a Rock Star...

~ VI ~

The damp sidewalk is lined with homeless people and transients. The humbled folks are dressed in a variety of hand-me-downs, donated clothing and anything else they could find on the backstreets of The Big Easy.

The worn down neighborhood rests on the edge of the bustling city. Most of the storefront windows appear boarded up with several others having their windows smashed out. The line of homeless people moves forward as if they were inching their way along a food line. However, it is not a meal they are waiting for.

The two-story bus seems drastically out of place in this part of town. Well, out of place nearly everywhere it travels. The customized vehicle stands nearly fifteen feet tall, eleven and a half feet wide and over forty-eight feet in length.

The medical laboratory on wheels is the size of a double-decker bus. Along the center of both sides, a large, red cross is seen, similar to the exterior of an ambulance. Painted along both side panels near the end of the bus;

MANCINI PHARMACEUTICALS, INC.

As a slow moving assembly line, the transients make their way from the sidewalk and approach the opened forward door of the towering bus. One by one, the treated vagrants exit the large vehicle from the opened rear door.

Crockett is a pleasant looking fellow, better dressed than some, worse off than others. He has all of his teeth and has a polite mannerism. He's just a guy who's lost his job, house and his wife. Crockett is just trying to get back on his feet. "Next!" A commanding voice echoes out from with inside the bus.

A homeless married couple exits the rear door as Crockett steps up and into the bus. He looks around the interior to gather his bearings, to assure himself there is no danger. To his immediate right, the forward driver's chair and forward passenger's chair have been curtained off.

Crockett makes his way along the central aisle, surrounded on opposite sides by secured, metallic table tops and work stations. The interior is brightly lit and strikingly similar to a doctor's examining room.

Further along, a set of four gurneys, two on each side, are seen. The wheels have been retracted with their side handrailings secured to the walls. The next areas are filled with windowed cabinets, filled with a wide variety of prescription drugs. "Good-morning. What can I do for you?"

Gio greets the homeless man as he extends out his hand to be shaken. Crockett smiles, as he approaches Gio and takes his hand. Gio's tailored shirt and tie appear under his white, medical jacket. "I'm Crockett."

"Doctor Mancini. But, you can call me Gio or Doc. I like to keep things informal."

"Right..." Crockett says, as Gio leads him to the examining chair. As Gio slides into a pair of latex free, medical gloves, Crockett takes a seat, remaining upright in the chair similar to what a dentist would have.

"Well, Crockett. Do you have a particular illness or medical problem you'd like to discuss?"

"No, not really. Just like to get a flu shot if I could."

"That's simple enough," Gio says, in a polite tone. He is not here to judge or ridicule. He only wants to provide the best care and medical service to the less fortunate. "Would you mind rolling up your sleeve?"

Crockett seems at ease in this traveling hospital, it's nothing like he had expected. Clean, sterile and friendly. As Crockett rolls up his sleeve, Gio takes a pen and clipboard in hand. "I need to take some vital signs for my records. Although I'm privately funded, I still have to keep up with the medical board."

"Yeah, no problem." Gio plops down on his wheeled stool, opens one of many drawers and retrieves and stethoscope, a blood pressure cuff and an electronic thermometer with a disposable probe cover.

"So, Crockett. What do you do for a living?" Gio asks as he begins his examination.

"I *was* a diesel mechanic for a car dealership. You know, people come in with their cars for a tune-up or repairs that are all under warranty."

"You sound more like a salesman than a mechanic."

"I *did* a little of both."

"I'm sure this is just a temporary situation. You'll bounce back."

"*This guy is alright,*" Crockett thinks to himself. Gio removes the blood pressure cuff and writes down his patient's readings.

"*I like this guy,*" Gio mumbles in his head. "*Good heart rate and healthy lungs. He'll make a perfect specimen.*" Gio slightly swivels along his stool and stares at Crockett with a concerned look. There's something wrong!

"What is it, Doc?"

"It sounds like you might have a heart murmur." Gio says, lying through his teeth. "I have the rest of them outside to see but I'd like you to come back later so I can run a few tests." With that, Gio injects a needle into Crockett's arm with what the patient thinks, is a flu shot.

"Is it bad?"

"It's nothing to worry about. It's probably nothing. We just need to make sure." Gio stands and motions for Crockett to rise. "How 'bout six-thirty? Is that alright?"

"Sounds fine. Thanks." Crockett gives Gio a slight nod, as he makes his way around the examining chair and heads for the exit. In the far corner of the medical area and adjacent to the rear door, a spiral staircase leads up to the second floor and living quarters of the bus.

"Next!" Gio calls out in a commanding voice. Crockett pauses a moment at the opened doorway as Gio removes his pair of latex free gloves and slides into a fresh pair.

Gio greets the next transient and is as polite and professional as he was toward his previous patients. Crockett begins walking away from the rear of the medical bus. *"There's nothing to worry about... right?"*

"You're on time. Come on in," Gio says as he opens the forward door of the medical bus. The damp street and sidewalks are void of life. The well placed lampposts shine their light downward, reflecting on the wetness of the mazes of concrete.

Crockett seems unsure as he steps up and into the forward door. He looks around as he did earlier in the day but something is different this time. Crockett suddenly feels like a rat in a maze. He has unknowingly become a test subject.

Crockett feels dizzy and nauseous. He looks at Gio who stands along the central aisle of the bus, tenderly placing his hand on the headrest of the examining chair. "You alright?" Gio pauses. "Didn't think so. The drugs are time released. They should be kickin' in right about now." Crockett drops to his knees.

"What did you do to me?"

"Nothing, really. I injected you with a cocktail of a muscle relaxants and truth serum. Here, let's get you into the chair." Gio swiftly moves toward Crockett and gathers him up in his arms. He drags him to the examining chair and heaves him into the seat. Gio seems to have a heightened sense of strength and power.

Crockett looks about the ceiling of the lower level of the bus and attempts to focus on his surroundings. He's quickly fading in and out of consciousness.

Gio takes a pair of surgical scissors and cuts Crockett out of his shirt then his pants. Sitting on his stool, he wheels himself toward the foot of the examining chair and removes Crockett's worn boots and wool socks. Gio leans his patient back in the chair. Crockett is now wearing only his dark colored boxer shorts.

Gio reaches under the examining chair and retrieves a thick pair of straps. He tightly fastens the straps around Crockett's ankles and wrists. Gio inserts both ends of the built-in locks. He retrieves another pair of straps and locks them around

Crockett's chest and the other around his waist, confining him to the chair. "What do you want from me"?

"On your time on the streets, have you heard of a man named Cyrus?"

"What?" Crockett continues to fade in and out. "What?"

"This will be the truth serum taking effect. What do you know of Cyrus?"

"He's a Voodoo Man from The Bayous. No one sees much of him."

"Where can I find'im?"

"He hangs out at a diner on The Bay Front. Thursdays from what I heard." Crockett wets his mouth. His tongue has become dry. "Whatta 'bout my heart?"

"There's nothing wrong with your heart. You were the mostly likely candidate."

"*Candidate* for what?"

"The muscle relaxants should be taking full effect by now."

"...can-di-date...for...what?" Crockett mumbles before nearly blacking out. Gio reaches up and squeezes Crockett's face. He's just this side of consciousness. Gio slightly turns and swivels on his wheeled stool.

He opens a cabinet and retrieves a large, customized oxygen mask which is attached to a thick, clear one inch hose leading to a modified vaporizer similar to an inhaler.

Gio secures the strap behind Crockett's head and places the oxygen mask onto his face. "Don't worry, my friend. I synthesized the compounds. You'll only have to go through this once, with no after effects. I *have* to know what the secret is!" Crockett's eyes explode open as terror fills his soul.

Gio reaches into a secondary drawer and retrieves a thumbnail size of a black and sticky paste. He loads the black paste into the carbonator of the vaporizer; an advanced and customized hookah. "This might hurt a bit..."

The doctor flicks on the switch. The vaporizer begins to percolate, creating a cloud of smoke inside of the humidifier size component. The black and sticky substance appears to burn, without a flame. "Here we go..."

With a slight movement of his forefinger, Gio flicks a switch and releases the mysterious smoke from the component, through the hose and into the oxygen mask. Crockett's lungs are instantly filled with smoke.

The chemicals of the mysterious black paste quickly seeps into Crockett's organs and races through his veins. He begins to thrash around the examining chair. But, to no avail. He's restricted from any escape. Then, the transformation begins.

From below the oxygen mask, Crockett's face expands outward and narrows. His face becomes covered with light brown fur as his ears rise upward and begins to slightly flatten and fan out.

Crockett's shoulders begin to narrow with his upper and lower arms mutating into light brown extremities. Although his wrists are still restricted to the arms of the chair, his hands attempts to free himself. His flesh transforms into light brown fur and surprisingly enough, retains somewhat of their human form with the addition of claws instead of fingers.

Crockett strains to raise his head only to see a thick, light brown tail mutating from behind, along his lower tailbone. The tail flops out from beneath him as his thighs continue to transform and grow larger.

He feels intense pain shooting through his feet as they mold and mutate into three distinctive digits. The larger one in the center with two smaller ones on opposite sides. "Well, *that's* a new one. Crockett, can you hear me?" Gio asks, as he stands and hovers over the marsupial.

The fully developed kangaroo seems to understand Gio as they look into each other's eyes. "Crockett, concentrate! Think hard on another animal. I want you to change. *Now*!"

The kangaroo shakes his head, attempting to free himself from the oxygen mask. His tail thrashes about, whipping from side to side. His constricted black claws scratch from the armrests, just trying to snag his captor. "Concentrate!"

The kangaroo remains. There are no other alters hidden deep inside of the homeless man. There are no other shapes or forms to take on. There is only the marsupial. "Blast it!"

Gio reaches up and removes the oxygen mask from the kangaroo's muzzle. The beast angrily shakes his head at the doctor as he whips his tail about. Gio retrieves a syringe from an opened drawer and approaches the examining chair.

He braces the kangaroo's forearm onto the armrest of the chair before quickly injecting the needle into his upper arm. The kangaroo thrashes about for a few moments then becomes slightly at ease. "When you wake up, this'll all be over. You'll think it was just all in your head."

The kangaroo's breathing shallows as his heart rate begins to slow. Deeper and deeper the mammal falls from consciousness. The light brown fur begins to dissipate with the human upper and lower extremities quickly returning.

The kangaroo's floppy ears mutate and shrink in size. Crockett's facial features replace the extended muzzle and light brown fur. Gio scurries about the floor, gathering the remnants of Crockett's clothing. "Great," Gio says to himself. "*Thursdays.* I have four more days to hang around here."

Regaining more of his human senses, Crockett strains to focus. His vision is blurry and vague. He is not sure what he remembers. He is not sure why he is here. "*Where is here?*" Crockett mumbles in his head before completely blacking out.

"Good-morning," a volunteer says with a cheerful smile. The basement of the church has been converted into a homeless shelter with rows upon rows of cots along the inner walls. A central walkway separates the makeshift sleeping area with dozens of transients rising up, welcoming another day.

Crockett runs his hands over his face as he swings his legs over and plants his bare feet on the cold floor. The volunteer gives Crockett a brotherly pat on the shoulder, "Had a little too much Vino, eh? You'll feel better after breakfast."

"Where are my clothes?"

"Don't know. You were brought in last night. I wasn't here yet."

"Who brought me in?"

"Don't know!" The volunteer snaps, becoming impatient with the homeless man. "I wasn't here yet." The volunteer turns and continues his rounds, greeting transients and homeless people as he makes his way along the central aisle.

Crockett suddenly extends out his hands to examine them. He quickly looks himself up and down. All of his human characteristics are present. There is no light brown fur, no floppy ears and no thick tail. "*That* was a weird dream."

"Good-evening ladies and gentlemen," the prerecorded, feminine voice echoes out over the well placed speakers. "The Zoo will be closing in thirty minutes." Larry glances down at his wristwatch then slightly looks up into the darkening sky. The full moon will beginning its three day cycle within the hour.

"Before leaving, please feel free to stop by our gift shop. Again, The Zoo will be closing in thirty minutes. Thank-you for coming and drive safely."

Larry is casually dressed with loose fitting jeans, loafers, a dark colored T-shirt and a sport jacket. He looks around the vacant walkways of The Zoo, beyond the soft glowing lights of the lampposts then back across the deep ravine. A large sign stands a few feet away from him;

THE CITY ZOO
PROUDLY PRESENTS
KEIKO & JAAKKO
CO-SPONSERED BY
THE JAMISON FOUNDATION
EXIBIT TEMPORARILY CLOSED
FOR MAINTENANCE

Keiko lays near the center of her artificial habitat, looking outward toward the familiar human. Her forepaws are crossed with her hind legs slightly tucked under and hunched.

The lioness's tail sways back and forth like she hasn't a care in the world.

The sounds of an annoying primate in the distance catches her attention. Keiko turns and sniffs the air. She wishes that silly monkey would just go to sleep. She turns and refocuses along the thick handrailing beyond the deep ravine. Larry is gone.

Jaakko strolls out from the cave opening along the back of the simulated containment area. He passes a few boulders and approaches his mother. The larger feline bats his forepaw at her, wanting to play. She snips at him and lets out a low growl.

Keiko abruptly stands and lunges at her offspring. She playfully bites at his neck and pins him to the ground. Jaakko rolls over onto his back and paws at her.

She licks him behind the ear and lovingly bats him in the muzzle. Keiko looks up into the sky and sees the rising moon. It's now only a matter of time.

"Sonja?" Larry calls out. "It's me, Larry." He stands at the handrailing, looking into the containment area. Larry has retreated from his hiding place in the shrubs. The last of The Zoo's employees thought they had made sure all patrons have departed. Keiko saunters passed a cluster of shrubs.

Larry looks along the dimly lit walkway in opposite directions. There is no one around. He grabs hold of the handrailing and powerfully thrusts himself up and over it. Larry seems to soar through the air, clearing the deep ravine then landing on the ground with nearly no sound.

Keiko sniffs the air as she slowly approaches him. Larry remains still as the large feline walks around him several times. She sniffs the human and she swings her tail. She purposely smacks him in the face with her tuft. "Yeah, it's good to see you, too."

Keiko raises up on her hind legs and places her forepaws on his shoulders which brings them face to face. Larry looks deep in her brown, saucer eyes. She cautiously moves in closer and recalls his scent from so many years ago. Her whiskers tickle his cheeks. She lets out a low growl, more of a grunt then lowers herself to all fours.

Keiko approaches the edge of the ravine and sniffs the air. She assures herself that Larry is the only human left in The Zoo. Keiko turns and makes her way back toward Larry. They stand there a moment just looking at each other.

Simultaneously, Keiko and Larry begin to lower themselves. Larry squats, then sits on the ground with his legs crossed. Keiko lays on her stomach with her forepaws stretched out in front of herself. Her tail sways for a few moments then lays motionless. Keiko releases a big yawn before the transformation begins.

The lioness's hindquarters shrink in length and width with the golden fur quickly dissipating, being vacuumed inward, not shedding. She arches her shoulders and stretches her spine. Along her back, the fur disappears as beneath her, the feline's ribcage becomes narrower.

The lioness and the image of the woman seems to be molding and transforming into one another. Larry can't make out where one entity begins and the other one ends.

Keiko rolls over onto her side, keeping her head upward, never taking her eyes off of Larry. The leathery pads of her paws mutates, revealing soft looking flesh. As the remaining fur along the tops of her paws vanishes, a pair of woman's hands appear.

Sonja's legs and thighs are smooth as the last of the golden fur fades away. The remaining traces of the lioness's tuft blends into her lower back at the base of her spine. Her tail is gone.

Larry smiles as he begins to recognize facial features. Her furry, round ears swivel from high around her head, falls into place and mutates into their human form. Her shoulder length, sandy blonde hair rapidly sprouts up along her head as a flower would bloom and grow, captured on a time-lapsed camera.

Sonja's dark colored, triangular nose softens and gives way to human characteristics. Her whiskers slide back into her cheeks as if being pulled back from inside of her mouth. Sonja bats her eyes, feeling her restored eyelids and lashes. "Hi..."

"Hey," Larry says with an uncertain tone. He quickly gets to his feet, reaches down and takes Sonja by the hands. Standing face to face, they awkwardly smile at each other.

Larry slips out of his sport jacket and places over Sonja's shoulders. She's quite amused at this gallant gesture. "What? It's not like you haven't seen me naked before."

"I know, it's just..." Larry fumbles for something poetic to say. "You look great," is all that comes to mind.

"Mom?"

"Jay, you're awake," Sonja says with a smile. She turns to see her son standing in the cave's opening. Jay has a towel wrapped around his waist. He's a bit more modest than his mother.

Jay is a strapping young man, looking more as if he were in his teenage years rather than ten years old. His blonde hair is matted and unkempt. Jay has his mother's face and his father's build. He'll be quite handsome when he grows up. "Jay, I'd like you to meet... Larry."

"Jay, it's a pleasure to meet you."

"Can we get something to eat?" Jay replies, completely ignoring Larry's greeting.

"Sure thing, sweetheart," Sonja says, as Jay turns and disappears into the darkness of the cave. "It's gonna take some time, Larry... for both of us." Sonja takes him by the hand and leads him across the containment area.

Approaching the boulder closest to the cave's opening, Sonja crouches down and rummages through a small cluster of shrubs. She removes the dirt around the bottom of the boulder and retrieves a set of keys.

The first key is large and flat. The second and third keys resemble ones used for the front door of an apartment or house. The last key looks as if it would unsecure a padlock of some kind.

Jay impatiently waits along the far side of the large cage. The accommodations for the feline mother and son are better than Larry had expected. The dirt floor has been freshly raked with no signs of animal droppings. Large mounds of straw lay along the inner walls with a matching pair of water bowls.

Sonja takes the key ring and selects the large, flat key. She reaches through the bars of the cage's door and slides it into the lock. Sonja swings the cage door open, leading Jay and Larry through. "They don't ask why you two are missing?" Larry asks.

"It's part of our arrangement. I'll explain later." Sonja secures the cage door and moves toward a military looking foot locker against the near wall. Taking the odd looking key, she unlocks a padlock and opens the small chest.

Sonja reaches inside and retrieves a neatly folded set of clothes. She tosses them to Jay before reaching in again and removes a one piece dress.

Sonja hands Larry his sport jacket then easily slides the dress over her head. She turns to see that Jay is already dressed in his jeans and T-shirt. "Would you mind giving us a ride home?"

"Home?" Larry asks.

"Yeah, we're not on display *all* the time," Sonja says with a mischievous smile. She motions for Jay to follow, as Sonja turns and heads through the back areas of the cages and pens. Larry follows close behind, wondering if he has made the right choice.

The car ride is quiet. No music plays from the stereo system. There are no conversations nor chit-chat. Larry steers north along the freeway with Sonja quietly sitting next to him. He glances into the rearview mirror from time to time. Jay sure does look like him.

Jay sits in the backseat, directly behind Larry. His eyes are wide open, looking out though the opened window. Jay takes in the wondrous sights and smells of The Emerald City. The last time he remembers being here, he was less than three years old. "You want to take this off ramp," Sonja instructs.

Larry slides into the far lane and eases off the freeway. The commercial and retail district quickly gives way to residential and housing tracks. Larry feels his heart beating faster as they draw nearer to their destination. "*What have I gotten myself into?*" he mumbles in his head.

"It's not much for now," Sonja says with an almost disappointed smile. "But, it's home." She forces the front door of her apartment open. Mounds of letters and mail clutter the floor, deposited from the mail slot in the door.

Jay follows his mother inside with Larry closing the door behind them. Sonja pauses a moment to see where she had left off when she was here less than a month ago.

The baseboards of the living room walls are covered by packed and unopened moving boxes. No paintings are hung. No shelves or knick-knacks. The only furniture is a standard coffee table with several large throw pillows in the center of the room. "Jay..." Sonja motions toward her son. Jay gives Larry an uncertain look as he follows his mother passed the bare kitchen and down the short hallway.

Larry walks through the empty living room and enters the kitchen. The counters have no appliances of any kind. He opens the refrigerator and sees empty shelves. Larry opens each of the cabinets and finds they have not been stocked either.

"We can fix it up any way you'd like," Sonja says. Jay stands in the doorway of his bedroom, trying to imagine what it'll look like someday. For now, he'll have to settle for the simple futon bed. "You have some clothes in the closet and there're towels down the hallway."

"Hey, where's your phone?" Larry calls out from the kitchen.

"Won't be hooked up till next week," Sonja replies, sticking her head out into the hallway.

"I'm gonna order pizza. Is that okay with you?" Jay turns toward his mother and gives her a discerning look.

"You need to spend some time with him. I think you'll like him."

"Do you like him?"

"I used to... a long time ago." Sonja leans down and kisses Jay on the top of his head. "Now, go get cleaned up. We only have three days."

"Pizza's on its way," Larry says, as he appears in the doorway. He slides his cell phone into his pocket and smiles at Sonja and Jay, waiting for a *thank-you*. Nope! Jay makes his way passed Larry and disappears into the bathroom down the hallway.

"Why didn't you tell me he *was* my son?" Larry and Sonja sit on the large throw pillows placed around the coffee table. In the background, the sounds of the running shower echo out into the hallway. The bathroom door appears slightly propped open.

"He *is* your son," Sonja sharply responds.

"I would've helped."

"Helped with what, Larry? Potty-training? When he was cutting his teeth? *Both* sets! How about the hours of colic? It's bad enough when you're human but when you're like *us?* Did you think about breast feeding?"

"Ouch!" Larry thinks. "*That must've hurt!"*

"I didn't *want* your help," Sonja says in an unconvincing tone.

"So, how does it work then?" Larry asks, ungracefully transitioning into the next subject. "All he has is three days?"

"Jay hasn't quite learned to control his alter, yet. He *was* born human. Then, when he was six months old, he changed. I couldn't keep him at home. I can only stay like this for a little while. They haven't found a cure yet."

"I'm sorry." Larry reaches across the coffee table and tenderly takes Sonja's hand. She almost smiles, remembering how kind and gentle Larry used to be.

"So, the only way to keep an eye on him was to form the *Jamison Foundation.* We're a package deal. I *own* Keiko and Jaakko. With public donations and *some* federal support, we go on tour."

"You're pimpin' yourselves out!"

"That was harsh!" Sonja snaps as she quickly releases Larry's hand. "Do you really think I like traipsing all over, putting us on display like freaks in a carnival?!"

KNOCK - KNOCK - KNOCK.

"Pizza's here!" Larry cheerfully says, attempting to lighten to moment. Sonja shakes her head. He just doesn't understand. Larry rises up, makes his way to the front door and greets the young deliveryman.

Down the hallway, the shower continues to run. Just beyond the slightly opened bathroom door, Jay carefully listens. He has overheard his mother and Larry's entire conversation.

"Look, I don't know you and you don't know me," Jay says as a matter of fact. He stands next to his mother with Larry directly outside of the opened front door. The coffee table behind Sonja and Jay is cluttered with paper plates, remnants of crusts and two half eaten pizzas. "But, I can feel my mother still has feelings for you. So, I'll give you a shot."

"Thank-you, Jay," Larry says, in a humbled manner.

"See you in the morning. *Early!"* Jay gives Larry a casual nod, turns and heads for his bedroom down the hallway. "Go ahead and kiss'er good-night if you want to," Jay loudly says over his shoulder.

"I guess I'll see you in the morning. *Early!"* Larry smiles. An awkward moment follows. "Good-night."

"G'night." Sonja's eyes flutter, as she hesitates then slowly closes the front door. Her son's comment rattles inside of her head. "*Go ahead and kiss'er good-night if you want to...*"

Chloe looks worn down and tired as she steps through the front door of her suburban home. Fiddling with a thick stack of mail, she bumps the door with her hip, closing it. Her casual business suit is slightly wrinkled from a long day at the office.

The living room is wide and spacious with modern looking furniture and tapestries. The lifeless fireplace and hearth above fills the wall across the room. In the center of the hearth, a familiar object is seen. The photo appears charred around the edges and rests inside of a common glass frame.

The image is that of a family. A happy family posing with the colorful and lively amusement park in the background. An athletic looking mother, a strikingly handsome father and a raven haired young girl with piercing green eyes and over than average sized ears. Everything in Chloe's home is where it should be. It appears her life is clean and orderly.

Chloe enters the kitchen and flicks on the overhead, florissant lights. She stops dead in her tracks. Chloe tosses the majority of the mail to the tiled counter top as she stares at one particular envelope. She reaches across the tile counter top and presses a button on the phone and message machine.

"Hey, it's Larry. I'm gonna be outta the office for a few days. Hold down the fort for me. Thanks," the recorded message says. Chloe tears the envelope open and scans across its contents. It's an eviction notice. Almost infuriated, Chloe reaches for the phone and quickly dials a number.

RING - RING.

RING - RING.

"Thank-you for calling Madam Zoey's. Please leave your name and number and I'll get back to you."

BEEEEP.

"It's me!" Chloe barks into the receiver. "Looks like the shop is three months behind in rent. I know you're getting a kick outta this gypsy-thing. But like I told you before, I'm not supporting your habit. Call me back when you get this!"

Chloe nearly breaks the receiver as she hangs it up. She stands there a moment, fuming. This is not the first time the mail was delivered to the wrong address. She's tired of receiving Zoey's trendy clothing magazines, junk mail and especially the late notices and bills. Chloe turns and approaches the closed door leading down into the basement.

She tenderly places her palm on the door, suddenly becoming saddened. "No, I'm *not* going to give in this time," she scolds herself. Beginning to unbutton her suit jacket, Chloe turns and heads down the hallway, leading into one of the three bedrooms.

The mysterious fortune teller's shop is dark and lifeless with the *CLOSED* sign hanging in the window. Along the floorboards of the picture windows, several filled, cardboard boxes are seen. The soft glow of the crystal ball rests on its wooden stand in the center of the round table and appears to be the only form of light.

The dresser and the room divider stand opposite from each other with the top of the dresser empty of all objects. The breadbox sized wooden chest has been packed away in a cardboard box resting on the floor. A stack of broken down cardboard boxes leans against the side of the dresser and have yet to be reassembled and used.

There is no trace of the raven haired, green eyed palm reader. Her absence seems to be permanent, unable to make the rent payments. It's just a matter of a few days until the shop will be completely empty and ready to lease to another tenant.

The Pacific Ocean spans out across the horizon for as far as the eye can see. The coastline stretches out a few miles away. From this distance, structures are unable to be defined, as amber and orange colors dance throughout the cloudless sky. It's going to be a beautiful sunset.

The rolling waves are speckled with crabbing boats and fishing trawlers. About their decks, the sea faring crews tend to their crab pots and spools of fishing nets. From time to time, migrating whales will surface, catching a quick breath before quickly submerging.

The dolphin swims along at a moderate speed with his dorsal fin cutting effortlessly through the surface of the ocean. His flippers direct him as if he were a majestic bird, soaring through the air.

He seems to slow his pace for a moment, coasting through the water. The dolphin senses a large school of fish ahead. He clicks his mouth several times before racing toward the fish.

The dolphin darts through the school of fish, not wanting to eat them, he just wants to play. The fish explode in all directions for a brief moment then rejoin each other. The school of fish want nothing to do with this mammal. They seem to speed up and vanish behind a reef of coral along the ocean floor.

The dolphin swims to the surface and replenishes the air in his lungs. As he returns to the ocean, something catches his attention. There is something far off in the distance. Something very familiar.

He swims further and further along the coast, heading south, away from the safety of The Sound he calls home. The dolphin continues searching, swimming in a weaving manner, back and forth, covering as much area as possible. He clicks his mouth several times, gathering his bearings. There it is again!

He is becoming more eager, carelessly swimming at a rapid pace. Faster and faster. The familiar presence is drawing nearer. He can feel it. He can feel *her*.

The dolphin is so overwhelmed with excitement, he doesn't sense the wall of extended fishing nets until he is upon them. His beak slides through an opening in the net as he maneuvers too late.

The net constricts the dolphin up passed his blowhole. He spins around, attempting to free himself. The net wraps around his flippers and tail, restraining him further. He thrashes around, trying to break free from the surrounding net. However, with each effort, the dolphin becomes more in peril. The net is beginning to drown him.

The dolphin begins to mutate and transform. Between his flukes, his tail separates and begins to shrink. The smooth surface of the dolphin quickly dissipates, revealing a man's pair of feet and legs, wildly kicking against the net.

The dorsal fin molds into Tez's lower back, all the way up between his shoulder blades. His torso narrows with his flippers regressing back to human arms and hands.

Tez violently pulls at the fishing net, searching for a way of escape. He's quickly running out of air. The dolphin's smooth beak retracts into his skull, reveling Tez's panicked facial features.

Tez claws his way to what he feels is the surface as the fishing net continues to restrain him. Unable to hold his breath any longer, his lungs are flooded with seawater. He's feels himself loosing strength. All hope is lost.

His body falls limp as he begins to sink deeper toward the ocean floor. A pair of woman's hands suddenly appear from behind Tez. She quickly takes hold of the fishing net, searching for an outer seam.

The mermaid pulls at the net with all of her might, loosening it from around Tez's neck and shoulders. Her long, red hair flows with the ocean current with wavy motions. Her set of gills behind her ears, provides the oxygen she requires for her aquatic travels. She is bare chested and appears human from the waist up.

Just above her hip bones, below her naval and above her tailbone, the top row of scales blends into her human flesh. The rainbow of blue and green scales tapers down along her lower extremity. Her tail ends with a wide fin with long, finger-like members inside, used for support and maneuvering.

Kaleen spins Tez around, bringing them face to face. He has lost consciousness with no signs of life. His breathing has completely stopped. She rips the fishing net from his waist and thighs. Then from behind, she wraps her arm around his chest.

With her freehand, she swims toward the surface, dragging Tez's lifeless body along. Her tail thrusts through the water, shooting them upward at an accelerated rate.

Kaleen powerfully lifts Tez above the surface as he remains lifeless and unconscious. She treads water with her tail swishing back and forth from below.

She tightly wraps her arms around Tez from behind and squeezes his chest several times. At first, there is no positive reaction. Then, a spout of seawater spews from his mouth. He violently coughs and regains consciousness.

Tez moves his arms through the water and begins kicking his legs, supporting himself along the surface. He lifts his face high into the air, feeling the warmth of the setting sun against his cheeks. Without turning around, he smiles, "Hey, *Ariel*. How you been?"

"Alright, *Flipper*. And you?" Kaleen loosens her grip on Tez. He continues to move his arms against the water as he turns and faces her.

"Thanks," he humbly says. "I wasn't sure if you were gonna show up."

"For the reunion or to save your life?"

"For both..." Tez smiles, reaches up and tenderly runs the back of his hand against her cheek.

"It's good to see you, too." Kaleen slightly leans forward and kisses him on the cheek. "Tag, you're it!" She suddenly pushes Tez away from herself then dives below the surface. She slaps her tail in front of Tez, splashing his face.

As a diver atop a tall platform, Tez extends his hands and arms upward, arches his back and submerges into the ocean. All that remains along the surface are ripples and slight waves. "Did you see that?" a fisherman asks.

"No and neither did you!" his crewmate answers. The pair of shipmates stands along the port side of their commercial fishing vessel. They clutch onto the ends of a fishing net, preparing to secure it and draw it in. The same fishing net which nearly drowned a dolphin a few minutes earlier.

"I see you're still living in the same place," Kaleen says as she treads water a few yards out from the shoreline. Tez stands facing The Sound as he continues to towel dry himself. The full moon casts its soft rays across his bare body.

"Yeah, I still like it here. But, you *knew* that." Tez reaches down, takes his pair of jeans from the sand and slides into them. He snags his pair of dark sunglasses from his wadded up T-shirt and places them onto his face.

Kaleen wades through the water and strolls up onto the shore. All of her human extremities have returned. He tosses her his towel before slipping into his T-shirt. "How was your trip?"

"Water was cold around Crescent City but I got used to it," she says as she blots the towel across her hair. "I was hoping I could crash with you," she whispers, as she wraps the towel under her arms.

"You always did pack light," he says with a smile. "Sure, come on. You know the way."

"You still have the couches we bought," Kaleen curiously says as she flicks on the light switch along the far wall. "I thought you would've replaced them years ago."

"Sentimental value I guess," Tez replies, as he makes his way around the back of one of the matching couches. His living room appears extremely organized and well thought-out. There is no unneeded furniture nor knick-knacks. The room is almost Japanese looking.

There are no framed pictures nor mirrors hanging from the walls. No shelves filled with books nor any other reading material. The television itself looks unused for some time now. "I've got to get ready for work. You can have my bed. No need for you to sleep on the couch."

Kaleen remains standing in the entryway with the towel still wrapped under her arms. She opens her mouth as if to say something. "I kept a few of your things. They're hanging in the closet," he says as he disappears into the bathroom around the corner. Kaleen smiles. It's kind of spooky how well he remembers her.

Tez leans against the wall of the shower with the hot water spraying down along the back of his head. He swivels his neck then raises his face, rinsing off the remaining soap.

Kaleen slides a one piece dress over her head as she stands facing the bedroom closet. Tez's clothes appear hung along a single horizontal pole, almost in an alphabetical order, very Albert Einsteinish. She sees a box along the upper shelf of the closet;

Kay

Kaleen reaches up and slides the box from the shelf. She sits on the floor and opens it. Inside, dozens of framed pictures of her and Tez; a camping trip, windsurfing, bungee jumping and of course... their wedding on the beach. "Like I said, sentimental value."

Tez walks across the floor and approaches an upright dresser along the far side of the room. He selects one of numerous pairs of dark sunglasses and slides them along the bridge of his nose. His queen sized bed is plain and well made, almost to military standards.

Kaleen remains seated on the floor, facing the closet with the opened box between her legs. She hears Tez drop his towel. Her eyes widen. She wants to turn around but can't force herself to. Well, maybe just one peek.

"I'll be home around nine. There's food in the fridge. Help yourself..." Tez slides into his jeans then grabs a tank-top from an opened drawer. He turns and makes his way passed the end of the bed, steps around Kaleen and takes a dress shirt from the closet.

"What happened to us, Tez?" Kaleen asks, as she looks up at him. He simply smiles as he half buttons his dress shirt.

HONK - HONK!

"I gotta go, I'm late for work. Make yourself at home, again." Tez quickly makes his way out of the bedroom and shuffles down the hallway. Kaleen sits there, just listening. A set of keys jingle as the front door opens then closes.

Kaleen sets down the opened box and stands. She reaches forward and gathers a large armful of Tez's hanging clothes. Kaleen deeply inhales. How she misses his smell.

"Hey, Paul. How you doin' t'night?" Tez asks, as he climbs into the backseat of the bright yellow taxicab.

"Great, Tez. N'you?" Paul, Tez's regular taxicab driver, says with a burly smile.

"Just another workday," Tez replies, as he shuts the taxicab's door. Paul sets the taxicab in gear and slowly steers the black and yellow checkered vehicle along the street of the shoreline community as Tez leans back, being chauffeured to work.

"Good-morning, Night Crawlers," Tez announces into the suspended microphone. He sits facing a massive control board with rows of levers and switches. The popular local radio station plays classic rock and roll in which Tez caters to. The disk jockey loves his fans.

A pair of turntables occupies the counter space to his left with a vast assortments of vinyl albums and compact disks filling the shelves directly behind himself.

The overhead florescent bulbs are void from light. The studio is dark for the most part. Over a half a dozen lava lamps appear strategically placed along the sparse counter tops. The oozing fluid of the lamps are in a variety of colors, slightly illuminating the hanging posters along the walls; Hendrix, Joplin, Dylan and Morrison.

"Before we get started tonight, I'd like to remind everyone that funeral services are going to be held for our beloved Dee Dee Sawyer at Jacobson Memorial this Friday." Resting on the top right edge of the extended control panel, a framed promotional shot of Dee Dee Sawyer. Tez's fellow disk jockey who had been brutally murdered under mysterious circumstances just a few days ago.

Tez cues up a compact disk in its player and flicks it on. A soft and slow rock ballad begins. "We miss you, Dee." Tez takes a breath. "You're tuned to The City's classic rock-n-roll station, one-o-one point three, K-R-W-L."

Tez flicks off the *on-air* button and eases back in his chair. "*What am I gonna play next?*" He thinks to himself. *"What am I gonna order for breakfast? What am I gonna do about Kaleen?"*

Large areas of flatlands and patches of desert appear for miles in all directions, speckled with towering cactuses and colorful rock formations. The sun hangs midday with no visible signs of civilizations for as far as the eye can see.

Along the desolate landscape, narrow dirt roads appear, winding along the sandy surface. One road spans out in an opposite direction, leading out to nowhere. One particular road extends off of the main highway, runs along for miles then dissipates over the edge of a hidden canyon.

Whiskey Ridge is pleasant this time of year. Not too hot and not too cold. The average temperature is around seventy degrees with little to no rainfall. The ridge itself hangs high above the lush canyon, kind of like a lookout point or lover's leap.

A slow moving river cuts through the heart of the canyon with sprawling trees and wild flowers. The slanting walls of the canyon provide shelter from the stale desert breeze above.

Along the near shoreline of the river, a campsite of sorts has been erected. The twenty yard flat area, spans from the water line to the tree line and base of the canyon wall. A community of tents stands along the edge of the tree line with numerous clotheslines spanning from limb to limb.

A few family members of Reggie's group hang their washed clothes along the clotheslines. Other bikers appear from the wooded area carrying armfuls of branches and fallen timber.

At the far end of the temporary camp, a row of parked motorcycles and even a few trikes are seen. The quiet machines are lined up beautifully as if they were parked on a city street along the curb.

Near the end of the assembly of bikes, Reggie's trike stands next to Dante's two wheeled ride. Just beyond the last cycle, the lower end of a narrow dirt road leads upward along the canyon wall at a gradual angle.

Oddly enough, for the number of motorcycles and tents, there are less than a dozen bikers throughout the camp. A silhouette steps away from the shoreline, carrying an armful of freshly washed clothes.

Amber is an attractive woman wearing a bikini top, jean shorts and cowboy boots. She approaches a clothesline and flops the damp attire along the outstretched cord. Amber begins separating the clothing, hanging them out to dry. "Pssssst!"

Amber looks over her shoulder as if someone was behind her. "Pssssst! Amber, over here," the voice calls out from beyond the tree line. Amber ducks under the clothesline and approaches a narrow separation in the trees.

"Gordon, is that you?"

"Yeah, it's me." Gordon pops his head out from behind a tree, keeping is bare body concealed. "I just *flew in* to see how the boys are."

"They'll be happy to see you. Well, not *that much* of you," Amber says with a giggle. "Let me get you something to put on."

Gordon and Amber walk along the shoreline of the river. His borrowed pair of jeans are loose and baggy. "Looks like you've been here for a few days."

"Yeah, Dante's resting up from his last fight. I think we're moving out tomorrow."

"So, how are you and Reggie gettin' along?"

"You know, one backwater town after another." The sounds of playful laughter fill the air as Amber and Gordon round the edge of the tree line.

The wide open area boarders the river's shoreline and the bottom of the canyon, about an acre. There are no rocks nor boulders for obstructions along the makeshift playing field.

Two teams run along the wide area, continuing their game of soccer. The players consist of the majority of the dwindling biker family and their offspring, kicking a worn and faded ball back and forth. It seems that it is the adults against the kids.

From the center of the field, Reggie, in jean shorts and barefoot, has the ball. He runs along, kicking it with several young opponents coming up alongside. Reggie passes the ball to one of his fellow bikers, Jimmy. A boy, around eleven years old, intercepts the ball.

The biker boy runs toward the end of the field, weaving the ball away from his adult opponents. Vince, a hulking man in a black leather vest, tends goal. He sees the boy quickly approaching and shuffles from side to side. The boy kicks the faded soccer ball; GOAL!

Cheers fill the air. The boy and his fellow teammates have won the game, again. As Vince approaches the center of the field, he sees Reggie give him a wink. The collection of bikers congratulate the younger men. Good game! The boy collects the game ball and leads the rest of his team back toward the camp. "Hey, Gordon!"

"Reggie, how you been?" Gordon and Reggie shake hands.

"We've been good. Ya' know."

"I'll let you boys catch up," Amber says before kissing Reggie on the cheek. She turns and follows behind the defeated team of adult bikers, back toward their primitive campsite.

"I see the family's not what it used to be."

"Yeah, our numbers are thinning out. People these days are more into the comforts of home instead of life on the road." An awkward pause follows.

"Where's Dante?"

"He's up over there with the rest of the kids." Reggie smiles, as he points beyond another bend along the shoreline.

"I'm next! I'm next!" one biker child calls out.

"No, I'm next Uncle D," another boy shouts.

"There's room for both of you," Dante says with a smile. The children swarm in front of Dante, waving their arms in the air as if to be picked up or carried.

~ VII ~

Throughout the centuries, the heredity of Sagittarians has evolved. They are no longer restricted to altering into just a horse. Some have the ability to transform into a deer, a caribou, an elk, a reindeer or even a moose. In Dante's case, a bighorn sheep.

Dante towers over the gathering of children, standing nearly seven feet tall. From their point of view, Dante's shoulders, rippling arms and ridged stomach appears human. His swollen eye continues to heal.

Just below his navel and above his hip bones, his flesh tapers into dark brown hair. Dante's thighs appear to be similar in size as his human extremities however his knees, shins and calves are slightly narrower.

Dante stands firmly on his forefront pair of hooves as he reaches down toward the closest child. He effortlessly swings the child upward and behind himself, revealing the rest of his quadruped altered form.

The first child straddles Dante's extended horizontal back, covered with dark brown hair. The boy slides himself forward, closer to Dante's human back. His thick dreadlocks hang just above his human tailbone which has mutated into the dark brown hair of his hoofed alter. Dante reaches down and swings two more children up onto his transformed, horizontal back.

Dante flexes his thick and hairy hind legs, adjusting to the weight of the three children along his back. He slightly stomps his rear pair of hooves into the dirt, preparing the children for a carnival-like pony ride. "Alright kids, here we go!"

The first boy slightly hangs onto Dante's dreadlocks as if they were a set of reins. Each of the children behind him have wrapped their arms around the next one's stomach, hanging on.

Dante trots along the shoreline of the river, moving his arms as if he were briskly jogging. The children giggle and wave toward the rest of the kids waiting their turn.

Dante gracefully turns away from the water's edge, trots along the opened area and across the valley floor. He sees Gordon and Reggie standing off to the side. Dante gives Gordon a subtle nod as he makes his way along the tree line and approaches the far end of the playing field. "Hold on. We're going to speed up now!"

The children hang onto each other as the first boy clutches onto Dante's dreadlocks, slightly pulling his head backward. Ouch! Oh well, the kids are having fun.

Dante begins to gallop along the shoreline with the trip around the large clearing taking less and less time. The children laugh out loud as Dante speeds up, now at a full run.

Dante's hooves shake the ground as if a lightning storm was quickly approaching with deep rumbles filling the air. He rounds the tree line one last time, passing Gordon and Reggie. He approaches the next set of young passengers and solidly plants his forward hooves. This might be the funest part of the ride.

Dante quickly lowers his hind legs causing his extended back to instantly drop. The children raise their hands in the air and slide back and downward. They laugh as they topple onto each other.

Raising his hind legs back into their upright stance, Dante reaches down and swings up the remaining children up onto his extended back. With the young passengers in place, he takes a deep breath and begins trotting toward the shoreline.

"I see you're still making money the old fashion way," Gordon says with a smirk.

"Yeah, beating it outta them," Dante replies. Reggie and Dante walk along opposite sides of Gordon as they make their way to the perimeter of the camp. For now, Dante has chosen to remain in his alter form.

The family of bikers take little notice of Dante's appearance. They appear is if it were a usual occurrence to have such a mysterious Sagittarian, hybrid bighorn creature living among them. After all, we all have secrets. "So, you boys headin' North?"

"Yeah, we'll make it," Reggie says with a smile. "The last show of the tour. We wouldn't miss it."

"We *all* gonna be there?" Dante asks, hoping *one* of their family of alters won't attend.

"Well, I haven't talked to him but I'm sure he'll make an appearance," Gordon replies with an odd tone. After all of these years, Dante and Gio still haven't called a truce. "I saw your television commercial a few months back," Gordon says, trying to lighten the mood.

"Oh, that one where I'm in the shower with that *two-things* body soap?"

"No, the *other* one! That *two-in-one,* bundling home and auto insurance." Gordon scowls up at Dante. "That's just one *more* rule you kids have broken."

"Hey, I don't know about the rest of'em but that was my only time! I was between fights and we were low on cash."

"I want your word, no more commercials."

"I can't give it to you."

"Dante!" Gordon scolds.

"How 'bout we race for it. Winner gets his way," Reggie chimes in.

"Hey, guys! Race for what?" Shelby interrupts as he quickly approaches.

"There's gonna be a race?" Vince blurts out. In a matter of moments, Gordon, Reggie and Dante are surrounded by wagering bikers. As usual, Shelby is the money man.

"Here's fifty on Dante!" Vince says, as he hands a ten and two twenties to Shelby.

"I'll take fifty on Reggie," Jimmy announces.

"I bet I can beat'em both. Two to one odds," Gordon says as he turns toward Dante. "No more commercials!"

"Wait, you don't have any money to bet with," Vince states as a matter of fact.

"I'll back'im," Amber says, as she makes her way forward and stands beside Gordon.

"Thanks, *dear*." Reggie scowls at Amber. She simply smiles and gives Gordon a playful kiss on the cheek.

"Hey, wait a minute," Jimmy interrupts. "You flew in, didn't you?"

"Yeah..."

"You got no bike. Whatta ya' gonna race with?"

"Let me worry about how I'm gonna race," Gordon says with a smirk. As the bikers continue to exchange bets, handing Shelby wads of cash, Gordon turns and heads for the nearest tree line. He slightly looks over his shoulder before disappearing into the trees.

Reggie dismisses himself from the wagering and heads toward his trike parked along the end of the row of motorcycles.

Vince and Jimmy bound for their bikes. They fire up their engines and lead a pack of bikers up along the narrow road. The line of bikers disappears along the gradual slope, heading toward the unseen finishing line.

Reggie throttles up and maneuvers his trike to the lower end of the road. The four pronged anchor dangles from the chain behind his rear seat.

Dante trots along, coming up alongside of Reggie. The few remaining bikers of the family stand on opposite sides of the road, supporting their racers. Reggie, Dante and... "Gordon! Let's go!" Reggie calls out over the low rumbling of his trike.

The ostrich appears from the tree line carrying a pair of borrowed, baggy jeans in his beak. The large bird stands nearly nine feet tall, towering over Amber as he releases the jeans into her arms.

She smiles at him, looking up into his large, saucer shaped, brown eyes. The majority of his lower body is covered with dark brown feathers with white feathers along his upper thighs, tips of his wings and tuft area. Although completely immersed in his alter form, Gordon still retains his inner human faculties.

He struts over toward the starting line and glances down at Reggie. Turning, he stands slightly over Dante and gives him a playful peck of his beak. "First one to Whiskey Ridge wins!" Amber announces.

She moves to the side and stands along the end of the road. Dante stomps one of his fore hooves along the ground as a house cat would claw at a scratching post. His powerful hind legs flex, preparing for a quick start.

Reggie tightens his grip on the clutch at the end of his handlebars and flicks his foot against the gears. He revs his engine. "I prefer *horsepower* myself!" Reggie revs the engine of his trike again; he's ready to go!

The ostrich takes his position next to Reggie, slightly ruffling his wings. The few remaining bikers eagerly wait, cheering and coaxing the three racers on. "On your mark..." Amber shouts as he raises her arm high into the air. "Get set..." Reggie winks at Amber as she quickly brings her arm down. "...Go!"

The ostrich bolts from the starting line followed by Dante who bursts into a gallop. Reggie releases his clutch and accelerates up the gradual incline; the race is on!

The road cuts along the wall of the canyon with the steep slope to one side and the vast tree line to the opposite side. The ostrich is at a full run with his powerful legs taking massive strides.

Dante gallops close behind, waiting for an opportunity to pass his feathered friend. Reggie is unable to change gears and make an attempt to pass them both. The road is too narrow with no extended stretches. He'll have to wait for the break in the tree line to make his move.

The ostrich quickly approaches a slight turn in the road, continuing up the gradual incline. Just as the ostrich takes the turn, Dante explodes forward and nudges the large bird.

Dante passes the ostrich and continues to pick up speed. Reggie accelerates for a few dozen yards then is forced to ease back due to another bend in the road. Yet, the ostrich is behind him now.

Just as Reggie takes the turn, the ostrich passes him. Dante thunders along a few strides ahead. The ostrich is gaining on the hoofed one.

Dante and the ostrich exchange the lead several times, playing leapfrog with one another. Trees whiz passed them as they leave clouds of dust in their wake. Reggie, still behind, knows his chance is coming.

Whiskey Ridge is pleasant this time of year. Not too hot and not too cold. Vince and Jimmy are the first to hear the dull roar of Reggie's trike from the distance.

The opening of the narrow road is seen near the center of the tree line and heads off in opposite directions along its border. There is no road across the wide opened area about the size of a professional football field.

A makeshift finish line has been constructed with a row of parked motorcycles and a few trikes facing each other. A wide opening stands between them for the arriving racers to pass through. Twenty or so yards passed them, the plateau and the abrupt edge dropping back into the canyon.

Dante is the first to appear from the road and tree line. Some of the bikers cheer and wave him onward. He runs at full speed into the opened area with the ostrich a few yards behind.

Reggie explodes from the wooded area and accelerates. He quickly changes gears and closes the gap between him and the ostrich. Dante and the ostrich are now neck and neck, each taking the lead, back and forth.

Reggie changes gears and yanks back on the throttle. The trike races forward, closer and closer to Dante and the ostrich. Then suddenly, Dante slows his stride.

His left, foreleg appears to wobble. Dante winces in pain. He has strained his old wrestling injury. He's so close to the finish line, too!

With as much grace as he is able to muster, Dante bows out of the race. His gallop turns into a trot then finally, a slow and painful walk.

Reggie and the ostrich battle for the lead. The large bird has a slight edge over the charming biker and his thundering trike. Has Reggie waited too long to make his move? There's only one way left to win.

Reggie changes gears and accelerates. The bikers waiting at the finish line jump up and down, waving their hands wildly through the air. The ostrich runs at full speed with Reggie and the trike gaining on him. Closer and closer to the plateau. And then-

Reggie crosses the finish line first with the ostrich a mere foot behind. Cheers fill the air. Reggie wins! The ostrich slows himself down, catching his breath. However, Reggie is traveling too fast toward the ridge to slow down.

Keeping his hands firmly in place along the handgrips, Reggie lifts himself upward and stands on the seat of his trike. He reaches down and releases his custom lever, similar to an emergency break.

Reggie and the trike roar to the edge of the plateau. The four pronged anchor breaks free from behind the back support of the rear seat. The chain rattles as the anchor bounces along the ground for several moments.

As Reggie and the trike continue forward, the anchor takes hold and sinks two of its prongs into the dirt. The slack in the chain tightens as Reggie and the trike approach the edge of the plateau. He releases the handle bars and stands upright with his arms spread out.

Due to his momentum, Reggie is thrust into the air and over the edge of the plateau. The anchor and chain pulls tight with the front wheel of the trike halted mere inches from the edge. The three wheeled cycle is safe.

Reggie freefalls like a skydiver, but without a chute. He is exhilarated with the wind flapping across his face. Looking downward, the canyon floor is drawing dangerously close.

Dante, Jimmy and Vince approach the plateau and look over the edge. "This is always the coolest part," Vince says with a smile. He points toward the treetops below. "Look... there!"

All that can be seen is a pair of jean shorts floating passed the tree limbs. There is no sign of Reggie. "Did he make it?" Gordon asks, as he approaches from behind.

The professor has a ragged towel wrapped around his waist as he too, looks over the edge. There is still no trace of Reggie. Oddly, they begin to look away from the canyon floor below and gaze up into the sky. "There he is!" Jimmy says as he points upward.

The condor is magnificent with a wing span of nearly ten feet. He effortlessly soars through the air in a wide half circle then banks. He flaps his wings several times as he climbs higher into the air.

The condor seems to hover a moment before abruptly diving in a weaving manner. He zigzags back and forth, flying in a manner which should be impossible for such a bird of prey. "Showoff," Dante mumbles.

"It's me!" Zoey stares blankly at her telephone and listens to the message on the machine. "Looks like the shop is three months behind in rent. I know you're getting a kick outta this gypsy-thing. But like I told you before, I'm not supporting your habit. Call me back when you get this!"

Zoey stands facing a catch-all table with the oddly painted portable telephone and message machine. She tosses her key-ring down which lands on top of a staggering pile of payment notices.

Zoey's place is very wide open, similar to a large studio apartment. The entire area is dark and dreary. If there were any windows, they have been blocked off by synthetic rocks. The walls look like the inside of a medieval dungeon.

Blue florescent lights hang from the low ceiling. There doesn't seem to be a traditional white light anywhere. Along the stone covered walls, an occasional framed picture is seen. Evil and dark looking clowns and scarecrows.

Zoey stands for a long moment along the far wall. Directly behind her, a closed door, probably leading outside. At her feet, a row of haphazardly packed cardboard boxes. All of her belongings and props from her fortune telling shop.

She forces herself away from the boxes, not ready to unpack just yet. Not ready to face another failure. Not ready to call Chloe and confront her, again.

Making her way into the spacious kitchen area, Zoey opens the fridge and takes out a wine cooler. Sipping on the bottle, she makes her way passed a closed door directly in the center of the sprawling living area.

The door itself is in the center of a small stretch of the stone covered wall. The bumpy surfaces turns the corners in opposite directions and runs along, creating a rectangular looking room of sorts. Possibly a walk-in closet or a storage area for linins or such.

Zoey turns the far corner of the self-contained rectangular room and enters her bedroom area. The centerpiece is eerie yet, somehow inviting. Her bed is a dark wooden coffin, supported off of the floor by eight inches with legs similar to the legs of a Victorian style couch, one at each of the six corners.

Both the lower and upper lids of the coffin remain opened revealing the plush royal purple interior. A full size pillow rests at the head area, wrapped in a black satin pillowcase.

Zoey faces an extended, horizontal pole attached to the wall with her wardrobe hanging from an assortment of hangers. Below the row of hanging clothes, a dark colored dresser.

Resting on the center of the dresser, a single picture is seen. Awkward looking at least. The dark colored, modern frame is a contrast to the severely burned edges of the older photo.

A fellow tourist snapped the shot. Herself, as a child, posing with her smiling, athletic mother and strikingly handsome father at an amusement park. In the photo, she looks quite normal. But now, this *living dead girl* seems quite obsessed with darkness.

Between the kitchen area and the bedroom, the living room takes up the entire corner. Zoey sits in the corner of a black leather, sectional couch. She's changed into her favorite black and white, skulls and crossbones pajamas.

A black glossed coffee table stands in front of the couch with an opened laptop computer resting on its smooth surface. Next to the laptop, an opened appointment book.

Zoey causally plays with the portable phone resting on a cushion next to her. She is reluctant to make the call. Finishing her fifth wine cooler, Zoey dials a number.

RING - RING.

RING - RING.

"Sorry I missed your call. Leave your name and number and I'll get back to you."

BEEEEP.

"Hey, it's me," Zoey timidly says into the receiver. "Sorry about the three months late." She swallows, choking on her words. "Well, I've already moved all of my stuff outta the shop. Looks like I'll be working from my truck for awhile." Zoey pauses a moment. "Just called to say sorry..."

Zoey tosses the receiver aside and looks blankly ahead. The large screen television sets directly across from her and continues to run it's late night programming. Mindless infomercials with the announcers trying to sell you something you really don't need.

Zoey leans forward and runs her finger down the page of the appointment book, finding the name of her next palm reading; Chuck McDaniels. She then focuses on her computer with her fingers quickly typing in the name with a website popping up on the screen.

The website is a public forum for friends to chat back and forth, leave messages, post photos, join various clubs, create musical playlists and countless other features. Everything you ever wanted to know about someone is available.

Zoey moves through Chuck's profile page, browsing along its content. "Alright, Chuck. Let's see what you're all about." She scrolls over to Chuck's listed friends and selects the top ten.

As she opens each of Chuck's friends profile pages, Zoey begins to take extensive, handwritten notes; favorite music, favorite food and drink, information about their lives and family.

Everything Zoey needs to know about Chuck and the most likely friends he'll be bringing along to his palm reading. Everything she needs to know about them even before they walk through her door.

"So, this is what you want to do on your last day?"

"Yeah," Jay replies with a smile as he unwraps his colorful towel from around his neck. Larry tosses him a wink then glances over to Sonja. Larry and Jay wear knee length shorts with Sonja in a pink bikini with a matching sarong around her waist.

"You two go and have some fun. I'm going to try and get some sun." Sonja playfully snaps her towel at Larry and shoos him away. With her filled beach bag in hand, Sonja turns and makes her way through the mob of sunbathers.

The replicated beach surrounds the activity pool with countless bodies splashing and bobbing through the rolling waves. Laughter fills the pool and beach area with joyous screams escaping from the nearby activities.

The waterpark sprawls across ten acres with a wide variety of aquatic attractions; five towering water slides, a steep speed slide, a casual river ride, three kiddy areas, concessions and lockers.

Sonja finds her spot along the beach area and activity pool. She tosses her towel onto a lounge chair and slightly looks up into the sky. It's a nice day with no clouds for miles.

Larry and Jay climb higher and higher along the steps of the tower. They reach the near top of the structure and fall in line along the platform. Other parents and children come up behind, extending the line of waiting thrill seekers.

The ride itself is a quick one. No inner-tube is needed, just a straight shot down an extremely steep water slope nearly one hundred feet. "Alright, guys. One at a time." The cute waterpark employee motions her hand toward the opening of the slide. "Feet first, cross your ankles and your arms."

Jay sits on the edge of the slide just inside of a short tunnel. He crosses his ankles, lays back then crosses his arms.

"Head back and hang on!" She says with a smile. Jay slightly pushes himself forward and disappears over the edge.

Jay explodes from the short tunnel's opening and races down the steep water slide. He appears to freefall for several moments with water splashing all around him. Traveling at an accelerated speed, the walls of the slide whiz passed him.

"Alright, you're up!" the attendant says, motioning Larry toward the edge of the slide. Larry plops down, crosses his ankles and arms then pushes himself into the short tunnel.

Jay approaches the bottom of the steep water slide and splashes into the pool below. He swims along the surface until reaching a depth he can touch the bottom. As Jay wades toward the far side of the pool, Larry approaches the bottom of the slide and splashes into view.

Jay lifts himself up onto the adjoining walkway, turns and sees Larry wading toward him. Jay realizes that he has a lot of water in his ears. As Larry approaches the side of the pool, he looks up toward Jay.

Jay vigorously shakes his head as a dog would just getting out of the bathtub. "*That's funny*," Larry thinks. "*Like son, like mother*." He is reminded of the moment he first laid eyes on Sonja so many years ago, descending down a rickety set of wooden stairs.

"That was great!" Jay reaches down and takes Larry's hand, pulling him up and out of the pool. "Now what?"

"This is *your* day. Lead on!" Larry looks Jay up and down. Ten years have gone by. He wishes he had known sooner. There has been so much time that has been lost.

"Are you sure about this one?" Larry and Jay stand at the lower entrance to a colossal water ride; The Abyss. The steps leading upward inside of the tower stands nearly one hundred and fifty feet.

The water slide itself is entirely enclosed with a dark tunnel from top to bottom. The slide winds downward from the top of the tower in a snake-like manner with several extreme banks.

"Sir, how old's your boy?" The waterpark attendant moves forward, blocking Jay from the ride's entrance.

"Why does it matter how old he is? He's clearly *tall* enough for this ride." Larry steps forward and stands face to face with the younger man. From deep within, Larry lets out a low growl.

"Here you go, sir." The attendant quickly hands Larry a two-man, bright yellow inner-tube. "Have fun," he nervously says to Jay.

Larry mocking smiles at the attendant as he takes the inner-tube and follows Jay inside of the tower's entrance. "You'll have to teach me that," Jay says.

"Love to," Larry replies. Jay and Larry begin climbing up the steps, higher and higher into the tower. They ascend along each level's platform until reaching the enclosed summit.

Jay looks through the cage-like observation deck. He's never realized that he's afraid of heights. Jay becomes visibly nervous. Although it's a nice day with mild temperatures, Jay begins to sweat. "You don't have to do this, Jay."

"Yeah... yeah I do," Jay says in a determined voice. He takes the two-man inner-tube from Larry and sets it down along the edge of the slide and entrance of the dark tunnel. The attendant takes hold of one of the many handles and braces the inner-tube in place.

Jay sits on the inner-tube and clutches onto his set of handles. Larry climbs aboard, sits next to Jay and takes hold of his pair of handles. "You guys ready?" the attendant asks.

Larry looks over to Jay. It looks like his head is going to explode. Jay's eyes are wide open and terrified. He takes deep breaths, psyching himself up for the inevitable. The attendant comes up from behind and slightly pushes the inner-tube over the edge.

Larry and Jay are plunged into darkness. The splashing water sprays against their faces and chests. Faster and faster they race along the winding curves of the steep water ride. Jay lets out a terrifying scream. This is too much for him to take!

Jay's ears begin to quickly mutate with golden fur sprouting up from his flesh. His jaw widens and reveals sharp feline teeth as whiskers emerge from just above his upper lip. "Jay! Jay, stop!" Larry shouts. It's too late!

Jay clutches onto his set of handles with his fingers transforming into claws covered with golden striped fur. With his legs bent at the knees, Jay's feet brace himself against the inner-tube.

The bottoms of his feet mutates into dark colored feline pads. His toes dissipate as sharp claws emerge. Jay attempts to yell out. But instead, the dark tunnel is filled with a deep and ominous feline roar.

Jay's hind legs have completely transformed into is alter. The tigon extends out his claws and sinks them into the inner-tube. The bright yellow fabric is shredded and quickly releases all of the air.

Larry and what's left of Jay's human features, slides down and along the end of the dark tunnel. The flattened inner-tube is useless. Larry and the large half-feline explodes from the lower opening of the tunnel.

They skim along the watery surface for several yards before coming to an abrupt halt near the center of the pool. "Look, mommy!" A child cries out, pointing to the large, waterlogged cat.

Larry quickly takes Jay by his human shoulders and dunks him into the pool. He takes a hold of the flattened inner-tube and covers Jay, attempting to conceal the half-boy half-feline from onlookers. From the appearance around the pool, a father is drowning his son. Screams for help fill the air.

Several attendants leap into the pool and frantically swim toward Larry and the flattened inner-tube. As they approach, Larry dives under the surface and takes Jay under his arms.

Larry and Jay resurface, gasping for air. All of Jay's human extremities and facial features have quickly returned. "Whatta ya' doin', buddy?" an attendant barks at Larry. The attendants aggressively rush Larry and shove him away from Jay. "You okay, kid?"

"Yeah, back off!" Jays says in a sharp tone, as he pushes the attendants away from himself.

"Jay, are you alright?" Sonja asks, as she stands at the edge of the pool. Jay wipes the water from his face then turns to see his mother hovering over them.

"Yeah, we're fine," he says with a smile. Jay and Larry begin wading toward the side of the pool as the attendants head off in another direction. One drags the flattened inner-tube along. "Hey, Larry..."

"Yeah, Jay?"

"Let's go again!" Jay says, with an eager tone. Larry smiles. He's proud of Jay. He's even more proud of his son.

Larry and Jay stand facing each other. The cage door has been secured with the floor all around them covered with hay and straw. Keiko circles Larry and Jay several times. She pauses a moment then nudges Larry's hand.

The lioness sniffs then licks Larry's hand, turns and lopes out through the simulated cave opening. Larry backs away as Jay slides his jeans through the cage bars and tosses them on top of the foot locker.

Jay squats down, leans to the side and supports himself with an elbow and his other hand. He lays sideways on the floor. "See you next month..." he says in a near whisper. He takes a deep breath and closes his eyes for a moment. Jay can feel the transformation approaching. The three day cycle of the full moon is nearly complete.

His shoulders begin to expand with his upper extremities lengthening. Jay's torso mutates with his ribcage nearly doubling in size. His thighs become more broad, covered with striped, golden fur.

Jay stretches out his mouth with strands of whiskers sprouting from above his upper lip. A thick tail emerges just above his tailbone with a black tuft at the end.

The tigon stands on all fours, wags his tail then circles Larry several times. The hybrid feline faces the human then stands up on his hind legs. The large cat tenderly places his forepaws on Larry's shoulders then licks his face. "Yeah, I'll see you next month..."

The pyrotechnic and firework show is phenomenal. Flames, smoke and sparks fill the air along the flashing orange and green footlights of the stage. The capacity crowd is an endless wave of bodies, rolling and moving throughout the sports arena. Everyone is on their feet! Every seat is empty!

The costumed concertgoers dance along the foot of the stage, waving their hands high in the air. The camels, zebras, lions, dairy cows, bunnies, giraffes, cheetahs, bulls, leopards and other wildly represented creatures reach up toward the stage.

Rafe hammers his chewed-up looking wooden drumsticks along the worn heads of his floor tom-toms. His feet furiously stomp on his foot pedals of his double-bass creating a low and constant thundering sound.

Rafe's only costume, as usual when their concerts sell-out, is a pair of mock cheetah ears upon his head. His basketball style shorts flutter as his legs continue to powerfully stomp on the foot pedals. His black tattooed spots covers his knees, shins, shoulders, torso, upper back, chest and arms.

T-Bone, dressed in his Texas longhorn attire, stands at the right side of the stage, banging his fist against the four strings of his giraffe printed bass guitar. He wildly moves his head up and down, thrashing it to the final chord of The Zøø Crüe's second encore.

Mark, at left stage, kicks his thick black boot into the air toward the screaming crowd. His zebra-type mohawk and mane dangles long his head and down his back. Behind him and slightly off to the side of Rafe's towering drum set, the glossy black and white striped grand piano.

Mark's left hand is but a mere blur as his fingers blaze across the strings of his single neck, zebra patterned guitar. Then... there's Jon Von Dutch.

He stands at center stage with his legs slightly spread apart and his arms extended out from himself as if her were expecting a massive bear hug.

Slung over his shoulders and head, his wolf's fur hide, head and skull. Dangling along his back from the thick guitar strap, the peacock looking guitar. Jon looks up toward the rafters and exploding lights above. "*Alright then,*" he thinks to himself. "*They came for a show... I'll give'em a show!*"

In unison, Jon, Mark and T-Bone charge forward, clutching onto their guitars. They slightly leap up into the air, glide for a moment then each land in the center of a strategically placed yellow trampoline along the stage.

The three costumed musicians bounce upward as they continue to play their instruments. Each of them complete an aerial summersault then land with a thud at center stage; the crowd goes wild!

One last series of explosions blankets the stage. The music stops and is overrun with boisterous rhythmic applauds and stomping feet of the raging crowds; *We Will Rock You!*

Mark and T-Bone are the first to exit the stage, greeted by Rick, in his top hat and ring master attire and a small army of roadies. Several stagehands appear from the shadows and begin removing T-Bone's horns and Mark's zebra-like mane.

Rafe manages his way from behind his gigantic, neon green drum set and disappears behind the drawn back curtains. He turns to see Jon remaining at center stage as the footlights go dark. The crowds continue their repetitive chant, wanting one more encore, one more song.

Jon slips behind the curtains of right stage and quickly removes his wolf's head and cape. He reaches for his custom, chrome stand and takes his double-neck guitar in hand. He swings the handmade strap over his shoulders and rests the top of the "X" shaped guitars in front of himself.

With the stage lights still dimmed and the raging crowd continuing to clap and stomp, Jon saunters his way back to the center of the stage. *"No, Jon!"* He hears his ex-wife Leslie pleading with him in his head. "*Not that song!*"

"Yeah, *that* song," Jon mumbles with a mischievous grin. Jon reaches up his left hand and tenderly clutches onto the neck of six strings of the guitar. He places his right hand around the four strings of bass guitar and pauses a moment. The orange spotlight slowly floods across his body.

"DE-DE-DE... DE-DING," says his left hand.

"DE-DE-DE... DE-DING," his right hand answers.

"DE-DE-DE... DE-DING..."

"DE-DE-DE... DE-DING..."

Jon's left hand rolls along the strings of his guitar as his right hand, along his bass, answers every note. Back and forth he continues his self-serving, solo encore. Jon continues the *Dueling Banjos* intro. At first, the pulsing crowd is unsure where he is going with this. Then, his fingers rip across the strings; he's been practicing!

Jon's fingers of his left hand lead-in and direct how his right, bass hand will answer. The screaming guitar solo fills the sports area. The costumed fans in the festival seating begin to get into the groove, dancing about in a hillbilly manner.

The right bass answers every note of the solo guitar. Back and forth. Jon begins to pick up momentum, dueling himself. Faster and faster. He closes his eyes for the briefest of moments, preparing himself for his transformation. The crowd is at a near frenzy until-

The deep floor tom-toms behind Jon begin to thunder, accompanying the dueling guitar and bass. Green spotlights burst to life, blanketing Rafe seated on his padded stool behind his massive double-bass drum set.

Rafe's foot pedals slam against the double-bass creating a low and constant roar. His hands move away from the floor tom-toms and begin racing against the mounted tom-toms and cymbals. Rafe is overtaking Jon's limelight.

Jon steps out of his orange spotlight as the brightness fades away. The center of attention is Rafe's colossal drum solo. The walls vibrate. The rafters shake. The countless rows of empty seating appear to be loosening from the bolted concrete as if the entire building was about to crumble. "*So, he wants to play?*" Jon mumbles in his head.

Along side stage, Jon quickly rests his double-neck "X" guitar onto its chrome stand and retrieves his single neck, oddly designed black and white guitar. Mark, T-Bone and Rick don't know what to do. "Hey!" Jon shouts at a sound and lighting technician. "Try to keep up, eh!"

Jon swings the guitar strap over his head and rests the guitar in front of himself. As he turns and walks back on stage, his fingers begin to squeal across the strings. Now, *he's* interrupting Rafe's solo.

Jon lets out a series of guitar riffs quickly answered, almost identically, by Rafe who then adds a drum pattern which is quickly answered, almost identically, by Jon.

The shadowed screen filling the entire wall of the back of the stage explodes with images. A raging storm with thunderous clouds and lightning bolts. The full moon hangs in the distance and slowly begins to grow larger.

Almost angrily, Jon screams his guitar at Rafe. The frustrated drummer answers right back with pounding drums and crashing cymbals. Back and forth, musician versus musician. Brother against brother.

Jon makes his way toward the footlights of the stage with the screaming costumed fans reaching out for him. He steps slightly off to the left with the orange spotlight following his every move.

A sudden surge of adrenaline rips through Jon's body. He breaks away from his duel with Rafe and begins a ferocious guitar solo. Rafe is no match for his older brother.

Jon's fingers race across the strings as the tops of his hands begin to sprout dark colored fur. His fingertips mutate into claw-like phalanges. The dark fur spreads up his forearms, biceps then out and over his shoulders.

His chest expands with his waist slightly tapering. The dark colored fur quickly covers his back and torso. Beneath his black spandex, Jon's thighs expand with his exposed shins and calves sprouting dark fur. Jon's bare feet quickly transform into large claws, scraping across the wooden stage floor.

As the beast continues his raging guitar solo, he arches his head back and stretches his neck. Jon's lower jaw, cheek bones and nose expands outward, transforming into a large muzzle. His flowing locks of hair seem to be vacuumed into his skull revealing dark colored fur.

His lobs and cartilage mutates upward, forming into large canine ears. His claws tear across the strings as the transformation is completed.

Mark and T-Bone are astonished as they look upon the legendary creature from the side of the back stage area. They thought that such mythological figures only belonged to books or in the movies.

Rick steps forward and moves aside the curtains to get a better look at Jon, or least the beast that was once the lead man of the band. Rick can't believe what he is seeing; a guitar playing werewolf!

The crowd pushes toward the stage, waving their hands in the air. Several costumed fans even begin to howl. Totally disgusted, Rafe tosses his worn drumsticks aside and storms off stage.

The large, upright wolf concludes his unbelievable guitar solo, silhouetted by the full moon and lightning behind him.

He slams the last, thundering chord with his right claw with his left claw moving across the upper strings. The wolf howls as he waves his right paw to the raging crowd, running back and forth across the front of the stage, soaking in all his glory.

"You were great!" T-Bone eagerly says.

"You're the coolest thing I've ever seen!" Mark blurts out.

"You're a sonuva-bitch!" Rafe declares as he slams the upright wolf against the large dressing room wall. Rafe and the wolf glare at each other. The wolf quickly shoves back at Rafe, causing him to nearly topple over.

Rafe regains his footing and charges toward the wolf. They slam into each other, powerfully clutching onto each other's shoulders. Rick, T-Bone and Mark back away, unsure what's about to happen.

"You should've told me, Jon!" Rafe says with a disappointed tone. "We're brothers!" Rafe hisses at the wolf. The deep hiss of a wild, jungle cat. Rafe powerfully releases the wolf. "You should've told me. I can change, too." Rafe turns and storms out of the dressing room. Rick is dumbfounded as he slowly approaches the wolf. Jon's reverse transformation has already begun.

T-Bone and Mark stand in awe with their eyes as wide a saucers. T-Bone takes a swig from a whiskey bottle as Mark pounds a beer. Rick steps closer to the odd looking, upright wolf, now almost completely human again. "Jon?" Rick timidly asks.

"Where's Rafe?"

"He split." Rick reaches up as if to touch Jon's shoulder, to assure himself of reality. "Man, I have so many questions." Jon turns and bolts out the dressing room door.

The small army of roadies scurry across the brightly lit stage. A pair of crewmen have already begun to disassemble Rafe's massive drum set along the back area as other crewmen carefully roll up the large screen.

The wide assortment of lead, rhythm and bass guitars have been packed up and stored. The roadies continue to roll up the cable cords and remove the massive speakers.

Patrols of facility workers make their way in and out of the vast rows of the upper seating areas. Another group of facility workers sweep their wide brooms across the vacant festival seating area, collecting empty cups, beer cans and empty booze bottles. "Hey, anyone seen Rafe!" Jon asks as he appears from the side of the stage.

Collectively, the roadies shake their heads *no*. Jon rushes to the edge of the center of the stage, looking out across the vast, empty rows of seats. The ringing in his ears continues. The blank expressions of the facility workers looks back at him. They know who he is but they just don't care. They're cleaning up after *him!*

Jon lowers himself over the edge of the stage and flings his bare feet over the side. Sitting there, he watches the facility workers continue their cleaning efforts. Behind him, he feels the movements of the roadies. Jon looks forward into the empty sports arena where less than an hour ago, was filled with screaming, costumed fans. "Great..."

"Can I buy you a drink?" Gio asks as he approaches a dimly lit booth toward the back of the diner. His professional appearance seems drastically out of place with his business suit contrasting with The Bay Front locals.

The scattered tables and chairs are sparsely filled with patrons wearing casual jeans, ethnically influenced shirts and shawls with most either barefoot or wearing handmade sandals.

The inner walls and wooden beam supporting posts are decorated in a Cajun style with fishing nets, Old World buoys and historical looking fishing rods.

Off to the far side of the room, Zydeco music filters into the diner. A trio of musicians continues to play their acoustic instruments; a fiddle, an accordion and a washboard.

Gio steps between two adjacent tables from the booth in the back. Sitting at each of the tables, two pairs of very large fellows dressed in outdated suits. Yet, with their dark complexion and obvious heritage, they pull it off.

Cyrus takes a sip of his Creole then slightly looks up and across the booth. The mysterious Voodoo Man is intimidating to most. His light and dark maroon, tailored made suit appears to be an exact representation of a plantation owner of the mid 1700's.

The lime green, nine foot boa constrictor lays peacefully along the back of Cyrus' neck and shoulders. The thick reptile slightly moves across the upper padded backrest of the booth, quite comfortable with its human companion. "Cyrus?" Gio inquires as he approaches the edge of the booth. "I'm Giovanni Mancini. I would like to have a word with you."

Cyrus looks passed Gio, giving his four associates a commanding look. They remain seated more than an arm's length away from their employer. Glancing over his shoulder, Gio realizes that he may have to do this the hard way.

Without an invitation, Gio slides into the booth next to Cyrus. The four bodyguards abruptly stand and moves in closer. Gio is uninhibited by their threat.

He looks directly at them and lets out a low, animalistic growl. Gio glares at them a moment then focuses his attention to Cyrus. "You're a businessman. I have a proposition for you. Tell me what I need to know and I'll let you live."

Cyrus calmly waves his hand to the side. The four bodyguards seem to be humbled as they turn and disperse into the diner. "Mr. Mancini, you have my full attention."

"I am searching for the secret of therianthropy."

"Shapeshifting?" Cyrus asks in a curious tone. "I sense you already have that ability."

"Yes, but not completely. I am limited to one being."

"And you think *I* have the knowledge to increase your powers? Why would you think that?"

"The history of your magic indicates that you would have this knowledge."

"Young man," Cyrus nearly laughs. "I don't know what you've been reading but it is not accurate. You see, our religion is passed down from word of mouth. There is no sacred book or written spells. You will have to search elsewhere for your answers."

A waitress approaches the booth and slides in two plates filled with lavish food in front of Cyrus. Gio stares long and hard at the Voodoo Man, waiting for the secret that never comes. "Do you mind? My meal is getting cold."

Gio maneuvers his way from the booth and stands facing Cyrus. With a polite nod, Gio turns, "Have a good-evening."

"You as well, Mr. Mancini..."

Gio closes and locks the rear door of his mobile medical center. The work stations, metallic countertops and examining area is dark and lifeless. He approaches the bottom of the narrow spiral staircase and begins his ascent.

The luxury apartment consumes the entire second level of the customized bus. Gio steps away from the top of the spiral staircase and enters the entertaining area. He walks along the central walkway passing a full living room set, complete with a large screen television set and an electrical fireplace.

The adjoining kitchen area is accented with hardwood cabinets, a four person dining table, stove, microwave and a double sink.

A two person hot tub fills the next area directly across from a shower stall and bathroom. Gio flicks on the wall light switch before slipping out of his suit jacket. He tosses it onto the foot of a king sized bed as he makes his way to his computer.

Gio sits at his desk and faces the screen. With several keystrokes, a United States map appears. Across the digital image, a defined route is seen. It begins in his home town and laboratory in Savannah, moves west to Alabama and then through Mississippi. From there, the route continues to head west to his current location in The Big Easy.

He studies the map, seeing that there are no stops along the way through Texas or New Mexico. Using the computer's mouse, Gio clicks on the next location along his route. "Looks like I'm off to Arizona," Gio mumbles to himself.

Kaleen lays fast asleep under the blankets of Tez's bed. The room is quiet and still with more and more sunlight peaking through the drawn curtains. She stirs and moves her head along his pillow, falling deeper into her aquatic dreams.

Tez stands in the bedroom doorway, leaning against the frame with his arms crossed wearing his ever present faded, leather bomber jacket and dark sunglasses. He quietly enters the room and approaches the side of his bed.

He stands over Kaleen, just hovering, listening to the shallow breathing of her slumber. Tez wonders, what would have happened if they would have stayed married? What would have happened if she didn't move away? He wonders if she's really happy with her life now, content with her career and where she lives.

Tez slightly leans over her and quietly inhales her scent. He's always loved the way her hair smells in the morning. Tez carefully extends out his hand, as if to tenderly take hold of her fiery locks of hair spread out across his pillow.

Kaleen's eyes flutter as she feels the presence of her ex-husband standing behind her. She wonders, what would have happened if they would have stayed together? What would have happened if he would have moved away with her? Kaleen wonders if he's still content with his life at the radio station.

Tez's opened palm is mere inches from the back of her head. Kaleen continues her shallow breathing, not wanting Tez to know she is awake. Again, her eyes flutter.

Kaleen quickly rolls over, tosses off the blankets and sits up, smiling at Tez. However, he is nowhere to be seen. She hears his quiet movements from the living room. The sounds of a spare blanket and pillow being tossed onto the couch. Then, the sounds of Tez plopping down and nestling in for a morning nap. Finally, the rattling sound of him placing his dark sunglasses onto the coffee table.

"That smells terrific!" Tez says, as he slides his shades onto the bridge of his nose. The early afternoon sun shines brightly into the kitchen with Kaleen standing over the four burners of the stove. The skillets are filled with simmering eggs, bacon and hash browns.

"Good-morning, sleepyhead," she says, in a cheerful tone. "Did I wake you?"

"Not at all. Six hours is more than enough."

"I hope you don't mind. I ran to the store and picked up a few things."

"...and you paid for them how?"

"I used your credit card."

"Didn't they ask you for ID?"

"...yeah."

"...and?"

"I told them I was your wife."

"How'd that work out? They all know me around here. They *know* I'm not married... anymore."

"Yeah, well. Ya' know."

"No, I don't know!" Tez sharply replies. "Why don't you explain it to me." Kaleen abruptly turns away from the stove and tosses the spatula into the sink.

"I *knew* I was right. I should've stayed with *Melissa* instead of coming here."

"What's wrong with my place? Oh, that's right! It's all about *you!*"

"I don't wanna to go over this again, Tez."

"*Again*? We never went over it the first time. One day I woke up and you were gone."

"I'm not the one who wanted the divorce. *You* wanted the divorce."

"No, I didn't. I *had* to stay here."

"No, you didn't! You could've gone nationwide by now. You could've had your own show, coast to coast."

"Right! Like program directors and general managers were knocking down my door, just waiting to hire the blind deejay!"

"Oh, this has nothing to do with you being blind! You got comfortable here in your little *safe zone* where no one could touch you. Not even me!"

"You could've stayed!"

"...and done what? Work at the local grocery store? Drive a school bus? Give up *my* dreams? No, Tez. It was all about *you*! Your *little area* where you felt safe was more important than me."

"That's not true!"

"Sure it is."

"There was *nothing* more important than you." Tez pauses a moment as he steps toward her, reaching for her hands. "...nothing more important than you."

"...sure got a funny way of showing it." Kaleen turns and heads for the backdoor. Tez reaches for her hands. She's not there. "Kay?" Tez calls out.

SLAM!
Kaleen is out the door...

"I'm sorry, Kay." Tez makes his way to the shoreline of The Sound, along the near end of the park. He squats down then sits next to her. Kaleen dips her toes into the water, slightly splashing. "How do we fix this?" Tez softly asks. "How do we fix *us?*"

Kaleen reaches over and takes his palm. She tenderly raises the back of his hand to her lips and kisses him. "We don't, Tez," she sadly replies. "We don't..."

~ VIII ~

"Hey, boys. It's good to see you again." The bubbly waitress, Anita, smiles as she makes her way through the roadside diner. "How do you want your eggs?" Reggie and Dante sit on opposite sides of the booth along the window with their cycles parked along the sidewalk just outside.

Anita stands over them and off to the side with her order pad and pen ready, waiting for Reggie to make up his mind as he scans over the menu. Dante gives Anita a polite smile then flips through the assortment of songs of their booth's *Select-O-Matic* style jukebox.

The quaint restaurant is a throwback from the mid 1950's. A black and white checkered tile floor and a matching counter along the far wall with round, leather padded stools complements the brightly lit diner.

The surrounding booths, tables and chairs as well as the dining counter is sparsely filled with fellow travelers, taking in a bite to eat before continuing their journeys. "I'll take the number three, over-easy," Reggie finally says to Anita as he hands her his menu.

"...and for you, hon?"

"Two number fives, runny."

"Hungry this morning aren't you?"

"Haven't had a home cooked meal in awhile."

"I'll have your coffee in just a minute." Anita jots down their order, turns and heads back behind the checker tiled counter. She slips their order slip onto the circular chrome rack then spins it toward the burly cook in the back kitchen.

"Today's Sunday isn't it?" Reggie asks.

"You *know* it is," Dante says, as he continues to flip through the song selection of the small jukebox. Reggie seems anxious. He keeps looking over Dante's shoulder, back to the pair of restroom entrances. Between the closed swinging doors, a payphone hangs from the wall.

Reggie focuses his attention to a wall clock hanging above the window area of the kitchen. It's almost twelve o'clock.

He glances away from the clock to see the cook, vaguely seen from the kitchen, continuing to prepare meals for his patrons.

RING - RING.

RING - RING.

Reggie nearly falls over himself as he springs from the booth and darts toward the payphone. He fumbles for the receiver as it rings one last time. "Hello?"

"Reggie, is that you?"

"Yeah, it's me, Blake. Whatta ya' have for us?"

"Is Dante around?"

"Yeah, why?" Reggie is caught off guard, *he's* the one who handles all of Dante's bouts and wagering. But now, Blake wants to talk to Dante. Something's not right. "Hey, Dante! Blake wants to talk to you," Reggie says, covering the receiver of the phone with his palm.

Dante takes a sip of his coffee before rising up from the booth and approaches Reggie. "He wants to talk to me?"

"That's what he said."

"That's weird."

"Yeah, that's what I thought." Reggie reluctantly hands Dante the phone. He raises it to his ear and pauses a moment.

"Blake? It's Dante."

"Is Reggie still there?"

"Ah, yeah."

"Let me know when you can talk." What Blake has to say is for Dante's ears only. Dante gives Reggie the *you're dismissed* nod and waits. Quite puzzled, Reggie looks over his shoulder as he slides back into their booth. Dante slightly turns his back toward Reggie and the rest of the diner.

"Alright, Blake. What's goin' on?"

"There's a *new guy* on the circuit, not one of mine. They say he's unbeatable." Blake stands at the wall of picture windows of his sky rise office. It's a traditional looking work area, similar to a vise president of a corporation or an elite stockbroker.

"Why are you telling *me* this?"

"Adolpho is managing him. I want *you* to fight for *me*."

"Now, *that's* a switch. What are the odds?"

"Let's just say I'll pay you one million, win or lose, to fight this guy."

"That's a lot of money."

"Yeah..." Blake turns away from the picture windows and approaches his desk. Cluttered along the oak finish desktop, there is a series of color photos. "Look, Dante. You can spread out the money to your family, you and Reggie can split it or..."

"...or?"

"...or you can keep all of it and start over somewhere. You can have your life back."

"Who *is* this guy?" Dante curiously asks. As Blake answers, Dante slightly turns and sees Anita bringing their plates of breakfast over to their booth. "Oh... *him!*"

"Yeah, Dante... *him*."

"Look, I *won* last time, but I didn't *beat* 'im."

"You can win. I *know* you can." Blake looks down at the colored photo on top of the stack. "Think about it, Dante. One million bucks, win or lose. Call me in a few days. If you agree, I'll set it up in Reno."

"I'll talk to you in a few days." Dante slowly hangs up the phone. As he makes his way back to their booth, he ponders what to say to Reggie. Does he tell him the truth? How much of the truth does he tell his best friend? Man, a million dollars... that's a lot of money!

"So, what's up?" Reggie asks, as Dante slides in across from him. Dante looks down at the two plates of food in front of himself. He's suddenly lost his appetite.

"Blake's setting up a fight. He's gonna back *me* for a change."

"That *is* weird." Reggie pops in a mouth full of hash browns. Dante takes a sip of his coffee then looks out the window. The highway traffic rolls along with the midday sun climbing higher into the sky. "Dante! What's goin' on!" Dante reluctantly turns away from the window.

"I *know* this guy," Dante says in a low and disconcerting tone. "He was my last professional bout. *He's* the reason I was forced into retirement."

"Your knee?"

"Yeah, my knee. It was a cage match in Philly with no time limit. We were about fifteen minutes into it when he picked me up and body slammed me. My leg was bent under when we landed and..."

"Yeah... I heard it was a great fight. Sorry I missed it. My tent didn't have cable."

"That's alright. That was about the same time Ma and Pa..." Dante pauses a moment. "I'm sorry I missed their funeral." Reggie slightly raises up, reaches over the tabletop of the booth and brotherly squeezes Dante's shoulder.

"It's better to burn out, than to fade away..."

The tropical jungle is darker than usual for this time of year. The three quarter moon struggles to break through the upper canopy of trees. Thick foliage covers the ground, making it difficult to see even ten feet ahead.

Oddly, there are no sounds. No chirping birds. Not even a growl of wild jungle cat. The gentle rolling sound of the wide river isn't even present, as if the water has simply stopped. Along the near shoreline, a clearing appears. Several pole-like torches flicker, providing the only light.

A grotesque creature explodes from the thick tree line and charges into the clearing. The beast roars as it drops down on all fours. What *is* this thing?

The beast's arms are covered with tan and white fur. It's claws are that of a three-toed sloth, almost useless on the ground. The creature's hind legs are that of a kangaroo. Thick and powerful.

A long, male lion's tail whips around from behind, swishing the dark colored tuft at the end. Orange, black and white strips cover the waist, torso and chest area of the beast, that of a tiger.

The head of the creature is an Old World monkey with a bright red and blue nose and face. The baboon's whiskers flex as the animal opens its mouth, revealing its sharp and pointy set of teeth. Along the baboon's head, a pair of canine ears are seen.

The hideous beast rears up and roars. It scans in all directions, sniffing the air for any predators. The mutation continues, shifting and altering the creature again.

The muzzle of the baboon molds and extends outward forming to the features of a massive wolf, completely overtaking the primate's characteristics. The canine's ears have been replaced by ears of an orange, white and black leopard.

The tiger stripes mutates and is replaced by dark hair along its waist, torso and chest. Silver hair of an aged gorilla covers the back of the creature. The three-toed claws of the sloth transform into smooth and flat flippers, that of an orca.

The thick and powerful hind legs of the kangaroo begin to expand upward and stretch. The tan fur dissipates and gives way to the dark colored, sprouting hair. Thick and coarse.

The kangaroo's tendons mutate into the hind legs of a majestic stallion. The beast stomps its pair of hoofs several time creating small clouds of dust.

A large, reptilian tail sways back and forth behind the creature, the appendage of a Komodo dragon. Crunching and crackling noises escapes from the canine skull with a full rack of mule deer antlers expanding upward. The wolfish head turns, hearing something approach from the tree line.

The black colored, orca flippers mutates and shifts, transforming into almost human looking limbs. The beast claws its hands through the air, awaiting for its prey to come to it. "Gordon, can you hear me?" Elez softly asks.

Gordon can hear her. Deep within his human consciousness, he knows he will not harm her. Yet, he is overcome with animal instincts. All of them. Every creature and beast he is able to transform into, runs through his veins. He still has not harnessed the ability to control his alters. "Gordon..." Elez timidly creeps her way forward.

The creature sniffs in her direction. He reaches out to her, baring his razor sharp claws just inches from her face. She takes the remnants of his human hand in into her palm and tenderly squeezes. The odd looking being growls at her.

Elez is unafraid as she steps closer. The beast appears to be soothed by her presence. He towers over the Native Pigmy. Then, he is overpowered by a carnivoristic urge. He viciously grabs her by the shoulders and buries his canine teeth deep into the side of her neck.

She screams out in sheer terror as intense pain shoots through her body. The beast continues to ruthlessly feed upon her flesh and tissue. Elez struggles to free herself, pounding her fists against the silverback's chest. She wildly kicks her legs as the creature lifts her off of the ground as blood begins to flow from her gaping wounds.

The beast gnaws at her collar bones and are crushed between his powerful razor sharp teeth. Elez screams as the creature continues to feed upon her. Raising his blood filled jowls, he slams his sharp teeth into her neck, preparing to sever it from her body-

"Holy crap!" Gordon exclaims, abruptly waking up from his nightmare. He is covered with sweat, gasping to catch his breath. Gordon sits up, sideways on his couch.

Gordon scans his back living room. The picture window and sliding glass door overlooks his deck and The Sound. The mounted, stuffed moose head over the smoldering fireplace and hearth. Dante's framed picture hangs on the wall. The Zøø Crüe's autographed guitars appear along the opposite side of the fireplace.

He extends out his hands to examine them. First, the tops of his human flesh. Gordon rolls over his hands, holding his palms close to his face. The lines and creases of his skin appear unaltered. He makes several fists, assuring himself of his human state of being.

Gordon takes a sigh of relief as he pushes himself up and off of the worn couch. He walks with stiff legs and a sore back, as if he were a laborer just finishing a sixteen hour work day.

He enters the kitchen area and flicks on the light switch on the wall. Again, Gordon scans the room, assuring himself that it was just a bad dream. He has returned to reality, unscathed by ferocious creatures and hideous beasts.

Gordon reaches for the refrigerator handle and opens the door. "Gordon, can you hear me?" Elez softly asks. Her severed head rests on the top shelf inside of the fridge.

Elez's tissue, neck muscles and chewed through bones slightly poke through the bloody grates of the shelf below. A large pool of blood has formed along the top of the lower crisper. He takes a deep breath, preparing to scream for help. Elez moves her lips. "Gordon..."

Gordon erupts from his nightmare within a nightmare from the couch! He's covered with sweat and struggles to catch his breath. He frantically looks around his back living room. The sliding glass door, the fireplace, the framed picture of Dante hanging on the wall and the autographed guitars resting in their chrome stands. "Holy crap!"

"Mommy, what's goin' on?" Dexter asks. The charming, eight year old boy sits in the rear seat along the passenger's side of the minivan. As he continues to look out the window into the afternoon sky, his mother, directly in front of him and his father, steering the family vehicle, curiously glance at each other.

"I'm not sure, honey," his mother replies. She turns away from father and looks out her passenger's side window. Father slows the minivan to a near crawl. The traffic is nearly at a standstill.

Up ahead along the side of the Wyoming highway, a parked convoy of State Trooper patrol cars are seen. Among the official looking vehicles, a handful of older style pickup trucks.

On the opposite side of the highway, numerous other parked vehicles are seen; Wyoming Game and Fish Department. A few families and travelers heading in the opposite direction has pulled off the side of the road to catch a better look at the ongoing events.

A uniformed Trooper stands in the middle of the highway, waving his hands as he directs the slow moving traffic in both directions. Dexter seems anxious as he peers out through his window. Along his side of the minivan, beyond the edge of the highway and passed the endless barbwire fence, a noticeable gathering appears, then another, then another. Five groups in all.

About fifty yards out along the flat grassy plains, several Troopers stand in awe. They are joined by members of the Game and Fish Department as they gaze down at the horrific sight.

The rancher, who owns the land and a massive herd of beef cattle, removes his sweat stained cowboy hat and slaps it against his thigh. This is just one of many that he's lost in the last few days.

The bull lays on its side, as if it were bound by the front and hind legs then violently stretched in opposite directions. Its throat has been powerfully severed from the attack, the fatal blow. The bull's stomach and internal organs lays about the blood soaked prairie grass. Who or whatever did this had no remorse for the slaughter.

A Trooper motions toward the remains of the slain animal. The attacker must have gutted the bull, went up through the ribcage and pulled out the liver and beef heart.

As father slowly steers along the highway, Dexter's attention is drawn away from the first group of Troopers and members of the Game and Fish Department. About another fifty yards away along the grassy plain, another gathering has formed over yet, another viciously slain bull.

Fellow ranchers shake their heads, as they stand over the dead bull. They speak in low voices. They've heard about things like this but never thought they'd be a part of it. It would be unthinkable for their competitors to do such a thing.

The ranchers and Troopers think it could possibly be just some cruel prank caused by local teenaged hooligans. Then, they think it could be a part of some kind of sadistic, religious ceremony or even could be an alien abduction and grotesque experiments.

But then they realize, it could be something much worse. A new kind of predator has come to their territory. A predator in which they have never encountered before...

"Zoey?" Jon says with urgency. "Zoey?"

"Jon? Is that you?" Zoey asks. She stands in her kitchen area wearing her usual skulls and crossbones pajamas. She props the receiver of the phone onto her shoulder as she continues making herself a snack. "Where are you?"

"In the next time zone, I think." Jon stands nearly naked inside of a poorly lit telephone booth along the side of a back road. He wears a makeshift pair of shorts constructed of several layers of discarded newspapers. It looks like he's covered himself like this before.

Directly behind him, a Mom-n-Pop gas station and general store, closed for the night. The back road is desolate and rarely traveled at this hour. The gas station's façade is dark and creepy looking as if it were plucked right out of a horror movie. "What's going on? You called collect. Can't you Rock Stars pay for your own calls?"

"I need your help," Jon says almost pleading. "It's Rafe." Zoey's hooked. That's all he had to say.

"What about Rafe? Is he alright?"

"I think so. I've been following his trail for over a week. Looks like he's eating well. He's just too fast to catch up with."

"What happened?"

"We, uh. Kinda had an argument."

"Oh, you mean your concert in Des Moines?"

"You know about that?"

"It's all over the internet! Half of the planet knows about it by now!"

"Zoey, I need your help to get'im back. We've canceled six shows already."

"Is that all you think about, Jon? *The concerts*? I'd be pissed off, too!"

"Zoey, please!" He knows she's his last hope. Zoey's always had a thing for Rafe but they never followed through with it. They just had bad timing.

"Alright, Jon... where are you?"

"A few hours west of Laramie."

"Fine, I'll be there sometime tomorrow."

"Zoey..."

CLICK!

"...thank-you." Jon humbly hangs up the receiver. He steps out of the telephone booth and surveys his surroundings.

Jon slightly lifts his head and sniffs the air. His brother has a distinctive scent which is unusual for this part of the world. He turns his head, thinking he may have picked up Rafe's trail.

Jon begins walking along the side of the back road, further away from the gas station and general store. As he slips deeper into the shadows, he begins to unravel his newspaper shorts. Layer by layer, Jon tosses the printed sheets to the side.

"You *wash* those before you give 'em back!" Zoey says with a sharp tone. Jon slips into a borrowed pair of jeans then slides into one of Zoey's black T-shirts.

"Thanks for comin'. I owe you."

"*You* don't owe me anything. I came for Rafe."

"...right."

"Where is he?" Zoey and Jon pause a moment before crossing the deserted Wyoming highway. It's late in the afternoon with the sun continuing to set along the horizon. From Zoey's travel route from the northwest, she's parked her pickup and camper along the far side of the paved, two-lane road. Her mode of transportation and shop-on-wheels is an interesting looking vehicle.

The extended cab pickup truck is black in color with custom paint along the hood and doors as well as the front and rear fenders. The images are not quite flames but more of magical swirls and waves.

The primary sleeping area of the camper nearly touches to roof of the cab. The interior of the kitchen, seating area, as well as, a sink and shower extend along the bed of the pickup.

A single door at the end of the camper, where the pickup's tailgate should be, allows access inside. Along opposite sides of the largest side panels of the camper, swirling letters have been hand painted;

Madam Zoey's
Fortune Telling & Palm Reading

Zoey and Jon approach the far side of the highway, walking down, then up a slight ditch and stand facing a barbwire fence that stretches out for miles in opposite directions. "He's out over there, about a half a mile," Jon says, as he points across the ocean of prairie grass. "Just follow the dead cattle."

Jon steps forward and carefully takes a hold of the barbwire between a set of sharp prongs. With his bare foot, he finds a gap between a lower stretch of wire and presses his weight downward.

Zoey leans over and steps through the opening of the barbwire. She pauses a moment, looking far off in the distance, trying to catch a glimpse of Rafe. Without a second though, she slips out of her shoes, then slides off her shirt. Zoey unbuttons her jeans, kicks them off then tosses them to Jon. She's never been the shy one.

Jon carefully takes Zoey's clothes and rests them on top of the nearest wooden pole, supporting the extended span of barbwire. He turns and heads back toward the camper. "*I wonder if she's got anything to eat*," he thinks.

The sun dips closer to the horizon with gray clouds beginning to roll in. A light breeze flows over Zoey's bare body. It's getting a little chilly.

She stands there a moment looking at the remains of a viciously slaughtered bull. It's throat has been torn out, it has been gutted and appears to have had its heart eaten while it was still alive. Zoey knows she's getting closer.

Suddenly from the shadows, the cheetah attacks. With full force, the large cat slams its forepaws against Zoey's chest causing her to violently fall backward. The cheetah pounces on her, pinning her to the ground.

The cheetah sniffs at Zoey's neck and shoulders. There's something familiar about this Gothic human. His black nose, muzzle and whiskers are covered in cattle blood.

The spotted feline opens his mouth, bares his sharp teeth and hisses. "Rafe, get off me!" Zoey demands as she shoves the cheetah to the side.

As she supports herself with one hand, attempting to get to her feet, the cheetah lunges again, knocking her to the ground. "Oh!" Zoey exclaims. "It's gonna be that way, huh?"

Zoey quickly gets to her feet as the cheetah races around her almost as if he were chasing his tail. The cheetah draws in closer, rubbing the side of his body against Zoey's thigh.

In an inviting manner, the cheetah bobs his head. "*Come play with me*," he seems to be saying. The cheetah raises up on his hind legs, carefully supports himself on Zoey's shoulders and licks her face.

"Whew!" The taste of the cattle's blood covers her lips. "Come on, Rafe! You know I'm a vegetarian." With that, the cheetah springs away and frolics through the prairie grass. "Rafe?" The large feline is gone. "...alright then."

Zoey lowers herself to the ground, supporting her weight on her hands and knees. She takes several deep breaths as she turns her neck, rolling her head in small circles.

Her body begins to double in size and density. Zoey's flesh, tissue, muscles and skeletal structure balloons outward like an instantaneous allergic reaction to a wasp or bee sting.

Black and white fur quickly sprouts from her skin and covers her hands, arms and shoulders. A wide band of sorts runs crossways along her back, seemingly connecting her shoulder blades. The black and white fur continues to spread along her hips and waist until completely covering her legs.

The rest of her transforming body is covered with soft white fur with the exception for her mutating ears and large round patches around her eyes. The panda's characteristics are nearly complete. Keen sense of smell, heightened vision and elevated hearing.

The panda rolls on the ground, as if to scratch her own back. Springing up on all four of her paws, she sniffs the air in an attempt to locate the cheetah. She turns and begins a casual gallop across the grassy terrain.

The cheetah bounds from a sparse tree line and playfully attacks the panda as she passes by. The cheetah and panda roll across the ground, over and over in a kind of wrestling match.

The panda maneuvers herself onto her paws as the cheetah springs on top of her back. She carries him for several yards before carefully shaking him off. The cheetah leaps forward and wraps his forepaws around her thick neck. The cheetah playfully nibbles at her furry black ear.

The panda reaches up and takes the cheetah by the back of his neck. She pulls the large feline away from herself and pins him to the ground. Pressing her entire weight downward, she has the cheetah right where she wants him.

The panda lowers her head and begins licking the inside of his spotted ear. The cheetah's tail wags back and forth. This kind of tickles. The panda releases her grasp and sits up, oddly human looking as a child would sit on a floor watching television.

The cheetah springs up and circles the panda. She playfully paws at him as he passes in front of her. The large cat nips at her furry shoulders from behind. Around and around the feline spins.

The panda presses her weight forward and stands up on all fours. The cheetah continues to nip at the panda as would a puppy starved for attention. The panda begins to lope across the prairie, back toward the highway with the cheetah never leaving her side.

"Thanks for coming and gettin' us," Jon finally says. He sits in the passenger's seat of Zoey's pickup listening to the light music escaping from the older model cassette deck.

Zoey focuses on the road ahead, steering along, cutting through the darkness. The dimly lit inner console of lights reflect across her face. She looks worn out and tired.

She's tossed on a black tank-top and faded jean shorts, perfectly comfy for the long journey ahead. Behind both of their heads, the back window of the pickup's cab appears completely slid open revealing the dark shadows of the rest of the inner camper. "I didn't come for you, Jon. I came for Rafe."

"Hold on a minute. What did I ever do to you?"

"Nothing to me, Jon. It's what you've done to your brother that pisses me off." Zoey snaps her head to the side and glares at him. "Oh, don't *even* give me that *deer in headlights* look. You know *exactly* what I'm talking about." Zoey looks away, refocusing on the desolate highway.

"I didn't *ask* him to quit school. He did that on his own."

"...and what, break up the band? Oh, *please*, Jon. Is that it? Is that the best you have? Outta everything, *that's* the *least* of your issues."

"What is it then?"

"Let's see. You took Leslie away from him. How's that workin' out? See the kids much?" Jon can hear the pain in Zoey's voice. "Then, Rick promotes *you* to lead vocals sending Rafe to the back of the bus."

"It wasn't like that."

"Wasn't it, Jon? Remember, I was there since the beginning. Let me tell you a little secret." Zoey pauses a moment, not really sure she should divulge anything more to Jon. "I *hate* the drums. I have no rhythm. Chloe got all the rhythm. I can't even do the two-step. I hate her..."

"I didn't know it was getting worse," Jon says, in an apologetic tone.

"Do you really think I enjoyed setting up and tearing down Rafe's drum set in school? No! I just liked being around him..." Zoey fights back the tears. "Bottom line, Jon. It was *you* that took him away from *me*."

"So, now what do we do?"

"*We*?" Zoey nearly laughs. *"We* don't need to do anything. *You* have a lot to work on."

"I can't trust him. He's not responsible enough to handle this."

"How would you know, Jon? You two need to get back to your roots. Get back to where you started. You used to be the Two Musketeers. Everything was equally decided."

"I don't know. Everything is more complicated now."

"Is it? Or are you just making it that way? You have to start somewhere. You have to trust him before he trusts you..."

Along the upper sleeping area of the camper, above the roof of the pickup, Rafe lays on his stomach with his waist and backside covered by a dark printed sheet.

His shins, calves and thighs are covered with the tattooed cheetah spots, similar to his shoulder blades, upper back and arms. His acute hearing has woke him up. Rafe's eyes have been open for some time now.

"Oh, great," Gio sarcastically mumbles to himself. "This should be fun." He sits behind the wheel of his custom, medical bus with the right turn signal flashing. He's dressed casually, quite comfortable for the many hours on the highway. Gio eases back on the accelerator as he slightly maneuvers the extended vehicle off of the paved two-lane road.

Due to the height of the of the med-lab on wheels, Gio slows to a halt along the roadside of the overhead awning of the modern looking gas station and general store.

Spanning out across a small clearing along the nearside of the general store, a row of parked motorcycles with a few trikes tossed in. In the distance, Jimmy and Vince play a haphazard game of toss with several of the biker children.

Shelby and a few others tend to their cycles, making sure their air pressure in their tires is correct, tightening any loose gears or wires. Amber sits at one of many worn and faded picnic tables, soaking in the midday's sun. Other children and biker babes, sit along the surrounding picnic tables finishing their lunches.

Under the overhead awning of the gas station, Reggie, Dante and Angus continue to fill up a short line of cycles. With their gas tanks full, their fellow bikers push their cycles from the gas pumps and collectively join the rest of the family. All that's left is Dante standing alongside his motorcycle and Reggie next to his trike. "Look who's here," Dante says with a sneer.

Gio flings open the forward side door of his bus and steps onto the concrete next to the gas pumps. He looks Reggie up and down then slightly tosses Dante a glance. "Hey, guys. How've you been?" By their attire and modes of transportation, nothing's changed much.

"Fine, Gio... and you?" Reggie asks in the most polite tone he can muster. Even before Gio can answer-

"I see you're still playin' doctor," Dante says, in a condescending manner; old feelings die hard.

"Doing what I can to ease pain and suffering."

"That's what Kevorkian said," Dante defiantly says. Gio and Dante stare at each other. An awkward silence follows.

"Hey, guys! Come on. We're losing the light!" Vince shouts from the small clearing. Never taking his eyes off of Gio, Dante turns and places his palms on his handlebars. He pushes his cycle from the gas pumps and joins the rest of his biker family.

"So, you headed for the show?" Reggie asks, as he replaces the nozzle back into the gas pump.

"Yeah," Gio replies as he unscrews the cap of his gas tank. "Gonna stick around here a few days. Have some things to take care of near San Carlos." Reggie gives him an odd look. "*Doctor stuff*," Gio adds with a smile.

"Yeah, well." Reggie wipes his palm off of the thigh of his worn jeans and extends out his hand. "We'll see you in a couple weeks." Gio and Reggie shake hands. They've never been real good friends but they don't have animosity nor contempt for each other.

Reggie bounds for his trike and straddles the seat. Using the electric starter, he fires it up and revs the engine several times. Reggie slowly rolls his trike along the edge of the small clearing where Dante and the rest of the family prepare for their departure.

The air is filled with thunderous engines causing the ground to tremble. Amber climbs on behind Reggie, leans forward and kisses him on the cheek. With a wave of his hand, Reggie motions his convoy forward.

Leading his family of bikers in a flock formation, Reggie heads out along the two-lane highway. Keeping close as his wingman, Dante follows along. The traveling band of misfits rolls along for several moments before disappearing beyond the growing waves of heat along the asphalt.

As the gas pump continues to fill the tank of the medical vehicle, Gio makes his way to the edge of the smoldering highway. The air is warm and stale with not even a light breeze. He lifts his head and closes his eyes as if he were trying to catch the scent of his prey, carefully stalking it.

The small, Native American based city is nestled in the southern central area of the Indian Reservation. The historical buildings, lined up along opposite sides of the main street, look as if they have no idea what century they are in. The structures have been simply trapped in time, when life was much simpler.

There is sparse traffic along the main and side streets with even fewer pedestrians. The blanket of dawn is quickly fading with the first rays of the rising sun peeking over the rugged terrain in the far distance.

One main roadway leads in and out of the desert city. However, there are a number of side and dirt roads leading out into the depths of The Reservation. Along one of these primitive northern routes, a faint trail of billowing dust follows behind a sleek, two-story bus, distinctively out of place.

Gio's med-lab stands parked alongside the western entrance of the Native community. The wide variety of mobile homes and trailers span out in organized rows for nearly ten acres.

Over thirty trees have been strategically planted many years ago and provide the only shade and foliage. A drastic contrast to the surrounding desert. The gathering of dwellings looks as if it had been simply dropped there in the middle of nowhere. Right, like this is the best place The Government could find!

Gio appears professional, in his white medical jacket, pressed slacks and latex gloves. He sits in a chair near the opened forward door of his two-story vehicle. Next to him, a small metallic table is covered with medical supplies and equipment; a tubular container of wooden tongue depressors, a disposable thermometer, a blood pressure cuff.

An awning has been raised, extending outward nearly fifteen feet and running the length of the bus. The awning protects the waiting Natives from the blazing rays of the midday's sun.

Gio takes a tongue depressor and moves it around a Native boy's mouth. The youth looks fit and healthy, despite the lack of constant medical care. Gio's bedside manner is calming as he remains courteous, providing medical advice as needed.

Giving the Native boy a clean bill of health, Gio politely nods to the boy's mother. She gathers up her son as the next dark skinned patient approaches Gio and finds his chair facing the doctor.

Gio slides out of his latex gloves, tosses them into a small trashcan next to him and slips into another pair. He smiles at the elderly Native, he's not quite sure if he speaks English or not. Just as well.

The elderly man extends out his hand as Gio slides the blood pressure cuff around his arm. With several brisk squeezes of the handheld pump, the cuff tightens around his bicep. As Gio looks down at the gauge, he feels a presence, as if someone were watching his every movement.

Gio looks up and beyond the shade of the extended awning. The sun is blinding. He squints and looks in all directions. Narrow roadways cut through the small community, in and out of the rows of trailers and mobile homes.

A handful of young Native boys kick a worn soccer ball around. A mother carries her newborn baby in a traditional papoose along her back as she totes her half filled, handmade satchel of groceries. A trio of teenage girls stand at the edge of one of the roadways, pointing and giggling at Gio and the odd looking two-story bus.

Gio's vision adjusts to the contrast of the awning's shade and the surrounding brightness of the sun. There, across the way, next to one of the towering trees, an image appears.

The shadowy figure can't quite be defined at this distance. All Gio can determine is that the man is taller than most with a cloud of smoke billowing out from a pipe. Gio turns to the elderly Native patient in front of him and nods. His blood pressure is fine.

Gio takes an otoscope from the metallic table, flicks on the small light and looks into the patient's ear. Seeing nothing out of the ordinary, Gio maneuvers himself to the man's other ear and looks inside.

Gio slightly pulls away from the dark skinned man and removes the disposable tip from the otoscope. As he replaces the device back onto the metallic table, he looks up. Beyond the awning and across the narrow roadway, the shadowy image is gone. All that remains is a faint trace of pipe smoke.

"Thanks for the business, mister," the young Native woman says with a smile. The common looking general store sits in the direct center of the trailer park. The wooden plank floor seems to slightly creek under Gio's feet.

The primitive aisles are filled with staples for the community. Nothing too fancy, just the basic needs. The refrigeration and freezer fills the far wall, directly across from the cash register and check-out counter.

Gio collects his paper bag filled with groceries from the counter. He smiles and slightly nods, as he turns and exits through the screen door.

Gio strolls through the narrow central roadway carrying his purchased items. The night air is humid, yet cool. A drastic change from earlier in the day. As he walks along, Gio tosses a glance inside of the passing trailers and mobile homes.

Some families wrap up dinner in their kitchen areas as others watch television in their living rooms. Inside one particular kitchen, a father sits down at the dining room table with his son, pounding out math problems of homework.

"Good-evening, Paleface," the Medicine Man says, in a jesting tone. The tall man sits in Gio's chair, just outside of the bus's opened front door and the metallic table. The awning remains extended with the attached outside lamplights creating a kind of patio effect. The wise, dark skinned man wears common attire with no feathered headdress nor beaded necklace.

His eyes are warm and welcoming. The man's facial features are a roadmap of wrinkles caused by the many years of sun and desert wind. He does not appear to be intimidated by Gio's arrival, making himself at home outside of the two-story medical bus. He takes a puff of his handmade pipe, as Gio steps under the awning. "Good-evening."

"I am Dahana. I knew you were coming."

"Do you have the sight to see into the future?" Gio asks, before setting down his sack of groceries just inside of the opened door.

"Naw," Dahana says with a smile. He reaches into the breast pocket of his worn, plaid button up shirt. Dahana retrieves a cell phone and holds it out for Gio to see. "I have a *friend* in New Orleans that told me you might be coming this way." He snickers as he slides the cell phone back into his shirt pocket. "What can I do for you..." he asks, fishing for a name.

"Giovanni Mancini." Dahana and Gio shake hands. The Medicine Man clutches onto Gio's grasp, feeling his energy. There's something not quite right about this visitor.

Gio finds his seat next to Dahana with the metallic table, the only thing separating them. "I am searching for a secret."

"Aren't we all," Dahana says, with a smile, puffing on his pipe.

"You're ancestors spoke of animal spirits. They spoke of how the animals carried them away. How they bonded with the animals and became as one."

"That's just the peyote talking. The stars tell us, a man *is* who he is. A man *is* what he is. A man can change his spirit, not his form."

"Well, I don't know about that..."

"At one point or another in all of our lives, we stand before our Maker. I have some time before that day comes. As for you, I see the day you meet your Maker is coming swiftly."

"You're speaking in riddles. Say what you mean!" Gio is becoming frustrated, this Medicine Man is sending him in circles.

"There is nothing more for you here." Dahana stands. "I do not expect to see you when the sun comes up." With a stern look, Dahana turns and begins walking away. In a matter of moments, the mysterious man vanishes into the darkness along the narrow roadway.

Gio stands and makes his way from under the awning. He slowly walks along the edge of a stone path which leads out and away from the last row of trailers and mobile homes. Darkness surrounds him. Gio pauses and looks up into the night sky.

He is blanketed by the vastness of stars overhead. Then, one by one, a handful of constellations come into focus; Libra, Gemini, Cancer and Virgo. Gio scans the stars until locating his Zodiac sign. His eyes follow along a stream of sparkly lights until resting on the brightest star in his constellation; Regulus.

"Hey, Larry." A fellow lawyer from down the hall enters the waiting area of the Assistant District Attorney's office. "What are you doing behind Chloe's desk?"

"I gave her some time off," Larry replies. "She had some *personal* things to take care of." Larry is dressed in his usual suit and tie. He looks somewhat out of place behind his assistant's desk, not really knowing where everything is.

Chloe has a certain way of filing things. Not necessarily in alphabetic order but more of the chaos theory. However, if she were there, Chloe would know where everything was. "It's about quittin' time. Wanna grab a drink?" the professional looking man asks.

"Thanks. I have some errands to take care of."

"Next time."

"Yeah, next time." Larry shuffles some paperwork across the desktop. The attorney pauses a moment in the opened doorway, just in case Larry changes his mind. He does not. Larry seems focused on returning Chloe's desk to the condition in which he had found it.

Larry looks up to see the younger attorney has vanish from the doorway. He casually turns and looks out through the picture window. An afternoon thunderstorm is approaching The City.

Larry rests his forearms against the handrailing of the lioness pit. The shoulders of his tan raincoat are sprinkled with sporadic raindrops. Small pools of collected rainwater lay scattered along the floor of the deep ravine.

The exhibit itself is empty. There are no signs of Keiko nor Jaakko. The natural habitat is void of all feline activity. The mist which fills the air slightly conceals the simulated boulders. A light drizzle blankets the surrounding trees.

The Zoo seems unoccupied with less than a handful of patrons roaming along the concrete walkways behind Larry. Yet, he remains focused, looking to the cave opening of the lioness pit. From inside, a low growl is heard.

Larry slightly raises up from the handrailing, waiting to be greeted by either Keiko or Jaakko. A secondary growl seeps out from the cave's opening. The mother and son are communicating with each other. They both can sense and smell Larry but neither wants to trudge outside to get wet.

Larry turns his head and looks in opposite directions. Fewer and fewer patrons remain. The drizzle is now a constant rain. He turns forward and releases a deep and commanding feline roar.

From just inside of the cave's opening, Keiko appears and looks out toward Larry. She remains just inside of the cave, protected from the increasing rainfall. Keiko slightly tilts her head to the side. "*What, are you kidding?*" she seems to be saying. "*Don't summon me!*"

"We have to talk!" Larry says in an elevated tone. This outburst catches the attention of a couple passing by. Oh, he's an odd one, talking to a lioness, as if they had just broken-up.

The couple quickly departs the area, afraid that the man is about to apologize then propose to the lioness. That's just too weird! Larry shrugs off the couple and refocuses on the lioness pit. Keiko stands in the cave's entrance for a moment before turning and defiantly swooshing her tail. She quickly disappears back into the cave. "Jay?" Larry calls out.

Jaakko peers around the corner of the cave's entrance. The rainfall has turned into a downpour. Larry stands on the opposite side of the handrailing, drenched.

The tigon lifts his forepaw as if to reach out toward Larry with a simple *hello.* Larry smiles as he waves back. It's going to be a long two weeks before he can see his son again.

"Alright, guys. Yeah, right over there is good." Larry directs a pair of young men across Sonja's living room. They are dressed in identical, light blue jumpsuits. The pair of men each hold onto an end of an expensive looking loveseat, slightly struggling due to the weight.

The pair of movers lean forward and place the loveseat onto the floor in the off-center of living room. The dwelling is a drastic change from before.

A pair of matching easy-chairs stands facing the couch and loveseat with a modern looking coffee table separating them. A large screen television sets hangs from the wall across the room with several hanging plants off in the corners.

An oak, roll top desk sits next to the closed front door. On the opposite sides of the door, a series of shelves houses rows of books as well as the main component of a stereo system.

Two other pairs of movers, wearing identical light blue jumpsuits, appears from the opened front door. One pair carries a queen size box spring with the other two carrying a mattress. They tromp passed Larry with his back toward them.

Larry looks into the kitchen to see another mover placing a wide assortment of pots and pans into the lower cabinets. The newly furnished and redecorated apartment is nearly complete. "Larry! What's going on here?" Sonja's voice seems to shred the air.

Larry turns from the entrance of the kitchen to see Sonja standing in the opened doorway of the apartment. She wears her slip-on dress she's stored in the locker at The Zoo. Yet, even with her matted hair and no makeup, Sonja still looks lovely. "Well, what are you doing?"

"I guess we're done here guys," Larry says to the movers. The younger men can tell they had better get out of there before it really gets interesting. Larry steps into the living room as the movers begin to shuffle toward the door.

Larry reaches into his pocket and retrieves a thick money clip. As the last mover makes his way passed him, Larry slips him several one hundred dollar bills. "This is for *you* guys. Get some pizza or something."

Larry follows the movers to the front door and closes it as the last one exits. Larry humbly stands in front of Sonja, searching for the right words to say. However, nothing poetic comes to mind. "I wasn't expecting to see you here."

"What gave you the idea that I *needed* your help? I don't *need* your help."

"I just thought..."

"No, you didn't, Larry. Jay and I have been doing fine without you. So, just because you pop back into my life doesn't mean everything's fine and dandy!"

"I wanted to..."

"Wanted to what? Make up for lost time? If you wanted to find me, you could have done it years ago."

"Wait a minute," Larry abruptly says going on the offensive now. "You're the one that left! We were going to move into The City so I could go to school. Then you just up and left."

"I was pregnant with Jay."

"And you didn't think I had a right to know?"

"I thought we would just get in your way. We'd be a distraction. Becoming a lawyer was so important to you."

"*You* were important to me. Now, you *both* are." Larry looks deeply into Sonja's soft brown eyes. He reaches up and tenderly takes her by the shoulders. They passionately kiss. Suppressed emotions overwhelm them.

Sonja embraces her once lost lover. Larry tastes her lips as if it were just yesterday. They gently part, still looking deep into the other's eyes. As if an unheard ballad was beginning to play from the stereo, Larry and Sonja begin to slow dance.

She reaches up and begins to play with his hair above the back of his neck. Larry softly pulls back a few loose strands of hair away from her face. He's decided to end this masquerade. "Where's Jay?" Larry finally asks.

"He's fine. He's still at The Zoo... asleep." As the soft ballad continues to play in their heads, Larry and Sonja kiss again, with more familiarity this time.

"Well, we know why *I'm* here," Larry says as he tosses a glance toward the newly arrived furniture and redecorated apartment.

"I slip out from time to time. Check the mail. Take a hot shower."

"A shower?"

"Yeah, a shower," Sonja answers with a smile. "A girl can only take so many tongue baths..."

~ IX ~

"Do you want anything from inside?" Reggie asks as he swings his leg over the worn seat of his trike.

"Yeah. How 'bout some road beer," Dante says. He slides his dark colored goggles from his face and hangs them on the handlebars of his motorcycle. Reggie saunters along, under the weather beaten awning of the roadside gas station and general store.

The midday sun is blinding with the vastness of the desert spanning out in all directions. The small oasis appears to be the only structure for miles and miles.

As Reggie steps up onto the wooden porch, a young man exits through the swinging screen door. Buster is a lanky fellow, wearing faded jeans and a traditional light blue shirt as a gas attendant would. "What can I git ya', mister?"

"Go ahead'n fill'em up."

"Sure thing," Buster says, in a cheerful tone. He makes his way toward the historical looking gas pumps, takes a nozzle in hand and begins filling Reggie's trike. Buster looks outward to see there is no traffic along the paved two-lane highway, just the endless waves of rising heat.

"Blake? Yeah, it's Dante," he says, with the payphone's receiver clutched to his ear. Dante stands along the outside wall of the side of the gas station. On opposite sides of him, the closed doors of the men's and woman's restrooms with the payphone hanging in between.

"Well, have you made a decision?" Blake asks, from the other end of the phone.

"Yeah, I'll take the fight." Dante pauses a moment. "One million win or lose, right?"

"Right! I'll set it up for Sunday at noon."

"Where at?"

"Do you remember when you fought Jack Diesel a couple of years ago?"

"Yeah, I remember the place. I'll see you Sunday." Dante hesitates as he hangs up the receiver. He runs his fingers through his matted dreadlocks. Dante slowly makes his way from around the corner of the building and steps up onto the wooden porch.

Arthur stands behind the checkout counter of the primitive looking general store. He is an elderly man, kind looking with gentle eyes wearing a pair of jean, bib overalls and a plaid shirt.

However, Arthur appears slightly on edge. Although he's seen all kinds of people come in and out of his store over the years, these biker-types still makes him nervous. "How'z it gonin'?" Dante politely asks as he makes his way passed the checkout counter and older model cash register. Arthur simply nods.

Along the back of the general store, Reggie hangs onto a twelve pack of beer with another tucked under his arm. He walks along the extended refrigerator doors and ducks into an aisle, playfully hiding from his riding buddy.

Dante takes a few bags of chips in hand as he rounds the end of another aisle. He looks over the half stocked items along the shelves as he strolls across the wooden planked floor.

Feeling quite spunky, Reggie springs out from around the corner of the aisle, dropping the two twelve packs of beer. He leaps onto Dante's back and wrestles with him. One of the twelve packs breaks open, spraying beer all over the place.

Dante drops the bags of chips to the floor and grasps for Reggie clinging to his back. They tussle for a moment until toppling each other to the wooden floor.

Laughter fills the air as the two best friends release tension from the long hours of the road. They wrestle and flip-flop across the floor, knocking canned goods and bags of pasta from the shelves. "Git off that boy!" Arthur shouts, as he levels his double barreled shotgun at Dante.

"Look, mister. We were just havin' some fun!" Reggie says as he slowly releases Dante and raises his hands in the air. "Sorry 'bout the mess..."

Reggie slides off of Dante with the two of them laying on their backs on the dusty floor. Arthur inches closer, pointing the end of his shotgun dangerously close to Dante's head.

Dante, ever so slowly, raises his hands in the air showing Arthur that he means the elderly man no harm. Dante moves his right hand to the side, slowly behind himself as if to reach for-

Arthur leans forward and pulls the trigger of the double barreled shotgun just as Reggie lifts his boot and kicks the barrel upward.

KA - BLAM!

The shot is fired into the ceiling. Due to the force of the shotgun blast, Arthur is sent reeling backward, falling to the wooden floor. The elderly man grabs his chest as the shotgun falls to the side.

Reggie and Dante slide across the floor and clutch onto Arthur. He's having a stroke. Arthur frantically looks up into their eyes. There's nothing they can do. He gasps for air, pleading for help. Then, death quickly finds him.

"Come on, we have to get outta here!" Reggie says with urgency.

"We just can't leave 'im here."

"Why not? It'll look like he had a heart attack! Let's go!" Reggie abruptly stands and takes Dante by the hand. He nearly drags him away from the lifeless elderly man. Dante moves his right hand to the side, slowly behind himself as if to reach for-

As he passes the cash register, he reaches into his wallet and tosses a few twenty dollar bills onto the counter for the gas.

Reggie and Dante burst from the front screen door. They scan the area for any onlookers or travelers. There are none. Reggie hops onto his trike and fires up the electrical ignition.

Dante flips back his chrome kickstand and straddles his bike. In a matter of moments, Reggie and Dante thunder out onto the heated, two-lane highway.

BEEP - beep - beep.

Buster crouches down behind the checkout counter, concealing himself. He is frightened and trembling as he holds the receiver of the telephone to his ear. A feminine voice responds from the other end, "Nine-one-one. What is your emergency?"

"What are you gonna to do, Reggie?" Amber whispers into his ear. Reggie coddles her in his arms and softly kisses her on her forehead. He turns and looks upon the concerned faces of his fellow bikers.

There are no campfires to warm them. No tents nor shelters have been set up for the night. The last traces of the setting sun casts yellow and orange colors across the sky.

The collection of motorcycles and trikes stands parked in a single row along the side of the highway, somewhat of a rest area. The majority of the biker family continues to bundle-up, slipping into their leather chaps, jackets and gloves. A dozen yards away, a road sign heading southwest is seen;

BOULDER CITY 5 MILES

Reggie and Amber seem to be standing at the forefront of the small assembly. Dante, Vince, Jimmy, Angus and Shelby fill in the rest of the circle. Their thoughts are quite with an uncertain future ahead of them. "Vince, I want you to take 'em northeast and catch Highway 169. You should be able to mix in with Garret and his family. The Bullet Run passes through there this time of year."

"What about you two?" Shelby asks.

"I have a fight I have to get to," Dante replies.

"You're still gonna fight? You know the cops'll be lookin' for you," Jimmy adds.

"That's why we're splitting up. No need to drag all of you into this."

"But we're family and family sticks together."

"Not this time, big guy." Reggie smiles as he reaches out and gives Vince a bear hug. "Take care of 'em for me." Reggie and Dante give brotherly handshakes and hugs all around. Without another word, Jimmy, Vince, Shelby and Angus head for the row of parked bikes in the background.

"Then what?" Amber asks. She nearly glares at Dante then toward Reggie. "After the fight, then what?"

"Win or lose, it's my last one," Dante confidently says. He and Reggie curiously smile at each other. "Then, we get a hold of the only lawyer we know..."

"Good-morning, Night Crawlers." Tez reaches up and slightly lowers the suspended microphone closer to his lips. "It's about ten after four and you're tuned to K.R.W.L., one-o-one point three, The Emerald City's *classic* rock-n-roll station."

Tez's leather bomber jacket hangs over the backrest of his swiveling chair. His casual attire is slightly retro with his ever present dark sunglasses resting on the bridge of his nose. "I'd like to give a shout-out to everyone who made it to Dee Dee's funeral. It was a lovely service." Off to the right of the extended control panel, the framed promotional shot of former fellow deejay Dee Dee Sawyer remains.

Tez reaches across the pair of slowly spinning turntables to his left and sets an album into place. Next to the furthest turntable, a stack of album covers. Unnoticed before, on each of the album's top right corner, a section of paper, no larger than a standard playing card. The paper is covered with aligned dots in small rectangular boxes; Braille.

The shelves directly behind Tez are filled with similar album covers and compact disk cases, all with secured labels with Braille writing; name of the album, group and song list. "I'd like to thank everyone who couldn't make it. Your cards and letters are appreciated."

Hanging between the large gaps of black-light posters, hundreds of mourning cards and tearful goodbyes. The wide assortment of oozing lava lights provides the only light throughout the cave-like studio.

Almost undetectable, the massive control panel resting in front of Tez has also been customized for his needs. The levers and knobs have been retrofitted with Braille indicators. Even the poster images of Hendrix, Dylan, Joplin and Morrison seem to sympathize with Tez's condition.

Tez takes his left hand and presses it against the outside edge of the nearest turntable causing it to stop. With his right hand, he ever so gently runs his over sensitive fingertips across the groves of the album.

Finding the song he was searching for, Tez sets the needle in place. "This one's goin' out to all the Night Crawlers in The Valley. I'm the Taz Man and you're tuned to one-o-one point three, K.R.W.L."

Tez releases the turntable allowing the record to play. As upbeat, rock and roll music fills the air, Tez flicks off the *on-air* switch. He removes the previous compact disk from its player and places it back into its case. Feeling the Braille label along the top right corner, he spins around in his wheeled chair and slides it back in its proper place along the filled shelves.

Tez pauses a moment and smiles. He slightly raises and leans his head to the side, sniffing the air; *White Diamonds.* Tez runs his over sensitive fingertips across the edge of the shelve. Feeling the Braille indicators, he removes an album cover from the inventory of music.

Kaleen stands in the doorway, watching the rock and roll deejay work. She's dressed down, having found one of her old dresses in Tez's closet. The cold tile floor doesn't seem to bother her bare feet.

Tez is flawless in his movements. He effortlessly slides a compact disk into the player and cues up the next song. Maneuvering over to the pair of turntables, he places an album onto the slow spinning surface.

"Are you gonna stand there all morning or are you gonna come in?" Tez asks in a playful manner. He slightly turns in his wheeled chair. "Kay?"

Kaleen has disappeared from the doorway. Tez pauses a moment as he continues to sniff the air. Is his mind playing tricks on him? Was his ex-wife actually there? He rises up from his wheeled chair and carefully makes his way to the doorway.

Tez leans his head out into the dimly light hallway of the radio station and moves his head in both directions. He's attempting to confirm if Kaleen had been there. Tez steps further out from the studio and stands in the center of the hallway, ever so quietly. Atop the doorway directly behind him, the red *on-air* light comes to life as the previous song begins to fade out.

"Good-morning, Night Crawlers. This is *Ariel Nation* and you're tuned to K.R.W.L., The Pacific Coast's *number one* rock 'n roll station." Undetected, Kaleen has made her way into the studio and has found her seat in Tez's wheeled chair. She sits there with the suspended microphone mere inches away from her lips. Tez makes his way through the doorway and gives Kaleen a quirky smile.

"What are you doing?" Tez asks under his breath.

"The Taz Man had to step out for a moment so I took the liberty of setting up the next song," she continues in the microphone. "Here's one to get you goin' this morning; *Kiss Me Deadly.* Rock-on, Night Crawlers!"

Kaleen presses play on the compact disk player. The studio is filled with the melodic voice of the Rock Goddess of the 1980's. In a matter of moments, loud guitars and drums shake the walls. Kaleen has turned up the volume nearly full blast.

Kaleen flicks off the *on-air* switch and bounds from the wheeled chair. She quickly takes Tez in her arms and begins dancing with him. He plays along for a moment, allowing her lead in the steps as she had done so many years ago at life changing party.

Kaleen and Tez bounce up and down to the upbeat music. They smile and laugh at each other. Tez takes Kaleen by the hand and spins her outward in a ballroom or rumba fashion. Tez spins Kaleen inward, they come face to face.

Kaleen can see her own nervous reflection in Tez's dark sunglasses. They draw closer together, almost nose to nose. Yet, the hesitation is just a bit too long. They no longer have the spark they had once shared.

"What happened to the spontaneous man I used to know?" Kaleen shouts. The sun continues to rise up across The Sound as the yellow taxicab pulls away. Kaleen skips toward the shoreline and splashes into the water up to her knees.

Tez remains at the extended curb of parking spaces bordering the spacious woodland park. He senses familiarity, his home is only a few hundred yards away. "Come on, Tez!" Kaleen nearly commands.

Tez reluctantly reaches down and pulls off his cowboy boots. He slides out of his faded leather bomber jacket and begins a pile of his belongings.

Kaleen wades through the water, now up to her collarbone. She easily slips out of her waterlogged dress and tosses it up onto the shore. Tez tosses his dark T-shirt onto the pile then shimmies out of his jeans.

From the tree line, a young Canadian boy appears. He stops dead in his tracks as he sees Tez flopping his jeans onto the pile of clothing. Tez finally removes his dark sunglasses, flings them onto the pile and darts toward the shoreline.

The young Canadian boy spins and disappears into the forest. He frantically races through the trees searching for his mother. The boy finds her along the edge of a small clearing examining a cluster of indigenous flowers. He reaches up and tugs on the sleeve of her raincoat. "Mummy, I just saw a naked American..."

The waters of The Sound are clear. With the heightened vision of her alter form, Kaleen can see for nearly a mile underwater. She effortlessly moves her scaly tail through the current, swimming along.

The dolphin glides alongside of the mermaid then maneuvers up and over the hybrid. She reaches out her hand and runs her palm along the underbelly of the dolphin. He lets out a series of clicking sounds as he speeds up then takes a sharp turn.

The dolphin quickly swims back toward Kaleen and swishes passed her. She giggles. With her set of small gills working perfectly behind her ears, Kaleen swims further away from shore. The dolphin has nearly exhausted the air in his lungs as he swims toward the surface.

Kaleen glances across the watery floor seeing sporadic crustaceans and sea life. Suddenly, she looks up. Kaleen thrusts her opened hands forward, slowing herself along the current. Her wide tail moves back and forth beneath her as she appears to be treading water, hovering in one place.

She squints, trying to see as far in front of her as she can. Beyond the shadows of the distant current, there's something there. Something ominous. Kaleen is startled as the dolphin suddenly rejoins her.

The dolphin swims around the mermaid in wide circles, coaxing a game of tag. He is playful and at the moment, unaware of the dark presence in the distance.

The sleek, custom two-story bus appears parked in a north to south manner along the side of the street. Lights illuminate outward from both floors of the medical bus with slight shadows of movement along the lower floor.

The far side of the street is lined with well kempt, historical looking homes, occupying the entire block. A few yards out in front of Gio's med-lab on wheels, East South Temple Street, a main artery through the predominantly Mormon city.

The Cathedral of the Madeleine faces Temple Street with sprawling trees and shrubbery all around. Although the place of worship is not currently having a service, sparse lights flicker from within the twin towers on opposite sides of the stain glass, main entrance.

From the depths of the cathedral, low and sinister sounds are heard. The organist prefers to practice his dirge late at night, to hide his mistakes and to avoid criticism. The haunting music seeps out from the massive pipes of the organ, out of the windows of the cathedral and across the grounds.

Gio removes a half filled beaker from a supporting rack, filled with similar glass instruments. He's oddly dressed, not in his usual medical white jacket, dress shirt and tie. Gio has on a mismatch of a silk pajama top and blue jeans as if he had suddenly woken up due to an epiphany.

Taking yet another half filled beaker in hand, Gio mixes the two dark liquids together. The surrounding metallic counters are in total disarray with a wide assortment of opened containers, vials and chemicals.

Gio places the beaker back into the supporting rack yet, separate from the others. He turns and opens the small refrigerator, retrieving a filled syringe. Ever so carefully, Gio releases the liquid compound from the syringe into the beaker.

Gio tosses the syringe to the metallic counter top and corks the beaker. He vigorously shakes the glass tube, mixing all three compounds together. With the corked beaker still in hand, Gio returns to the fridge and removes an additional beaker filled with blood.

He shuffles along his chaotic work area and abruptly sits on his wheeled stool. Gio places both beakers into a smaller supporting rack, sparsely filled with similar, empty tubes.

Gio uncorks both beakers then takes and empty syringe in hand. He extracts an equal amount of the odd colored compound and the blood sample, filling the syringe. Taking a small section of clear glass used for microscopes, Gio releases the new mixture onto its surface about the size of a dime.

He reaches up and opens the door of an electronic synthesizer, looking similar to a common household microwave. Gio places the new sample into the device and closes the door. He turns several knobs, setting the electronic scanner to take the proper readings.

Gio runs his fingers across the keys of his computer's keyboard causing the synthesizer to come to life. Blue and yellow lights scan the sample with data and formulas popping up on the computer screen.

Gio leans forward and studies the results. As if he were following the words of his favorite novel, he runs his forefinger across the screen. Gio's lips slightly move, reading the newly discovered formula. "I've found it!" Gio says with an evil grin. "Now that I've *discovered* it, what do I *do* with it?"

"Glad you could make it," Blake says, with a slightly concerned tone. He and Dante shake hands as Reggie approaches them from the side. Slung over Reggie's shoulder, Dante's worn saddlebags from the back of his motorcycle. "Where's the rest of the family?"

"We ran into a little bit of trouble," Dante replies. "We'll meet up with them in a few weeks."

"...if we can," Reggie adds, under his breath. "Is everything set?" Reggie asks, as he faces Blake. There is no money to be handed off. There is no briefcase to exchange. Blake seems to be holding all the cards.

"Yeah. Take as much time as you need." Blake motions his hand, "You're over here."

Blake leads Dante and Reggie across the dirt floor of the abandoned blimp hangar. The massive building stands along the furthest outskirts of The Biggest Little City in the World. The building itself is colossal.

The gigantic structure is over eleven hundred feet long, three hundred feet wide, over two hundred feet tall and takes up the area larger than eight professional football fields side-by-side.

At opposite ends of the massive hanger, the identical doors have been closed. The panels of the doors are secured in six sections and roll along a singular railroad track. Running the full length of the upper areas of the hangar, decaying catwalks, now unstable to support any spectators.

Like the sidelines of a professional football game, the opposite areas of the dirt floor are filled with a wide assortment of luxury cars, limousines and lavish motor homes with the arena standing in the direct center.

Blake and his entourage represents the visiting team with Adolpho and his massive assembly representing the home team. On opposite sides of the blimp hangar, behind the rows of luxury cars, limousines and expensive motor homes, a pair of matching trailers are seen, the size of a common two horse trailer. Not large enough for camping but large enough for a dressing room of sorts.

Adolpho is an average sized man. However, he is commanding and ruthless in his three thousand dollar dress suit. He laughs and jokes with his obedient subjects before sauntering toward the center of the arena. "Blake," he calmly says. "Is your boy ready?"

"Yeah, he's ready," Blake says with confidence as he approaches his nemesis. They politely yet, with hesitation, shake hands. "I see you pulled out all the stops," Blake says as he motions his head toward the nearest dressing room trailer.

"I figured if you're gonna go down, might as well go down in style."

"Are you referring to Dante or your man?"

"We'll see. A no time limit fight brings many surprises."

"That it does." Blake pauses a moment. "Good-luck." Again, Blake and Adolpho shake hands with much reluctance.

"...and to you," Adolpho sneers as he turns and makes his way back toward his gathering of followers. Flunkies for the most part. Well dressed but flunkies.

A horde of barely dressed women swarm Adolpho, vying for his attention. A model looking woman hands him a glass of champagne. He takes a sip, feeling confident in his astronomical wager.

"Here's your gear," Reggie says as he opens the saddlebags then hands Dante his flaming and flamboyant costume. The red, yellow and orange boa, the fiery dark sunglasses, the yellow knee high boots and of course the gold champion belt with the red, white and blue elastic waist band.

"I'm *not* wearing that crap!" Dante announces as he stands from the padded seat along the inside of the trailer. "If I'm goin' down, it's gonna be on my terms." Dante pushes the flashy costume aside. He hands Reggie his black leather vest with an assortment of patches and insignias.

Dante slides out of his T-shirt and tosses it to the side. He stands there in his worn boots and faded blue jeans, nothing else but his knee brace underneath. "Well, this is it."

"Yeah..."

"Who'd you bet on?"

"Who said I made a bet?"

"C'mon, Reg! I saw you talkin' to Adolpho's zombies." Dante pauses a moment. "Who'd you bet on?"

"I bet on the best man." Reggie smiles, "Let's get goin', bro." Reggie leans to the side and moves toward the trailer door. "After you..."

Over two hundred well dressed spectators have gathered around the large semicircle. The rows of luxury cars, limousines and motor homes appear empty behind the eager crowd. From across the arena, Blake and Adolpho politely nod at each other. It's time! Adolpho raises his hand and slightly waves.

Among the parked convoy of motor homes, a door suddenly opens. Michael Buffer, celebrity ring announcer, makes his entrance. He is a tall and handsome man wearing an immaculate tuxedo and high glossed shoes.

Due to Michael's booming voice and the perfect acoustics of the blimp hangar, he has no need for a microphone. "Ladies and gentlemen! In the near corner, the pride of Odessa, Texas! Standing at six foot, one inch, weighing in at two-hundred and three pounds... Dante's Inferno!"

Michael swoops his hand, pointing in Blake's direction. The crowds part, creating a wide walkway from the small trailer toward the center arena. The trailer door opens with Dante stepping outward with the red, white and blue elastic waistband, gold championship belt slung over his shoulder.

Reggie follows Dante close behind, acting as his coach and wingman. Cheers and applause fills the air. Entering the arena from another direction, Blake approaches Dante and Reggie. The multi-millionaire smiles at the fighter; alright, no costume!

Adolpho turns to the side and motions his hand toward one of the many luxury motor homes. From on top one specific RV, six mounted speakers are seen, each are about the size of a standard home dishwasher. They begin to rumble as a loud guitar introduction begins. The solo grows louder and louder then is accompanied by drums; *Thunderstruck*!

"Ladies and gentlemen! In the far corner, coming to us from Dhirana, India! Standing at a mere seven feet, two inches. Weighing in at four-hundred and two pounds... Thunder Clause!"

Michael motions his hand in the opposite direction. The music continues to grow louder, now with vocals and additional instruments; the theme song for the opposing fighter. The second trailer's door opens. A pair of massive hands appear and takes a hold of the door frame. Due to his towering height, the fighter is forced to lean over to exit the trailer.

Thunder Clause steps outward, one foot then the other. The springs of the trailer abruptly rise up, relieved of the fighter's weight. Thunder stands upright as he releases the door frame, he stands a few inches above the top of the trailer.

Thunder is a descendant from India with a dark complexion. His facial features appear ghoulish with hints of a Neanderthal man. Thunder's black, wavy hair hangs loosely along his shoulders and appears slightly damp.

The towering man's attire is not unusual for a professional fighter. Black, knee high boots with white fox fur around the top openings. His red velvet pants cling tightly around his waist.

Thunder's matching red velvet jacket remains opened, revealing his massive chest. Similar white fox fur runs along the lower seam of the jacket with fur also around the cuffs. Atop his head, a traditional red velvet hat with a ball of fur at the pointy end.

The cheering assembly parts, allowing Thunder passage into the arena. "Jeez, Dante," Reggie manages to says. "That's the biggest Santa I've ever seen."

"I forgot to tell you," Dante leans over and whispers in Reggie's ear, "... his mother is Sasquatch."

Seeing that Dante has refused to don his own costume, Thunder quickly removes his red velvet cap and jacket and tosses them to the side. He reaches down and pulls his velvet pants from the front. The sewn in Velcro along the seams allows easy removal.

Thunder tosses his pants onto the red velvet pile. He stands there for a moment and adjusts his black, spandex pants. The ground nearly shakes as he begins walking toward the center of the arena.

Adolpho comes up alongside and joins Thunder. They slow their pace and stand directly in front of Dante, Reggie and Blake. Thunder looks down toward Dante standing nearly one foot taller. "Ladies and gentlemen!" Michael announces. "Let's get ready to rum-baaaaaaaaaaale!"

There are no handshakes, just lingering animosity. There are no rules; for this is not a sanctioned bout. Dante and Thunder never takes their eyes off of their opponent as they begin to back away from each other.

Blake and Reggie join their group on their side of the arena as Adolpho takes a glass of champagne in hand along the opposite side. Finished with his part of this fiasco, Michael returns to his motor home. The loud rock and roll music fades with cheering and wild applause filling the air.

Dante and Thunder begin to circle each other. At first, twenty feet away. Slowly, the area begins to close in on them, fifteen feet then ten feet. They continue to circle, now about five feet apart. Thunder is nearly in arm's reach of Dante. A deathly silence blankets the hangar and then-

Thunder is the first to attack. He lunges toward Dante who easily evades Thunder's grasp. Dante quickly sidesteps and delivers several fist blows to Thunder's ribs. This causes no effect to the hulking man.

Thunder swoops his clutched fist in a backhand motion, attempting to connect with Dante. Although the towering man is much stronger than his opponent, his agility is greatly lacking. Dante maneuvers around Thunder, facing him with his fists clutched.

As a boxer would bob and weave, Dante dances in front of Thunder. He delivers several left jabs to the face then follows with a right cross. Due to his arm reach, this was a lucky punch. This seems to catch Thunder slightly off guard. He steps back a moment then charges forward.

Dante swings again and again. This time, Thunder easily bats Dante's fists away as if he were swatting flies. Changing tactics, Dante swings his leg upward and kicks Thunder in the stomach. The towering man was waiting for this maneuver.

Thunder quickly reaches down and takes Dante by the leg. Dante delivers wild fist blows to Thunder's stomach and ribs. Thunder picks Dante up off the ground as he wraps his other arm around his chest.

Tipping his entire weight forward, Thunder begins to fall. Dante frantically attempts to free himself from Thunder's grasp. In a desperate effort, Dante manages to wiggle himself around, now on top of Thunder as they hit the ground. Dante's weight is no more than a marble dropping to the floor.

Thunder shoves Dante off of himself. Dante is sent reeling across the dirt floor of the hangar. The semicircle of spectators has drawn in a bit. Adolpho and Blake's groups has blended in with each other, now placing a flurry of side bets.

Dante leaps into the air and collides into Thunder from behind. He wraps his arms around Thunder's massive neck, attempting to secure a chokehold.

Thunder reaches up and around, grasping for the annoying little man on his back. Dante squeezes tighter and tighter. The crowds cheer. The side betting becomes more fierce. Thunder feels himself running out of air. Dante bears down on larger man's neck and throat.

Thunder charges across the arena, toward the edge of the roaring spectators. They see him closing in on them and instantly separate. Thunder continues onward with Dante recklessly clinging to his back.

Thunder spins around and slams Dante up against his trailer. The impact causes the trailer to tip upward. Over and over, Thunder slams Dante against the outside of the trailer. Intense pain rips through Dante's body.

Thunder takes a powerful step forward as he reaches up and behind himself. Taking two handfuls of his opponent's dreadlocks, Thunder rips Dante from his shoulders.

Dante is flung through the air like a simple ragdoll, seemingly helpless as the hard, dirt floor of the hangar draws near. He lands with a thud and topples for several moments. The enthusiastic crowd continues to cheer. Dante manages to get to his knee then to his feet.

Thunder is outraged at Dante's persistence. He turns and slams his opened palms against Dante's trailer, tipping it completely over onto its side. Thunder roars as he charges toward the littler man.

Dante clutches his fists and attempts to weave back and forth. His movements are becoming more sluggish. Thunder approaches him and swings his fists several times, each becoming more and more deadly.

Dante delivers a series of fist blows to Thunder's chin with minimal effect. Thunder slams his forearm into Dante's jaw sending him reeling to the ground. The gigantic man lunges toward Dante and straddles him.

K-WACK! K-WACK! K-WACK!

Dante's face is plummeted. He spits out a mouthful of blood then slumps to the dusty hangar floor. Thunder quickly raises up and thrusts his fists high into the air. He bellows out a triumphant battle cry as he turns to face the applauding crowds.

Blake and Reggie exchange a disconcerting look. Adolpho gloats as he extends his empty champagne glass for a refill. Thunder continues to wave his fists in the air, absorbing the approval of the on looking spectators.

Suddenly, the air falls deathly still. The constant cheering and applauds ceases. "Hey!" Dante shouts. "I'm still standin' here!" Thunder lowers his fists and slowly turns.

Dante stands upright with his fists tightly clutched at his sides. His breathing is heavy causing his chest to move up and down. Dante now stands nearly eye to eye with Thunder. The inner powers and strength of his alter have been revealed.

Dante has been anointed with the ability to mutate into not one, but two of his ancestors; the Sagittarians and the Arians. Like the time at Whiskey Ridge, Dante finds it fun, galloping along the riverbank with his biker family's children along his extended, bighorn sheep back. However today, this quadruped has chosen his other alter form.

Dante's pair of hooves are planted solidly along the dirt floor of the hangar. He slowly reaches down and takes the hanging waistband of his shredded jeans in hand as the faded blue fabric dangles along his hips.

Dante removes what's left of his jeans and tosses them to the side, into a pile next to his discarded and damaged boots. Never taking his eyes off of Thunder, Dante leans over and rips lose the securing Velcro straps of his knee brace. He adds the brace to his pile of belongings as he stomps a hoof in the dirt, causing a slight poof of dust.

Dante's shins and calves have slightly tapered. His thighs have expanded and appear to be covered with coarse, tan hair which becomes darker and runs all the way down to the crest of his sharp dark hooves.

The tan hair wraps around his entire waist and mysteriously blends into his flesh along his stomach, sides and lower back. Dante's human torso, arms and facial features remain intact. He slightly moves his neck from side to side, adjusting the newly acquired weight to his head.

Atop his forehead and directly below his forward hairline, a set of curved horns has emerged from within his skull. Each of the horns spiral and come to a curved tip, as those of a fully matured, male bighorn sheep. The Arian snorts.

Thunder cannot believe what he is seeing with this odd, mythological creature standing in front of him. He inches his way closer, slightly raising his clutched fists. Dante begins to slowly circle Thunder.

Now about ten feet away from each other, Dante arches his shoulders and brings his arms back. He lifts his right leg and lowers his head. Dante slams his hoof against the ground and charges forward.

Attempting to avoid the painful head on impact, Thunder reaches up and powerfully latches onto Dante's curved horns. The crowd go wild. The fight is still on!

Dante and Thunder circle each other, face to face. Dante feels that his body has been rejuvenated. The blood of his true heritage courses through his veins. He now feels stronger and more agile.

With Thunder's attention focused on the pair of curved horns, Dante is free to deliver a ruthless series of fist blows to his opponent's stomach and ribcage. Thunder painfully releases his grip. Dante slightly steps back a moment to survey Thunder's injuries. Then, he charges forward to end this fight.

LEFT - LEFT - RIGHT.

LEFT - LEFT - RIGHT.

LEFT - LEFT - K-BLAM!

Dante's uppercut to Thunder's lower jaw sends him reeling backward. The hulking man has been completely lifted off of his feet. He seems to be suspended in midair for a moment then crashes to the hangar floor. The sidelines of the arena reach a near frenzy. Dante is declared the winner!

Reggie races toward Dante to congratulate him. The Arian stands over one foot taller than his best friend. The side betting in the background has concluded. Adversaries pay-up their misguided wagers.

Adolpho stands hovering over Thunder who groans in pain and is still quite dazed. Eight well dressed associates of Adolpho approach Thunder, lean down and strain to lift him up off of the ground. They carry the large man out of the arena and toward the nearest luxury motor home.

Standing alongside of Dante and Reggie, Blake smiles at Adolpho; a mischievous smile. "Neat trick, Blake," Adolpho sneers as they shake hands. Although they are from opposite sides of the tracks, they are admirable competitors. A bet's a bet. Adolpho slightly raises his hand in the air.

From Adolpho's motor home, three well dressed associates appear, each carrying a pair of dark briefcases. They tote them through the departing luxury cars and limousines toward Blake's sleek home-on-wheels. "I see you made out alright, Blake," Dante says, with a smirk as he motions his head toward the six briefcases.

"So did you," Blake replies. His seductively dressed mistress comes up alongside of them carrying a camping style backpack. She hands it to Dante.

"I thought it'd be bigger."

"I can't say the same thing about you." Blake is still in awe at Dante's appearance and mysterious transformation. He reaches up and touches one of Dante's curved horns. Blake studies the blend of flesh and tan hair along Dante's waist then lower to the haunches and finally the sharp dark hooves.

"Don't even *think* about it!" Dante snaps.

"Think about what?" Blake answers with a curious tone.

"I can see the wheels in your head turning. This was my *last* fight. Win or lose."

"Well, you won. Let me know if you change your mind." Blake turns and begins heading after his mistress toward his motor home. "Good-luck, boys," he shouts over his shoulder.

Dante stares down at his newly acquired backpack for a moment. He smiles to himself and mumbles in his head, "*Win or lose, this was my last fight...*"

The massive blimp hangar is silent and losing light. All of the luxury cars, limousines, lavish motor homes and the pair of dressing room trailers have long departed.

Reggie sits sidesaddle on his trike next to Dante's motorcycle. Dante takes the last few stacks of money from the backpack and slides them inside of the opened flap of his saddlebags. "You put up a great fight," Reggie says with a smile.

"So, how'd you make out?" Dante asks, as he pulls his dark T-shirt over his head.

"I did alright," Reggie says as he reaches into a compartment along the rear fender. He retrieves a large roll of one hundred dollars bills. "I bet my trike you'd win."

Dante has fully mutated back into his human form. He slides into his black leather vest covered with patches and various insignias. Dante adjusts the waistband of his spare blue jeans resting on his hips as he walks across the hangar floor barefoot. He is unusually quiet. "Hey! What's the matter?"

Dante pauses and leans over. He retrieves his shredded pair of jeans and examines them a moment. Flinging the jeans over his shoulder, he leans down again and picks up his damaged boots. "I beat'im," he says, to himself.

Dante turns and begins heading back toward his parked motorcycle. Reggie can see there is something bothering his friend. "I *didn't* win... I *beat'im*!" Dante says as a matter of fact.

"Then what's wrong?"

"I trashed my last pair of boots..."

The autumn carnival is in full swing. The smell of fresh hotdogs and cotton candy fill the air. Children playfully squeal as the Ferris Wheel continues to spin around. Oceans of colorful light illuminates the sprawling area. Carney workers bark out their trade inside of their various booths of chance, inviting the countless families to try and win a prize.

The rattling tracks of the distant rollercoaster shakes the ground. Screams and laughter are heard all around as clowns and jugglers roam freely along the wide dirt pathways.

Several children attempt to snag the gold ring as they continue to ride the well preserved carousel. Hand carved mermaids, dolphins and mystical sea creatures appear to dance around in circles with clapping and waving parents looking on.

A circus like tent is seen toward the far end of the carnival. The red and white fabric is tightly secured to a series of thick poles and cables. A ring master sporting a black top hat and coattails stands at the opened flap of the tent, smiling and greeting people as they curiously enter. A sign hangs above the main entrance of the tent;

FREAKS OF THE WORLD

Standing at the opposite side of the ring master and opened flap of the tent, a Carney worker gathers tickets from the children and families as they creep inside, wondering what hideous creatures they are about to encounter.

With his leather satchel slung over his shoulder, tabloid writer Mason Spader appears at the end of the line of spectators making their way inward. He pulls in his jean jacket closer toward himself. The outside air is clear and chilly.

Mason smiles at the Carney worker as he flashes his *press badge.* The Carney worker motions Mason inside as the sleazy reporter clutches onto his satchel, concealing his camera inside. Just as Mason is about to enter the opened flap of the tent, a screech from the distance catches his attention.

A pair of twins playfully shove and push at each other along one of the wide dirt pathways. Jason and Julie, nearly sixteen years old, are a charming looking pair, casually yet warmly dressed, dark hair and dark eyes. They are a spitting image of their mother, Robbin.

Her athletic frame is hidden under the layers of shirts and a sweater. Robbin's long dark hair is secured in a ponytail allowing her pleasant facial features to shine through. From this distance, Mason can faintly make out their conversation-

"Mrs. Baxter," a Carney worker smiles. "It's good to see you. I see the kids are old enough this year to give it a try."

"Yes," Robbin says as she and the twins pause along side of the Carney worker, handing him their tickets. "I think they're finally big enough to go inside and… it's Ms. Baxter now."

"Yes, of course," the Carney worker humbly smiles. "Have fun and welcome… to The Tunnel of Terror!" The Carney worker evilly laughs.

Mason slightly ducks his head as he enters the red and white tent. The air is damp with a taste of lingering mildew. Atop tiki-like poles, lit torches appear along the winding pathways, creating eerie shadows across the inside areas of the large tent.

Mason joins a small gathering of people as they watch a very tattooed man swallowing the two foot blade of a sword. Mason slyly reaches into his leather satchel and retrieves his camera. So as not to draw too much attention, Mason casually snaps a few pictures without actually aiming. He stuffs his camera back into his satchel as he turns and strolls along the pathway of the odd exhibits.

Rounding the next corner of the tent, Mason comes across The Bearded Lady with The Dogboy sitting next to her.

Underneath her layers of facial hair, The Bearded Lady looks somewhat attractive and even tosses Mason and flirtatious wink.

The Dogboy is not as accommodating. He looks strikingly similar to a light brown Pomeranian. The odd looking creature lets out a growl toward Mason. The Dogboy bites in Mason's direction as the reporter snaps a few quick pictures then moves on.

Mason enters the next area and joins another group of spectators. Seated in matching throne-like chairs, a leopard tattooed man and a cat woman.

The inked man is normal looking enough. He is completely shaven, from head to toe. Over ninety percent of his body is covered with leopard spot tattoos. His entire head, face, neck and all other exposed areas are covered by the black, orange and tan spots.

However, the woman is quite creepy looking. Her extensive plastic surgery has somewhat disfigured her face.

Implanted whiskers protrude outward from above her upper lip with her cheekbones filled with saline forming lioness facial features. Her implanted fangs were to look like a wild jungle cat but instead look like a goblin.

Mason casually takes a few pictures of them then heads toward the next adjoining exhibit. He turns the corner of the red and white fabric and enters a slightly larger room. The surrounding lit torches cast dancing shadows across the inner tent with a large tank of water in the center of the area.

The aquarium of sorts is nearly fifteen feet long, ten feet wide and about ten feet deep. A handful of spectators stand around the large tank, looking at the Mermaid swimming inside.

Mason steps closer to the front of the tank, getting a better look at the half-woman-half-fish inside. The Mermaid is an obvious fake with a glued on tail attached around her waist. She constantly raises to the surface to fill her human lungs with air.

Mason studies the countless flaws in the Mermaid as she awkwardly swims inside of her tank. A newly arrived spectator slightly catches Mason's attention as he stands next to him.

Mason looks the tall man over, head to toe. He's charming looking with his long silver-gray hair tied back in a ponytail. His casual suit jacket and slacks dictates he's some kind of professional.

He's possibly an executive at the local computer corporation. Maybe a vice president at the home base of the coffee franchise. He could even be a senior foreman at the airplane factory that has been recently been laying off workers. Mason prides himself on being able to size people up. "So, what do you think of her?" Mason asks.

"Not too sure. I know she's not real."

"That's kinda obvious." Mason continues to study the tall man. He appears slightly offended by the Mermaid's façade. "You strike me as a man who's seen his share of strange things."

"You have no idea," Gordon says with a smile.

~ X ~

Brisk early morning traffic continues to roll along the interstate highway. Minivans carrying families to their favorite vacationing spots. Businessmen traveling to their next sales meetings. Semi trucks hauling an assortment of goods and livestock to a variety of markets. And of course, a rock and roll band heading to their next concert.

The Zøø Crüe's convoy is nothing less than spectacular. Four semi trucks with trailers and one custom bus for the band members. Each of the semi trucks and matching trailers are painted with their own motif; zebra, leopard, giraffe and peacock

The custom bus is painted with bright green colors, as if onlookers were standing in the middle of a jungle. Tropical trees, a waterfall and a wide assortment of plant life. Bringing up the far end of the convoy, Madam Zoey's pickup and camper.

Backstage is a flurry of activity with roadies and stagehands scurrying about. The background noise of the outdoor amphitheater is filled to capacity with chanting fans and stomping feet; they're ready for the show to begin!

Jon stands facing the extended mirror along the far side of the lavish dressing room, staring at himself. He has chosen not to wear his wolf's clothing. No furry chaps nor wolf's head and arm dressings. He simply wears black spandex pants and a loose fitting, dark colored tank-top.

Rafe's reflection appears in the mirror and approaches Jon from behind and the side. He twirls his pair of drumsticks along his fingers, limbering up his hands. Jon and Rafe exchange looks in the mirror with each other, turns away and stares at their own image in the smooth surface.

The tattooed cheetah spots covers Rafe's neck, chest, shoulders, arms and stomach. He reaches down and slightly adjusts his professional style basketball shorts of his favorite team. "Hey, Jon. Are you gonna vamp-out during the show?" Mark asks, as he continues to tune his six string guitar.

"No!" Jon says with a sharp tone. "That's the wrong legend."

"Sorry..." Mark shrugs his shoulders. He's already dressed out for the concert. Zebra spandex pants, black mohawk mane and matching black and white striped guitar.

Zoey is quite amused as she watches T-Bone pace across the lush carpet floor with his giraffe print bass guitar hanging loosely in front of himself. He seems to be murmuring to himself, possibly going over the lyrics of all the songs running through his head.

T-Bone's costume is slightly different than his earlier concerts. Instead of donning his large, Texas longhorn headgear, he sports a smaller pair of horns, similar to a musk ox with his hairy, Pan-like legs secured by suspenders hanging over his shoulders.

Zoey stands from her thick cushioned chair and approaches Rafe from the side. She looks herself over in the mirror. The Gothic schoolgirl-look really works for her.

"Alright, guys! It's show time!" Rick announces, as he bursts in through the dressing room door. He adjusts his black top hat, completing his ring master costume.

T-Bone and Mark are the first ones out the door. They race down the smooth, concrete hallway behind Rick. The thundering applauds and cheering fills their ears. A small army of uniformed security guards holds back the screaming, costumed fans as they all want a piece of The Zøø Crüe.

Jon, Rafe and Zoey explode from the dressing room door. They are consumed with adoring fans. The mishmash of spectators swarm the three of them as they attempt to make their way to the stage. With Jon taking the lead, Rafe and Zoey are slightly separated. "Rafe!" Zoey calls out, as a security guard pushes her back toward the concrete wall.

"Hey," Rafe barks. "Lay off. She's with me!" Rafe rushes toward the security guard and stands toe to toe. He lets out a low growl, greatly intimidating the security guard. Taking her by the hand, Rafe leads Zoey through the screaming mob. Zoey smiles.

"*She's with me,*" she replays in her head.

"Hello, Nampa!" Jon yells into his microphone headset. He swings his peacock printed, single neck guitar in front of himself. The mass assembly of concertgoers are on their feet. A wave of bodies flows across the full capacity, horseshoe shaped outdoor amphitheater.

T-Bone finds his mark at right stage, as Mark makes his way to left stage, finding his position slightly in front of the black and white, zebra striped grand piano. T-Bone begins and repeats a low bass line as a spotlight softly shines on him-

THUMP - THUMP - THUMP - THUMP.

THUMP - THUMP - THUMP - THUMP.

THUMP - THUMP - THUMP - THUMP.

THUMP - THUMP - THUMP - THUMP.

Ever so softly, Mark joins in with an eerie guitar solo and introduction with an additional spotlight bringing him into view along the opposite side of the stage. Jon stands center stage, waving his hands toward the costumed concertgoers amassed in the festival seating area. Suddenly, the music stops and is overtaken by a hypnotic drum pattern.

Rafe's double-bass and drumsticks pound out the rhythmatic sounds of a Native war chant. Slowly, ever so slowly building. Jon, Mark and T-Bone recklessly dance across the stage as Rafe continues to intensify his thundering and hypnotic drum pattern.

In unison, Jon, Mark and T-Bone turn and leap into the air with their cordless instruments slung over their shoulders. They each land onto their well placed, yellow trampolines positioned in the floor of the stage.

The three musicians complete their summersaults then land solidly at the front of the stage as the footlights explode with brightness.

Mark and T-Bone strum their guitars to Rafe's drum pattern as Jon leaps from trampoline to trampoline, hurling himself wildly through the air. Rafe's drum beat gracefully changes and continues to repeat itself like the sounds of a low heartbeat-

BUM - BUMP.
BUM - BUMP.
BUM - BUMP.
BUM - BUMP.

Jon springs through the air, leaping from trampoline to trampoline. Completing a full summersault, he lands at center stage facing the cheering audience. Jon waves his hands in the air in a coaxing manner, "*Let-me en-ter tain-yooou! Let-me en-ter tain-yooou!*" Jon seems to be singing with his wild body movements.

A thundering series of explosions and pyrotechnics fills the stage. T-Bone rolls his fingers across the strings of his bass as Jon and Mark join in with lead and rhythm. Rafe pounds away at his drums. Let the spectacle begin!

"Well, Rafe," Jon says, as he catches his breath from the last song of the set. Rafe and Jon stand off stage, just beyond the drawn back curtains with T-Bone and Mark close by. "Are you ready?"

The audience has reached a near feeding frenzy. They chant and stomp their feet for another encore. The stage is dark and empty. All that remains is Rafe's towering lime green drum set along the back center of the outdoor amphitheater.

"Let's rock!" Rafe says, with an eager smile. T-Bone and Mark are puzzled as they remain off stage. What are the brothers up to? Rafe and Jon slip through the shadows and disappear into the darkness as the ranting crowd continues to cheer. The stage is dark and quiet for several moments and then-

Rafe begins a low and ominous drum solo. He is blanketed by the soft green spotlight as it continues to slowly brighten. The double-bass drum shakes the floorboards of the stage. His sticks hammer against the deep floor tom-toms creating a hypnotic pattern.

The strings of Jon's custom "X" guitar screech as would sharp fingernails across a chalkboard. He steps into view with his orange spotlight centered on him. Jon remains at right stage, usually where T-Bone stands. He smiles at Rafe and gives him an approving nod.

Rafe releases a drum riff across the row of mounted tom-toms. Jon answers back with a thundering replay of the four thick strings of his bass guitar. The three-way duel begins!

Rafe begins a constant bass drum pattern, almost tribal and savage. With his drumsticks, he pounds out a melodic pattern against the mounted tom-toms. Jon mimics the invitation with his bass guitar.

Although both instruments are quite dissimilar, they are almost identical with the melody. With his left hand, Jon flies his fingers across the six strings, echoing the previous bass guitar riff.

The pace quickens. Once extended measures of music battling back and forth are now swifter replies. The three-way duel is not to be better than ones brother but to bring out the best in each of them. They are working together. The brothers sound like they had at the University.

With a flurry of crashing cymbals, Rafe subdues his drum solo and simply focuses on his left footed high-hat. The speed of his foot looks similar to a basketball player dribbling a basketball at a high rate-

CLICK - CLICK - CLICK - CLICK.

CLICK - CLICK - CLICK - CLICK.

Jon has repositioned himself and stands at forward center stage. The costumed fans consuming festival seating wildly dance about, screaming and waving their hands into the air.

Jon's fingers race across both sets of strings of his guitars. Faster and faster as they continue to beautifully blend together with the drum pattern.

His fingernails mutate, taking the form of claws. The tops of his hands quickly sprout dark colored fur which rapidly spreads all the way up his arms then across his shoulders, back and torso.

Jon's chest expands outward forming into the ribcage of a massive wolf. Beneath his black spandex pants, his lower extremities are covered with dark fur. Jon's bare feet have transformed into claws which support the upright wolf-like creature.

He raises his head and arches his back. Jon's lower jaw and cheekbones extend outward forming into a fully developed wolf's muzzle. The beast howls as he slams down the last ringing chord of his raging guitar solo and bass guitar riff.

The upright wolf slightly wags his furry tail as he lowers his custom "X" guitar and steps to the side of the stage allowing Rafe the limelight. Rafe's feet hammer against the foot pedals of his double-bass drum. It's now his turn to shine.

Rafe's hands clutch on to his chewed-up looking drumsticks, pounding at the mounted tom-toms. The thundering double-bass continues to shake the stage. Rafe's flesh begins to mutate.

It appears that Rafe's tattooed cheetah spots have been strategically placed. Short, tawny brown fur with a hint of yellow quickly spreads out and across his back and shoulders. Hundreds of black spots emerge from his fur, almost identically where his human counterpart has been tattooed.

Rafe's non-retractable claws grasp onto the drumsticks with a flurry of pounding drum riffs. His stomach tapers with his spotted chest expanding and becoming more deep. From the rear waistband of his basketball shorts, a thick round tail appears. The light brown fur of his tail is covered with black spots and a white tuft at the end.

Rafe's eyes have transformed in color and now appear orange with circular pupils. His head has slightly narrowed with small, round ears covered with black spots. A set of white whiskers sticks out from above his mutated upper lip with a dark colored, heart shaped nose.

A common characteristic of a cheetah, a pair of teardrop strands of black fur run down from the inside corner's of the feline's eyes, down the opposite bridges of his wide nose and taper to the corners of his mouth.

The cheetah remains seated on the drum set's swiveling stool. He blasts out a furious series of cymbal crashes and tom-tom riffs. His forepaws and lower claws are but a mere blur.

From side stage, the wolf screams a guitar chord, slams a bass guitar note and strolls back into view. Simultaneously, the strange canine and the odd feline slam the last chord. The stage falls dark; the crowd is uncontrollable!

Directly off the side of the stage, Rick, T-Bone and Mark are dumbfounded with the jaws gapping open; they had no idea that Rafe had similar talents as his brother Jon. Zoey simply smiles. The thunderous cheers and applauds of the spectators is nearly deafening.

Then, from the darkened shadows of rear area of the stage, a familiar drum solo and intro begins. The beating drums of the cheetah is quickly joined by the melodic sounds of the wolf's accompaniment. It's the beginning of a song that Mark and T-Bone know well.

It's an upbeat, rock and roll tune The Von Dutch Brother's managed to get on the air at a local radio station when they were just starting out. It did very well on the charts as well.

The wolf stands at forward center stage as the lights slowly come up. He has opted to switch out the custom "X" instrument with his oddly designed black and white, single neck guitar. The furry beast seems to be smiling as he waves Mark and T-Bone to join them.

T-Bone slings his bass guitar strap over his shoulder and steps onto stage. His fingers glide across the four thick strings as he flawlessly picks up with the drum solo and guitar introduction of the song.

As T-Bone finds his place along the right side of the stage, Mark strums along the strings of his zebra print guitar providing the lead. The wolf nods over to T-Bone then to Mark.

The creature seems to be coaxing them to sing the lead vocals. With the extensive transformation of certain parts of their anatomy, Rafe and Jon are now unable to sing. However, they are more than happy to provide an occasional growl and hiss.

The loud, upbeat tune is rough and animalistic, as if The Zøø Crüe had been *unchained*!

Continuing their encore, Mark and T-Bone supply the harmonic lead vocals. As they continue to play their instruments, they toss casual glances at their altered fellow band members. What does the future hold for a rock and roll band with a drum playing cheetah and a guitar playing werewolf?

A light breeze rolls through the landscaped trees of The Zoo. There is a chill in the air as the nearly full moon hangs low in the nighttime sky. It is mysteriously quiet throughout the various exhibits, pens, cages and artificially constructed natural habitats.

A group of primates appear slightly nervous as they huddle together. A family of zebras anxiously gallop around in wild circles. An elephant mother tightens her loving trunk around her calf. The timid giraffes swiftly turn in for the night. The macaws aren't... macawing.

A pair of night janitors, wearing matching, dark blue jumpsuits, appear along the concrete walkway totting their extended push brooms over their shoulders. Their way is guided by the illuminated lampposts strategically placed throughout the walkways of The Zoo.

As quickly as the janitors had appeared, they vanish around the corner of the walkway. A low roar from the nearby lion's exhibit echoes through the darkness. A slight rustling causes a gathering of shrubs to part.

A dark clothed figure steps out from the shadows. From the outline and movements, this intruder is a man. He is dressed from head to toe in a snug fitting black outfit and black leather gloves. Dangling from his left hip, a black pouch, no larger than a grocery store's loaf of bread.

The man wears a utility belt of sorts around his waist, similar to a police officer with filled pouches, an assortment of black carrying cases and a holstered weapon at his right hip. A black knit ski mask conceals his facial features making him almost Ninja looking in appearance.

As the man cautiously makes his way along the walkway, he passes by the lion's exhibit. The male lion studies the man as he makes his way along the handrailing lining the spectator area of his domain. The lion can sense that this outsider is up to no good.

The dark clothed man pauses as he faces The Zoo's featured exhibit, Keiko and Jaakko. There's no sign of movement beyond the deep ravine and throughout the habitat of trees and boulders.

The man reaches into the black pouch along his left hip and retrieves an extremely thick, raw steak. He hurls it across the ravine. The steak lands near the opening of the cave leading deep into the caged containment areas. A low growl seeps outward from deep inside the cave.

Keiko timidly peers her head outside. She sniffs the air, absorbing the scent of the steak. Keiko cautiously steps forward and takes a lick of the steak. Her human instinct knows better.

As she sniffs the steak again, the man reaches for his right hip and draws a tranquillizer gun. Just as Keiko takes the steak into her wide mouth, the man fires a dart.

The needle pierces her tan fun along her right, upper shoulder. She bolts back into the cave with the steak clutched in her mouth. From the darkness of the stone and concrete dwelling, Keiko lets out a defeated roar.

Without hesitation, the man leaps into the air, effortlessly clearing the top of the handrailing and deep ravine. He lands with the utmost stealth, never making a sound. As he quietly makes his way toward the cave opening, he reloads the handgun with another tranquillizer dart. From inside the cave, a frightened roar blurts out.

Jaakko lunges from the darkness. His forepaws are fully extended outward with his razor sharp claws preparing to attack the intruder. The man swiftly raises his gun and fires a dart.

The needle is embedded into Jaakko's neck, close to his furry throat. The large feline is suspended in midair for a moment as the tranquillizer quickly takes effect. Jaakko loses all bodily control as he falls limp and crashes to the ground at the man's feet.

The man squats down near the tigon's head. He reaches into one of his many pouches and retrieves a needle and syringe. Making sure he has found one of the main arteries of the large feline, he injects the odd colored serum.

The man returns the empty syringe to the pouch then removes a thin, aluminized emergency blanket from yet another pouch around his waist. The man covers Jaakko with the blanket and remains crouched over him.

The man is eager to see the results of the serum he's spent years developing. He's discovered a combination of elements that greatly effects beings who are able to shift their bodies, forcing them to return to their human form.

The man has traveled for nearly a decade, traveling around the country in a two-story laboratory on wheels. He has provided much needed medical assistance for the homeless population while conducting his less than ethical experiments on others. However, that's not all he's discovered.

The serum runs through Jaakko's veins causing him to transform. The tigon's tail disappears under the shiny blanket. His body mass retracts in size. His black, triangular nose, whiskers and muzzle mutates into human facial features.

From along the edges of the blanket, Jay's feet, ankles, arms and hands begin to take form. The light tan and orange fur with traces of black stripes vanishes into his flesh.

Now able to handle this human boy and not a four hundred pound feline, the man reaches down and wraps the silver blanket around him. With the three day, full moon cycle approaching, Jay will be much easier to handle and control. The man heaves Jay up and over his shoulder. He walks to the edge of the ravine and leaps into the air.

The man lands on the opposite side of the handrailing and spectator area. He pauses a moment. There are no spying eyes to witness his abduction. He adjusts Jay's weight on his shoulder and dashes toward the shrubs.

As he and the kidnapped boy disappear into the darkness, a mother begins to stir and lets out a painful roar. She's realized that her only offspring has been taken from her.

Gordon stands on his back deck sipping on a steaming mug of coffee. He appears happy and content with his surroundings as the rising sun peeks its orange head up and over the distant horizon of The Sound. The growing rays of light sprinkle across the rolling water and begin to warm Gordon's cheeks.

RING - RING.

RING - RING.

Gordon tightens his bathrobe's loosely tied belt around his waist before turning and entering his back living room through the opened sliding glass door. He moves across the floor, shuffling his cartoon character slippers over the thinning carpet. Just as the telephone rings again, Gordon picks up the receiver. "Hello?"

Gordon's carefree attitude quickly fades away as he listens to the voice on the other end of the phone. The color from his cheeks and the warmth of the morning sun dissipates.

Gordon sets his mug onto the wooden planked coffee table. Nearly in shock, he slowly sits down on the couch, carefully listening to his instructions.

"It's really nice to have you back, Chloe," Larry says with a cheerful smile. He's as damper as usual sporting his professional looking attorney's suit.

Chloe sits behind her desk with the morning sun filling the picture window directly behind her. She's dressed in a light lavender business jacket, white blouse and a dark colored, knee high skirt. Chloe looks refreshed and full of energy. "It's good to be back, Larry."

"I hope you worked out what you needed to."

"Well," Chloe smiles. "Let's just say it's an ongoing project." She looks at the thick case files in Larry's hand. "I assume those are for me." Larry places the thick stack of case files on the corner of her desk.

"We have a lot of work to do," Larry says with wink. He saunters away from Chloe's desk and approaches the opened door of his office. Larry turns and looks over his shoulder. "How 'bout lunch? To catch up on what you've been up to?"

"Lunch? I don't think we'll have time. *We have a lot of work to do*," Chloe playfully mimics, as she waves the thick case files at Larry. The Assistant District Attorney smiles and enters his office.

"*Yeah, it's really nice to have you back*," he thinks.

Chloe's lavender business jacket hangs on the backrest of her chair. Remaining seated behind her desk, she places a folder of documents onto the stack of completed case files. The stack of files is dwindling. She looks up and into Larry's office.

Larry paces back and forth across the custom Persian floor rug. He has removed his suit jacket and loosened his tie. Chloe is amused with Larry's animated hand movements.

His lips move as if he were speaking to a judge or addressing a jury. Chloe loves watching Larry rehearse for an upcoming trial. "Larry!" Sonja shrieks, as she charges into the waiting room. Chloe is startled and nearly leaps out of her chair.

Sonja races passed Chloe without acknowledging her. Her one piece, older style looking dress flutters behind as she crashes into Larry's office. "Sonja, what's wrong?"

"Jay's gone," Sonja says with tears in her eyes. She falls into Larry's arms. "When I woke up this morning, he wasn't there!"

"Did you tell the staff?"

"I couldn't tell them. I closed the exhibit instead. It's the full moon tonight."

"We need to call the police," Larry insists as he moves toward the telephone.

"...and tell them what? My ten year old son is roaming the streets of The City? Put up posters. *Missing - four hundred pound tigon - if seen, please call The Zoo*?"

"That's not what I meant, Sonja. Maybe he just wants to explore alone."

"That's just it, he's *alone*!"

"Larry..." Chloe timidly says, as she peeks her head in through the opened door of his office. Larry picks up the receiver of the telephone and begins to dial the police. "Larry!" Chloe says with urgency.

"What, Chloe?" Larry snaps.

"You have a call waiting on line three."

"Now's really not a good time."

"Larry." Chloe's tone is saddened and almost remorseful. "You *need* to take this call." Larry and Sonja exchange a frightened look. Is it Jay? Larry slowly brings the receiver to his ear as he presses line three on the multi-line telephone.

"Hello?"

"Hello, Larry," Gio says from the other end. "Busy day so far?"

"Where's Jay?"

"Oh, he's with me. He's safe and sleeping right now." Gio becomes arrogant and quite smug. "You know growing boys need their rest."

"What do you want?"

"That's what I've always liked about you, right to business. Here's the deal. Gordon has something that I want and I have something that you want." Gio pauses. "How 'bout a trade?"

"When?"

"Tomorrow night. You don't even need to ask where. You *know* where."

CLICK!

Larry is quiet as he hangs up the receiver. He looks at Sonja. She's trembling with her eyes filled with fear. Larry moves toward Sonja and lovingly takes her in his arms. Feeling dismissed, Chloe moves from the opened doorway of Larry's office. "Chloe?"

"Yes, Larry?"

"This concerns you, too." Larry smirks. "Ready for a little road trip?"

"Dinner smells great! Whatta we havin'?" Kaleen asks, as she makes her way into the kitchen. She sports Tez's favorite professional football jersey. A Dallas, Texas blue star with white trim along the top of each of the short sleeves.

"Chinese okay with you?" Tez smiles, as he scoops a large spoonful of noodles from a white, square takeout box. He's half dressed for work. Faded blue jeans, a rock and roll band's T-shirt and his dark sunglasses.

"Yeah, that sounds great," Kaleen says, as she tosses her fingers through her damp, loose hair draped along her shoulders. As quietly as she can, Kaleen moves in toward the counter and reaches for a fortune cookie. Without missing a beat, Tez playfully smacks the top of her hand.

"Not till *after* dinner," he says, with a smile. Shaking her head, Kaleen takes her plate of food from the counter and finds her chair along the dining room table. She's still amazed in some of the things Tez is still able to do. His other senses are much more acute than hers.

He has no need of a seeing-eye dog nor the use of a white and red tipped walking stick. As other sight challenged people, who are forced to memorize how many steps it is to the bathroom or how many steps then turn left into the kitchen, Tez has tapped into his altered state abilities.

Tez roams freely around the kitchen. His sonar frequencies of his alter form notify him of various obstacles and potential dangers. With a plate of noodles and sweet and sour pork in hand, he gracefully walks toward the dining room table as a sighted man would, sits and joins Kaleen for dinner.

"So, I see you're still working at Ce' Laguna," Tez says with a mouthful of sweet and sour pork. She has a puzzled look on her face. "Ce' Laguna's website also lists its staff." Tez pauses a moment. "I'm sorry to hear about your friend, that trainer who was killed by that orca."

"Yeah, me too..." is all Kaleen can manage to say. She appears slightly distracted, as she takes a bite of spicy noodles.

"Are they gonna release it back into the ocean or put it down?" Tez can feel Kaleen scowling at him. "Sorry, subject change. Duh!"

RING - RING.

RING - RING.

"I'll get it." Kaleen raises up from the dining table and shuffles across the kitchen. She snaps up the receiver from the mounted, cordless telephone hanging from the wall. "Hello?"

Kaleen smiles as she hears a friendly voice she hasn't heard from in years. "Yeah, Larry. It's Kaleen. How've you been?" She pauses a moment. "Yeah, he's here. Hold on a sec." Kaleen cups her hand over the phone's mouthpiece as she makes her way over to the dining table. "I didn't know you and Larry were keeping in touch."

"Neither did I." Tez wipes his mouth and takes the receiver from Kaleen. "Hey, Larry. It's been awhile." At first, Tez appears cheerful, hearing from an old friend. Then, his expression changes, that of concern and imminent danger. "Yeah, we'll be there..."

"You two were the last ones *I* expected to see here," Gordon says with a welcoming smile. "You left the gate open." He shakes hands with Reggie then Dante. Gordon's casual attire seems fitting for his rural dwelling; jeans, a sweater and loafers.

Dante and Reggie begin to feel the effects of the late afternoon air. Their black leather vests with various patches and insignias provides little protection from the setting sun outside.

The rustic living room is dark and unlived in like vacationers who had just arrived at their summer home. "Why are you creeping around with the lights off?"

"We, ah..." Reggie hesitates.

"We're kinda on the run," Dante adds.

"Well, either you *are* or you're *not*." Gordon smirks.

"We're on the run," Reggie says, as a matter of fact as he heads for the closed front door.

"It really wasn't our fault," Dante chimes in as he follows Reggie out onto the front porch. Gordon appears from the shadows of the living room and stands along the wooden handrailing of his wraparound porch.

"We're supposed to meet up with Larry to see if we can't clear this up. We thought we'd hangout here till then."

"...if you don't mind," Dante humbly says.

"I don't mind at all, boys. Stay here as long as you need to." Gordon looks out across the field separating his home and the two-story barn in the near distance. His older model, red and white VW microbus appears parked a few yards away from the closed, large double doors of the barn.

"We put the bikes inside," Dante says as he steps off the porch. He quickly turns and looks up at Gordon who remains leaning over the handrailing. "Whatta *you* doin' here, professor?"

"It's funny you should ask..."

"She looks exhausted, Larry. You're not *working* her too hard are you?" Sonja asks in a playful tone. She looks directly at his reflection in the rearview mirror attached to the front windshield. Chloe sits in the backseat of Larry's expensive automobile with her head propped against the rear window. She's fast asleep.

Chloe's half covered up with a borrowed comforter. Her matching, light colored sweat outfit keeps the chill away. The cool, nighttime air slips inward from Larry and Sonja's slightly rolled down front windows. "Not working her too much at all. She's just returned from a..." Larry struggles to find the right wording. "*An extended leave of absence,"* he finally replies.

Larry fiddles with the leather steering wheel as he continues to drive along the desolate highway. He's dressed as if he were on his way to the gym for a workout with gray sweats and tennis shoes. "She's still having issues with Zoey."

"I thought she would've outgrown that by now. She needs some professional help, Larry." It appears that before they departed The City, Larry and Sonja made a quick pit stop at a local boutique. Sonja's colorful, snug fitting dress complements her curvaceous figure.

"She'll work it out when she's ready to work it out," Larry says in a fatherly manner. Sonja glances at the digital clock along the center console just above the quiet radio.

"We're running late," Sonja says. She looks out through the passenger's window and takes in the familiar surroundings. "A few miles up ahead, there's a shortcut."

"I don't think that's a good idea, Sonja."

"Why not? We need to make up some time." Larry tosses her a playful smile.

"The last shortcut I took, I almost ended up married..."

"I wasn't sure if you two were gonna make it," Gordon says, shaking Jon's hand.

"What? *Us* miss one of *your* parties? Not a chance!" Rafe steps forward and likewise, greets their former professor. Directly behind them, their recently unretired, brightly painted, custom van is seen parked near Gordon's microbus;

♫ ♪ ♫ The Dutch Brothers ♫ ♪ ♫

"Look, the Rock Stars made it!" Reggie smiles, as he rushes toward Rafe and gives him a bear hug. Dante and Jon shake hands. Gordon is slightly distracted and turns his head. A pair of headlights pierces through the darkness, running along the narrow roadway heading closer to the sprawling property.

The yellow and black checkered taxicab rolls to a halt at the edge of the clearing. Jon approaches the rear passenger door and flings it open. Kaleen steps out and gives Jon a big hug. "How've you been? You look terrific," Jon says.

"Hey, dude." Reggie extends his opened palm and takes Tez by the hand, assisting him out of the other side of the taxicab.

"Reggie? It's good to see you," Tez replies with a satirical tone.

"Yeah, you too." Reggie leads Tez away from the taxicab and shuts the rear door with his hip. He maneuvers Tez around the front of the taxicab and joins the rest of the group.

The air is filled with sporadic chit-chat and greetings from the long lost group of friends. Each catching up on the other's lives, what's been going on. Oh, you've lost some weight.

The taxicab completes a turnaround and begins heading out and along the narrow roadway. The brake lights flicker as the taxicab is forced to the extreme side of the roadway.

Appearing around the tree lined curve, a massive set of blinding headlights. The taxicab honks a few times before managing to steer around the curve and disappears from sight. The headlights pause a moment then slowly continues forward. "There goes the neighborhood..." Dante mumbles.

Gio steers his two-story, med-lab on wheels into the clearing. He rolls to a halt, away from the barn and parked vehicles. There is a mysterious hesitation throughout the group of friends. Gordon steps forward in an attempt to show he's still in control of the situation.

The bus's front door opens. Gio appears from within and plants his bare feet onto the ground. He wears a matching white, silk sweat suit with a pair of black stripes running down the outer sleeves and legs.

There are no greetings nor polite chit-chat. There are no welcoming smiles. He closes the bus's door then slowly makes his way into the clearing.

Gio turns and faces Gordon. Defiantly, he motions his hand for his former mentor to join him. "Let me take'im," Dante whispers in Gordon's ear. Reggie comes up alongside of Dante.

"Kick his ass... *again*!"

"What? You don't think I can hold my own?" Gordon asks the younger gladiator.

"It's not that," Dante says, in a concerned tone. "It's just that you're..."

"*Old*?" Gordon smiles.

"I wasn't gonna say that." Dante is embarrassed. "I was gonna say, *well aged*."

"I have to do something to help my nephew." Gordon pats Dante on the shoulder. "It'll be alright." He glances over the concerned faces of his former students. Gordon turns and begins heading into the clearing.

Gio halfway unzips his sweat suit jacket and rolls his shoulders. Never taking his eyes of off Gordon, he slowly approaches the elder man.

Gordon slides out of his sweater and hands it to Kaleen. Without missing a step, he kicks off his hippy-style sandals. He and Gio now stand only a few yards away from each other. "Where is he, Giovanni?"

"He's in the rig. I would've never hurt him." Gio takes a few steps forward. "All I wanted was the secret."

"There *is* no secret! How many times do I have to explain that to you?"

"That's *not* what my father told me."

"You're father?" Gordon takes an unsure step forward. "I don't know your father."

"Reece Taylor was my father..."

"*Was*?"

"He died about six years ago. But you would've *known* that if you would've kept in touch... *if* you were friends."

"I'm sorry."

"Are you?" Gio snaps. "You're probably relieved that he died. Relieved that he met his Maker before he could tell me the secret."

"There *is* no secret!" Gordon realizes that there is no convincing Gio of this. "Fine then, let's get this over with." Gordon and Gio slowly begin to circle each other, the predator and the prey. However, which is which? Gio slightly arches his shoulders back and positions his hands outward preparing to attack.

HONK - HONK.

Gio eases his stance and turns his attention to the narrow roadway. A pair of beaming headlights race along, quickly approaching them. Larry skids his car to a sideways halt causing a cloud of dust. Gio sneers.

Larry steps through the settling cloud of dust as a Western gunslinger would appear along Main Street for a final shootout. "Sorry, I'm late. I took a shortcut."

"You didn't end up married, did you?" Gordon playfully asks.

"No, but thanks for asking." Gordon approaches Larry and gives him a fatherly handshake. Suddenly, Sonja bounds from the car and glares at Gio.

"You sonuva-bitch! Where is he?"

"He's fine, dear," Gordon says, as he tenderly kisses Sonja on the forehead. Reggie and Dante toss Larry a welcoming nod. Rafe and Jon casually wave hello. Chloe appears from along the opposite side of Larry's car. Rafe smiles. Kaleen tightens her grip on Tez's arm. She is anxious to witness the coming events.

"Smells like the gang's all here!" Tez announces in an attempt to lighten the mood. However, his attempt has failed. Larry leans back, against the hood of his car and slips out of his tennis shoes.

"Larry..." Dante approaches Larry and places his hand on his shoulder. "You don't have to do this. It's *not* your fight."

"Yes, it is." Larry smiles, "Jay's my son..."

~ XI ~

"Jay? Wake up," Sonja whispers into her son's ear. Jay is restrained at the wrists, tightly strapped to the armrests of the examining chair inside of Gio's dimly lit, medical bus. His ankles are likewise bound to the lower leg rests of the chair. Jay is covered in a light blue, hospital type gown, tied in place under his arms and at the waist.

Jay slightly moans with his eyes fluttering. The combination of tranquilizers and the specially developed serum is wearing off. "Mom? Where am I?"

"It'll be alright, Jay." Sonja tugs at the restraints around his wrists. The built-in locks of the straps won't budge. She raises up from him and begins searching the surrounding counters and drawers for the keys or something to pry open the restraints.

As she frantically makes her way passed the metallic counter top, she approaches the glass door of a small refrigerator. Inside along the shelves, Sonja sees the rows of laboratory racks filled with small bottles of pharmaceutical drugs, medications, raw chemicals and serums. She turns pale.

Sonja opens the refrigerator door and takes a small bottle in hand. She carefully examines it and reads the handwritten inscription;

Sonja Jamison

"I'll be right back," Sonja says before kissing Jay on the forehead. Clutching onto the small bottle, Sonja storms toward the bus's rear door and bolts outside.

"Gio!" Sonja angrily shouts. "Gio, what is this?" She waves the small bottle at Gio as she quickly approaches him standing in the center of the clearing.

Dante and Reggie exchange a curious glance. Directly across from them, Kaleen continues to cling to Tez's arm. Around the semicircle, Jon, Rafe and Chloe. Completing the spherical gathering, Gordon and Larry eagerly watch Sonja and Gio's verbal confrontation. "That's for you, Sonja."

"What is it?"

"I've discovered the cure for your disease," Gio says in a gloating manner. "In a few weeks, that drug will purge the disease from your system. You'll be completely healed."

Sonja is at a loss of words. Her heart is filled with conflicting emotions. She is angry with the abduction of her son and joyous that soon she will be cured. "But, why?"

"It was the only way Gordon would tell me the secret. I would've never hurt the boy." Gio reaches into the pocket of his white sweat pants and retrieves a set of keys. He tosses them to Sonja. "The thing is..." An evil smiles rolls across Gio's lips. "The combination is very tricky. Only *I* know the proper dosage."

Gio focuses his attention to Gordon and Larry. Gio steps forward and faces them. "I win, you give me the secret," he says to Gordon then turns toward Larry. "You win, Sonja gets to keep the cure."

"I can live with that." Larry smiles at Gio then at Gordon. "Can you live with that?"

"Yeah, I can," Gordon says with a smirk. "Good-luck." Gordon fatherly pats Larry on the shoulder. Gio and Larry never take their eyes off of each other. They step away from Gordon and inch their way to the center of the clearing.

Looking over his shoulder, Larry gives Sonja a tender smile. "*It'll be alright,*" he seems to be saying. With the keys in one hand and the small bottle in the other, Sonja turns and races back toward the opened rear door of the medical bus. From about five feet away, Gio and Larry begin to circle each other.

Gordon and his former students spread out along the perimeter of the clearing creating a large circle. Gordon appears to be guiding them into place using unspoken commands and subliminal directions. Unbeknownst to all of them, they stand positioned along their proper placement of the Zodiac Chart.

Oddly, Gordon stands in what appears to be in between two signs, Sagittarius and Scorpio, as if there is one astrological sign missing.

Freed from his restraints, Jay appears from the opened rear door of the bus. Clutching onto the small bottle containing her cure, Sonja follows behind as they join Rafe along the bottom right corner of the circle. Although the three of them are separated by their variety of alter forms, they collectively share the same sign.

An eerie stillness fills the air. In a fatherly manner, Gordon nods at Larry who simply smiles. The assembly of watchful eyes follows Larry as he continues to slowly circle Gio.

The doctor slightly raises his hands and holds them out in front of himself as a wrestler preparing for an attack. Larry and Gio glare at each other and then-

Gio delivers a series of punches that miss Larry. He swiftly maneuvers himself around and throws several jabs that find their target. Larry is slightly caught off guard as he takes a few steps back. He reaches up and wipes away a trail of blood from the corner of his mouth.

Larry charges forward and delivers several fist blows to Gio's face then stomach. Gio is stunned as he reaches up to his broken nose, slightly wiggling the damaged cartilage.

Gio rushes Larry and tackles him. The two competitors wrestle in the dirt, struggling for control amidst a growing cloud of dust. They each fight to gain the advantage. Around and around with sporadic knee blows and punches. From within the dust cloud, a low growl is heard.

Larry and Gio manage to get to their feet, facing each other as they grasp onto the other's arms and shoulders. Larry's hands begin to mutate and enlarge. Orange fur sprouts out from his flesh and quickly covers the tops of his hands.

Gordon is filled with apprehension as he continues to watch Larry and Gio battle. He feels a slight patter on his shoulder. Looking upward and slightly around, Gordon sees that it has begun to drizzle. More of a heavy mist blanketing the area.

Gio digs is transforming fingers into Larry's shoulders. The thick, black claws powerfully rips his sweat jacket from his back. The damaged garment falls to the ground.

Larry swoops his tiger claws outward, swiping Gio's face. Three precise incisions appear along Gio's cheek and jaw line. He roars at Larry.

Gio's chest expands with his waist beginning to taper inward. His ears mutate upward along his head, shaping and molding into feline characteristics. Smooth, black fur overtakes his scalp and continues along the back of his neck. Gio's face expands outward, quickly taking the shape of a muzzle.

Below his pink, triangular nose, light colored whiskers sprout from Larry's upper mouth area. The opposing black panther moves his head to the side, attempting to bite the transforming tiger along the neck. Both of the large felines remains upright, supporting themselves on their mutating hind legs.

The tiger bares his black claws into the panther's shoulders, powerfully shredding the white silk sweat suit jacket. The panther lands on the ground on all fours. He swipes his sharp claws several times along the tiger's gray sweat pants.

The tiger viciously bites at the panther. He takes a firm grip at the panther's hind leg, tearing away the white sweat pants. The accumulating drizzle has grown to a light rain, causing the dust to settle and begins to create small mud puddles. Gordon can clearly see that the transformations are complete.

The tiger lowers his head and growls at the black panther. In an almost playful manner, the panther bats his forepaw at the tiger, taunting him to attack. Throughout the panther's coat of fur, leopard spots are faintly made out. The large felines rear up on their hind legs and lunge forward.

The predators collide into each other with their wide mouths chomping. Their sharp black claws slash at each other as they topple across the ground. The tiger's orange and black stripped fur begins to be covered with mud. The black panther's fur is likewise muddy but not as apparent.

The tiger springs up and lands on all fours. He swiftly maneuvers around and powerfully lunges out his forepaw. The tiger's extended claws scrape the panther's shoulder.

The panther rears back on his hind legs and thrusts himself at the tiger. The panther clamps hard onto the tiger's shoulder, knocking him completely backward. The tiger struggles to maintain control as he lunges upward and bites down on the panther's throat.

The panther thrashes around, attempting to free himself from the tiger's tightening bite along his throat. However, it is no use. The tiger continues to sink his sharp teeth deeper and deeper into the black panther's throat.

The panther loosens his claws from the tiger's muddy shoulders. The tiger pushes himself upward with his hind legs, never loosening his grasp around the panther's throat. The tiger maneuvers himself around, now straddling over the helpless panther laying on his side.

The black panther's forepaws and front legs begin to mutate back to their human form. The tiger bites down, preparing to deliver the fatal blow. In a matter of seconds, Gio's muddy, human hand appears and slightly raises off of the ground.

TAP-TAP!

The tiger releases his powerful jaws from around the panther's throat. The tiger slowly begins to circle the defeated feline as the reverse transformation continues.

The black fur seems to dissolve into Gio's flesh. His thick black claws of his hind legs disappears into his mutating human toes. An ankle then a calf appears. Gio's human thighs and hips.

Battle wounds and cuts appear scattered across Gio's muddy torso, arms and legs. Across his cheek, three deep incisions left behind from the tiger's wrath. Gio places his hand on to the ground as if to push himself upward.

The tiger lunges toward him and powerfully presses his forepaw against Gio's chest. Without extending his claws, the tiger shoves Gio onto his back. The tiger lowers his head and looks deep into Gio's eyes. The tiger lets out a low growl. This has been a warning!

"Alright, Larry," Sonja says as she approaches Gio with a damp blanket. "You can let'im up now." Sonja reaches down and lovingly scratches the tiger between his ears. He steps off of Gio and backs away.

Sonja crouches down, faces Gio and wraps the blanket around his shoulders. She leans in and embraces him. A forgiving hug. "I would have never hurt the boy," Gio humbly says.

"I know you wouldn't have."

"All I wanted was the secret," Gio says in a near mumble. One by one, Gordon and the rest of the group approach Sonja and Gio near the center of the clearing. Jay sticks close to Rafe, like kittens from the same mother only different liters. They seem to share a common bond; hereditary siblings.

The light rain has dissipated revealing a clear sky and the nearly full moon overhead. "Giovanni," Gordon says in a fatherly tone. He reaches down and takes hold of Gio's hands, helping him to his feet. "There *is* no secret. No potions or spells. There are no serums or injections."

"But I've *seen* you change into at *least* a dozen alters."

"I was born under the thirtieth sign. Serpentarius... The Serpent Bearer. I have no limitations. For I..." Gordon pauses. "For I am Ophiuchus!"

Larry puts on what's left of his grey sweat pants. He is covered in blotches of mud with very few war wounds and scratches. Larry enters the circle and approaches Gio. They stand there for a moment, human to human.

With a devilish grin, Larry extends out his hand. Gio slightly smiles and nods. Larry and Gio shake hands then brotherly embrace. "Let's get you two cleaned up," Gordon says as he motions the group toward his rustic house in the background.

"This might hurt a bit," Gio says with his best bedside manner. He has showered and wears his professional looking white doctor's jacket and slacks. Across his cheek, a set of three tiny stitches he had to sew himself.

Sonja sits in Gio's examining chair toward the rear center of his medical bus. The lights are bright, almost blinding. Jay stands off to the side, cautiously keeping an eye on the mysterious doctor.

Gio carefully inserts the tip of the needle into Sonja's vein at the bend of her arm. He releases the tied off rubber tubing around her upper arm.

Sonja tightly squeezes her eyes and wrinkles her nose. Gio slowly empties the entire formula filling the syringe. "Also, I'm setting up a prescription for you at my pharmacy near Tacoma General Hospital. You'll want to see Doctor William Grant. I'll give him specific instructions for you."

"What about Jay?"

"Well, while we were *spending time together*," Gio pauses. Although Sonja has forgiven Gio for kidnapping her son, she's still a little miffed. "I had the opportunity to run extensive blood work on him."

"...and?"

"And, it appears that Jay's dominant genes are those of his father. Jay shows no signs of your disease or condition. If it would make you feel better, I can give him a kind of... *booster* shot." Sonja smiles.

"What do *you* think, Jay?"

"I guess that'll be alright," Jay answers. Sonja stands from the examining chair with her son taking her place. Gio maneuvers around on his wheeled stool. He retrieves a small, chilled bottle from the refrigerator and an unused needle and syringe from a drawer.

Gio wheels himself closer to Jay. The young man is unafraid, as he extends out his arm. Gio takes the rubber tubing and secures it tightly around Jay's upper arm. Taking the small, chilled bottle in one hand and the syringe in the other, Gio draws out the proper dosage of the customized serum.

"Well, guys. That was pretty *dumb* on your part running from the scene." Sitting along the end of Gordon's living room couch, Larry leans forward and takes a drink of his Scotch and water. He places the stout glass back onto the familiar wooded planked coffee table. Larry's cleaned himself up and wears a set of Gordon's borrowed clothing.

"We didn't know what to do," Dante nervously says. He sits at the other end of the couch with a beer in hand. Resting on the cushions next to him, his worn saddlebags.

Reggie sits in the chair diagonally across from Larry and Dante. "You know what the cops would have done to us when they showed up," Dante says as a matter of fact.

"And you thought running was the better option?" Larry snaps.

"We didn't *kill* the old guy. It was his heart or sump' thin," Reggie chimes in.

"Alright, guys," Larry says in a commanding voice. "You two have to turn yourselves in. I need a few days to set it up."

"Would you mind hanging on to this for me?" Dante asks as he hands Larry his saddlebags.

"What's in it?"

"Our future," Dante says with a smile.

"Yeah, alright," Larry replies, taking the saddlebags from Dante. Larry turns toward the kitchen, "Hey, professor!"

Gordon steps slightly out of the kitchen area and pops his head into the living room, directly at the bottom step of the wooden staircase leading up to the second floor. He casually nods his head upward. "*What's up?*" he seems to be saying.

"Would you mind if they held-up here for a few days?"

"No parties!" Gordon says with a smile as he shakes a stern finger at Reggie and Dante. The pair of bikers wearing black leather vests, covered with patches and insignias turn to each other.

Reggie and Dante exchange a mischievous smile with each other. They seem to be thinking the same thing. "*Well, just a little party...*"

"Hey!" Jon calls out from Gordon's rustic, wraparound porch. Tez and Kaleen walk along the perimeter of Gordon's two-story barn. They are extremely close to one another with Tez slightly hanging onto her arm.

However, it is not an embrace of affection but simply a necessity for direction. He doesn't remember Gordon's property very well. It's like Tez's inner sonar has been interrupted. He is unfamiliar with his surroundings and has become quite anxious.

Rafe and Chloe appear from the shadows of the wraparound porch. They approach Jon at the log handrailing and look out into the clearing. Tez and Kaleen continues to make their way closer to the house. "We're about to head out. You two wanna catch a ride?" Jon asks.

"That sounds great. Thanks!" Tez says with a smile. Sonja and Jay make their way from Gio's med-lab in the distance. Gio remains standing at the forward opened door. He feels strangely out of place. There are no farewells nor good-byes. Gio turns to enter his bus.

"Hey!" Jon calls out from the bottom step of Gordon's porch steps. Gio turns. "You still got your ticket for the show?"

"Yeah..."

"When you get there, find Rick. He'll have a backstage pass for you!"

"Thanks," Gio says with a comforting smile. He slightly gives the group a wave then disappears into the bus.

"I'll see you two in a few days," Larry says as he, Reggie and Dante exit through the opened front door. Larry joins up with Sonja and Jay as Gio completes a wide turn along the clearing and heads for the opened gates.

HONK - HONK.

Gordon and his students wave at the departing medical bus. In a matter of moments, Gio's red taillights pass through the opened gate then vanish into the darkness along the narrow dirt road.

Sonja and Jay begin heading toward Larry's parked automobile next to Jon and Rafe's van, as well as Gordon's microbus. As Larry makes his way across the edge of the clearing, he realizes that he's one passenger short. He turns to see Chloe at the bottom of the porch steps. She seems to be having an internal conflict. Does she return to The City with Larry or with Rafe?

Kaleen climbs into the opened side door of Jon and Rafe's van. Jon places his hand on the top of Tez's head, indicating the safe clearance. Kaleen pulls Tez inward with Jon sliding the side door closed. He makes his way around the front of the van, waiting for his brother.

Rafe casually strolls around the edge of the clearing and approaches Chloe. They stare at each other for a long moment, an awkward moment. "Well, I guess this is good-bye."

"Not good-bye, Rafe," Chloe says with an uncertain smile. "I'll see you at the concert."

"Right..."

"...right," Chloe whispers. "See ya'."

"C-ya'..." Rafe turns and heads for the passenger's door of the van. Chloe makes her way to Larry's car and gets in the backseat with Jay.

Behind the steering wheel, Larry glances toward Sonja seated next to him then looks at Chloe's reflection through the front windshield's rectangular rearview mirror. "Are you alright, Chloe?"

"No, but I will be..." Sitting next to Jay, Chloe says nothing more. She slides into the seatbelt and settles in for the ride home. Larry backs his car along the edge of the clearing then pulls forward. He sticks out his hand and waves as he steers out through the opened gates.

"You alright, bro?" Jon asks, as he sits behind the steering wheel of their van. Rafe is quiet for several moments then answers Jon, still facing forward and blankly looking out through the windshield.

"No, but I will be..."

"You know, Rafe," Jon says, as he starts up the van. Tez and Kaleen sit next to each other on scattered pillows the floor near the middle of the van. They are staying out of this conversation. "They're *both* in love with you. One of these days you're going to have to *pick* one of 'em."

"Yeah, I know..."

"Well, Gordon," Rafe eagerly says. "Are you gonna help us out or what?"

"I'm still thinking," Gordon answers in a reluctant tone. He looks across the round table. The table top is supported by an aged keg, used for transporting bootleg wine or outlaw beer back in the day.

The waterfront tavern is off the beaten track. A favorite spot for locals and a souvenir trap for tourists. Low ceiling fans slowly spin overhead and occasionally cause the sawdust floor to stir.

A waitress, wearing a black and red, plaid flannel shirt, black shorts and mountain boots, makes her way through the tavern. The well known establishment is filled with a variety of customers and even a few families sitting around the beer keg tables. From time to time, a parent will motion over toward Gordon's table, pointing out the local celebrities to their children.

The made-to-look aged walls are cluttered with historical logging memorabilia, giving the large rustic room the feeling as if Paul Bunyan himself had called this place home.

Gordon slowly looks at them. Jon, Rafe, Mark and then T-Bone. The rock and roll band is casually dressed, not really trying to conceal their identities. All the local residents in these parts knows who they are. "Please, Gordon," Jon humbly says. "The crowds loved it! They went into a frenzy. We've sold out the rest of the tour and Rick is even talking with a bigger record label."

"Please..." Rafe quietly joins in. Gordon leans up and over the table and hovers mere inches away from Jon and Rafe.

"I taught you two how to shift for a reason." Gordon's voice is low and gruff. "It was *not* for financial gain and *not* to be freaks to be put on display!" Gordon stares at them for a moment before sitting back down.

"Well, we've already broke two of the rules. Why not go for all three?"

"Rules? What rules?" Mark asks.

"Never mind that now," Gordon snaps.

"So, I have a question," T-Bone says. "If you eat someone in your altered state, does make you a cannibal?"

"Man, that's great! You just ate Bob!" Mark laughingly says. "Wait-wait! I've got one! If I turn into a snake, how am I gonna play guitar?" Mark flicks out his tongue as he tucks in his arms and bobbles around as if he were without his upper limbs. Mark and T-Bone nearly fall out of their chairs with laughter.

"That's it!" Gordon abruptly stands from the table.

"Come on, guys! This is serious!" Jon angrily says. Surrounding customers have become slightly uneasy by the boisterous activities of the rock band.

Almost simultaneously, Jon and Rafe smack Mark and T-Bone in the backs of their heads. This appears to quiet them down a bit. "Please..." Jon says in a quiet voice as he motions Gordon to take his seat.

Reluctantly, Gordon sits back down, still glaring at Mark and T-Bone. Jon and Rafe scowl at T-Bone and Mark, urging them to keep still. "So, seriously," Mark says. "I'd like to change into a jaguar or a mountain lion or a bear. Sump 'thin that's cool!"

"Like I told you earlier, you do not choose your alter. Your alter chooses you," Gordon sternly says. From around the surrounding tables and booths, parents collect up their children and begin heading toward the door. All this talk of cannibalism and sacrificial altars is just too much, even for a rock and roll band.

"I think we'd better finish this later," Rafe whispers to the group.

"I think you're right, bro," Jon says. Mark polishes off his mug of beer and motions toward the waitress for another round for their table. Gordon looks the boys over-

Mark is the loud prankster.

T-Bone is the large mischievous one.

Rafe is quick witted yet reserved.

Jon is the leader of the pack. "*Great,*" Gordon thinks to himself. "*What have I gotten myself into?*"

"Is everybody in?" Gordon says, standing at the far end of the familiar wooden planked coffee table. "*Is every-body in? The ceremony's about to begin.*" He looks around at the eager faces. Jon sits next to Mark with Rafe sitting next to T-Bone. They hover around the odd looking coffee table built from remnants of an old sailing vessel.

Resting on the center of the table, the tall, lavender hookah with four separate hoses branching out from the main body of the glass smoking device. The singular bowl stems out near the base of the pipe with four, glass mouthpieces at the ends of the hoses.

Gordon reaches into his lap and opens a folded block of tinfoil, the size of a standard deck of playing cards. Inside, a black, sticky substance of his own design and creation. Gordon pinches off a piece of the substance and loads it into the hookah's bowl.

Mark looks around Gordon's back living room. Hanging along the wall, Dante's framed promo shot with an orange, yellow and red boa and flaming sunglasses. On the opposite side of the lifeless fireplace and hanging moose head, the symmetrically placed, autographed guitars and pair of worn drumsticks are seen under the framed *Rolling Stone* cover.

T-Bone glances over to Mark then focuses his attention toward Rafe. He'll be his instructor and guide for the night.

Gordon lights the end of an extended stick, the size of an average drinking straw. He lowers the flame to the dark, pasty substance cradled inside of the bowl of the lavender hookah.

Rafe and Jon each take a glass mouthpiece in hand. Rafe hands it to T-Bone as Jon, likewise, hands his mouthpiece to Mark. "Here goes nothing..." T-Bone says with a smile.

"No, here goes everything," Gordon replies, with a devilish grin. Mark slips the glass mouthpiece between his lips and deeply inhales. T-Bone pauses just for a moment then follows Mark's lead.

T-Bone and Mark continuously smoke. Jon and Rafe remain seated next to them. The brothers toss each other an occasional smile. The uncertain future is approaching. The excitement and apprehension. What are T-Bone and Mark to become? Yeah, Jon and Rafe remember their first time, too.

The back living room is filled with thick smoke as Gordon reloads the hookah's empty bowl with more of the black, sticky concoction.

"This is stupid," Mark says.

"I feel like a popsicle," T-Bone manages to say with chattering teeth. "I'm freezing my butt off."

"No," Rafe playfully replies. "You still have a little butt left."

"Shut-up!"

"Alright, boys. Let's settle down." Gordon sits on the ground with his legs crossed. The flickering campfire does not seem to be providing any warmth. T-Bone and Mark are completely naked as they crouch down near the flames.

"I don't feel anything yet," Mark says to Jon.

"Is it gonna hurt?" T-Bone asks Rafe.

"Just a bit."

"Just a bit!?"

"Yeah, but you get used to it," Rafe says in the most comforting tone he can muster. Gordon looks beyond the campfire. Directly behind him, the back of his house and wraparound deck. In front of him, the soothing water of The Sound and the hanging full moon.

"What are *you* looking at?" T-Bone curiously asks.

"Dude, you look weird!" Mark replies. Suddenly, horrific pain shoots through Mark's body. He struggles to keep focused on T-Bone who has already began to transform.

T-Bone falls to the ground, now unable to support his mutating body with his human legs. His flesh is quickly consumed with thick, coarse hair, almost bristly. T-Bone's head size nearly doubles. His ears begin to expand and flatten.

Mark's hind legs slightly shrink in size, becoming more defined and powerful looking. His skin is blanketed by tan fur with dark spots, similar to Rafe in his altered state yet distinctively different. Mark's fur is coarse and not as smooth as a cheetah's.

T-Bone's face has mutated into a large muzzle, more of a snout. At this stage of his transformation, it is unclear what creature he is becoming; feline, canine, marsupial or quadruped.

Mark crouches down, now standing on all fours. His mutating paws get the feel of the ground and dirt below. Mark's arched back is covered with tan fur and sporadic dark spots. The transforming creature raises up on his hind legs and extends his forepaws out toward Jon. With the last of his human facial features, Mark manages to ask, "How am I gonna play guitar?"

"T-Bone! Look at me!" Rafe commands. The drummer crouches over the mutating beast. Rafe takes the creature's snout in hand and forces him face to face. "Watch!"

Rafe extends out his hand and concentrates. His entire body remains human with the exception of his hand and arm. Light tan fur explodes from his flesh with a complete cheetah's arm and paw replacing his human limb. "You have control over it. Just focus on it, T-Bone."

The transforming creature looks into Rafe's eyes, he seems to be understanding the human. The beast lifts his weight upward and stands on its hind legs. The creature is odd looking, retaining his human consciousness yet, with the external characteristics continuing to take shape in his alter form.

"Look at it this way, Mark," Jon says as he slides out of his blue jeans. "At least you're not a snake." Jon takes a deep breath and briefly closes his eyes. He bares down, concentrating on his extremities. Jon has nearly perfected the art of instantaneous transformation. The upright wolf appears in a matter of moments.

The cheetah walks around the flickering campfire on his hind legs. Rafe's human consciences contains his feline exterior. The cheetah and the wolf appear to be greeting each other.

T-Bone and Mark are still at odds with their newly transformed bodies. They curiously gaze upon their upper extremities, where their hands and fingers had been just minutes ago.

Mark wags his tail. "*That's different...*" he thinks to himself. The wolf and the cheetah make their way around the crackling flames of the campfire. The four odd, upright beasts examine each other. The wolf and the cheetah seem to be welcoming the creatures that had recently been T-Bone and Mark into their pack.

"Hey, boys!" Gordon calls out from the shadows. The wolf and the cheetah turn to see Gordon approaching. In one hand, he carries T-Bone's autographed, first edition, giraffe printed guitar. In Gordon's other hand, Jon's autographed, first edition, peacock printed guitar as well as Mark's signed zebra printed guitar.

Gordon hands the bass guitar to the beast that was once T-Bone. The mutated creature slings the guitar strap over his shoulder. Gordon hands the lead and rhythm guitar to the wolf and the creature that was once Mark. Gordon reaches around to his back pocket and hands the cheetah a pair of worn, autographed drumsticks. "Alright, now practice!"

"That's it for me, Night Crawlers," Tez informs his radio audience over his suspended microphone. "Just a reminder, there's still a few tickets left for the Zøø Crüe's homecoming concert tomorrow night. I hope to see you there!" Tez pauses a moment. "I'm Tez Madon and you're tuned to The Emerald City's *classic* rock-n-roll station, one-o-one point three... K.R.W.L."

Tez flips off the red *on-air* switch and begins rolling through a series of prerecorded commercials. The scattered lava lights around the dark studio cast odd shapes across the walls and ceiling. "Morning, Tez," the casually dressed morning disk jockey says, as he flicks on the light switch.

Jack Jones saunters into the studio with the overhead florescent lights flickering to life. Behind his dark sunglasses, Tez does not notice the sudden bombardment of light.

Jack is a middle aged man, pleasant looking and slightly charming. "Morning, J.J.. I have your first set all lined up for you." Tez reaches over to the side counter area and pats a stack of compact disk cases.

A pair of albums rest in the center of the pair of motionless turntables. A needle and arm has been placed and cued up on each of the albums, allowing Jack to simply slide in and take over for the graveyard disk jockey.

Tez stands and turns, effortlessly replacing a series of compact disk cases into their proper locations along the filled shelves behind the main control board.

Jack plops himself down onto the wheeled chair and spins around. He quickly moves several knobs and levers along the control board. The series of prerecorded commercials is nearly over. Jack flicks the red *on-air* button. "Good-morning! J.J.'s in the chair!" he announces into the suspended microphone.

Tez makes his way to the opened doorway, slightly turns and gives Jack a departing wave. Jack nods with a smile then returns to the main control board. "If it's too loud, you're not hung-over enough! Let's get things goin'! I'm J.J. in the morning and you're tuned into The City's *home* of *classic* rock-n-roll, one-o-one point three... K.R.W.L!"

The studio is filled with the sounds of a snare drum. The upbeat, rock and roll tune's introduction nearly shakes the walls. The song's lead vocals kick-in with Jack vigorously dancing about the studio. Tez's not the only disk jockey who is enthusiastic about his job.

Tez feels his way down along the radio station's outside walkway and handrailing. It's still dark outside with the rising sun not quite awake yet. Tez reaches forward and presses his opened palm against the rear window of the parked taxicab. Tez open's the rear passenger door, "Hey, Paul. How'zit goin?"

Paul glances over his shoulder and smiles. "Good, Tez. You had a great show. I rocked out all night."

"Thanks." Tez lowers his head and slides into the rear passenger's seat. Closing the rear door behind himself, he sits there a moment.

At first, Tez focuses his attention through the thick protective glass separating the forward and rear areas of the taxicab. Tez smiles as he sniffs the air. "I see you've already picked up another passenger." A feminine hand seductively reaches across and squeezes Tez's thigh.

"Wanna go for a swim?" The woman asks in an enticing tone.

"Naw, I better not. The Ol' Lady will have my hide if I'm home late."

"*Ol' Lady*?" Kaleen says with a giggle as she slaps Tez's arm. Her one piece dress flutters as she lunges toward Tez and begins playfully beating him with her fists.

"Help! Help!" Tez pleads to Paul. "I'm being assaulted! What kinda people you pick up anyway?"

"...as *weird* as you? Not too many!" Paul says.

"Gee, thanks!" Tez retaliates, tickling Kaleen back.

"Home, James," Kaleen orders.

"*Paul...* not James."

"Whatever..." Kaleen mumbles. Tez quickly reaches over and resumes his tickling torture. They roll around the backseat of the taxicab, laughing. Paul places the vehicle in gear and begins to pull away from the radio station.

"Here you go, kids," Paul says, as he slows his taxicab along the far area of the woodland park bordering The Sound. "I'll put it on your tab."

"Thanks," Tez says as he opens the rear passenger door.

"...it was good to see you, Kate."

"*Kaleen...* not Kate," she insistently says.

"Whatever..." Paul replies with a devilish grin. Kaleen leans her head forward, looking through the separating glass. She and the taxicab driver smile at each other. It's been over three weeks and they're finally starting to get along.

"Come on, Kay! The water's great!" Tez yells out from waist high along the water, offshore from The Sound. His pile of clothes and dark sunglasses rests on the rocky beach. He blindly waves in her direction before turning and disappearing below the surface of the chilly water.

Kaleen makes her way to the tree line and looks about. There is no one else around. She quickly lifts her dress over her head and tosses it on top of Tez's pile. She darts toward the shoreline, splashes into the water and quickly plunges below the surface.

The dolphin and the mermaid effortlessly swim through the ocean, well passed the coastal cities of Victoria and Port Angeles. The Pacific water is cool for this time of year. Yet, the aquatic pair doesn't seem to mind too much.

Kaleen flips her tail causing her body to seemingly soar through the water. Her reddish hair flows behind herself with her remaining human torso and upper areas gliding along.

The dolphin swims in circles around the mermaid. Up and down, around and around. Kaleen smiles as she reaches out and runs her opened palm passed his blowhole and dorsal fin. The dolphin slightly turns and motions his head toward her as would a puppy looking for affection.

Kaleen runs her opened hand down along his tail as the dolphin banks hard to the side and swims away from her. The dolphin completes a full, sideways loop to the side and swims back toward the mermaid.

She smiles as the mammal approaches. Suddenly, Kaleen thrusts her opened hands forward and sways them back and forth. She appears to be levitating several yards off of the ocean floor.

At first, the dolphin is unaware of the dark image as it appears from the depths of the water. It hovers a moment, sensing its prey. Kaleen attempts to blurt out a warning. However, due to the constant flow of water through her gills and vocal cords, she is unable to warn the dolphin of the impending danger. Then, instead of attacking the dolphin, it attacks the mermaid!

The enormous great white shark bites down on the left side of Kaleen's lower extremity. Her single fin is now severed at the upper thigh area. Kaleen's blood flows freely through the ocean water causing the shark to enter a feeding frenzy, it violently chomps down on her again.

The great white effortlessly thrashes the mermaid around. She is helpless. The shark releases its mighty grip only to clamp down upon her thigh area again, just above where her human knee should be.

Kaleen struggles to swim toward the surface. But, all in vain. The surrounding water is filled with blood. The current is not helping. The blood appears to be remaining in one location, covering Kaleen in a blanket of appetizing film.

The shark powerfully hurls Kaleen to the side. It releases its mighty grip, opens its razor sharp jaws and violently swims toward the helpless mermaid.

Just as the great white charges forward to deliver the fatal blow, the dolphin races forward. The dolphin slams his beak into the shark's gills, over and over.

The great white is stunned at first, ceasing its attack upon Kaleen. The shark floats backward for what seems a second or two then rears its powerful jaws toward the dolphin.

Just as the shark turns and lunges toward the dolphin, Kaleen reaches out with both hands at grasps onto the shark's tail. The cold blooded fish thrashes around as the dolphin powerfully slams his beak into the shark's gills.

Tez's human instincts takes over. He reverses half of his mutation. Similar to Kaleen's lower, singular fin, Tez retains his dolphin's lower fin and flukes. His human waist, torso and arms transform and appear. Tez looks strikingly familiar to a merman.

Tez powerfully maneuvers the great white onto its back, thrusting it to the watery floor. Tez holds the shark down, beginning to drowned it. The fish thrashes about. Biting, biting and biting.

The great white falls limp. In his half altered state, Tez shakes the shark; it's dead. The merman releases the shark and swiftly swims toward Kaleen. She floats slowly upward, toward the surface of The Sound.

Tez reaches under her arm and carries her toward the growing light of the rising sun. He gasps for air. A fishing vessel speeds along the surface. Tez takes a deep breath of air before dashing to the side, attempting to avoid a collision. He's lost contact with Kaleen.

The keel of the fishing vessel speeds along, heading out to sea. Now completely in his human form, Tez treads water. He senses across the surface of the rolling water. Tez cannot smell nor hear Kaleen. He begins swimming toward the shoreline, "Kaleen!?" Tez gasps, spitting out a mouthful of seawater. "Kay!?"

Tez frantically swims freestyle toward the shoreline. As he twists his head from side to side, Tez still cannot smell nor sense her. "Kaleen!?" He feels the sand of the shoreline. Tez claws his way upward as he crawls on all fours. He is blind as a bat and helplessly frantic. "Kaleen!? Where are you?"

Kaleen's motionless body washes up on the shore only a few yards away from Tez. Her hair is matted with her human form completely intact, except for her left hip and left thigh.

All that remains of her left leg is bloody flesh, mutilated bones and grotesque bite marks left behind from the carnivorous great white shark. Kaleen's blood flows into the rolling surf. "Where are you!?" Tez hesitates a moment then frantically continues to search the shoreline. "Kaleen!?"

"She's lost a lot of blood!" the paramedic urgently says. An emergency room doctor approaches the side of the gurney. Kaleen is unconscious and covered in a sheet. Although bandaged, her severe injuries continue to seep blood, drenching the lower area of the sheet.

The doctor shuffles alongside as the paramedic wheels Kaleen's gurney along the backend as a secondary paramedic guides it along the front. They race from the opened backdoor of the parked ambulance into the sliding doors of the emergency room. "Sir, let me help you," an orderly says, as he exits the emergency doors.

The orderly reaches out his hand as Tez attempts to step out of the back of the ambulance on his own. Tez only had time to put on his leather jacket, jeans and dark sunglasses. He steps onto the pavement as the orderly takes him by the arm. "This way, sir."

The orderly leads Tez through the emergency room's sliding doors. A flood of chaotic sounds fills the air. Doctors shouting out orders. Scampering feet from nurses and other orderlies. Random squeaky wheels of occupied gurneys. "Where is she? Take me to her!" Tez commands.

"I can't do that, sir," the orderly says in his most comforting tone. "She's probably already in the E.R.."

"I don't care! Take me to her!"

"I'm sorry, you can't see her right now." The orderly leads Tez around the corner and enters a large, brightly lit waiting room. "You'll have to wait here, sir." The orderly carefully leads Tez to one of the few empty chairs. "If I hear anything, I'll let you know."

"Thanks," Tez replies, attempting to be polite. As the orderly leaves, Tez finds his seat and places his hands on the armrests. He beings to gathering his bearings. He takes a deep breath as if to begin intense meditation.

The chairs and couches lining the walls of the waiting room are filled with a wide assortment of distraught people, all awaiting news.

A wife, waiting to hear if her husband survived his heart attack. A mother and father, waiting to hear if their son lived through a horrific fall. A group of young men, all wearing matching black leather jackets, waits to hear if their friend made it through the motorcycle accident.

The low roar of the waiting room filters into Tez's ears. At first, soft whispers and painful crying. For Tez, the sounds intensify, growing louder and louder although in reality, remaining at the same level.

The wife casually looks over toward Tez. Then, the mother and father. Finally, the group of young men toss a glance in Tez's direction. The graveyard disk jockey appears to have become a seated statue, ridged and motionless.

Deep inside Tez's consciousness, the waves of noise rage on. Louder and louder. He's become frightened and anxious. Tez is unfamiliar with his surroundings. He realizes that up until recently, his life has become routine. The radio station, home and The Sound. The radio station, home and The Sound. The radio station, home and The Sound.

Tez has come to the abrupt conclusion that Kaleen was right. He is at the moment, out of his safe zone. He has become too regimented. He has become too comfortable with the routine of his life. Yeah, Kaleen was right.

Tez begins breathing heavily, trying to keep it to himself. However, the nearby wife notices his panicked condition. The mother and father look concerned for Tez. The group of young men wearing the black leather jackets slightly nod to one another. They understand what feelings Tez must be having right now.

The mother turns toward her husband. He slightly smiles and gives her an approving nod. The mother stands and slowly makes her way over to Tez. She pauses a moment, seeing his grief.

She calmly sits next to Tez and directly looks at him. "My name is Kathy." She tenderly places her hand on top of Tez's hand, resting along the armrest. "...and I'm waiting, too."

Tez suddenly comes to his senses, realizing that he is being spoken to. He feels Kathy's hand on top of his own. She tenderly squeezes. With his other hand, Tez slowly reaches up toward her face and carefully runs his fingertips across her cheeks, forehead and eyelids. She has the face of a concerned mother.

Tez pulls his hand out from under Kathy's hand then places it on top. He gently squeezes. A single tear rolls from out under his dark sunglasses. Then, another and another.

Kathy leans over and embraces Tez. He wraps his arms around her. She holds him as if Tez were her own. This seems to comfort Kathy as she waits for the outcome of her son. Tez has become a temporary surrogate.

He loses control. Tez begins crying on Kathy's shoulder. She draws him in closer and motherly pats him on the back.

Tez had no idea that he still had these kind of feelings for Kaleen. He should have nurtured them, allowed them to expand and grow. Tez should have never let her leave in the first place. There was no need for their divorce so many years ago.

He should have listened to her more and considered her thoughts and her feelings. Now, he may never have the chance to tell her how he feels. Yeah, Kaleen was right.

~ XII ~

"Good-morning and thank-you for calling S.P.D." The tall, pleasant man in uniform stands behind the booking desk with the telephone's receiver pressed to his ear. "This is Sergeant William Dodds, how can I help you?"

"Bill? It's Chloe."

"Chloe? It's been awhile. How have you been?" Dodds shifts his weight from polished shoe to polished shoe, standing behind the extended desk. He casually looks forward, through the windowed front entrance of the Police Station. It's a nice day outside for a change with the sun shining brightly.

Behind Dodds, a matching pair of aisles runs along bland looking carpet. Along the aisles, well dressed detectives appear in their cubicles as they continue to fill out their paperwork and complete their reports.

At the end of the far aisle, along the back wall of the main room, a thick secured door is seen. The door is intimidating and leads to the restricted areas of the Police Station. More importantly, the door leads to the detaining area and cells. "I'm fine, Bill. How's the kids?"

"Great! Billy's graduating from The Academy next month and Carolynn's expecting her third sometime in February."

"How's Madeline?"

"Maddy and I are going on our first cruise next summer after I retire."

"That sounds wonderful, Bill." Chloe sits behind her desk with the picture window directly behind her. The closed door to her right leads out into the hallways of the sprawling building with the left closed door leading into Larry's office. She looks professional in her snappy business suit and even looks well rested. Chloe shuffles through a small stack of legal papers.

"Well, Chloe..." With the pleasantries over with, Dodds' tone changes, professional and to the point. "What's going on?"

"Larry's representing a couple guys, Reggie and Dante. They're coming to town and have been involved in a little, *misunderstanding*. I'm going to fax over a Notice of Surrender as well as a Cease and Desist Order. We'd appreciate it if you'd spread the word."

"Sure thing, Chloe. We'll let you know when they get here."

"Thanks, Bill."

"Talk to you soon." Chloe hangs up the receiver of her phone then returns to her stacks of paperwork. She glances around a moment. The rows upon rows of legal books fills the bookshelves. Her familiar desktop and comfy leather chair. It feels good to be back to normal.

Dodds looks over his shoulder and sees the fax machine along a desk area next to a police scanner as well as several other computer components. The fax machine remains quiet.

The police sergeant looks up from his paperwork and sees a squad car pull up to the front of the Police Station. The pair of uniformed police officers slide out of the front seats of their black and white and both approach the same side, rear passenger's door.

As the rear door opens, a hulking image is shadowed in the backseat. The officers cautiously reach inward and carefully remove the notorious criminal from the back of the squad car. Due to his massive size, two pairs of handcuffs, linked together from behind, were needed to restrain him.

Seymour Clay; arsonist, bank robber, grand theft, disorderly conduct, forgery and counterfeiting as well as various weapons violations... and that was just for last week.

Standing over six feet tall, Clay towers over the officers on opposite sides of him as they escort him through the front glass doors of the Police Station. The repeat offender slightly smiles as he is maneuvered in front of the booking desk. "Dodds, you're looking well."

"Clay," Dodds says, in a polite tone. "Looks like you've lost a few pounds."

"Thank-you, Sergeant." The pair of younger police officers remove Clay from in front of the booking desk and begin to escort him along the far aisle. Being in this position on numerous occasions, Clay knows that he's going away for a very long time. He has nothing to lose.

Still restrained behind his back, Clay slyly crisscrosses his wrists. He slides the single part, ratchet, of one set of handcuffs into the double part, cheek plate, of the other set of cuffs. Twisting his wrists, the pair of handcuffs creates a lever and prying action. The second pair of handcuffs snap open.

Clay slams his left elbow into the first officer, sending him reeling over the countertop. Taking the released pair of handcuffs, Clay swings them toward the second police officer in a hooking manner. The cuffs powerfully hit the officer in the head, sending him to his knees.

Dodds rushes toward Clay and attempts to wrap his arms around him. Dodds and Clay struggle for control as a group of nearby detectives rush the scene.

RING - RING.

RING - RING.

The fax machine resting on the countertop begins to hum. Clay wildly flails his arms through the air. Dodds and the detectives surround the large criminal and slams him onto the countertop. The fax machine is crushed under all of the weight and shatters into pieces onto the bland carpet floor.

Dodds and the detectives have gained control over Clay. Four of the detectives powerfully restrain Clay on top of the counter as the pair of younger police officers tightly clutch onto his legs. Acting quickly, Dodds removes several pairs of handcuffs from the nearby detective's belts.

Dodds swiftly handcuffs Clay behind his back. This time, using four sets of two linked pairs of handcuffs. All taking a tight grasp of Clay, Dodds, the police officers and detectives surround him and escort him along the far aisle toward the ominous closed door.

The fax machine lays in shambles on the bland carpet floor. No paper has been ejected. No Notice of Surrender and no Cease and Desist Order.

"How is she?" Gordon eagerly asks, as he darts along the brightly lit hallway of the emergency room's waiting area. He's dressed as if he had just been pulled off of a logging run. A flannel shirt, dusty jeans and work boots.

"I don't know," Gio replies. "I haven't heard anything, yet." Gio's white medical jacket hangs over the backrest of one of the many chairs along the waiting room. He sports his professional attire with a dress shirt, tie, pressed slacks and polished shoes. "Tez is in with her now."

"Have you got a hold of everyone else?"

"Larry and Chloe are on their way to pick up Sonja and Jay."

"What about Jon and Rafe?"

"They're stuck in traffic. Reggie and Dante are... *missing in action*. They're supposed to turn themselves in today."

"That's all of us then."

"So, now what do we do?"

"We wait..."

"The doctors say that you're gonna be alright," Tez nearly whispers with his best poker face. Kaleen's not buying it. Even under his dark sun glasses, she can see the concern in Tez's expression.

"You never were a good liar," she says with a smile. Tez tightly clutches onto her hand, still shirtless and wearing his faded, leather jacket and jeans.

Kaleen lays halfway propped up in bed wearing a light green hospital gown with annoying tubes and wires sticking out of her arm. The intensive care room is for the most part quiet with the exception of the annoying sounds of the attached heart monitor.

Tez reaches up and brushes the back of his hand across Kaleen's cheek. He can tell she's been crying. Kaleen is more pale than usual. She had suffered a massive amount of blood loss from the great white shark attack. However, that's not all Kaleen has lost.

Beneath the light colored blanket, the outline of her figure runs down along the propped up hospital bed. Chest, stomach, waist and hips. Then, halfway down her upper thighs, the curvature of the blanket abruptly changes. Due to her extensive injuries, Kaleen's left leg had to be amputated twelve inches above of her knee.

Kaleen stares at where she thinks her left foot should be. She strains to feel her toes wiggling. They do not wiggle. Tears begin to well up in her eyes. Tez lovingly reaches up and brushes a few loose stands of hair away from her face. "We'll get through this, Kay."

"Oh, we'll be a sight to see," Kaleen angrily says as she wipes away the tears. "The Cripple and The Blind Man! Sign me up for the circus!"

"Kay, you're gonna be alright!" Tez raises up from the side of the hospital bed and moves inward to embrace her. Kaleen is becoming hysterical and slightly hostile. She wildly moves her arms through the air, keeping Tez at a distance.

"I don't wanna be *alright*! I wanna be the way I *was*!" Underneath the hospital blanket, Kaleen begins violently kicking her feet. They do not both kick. The movement underneath the blanket is that of her right leg and the thick nub, her left amputated limb, pathetically bobbing up and down like a fish out of water.

Tez lunges forward and tightly wraps his arms around her. Kaleen begins to uncontrollably weep. At first, she struggles to push him away. Tez squeezes her tighter. Kaleen's arms fall limp and drop to the blanket. He holds her up like a ragdoll as she continues to cry.

Ever so slowly, Kaleen lifts her arms and embraces Tez. Deep down inside, Tez knows what she is feeling. He recalls how it felt when he lost his sight. Tez remembers the difficult, life changing adjustments he had to make. Tez knows what she is feeling. The only difference is, Kaleen will never be able to change into her alter again.

"Are you ready to do this, Reg?" Dante asks in a concerned tone. He's dressed as usual in his black leather vest, faded jeans and cowboy boots.

The overhead, florescent lights of the connivance store and gas station's outside canopy begins to flicker. Dante slides the gas nozzle back into the cradle of the gas pump. He glances at his surroundings.

The sun continues to set over the horizon with the thick layer of mist blanketing the area. The streets have become damp and slippery. The impending evening air rolls over Reggie's skin. His black leather vest covered with patches and insignias provide little protection.

Reggie screws on the gas cap of his trike then straddles the worn in seat. The canopy lights burst alive, sustaining light throughout the perimeter of the connivance store and gas station. "You want anything? I'm gonna go get the change."

"Naw, I'm good," Reggie says with a smirk. Dante shuffles away from his motorcycle standing next to the gas pumps. Reggie tosses him a nod before sliding off of his trike's seat and begins checking the air in his tires.

A family sport utility vehicle rolls up along the adjacent island of gas pumps and stops. The father hops out from the driver's side and removes the nozzle from the pump. With Reggie preoccupied checking the air in his tires, he doesn't see the police patrol car roll up to the front of the gas station.

The uniformed police officer steps out of his cruiser and pauses a moment. He sees the ruffian biker stand from one of his rear wheels, walks around the back of the trike and squats in front of the opposite rear wheel. The police officer thinks the biker is strikingly familiar.

The police officer climbs back into the driver's seat of his patrol car. The officer takes the computer style keyboard in hand and quickly types in several codes. In an instant, a heading pops up on the monitor;

**** MOST WANTED ****

A series of criminal mug shots and booking photos race across the monitor. Suddenly, an image of Reggie appears. The police officer presses the forward arrow of the keyboard with a photo of Dante filling the screen. As the officer steps out of his patrol car, he releases the safety strap of his holstered automatic weapon.

From inside of the connivance store, Dante looks away from the clerk as he stuffs his change into his front pants pocket. Dante sees the police officer carefully inching his way from his patrol car with his weapon drawn and leveled. "*No-no-no*," Dante thinks to himself. "*It's not supposed to go down like this.*"

"Police! Put your hands in the air so I can see'em!" The police officer creeps closer toward Reggie as the gas pump island slightly blocks his clear view.

"Hey, put that away!" Reggie says in an elevated voice. "We were just on our way to see you guys!"

"Hold it right there!" The rookie police officer's voice trembles. His leveled automatic weapon begins to shake. The father of the sport utility vehicle panics. The last thing he wants to do is jeopardize his family. Without removing the nozzle from the gas pump, the father dives behind the wheel and slams on the accelerator.

The sudden departure of the sport utility vehicle catches the police officer off guard. He is distracted for a split second. Dante charges up from behind and powerfully takes the officer's wrist in hand. Dante forcefully shoves the automatic weapon upward a moment too late.

BLAM - BLAM!

The pair of bullets shred through Dante's gas tank. Yet, it does not explode. Gasoline begins to pour out from Dante's tank. The sport utility vehicle screeches away from the gas pump island causing the break-away nozzle to violently dethatch.

As the end of the break-away nozzle skids across the pavement, sparks appear. Reggie leaps onto his trike, fires up the engine and speeds toward Dante who continues to struggle with the police officer. "Dante, get down!"

KA - BLOOM!

The force of the explosion causes Dante and the rookie police officer to be hurled through the air. Dante's motorcycle is obliterated. The pair of bodies haphazardously topple to the pavement. The police officer is knocked unconscious as the sport utility vehicle speeds away into the darkness.

Raging flames consumes the gas station and quickly threatens the convenience store. Dante effortlessly drags the motionless police officer near the edge of a grassy area, a safe distance away from the intense heat and flames.

From the back door of the connivance store, the young clerk bolts outward and continues running for his life. "Dante, come on!" Reggie yells.

"We should stay. It's not our fault!"

"C'mon!" The islands of gas pumps are engulfed in roaring flames. It's only a matter of time before the below ground gas tanks are ignited. Dante rushes toward Reggie and leaps onto the back of the trike. Reggie slams back on the hand accelerator. The trike screams onto the damp side street.

The thick mist has transformed into a light drizzle. Reggie and Dante race along a series of dark, back alleys. In the near distance, the sounds of police car sirens continue to wail. Cutting across traffic and the mazes of side streets, Reggie maneuvers his trike deeper and deeper into The City, closer to the edge of The Sound. "Hard right!" Reggie commands.

Reggie and Dante heave their bodies to the right as Reggie banks the trike in a similar direction. Reggie, Dante and the trike thunder along Route Ninety-nine, otherwise known as Battery Street. The Sound whizzes passed them along their left as clusters of office buildings speed passed to their right.

Closing the gap behind them, a squad of police cars continues their pursuit with lights flashing and sirens blasting. This is extraordinarily out of place. This kind of police chase belongs in other California cities, not here.

Reggie gears down and takes a hard left, almost tipping the trike over. Dante hangs on for dear life as Reggie again accelerates and speeds along Denny Way. "This isn't working," Dante yells.

"Right!" Reggie shouts back over his shoulder. "Time to pull out the ace! Hold on!" The intersection of Denny Way and North Fourth Avenue is quickly approaching. Reggie is planning to take the extreme, ninety degree angle hard right. There's no way they're going to make that turn.

Reggie reaches down and takes a hold of the trike's emergency looking hand brake. He takes a deep breath before pulling up and back on the lever. The four prongs of the rear anchor break free from its secured latch behind Dante's backrest.

The anchor rattles along the concrete with sparks flying through the air. The linked chain flops back and forth with the anchor reaching for anything to grab a hold of. Then, then chain slams against a corner lamppost causing the four pronged anchor to whip around the links.

As Reggie continues to speed along, the slack in the linked chain becomes taunt. The anchor wraps itself around the chain creating a slingshot effect. Reggie, Dante and the trike are whiplashed around the ninety degree corner and are hurled along North Fourth Street. Reggie swiftly reaches down and releases the attached end of the linked chain. "Oh, crap!"

Reggie looks toward his left then to his right. Squads of racing police patrol cars are quickly approaching the intersection from the north and south of Broad Street. With North Forth Avenue coming to an abrupt halt, there is nowhere for Reggie and Dante to go. "We have to make a run for it!"

"Later, bro!"

"Later!" Reggie swoops his left hand across his chest and lifts it for Dante to see. He clutches his fist. Likewise, Dante clutches his fist and *pounds* Reggie's fist.

The police squad cars violently screech to a halt, skidding sideways, blocking all traffic along Broad Street in both directions. Reggie has a clear path to nowhere. "Here we go!"

Reggie heaves back on the accelerator and races toward the approaching containment wall. He and Dante hurl themselves up into the air, away from the thundering trike.

KA - BLAM!

Reggie's trike is instantly incinerated due to the violent collision into the containment wall. The swarm of police officers charge from their patrol vehicles with weapons drawn and leveled. They surround the destroyed trike engulfed in flames only to find, their fugitives has eluded them.

Reggie and Dante weave their way in and out of a lightly wooded area. In the distance, they can hear the wailing sirens of the police patrol cars. They pause just a moment to catch their breath.

Looking through the dimly lit trees, Reggie can see the smoldering flames of his trike along the opposite side of the containment wall. Now, he has nothing left from Ma and Pa. "Sorry, man," Dante says as he brotherly pats Reggie on the shoulder.

Scanning the surrounding area, Reggie and Dante see silhouettes racing toward them through the wooded landscape. "Maybe we should split up."

"You think that's a good idea?" Dante smiles. "The last time we split up, I blew out my knee."

"It'll be alright. We'll met up at Gordon's in the morning." The flickering flashlights of the approaching police officers are becoming dangerously close. Without another word, Reggie and Dante burst in opposite directions.

Dante heads west into the darkness. The wide area of trees appears to be some kind of undeveloped city park or soon to be developed wooded and secluded, luxury community.

His rate of speed is increasing. Dante feels his heart pounding. His legs and thighs surge with power as they mutate into his alter's lower extremities. Dante feels a shred along his transforming thighs and is followed by a series of rips and tears. "Ah, man," Dante says under his breath. "There goes another pair of boots..."

Reggie abruptly appears from the surrounding tree line. He is flooded with light coming from above. Reggie stops suddenly, his attire seems quite out of place.

Throughout the courtyard of the plaza, families and sporadic couples pause a moment to see the ragged biker catching his breath. From the panicked look on his face, he is in trouble. Fathers and mothers collect their children and shuffles them away. The couples turn their heads as if they hadn't seen Reggie and continue along the concrete walkways.

Reggie looks in all directions. Coming up from behind, the police officers pursuing him on foot maneuver their way through the trees. Their flashlights wildly moving from side to side. In the distance to his left and right, additional police patrol cars speed into view and skid sideways to a halt. The police cars have blocked all routes, in or out of the historical landmark.

Reggie looks directly forward. His face seems to be illuminated. First, his eyes begin to slowly look upward. Reggie begins to move his head following the direction of his eyes.

He looks up and beyond the concrete and steel supporting beams. Reggie can faintly see the blinking red aircraft warning beacon above the spherical restaurant level as well as the observation level. Up, up and up seems to be the only way of escape.

Reggie charges into the plaza on the ground floor. He is surrounded by tourists as well as local families. They appear frightened as they back away from the winded biker. Quickly looking over his shoulder, he sees a small army of police officers approaching the outer glass doors.

Reggie shoves his way through the panicked crowds and makes his way to the backside of the plaza. He frantically presses the button to one of the three elevators. Reggie scans to the left and then to the right. The numerous police officers are closing in on him.

BING!

The elevator door slides open. Reggie forces his way inside the lift as the terrified passengers swiftly exit and dash away into the plaza. The elevator door begins to close. Reggie presses his back against the wall just as a squad of police officers rush toward him. The door closes! Reggie takes a sigh of relief, it's only forty-three seconds to the top.

BING!

Reggie steps through the opened door of the elevator as if he belonged there, like he has a standing reservation with a table by the window. He casually walks through the foyer leading away from the closing elevator doors and approaches the edge of the stationary floor.

In front of him, the slow, revolving area of the circular restaurant. "Excuse me, sir. May I help you?" The pleasantly dressed hostess approaches Reggie from the side. She looks him up and down. "*This will not do,*" she thinks to herself.

Tank-tops or muscle shirts for men are not acceptable at SkyCity Restaurant. This hooligan is shirtless with a black leather vest covered with various patches and insignias. "*No way!*"

"Where's the bathroom?" Reggie asks in an urgent tone.

"Sir?"

"Sorry, I got lost! I really gotta go, miss."

"Sir!" The hostess moves toward Reggie as if to return him to the elevator. The outer restaurant area continues to slowly rotate. Seated patrons along the windows have noticed the commotion and have become slightly unnerved. Reggie looks in all directions. There is no escape from this level.

BING - BING - BING!

The three elevators have simultaneously arrived at the restaurant level, assuredly all filled with eager police officers. Reggie bolts from the foyer and charges directly toward the nearest elevator. At first, he thinks he will attack the police officers, catching them off guard. Nope, that's a dumb idea!

Reggie sidesteps the opening elevator door and crashes through the exit leading into the stairwell. He hesitates for a moment. Should he go up or down? "He went through there!" the hostess shrieks from the restaurant.

Reggie hears the thundering footsteps of the police officers running across the foyer. He takes a hold of the handrailing and heads upward along the stairwell, taking no less than three steps at a time.

The swarm of police officers charge through the exit door and scan the stairwell for Reggie. For a split second, all is quite. Then, the officers hear the above exit door click shut.

Reggie darts across the plush carpeted floor of the inner, enclosed observation level. The round room is well lit and almost blinding. He shoves his way through a group of college aged spectators as he makes his way to the spherical wall of thick Plexiglas.

The police officers burst through the exit door. "There he is!" one officer shouts. Reggie bolts from his position. He frantically runs along the enclosed observation level until he abruptly finds an outer entryway.

Reggie skips over the small set of steps leading out onto the exterior observation deck. He suddenly changes directions and races back in the direction he had come. On the opposite side of the Plexiglas, the police officers see him and run toward the entryway.

The on-looking tourists and spectators back away from Reggie as he races along the outer perimeter of the observation deck. Over the years, the historical landmark had to make some drastic upgrades. There has been far too many suicidal jumpers as well as accidental falls from his level.

The entire observation level is enclosed with a well knit series of upside-down, "L" shaped steel supporting beams holding together horizontal cables. Just above the handrailing spanning between the lower areas of the supporting beams, sections of Plexiglas enclose the wider areas of the horizontal cables.

Connected to the tops of the supporting beams and the top curved edges of the enclosed observation level, a checkerboard looking mesh of cables which prevent anyone from slipping over the top. The combination of supporting beams and cables looks like a gigantic bird cage.

Reggie darts along the handrailing, looking over the side. The curvature of the extended sun louvers completely surround the outer area of The Needle, providing shade for the restaurant level directly below. There, he sees it!

Reggie skids to his knees and grasps onto the upper edges of an access panel. It is tightly bolted to the inner wall. He strains as he pulls at the panel. Reggie can hear the footsteps of the police officers approaching him from opposite sides. Suddenly, the access panel gives way.

Tossing the panel to the side, Reggie dives head first through the opening. A pair of police officers lunge forward and snag Reggie by the boots. They struggle for a moment.

Reggie's weight slides downward along the top surface of the sun louvers and causes the officers to lose their grip. They are forced to release Reggie. His body spins completely around as he slides further down along the top of the sun louvers.

The toes of his boots snags the utmost end of the sun louvers. He is mere inches away from sliding off the edge. His fingertips claw into the smooth surface providing little support. "Hey, man!" one officer yells. "Hold on! You don't wanna go out like this. We can help you!" The officer holds out his hand.

Reggie looks up at the officer as he creeps his way outward and through the access panel opening. A secondary officer slips in behind the first with two more officers clutching onto their duty belts. They have formed a human chain.

The first pair of police officers are ever so close to Reggie as they reach out for him. However, the precarious man seems that he doesn't want to be rescued. Reggie releases his fingertips as he slightly raises the toes of his boots. He begins to quickly slide off the edge of the sun louvers.

The police officers dive toward Reggie and grasp onto the upper shoulders of his vest just as he goes over. Reggie dangles over the side of the sun louvers, kicking and thrashing around. The police officers struggle to hold on to him.

Reggie calms his movements. He realizes that the officers will not let him go, they're trained for this kind of thing. As the pair of officers continues to cling onto the upper shoulders of his vest, Reggie slowly looks up, winks then smiles at the nearest officer. "Don't try this at home..."

Reggie quickly raises his arms upward causing him to completely slide out of his vest. In an instant, Reggie is gone.

The horrified patrons filling the seats along the windows of the below restaurant level, see the shirtless biker freefall passed them. Screams fill the air.

With a police officer on opposite sides of him, Dante is escorted across the courtyard of the plaza. He is barefooted and has his hands double handcuffed behind himself. As they approach an awaiting police patrol vehicle, a frantic voice yells across their issued radios. "He jumped! He jumped!"

Dante and the officers pause and look up. The nighttime floodlights surrounding the upper areas of the towering building are blinding. An awkward silence follows.

All that Dante and the officers sec hit the concrete walkway of the courtyard is a worn pair of boots and a faded pair of blue jeans.

Dante looks up towards the sky. He scans the clouds for any signs of his feathered friend. An odd smile rolls across Dante's face. He thinks back to a time when he and Reggie were on the road.

Dante thinks of a melody he and his best friend used to sing along with all the time. "*'Cause I'm as free as a bird now, and this bird you cannot change...*"

"Jay!" Gordon calls out in a fatherly tone. "Don't go too far, now." Gordon makes his way along the wooden planks of his wraparound porch. He's casually dressed in a pair of worn house shoes, jeans and a fuzzy robe. Gordon slides his hand across the primitive, log handrailing and comes to a halt. Gordon smiles as he looks out and beyond the clearing.

The tigon frolics along the grassy area, just passed Gordon's two-story barn. The faint dark stripes of the large orange and tan feline slightly reflect against the morning sun. The tigon bats at a fluttering butterfly.

The tigon appears to have no regard to its own size. He leaps through the air attempting to snag the butterfly as if he were a simple house cat and not a four hundred pound predator.

Gordon surveys his property from one end to the other. Jaakko continues to play with the butterfly, approaching the far tree line of the thick wooded area surrounding his rural home. The two-story barn stands quiet with its wide double doors wide open.

Scattered throughout the clearing, nearly a dozen wooden cable reels are seen. Each of the empty reels lays on their sides, six feet in diameter and standing over four feet tall.

Chasing the butterfly, the tigon effortlessly maneuvers in and out of the randomly placed wooden cable reels. From time to time, Jaakko leaps up onto the round surface a reel, attempting to gain the advantage on the elusive bug.

Gordon's red and white, VW microbus appears parked off to the side of the barn's opened doors with Gio's medical bus parked just this side of the narrow roadway. The forward, side door of the bus appears propped open with no movement from inside.

Just passed the opened gates of the roadway, Larry's sleek automobile appears. It gracefully rolls along the dirt road and comes to a halt behind the two-story med-lab. Gordon steps off the wooden planked porch and begins crossing the opened clearing.

Larry steps away from his dusty luxury car and tosses a curious glance toward Gio's bus. Larry is ready for work, dressed in his flawless business suit and polished shoes. "What's *he* doing here?" Larry asks. Gordon simply shrugs his shoulders.

"Hey!" Sonja playfully calls out from the bus. Larry turns to see Sonja bounding toward him. Her light colored, flowery dress seems to effortlessly float behind her. Sonja approaches Larry only to see a confused look on his face.

"Like I said, what's *he* doing here?"

"He's just running a few tests on me and Jay. Making sure everything is alright."

"...and?"

"Everything is fine, Larry," Gio announces as he exits the forward side door of his bus. He is unusually dressed for his standards. Gio wears a full length, silk robe, as if he had just crawled out of bed. Larry curiously look him over as Gio approaches. "Sonja is showing no residual effects. Just like I said."

"... and Jay?"

"He's fine, too. There's nothing to worry about." Gio smirks at Larry, turns and heads out into the clearing.

"You two seem to be getting along rather well," Larry says in a disgruntled voice. Sonja is caught off guard.

"Is Larry jealous?" Sonja thinks to herself. She looks deep into Larry's big brown eyes. "*Yes, I think so*!"

"Well, I'm glad that you two are alright," Larry finally manages to say. He and Sonja awkwardly stare at each other for a long moment. Slight movement in the corner of their eyes distracts them.

Out along the edge of the clearing, just beyond a pair of cable reels, the tigon and black panther playfully bat at each other. They each bare their razor sharp teeth and growl. The tigon leaps forward and spins to the side. The tigon tackles the black panther.

The black panther rolls over to his side and wraps his forepaws around the tigon's shoulders as is to give him a big hug. The black panther and tigon roll over and over.

The tigon springs up and charges away. The panther leaps up onto all fours and chases after the tigon. Taking large strides, the black panther catches up with the tigon.

The tigon spins and lunges upward on his hind legs. Likewise, the panther springs upward. The pair of large felines playfully collide into each other as if they were in the middle of a Sumo wrestling match. "That's just too weird," Larry says shaking his head toward Sonja.

"What is?"

"*Uncle Giovanni,*" Larry sarcastically replies.

"Well, it beats trying to kill each other."

"I guess you're right."

"So," Sonja shifts her weight from one foot to the other. She appears slightly on edge, almost fidgeting. "What did you want to talk about?"

"Me?" Larry is distracted for a moment. The tigon and black panther leap from cable reel to cable reel as if the pair of large cats were crossing a river from boulder to boulder. "I didn't want to talk about anything."

"Gordon said you wanted to talk to me."

"No..." Larry turns toward Gordon. "What's going on, professor?" Gordon reaches into the front pocket of his fuzzy robe. Taking a set of house keys in hand, he tosses them to Sonja.

"There's plenty of room to roam for you three. No sense in you and Jay traipsing across the country anymore. Besides, I have my other house in The City."

"I don't understand," Larry says. "Why now?" Gordon looks at Larry then toward Sonja. Gordon fatherly takes their hands and clasps them together as if he was a priest finalizing a wedding.

"You weren't looking for her," Gordon says to Larry. He then turns toward Sonja, "...and you didn't want to be found." Gordon's facial expression changes. He is saddened. "Don't waste another ten years. There's still time for you."

"There's time for you too, Gordon."

"No..." Gordon sadly shakes his head. "For some of us... time runs out." He painfully smiles at Larry. "I'll go see if Reggie is out of the shower." As Gordon heads back toward his house, a mischievous smirk rolls across Larry's face.

"What, Larry?" Sonja asks.

"There's *always* time." Larry leans in and kisses Sonja on the cheek. "When I get back to the office, there's a phone call I need to make."

"Why aren't you behind bars?" Reggie asks as Larry and Chloe escorts him into the lobby of the police prescient. Reggie has cleaned up a bit sporting a borrowed dress shirt, necktie and jeans.

In his black leather vest covered with various patches and insignias, Dante stands off to the side of the booking area.

Resting on the counter, Reggie's pair of boots, faded jeans and his black leather vest.

Sergeant William Dodds shuffles the stack of Dante's release papers and hands them to Chloe. She smiles at the well aging, senior police officer. Chloe's snappy, lavender business suit seems to compliment her green eyes. "It's good to see you, too," Dante sarcastically replies.

"What's going on, Dodds?" Larry asks.

"Well, you're boys have been cleared of murder charges."

"I don't understand."

"We've been given a *full* confession." Dodds smiles and gives Larry and Chloe a nod, motioning back and behind them. They turn to see Buster standing from the row of chairs along the far side of the main door.

The young gas station clerk appears humbled and almost embarrassed. He knows he should've came forward sooner. "I told them everything," Buster says to Reggie. "I said that you guys didn't have anything to do with Grandpa dying. It was all an accident."

"There *are* a few loose ends we're gonna have to tie up, Larry," Dodds says. "Evading police officers, resisting arrest, damage to property... *indecent exposure*!"

"None of that would have happened if you would have received my faxed Notice of Surrender and the Cease and Desist Order," Chloe states. Dodds thinks for a moment. Every eye is upon him.

"But, none of that would've happened if I had the fax..." Dodds turns toward Larry. "We'll work it out, Larry."

"Thanks, kid," Reggie says, as he shakes Buster's hand. He glances over toward Larry and Chloe then turns toward Dante. "Let's get outta here before they change their mind!"

"Thanks for coming, guys." Dante gives Chloe a hug then pats Larry on the shoulder.

"That's what friends do." Larry looks the group over. "Lunch anyone?"

"Sounds great," Reggie says with a smile. He reaches up and wiggles out of his constricting necktie. Reggie stuffs the tie into his pocket before quickly unbuttoning Gordon's dress shirt.

Reggie tosses the shirt onto the counter and retrieves his vest. He slides it over his white T-shirt and takes his jeans and boots in hand. "Son," Dodds says in a cautioning tone. "You might wanna finish changing your clothes elsewhere." Reggie looks around. Oops, he's not out on the road somewhere.

"Right! Thanks, Sergeant!" Reggie turns toward Larry and Chloe. "Let's eat!"

"Hey, Larry," Dante says, with a hint of concern. "There's just one more thing we have to ask you."

"What's that, Dante?" Larry sounds irritated.

"Can we catch a ride with you?"

"How ya' feelin', kiddo?" Jon asks, as he and Rafe enter Kaleen's private hospital room. The brothers make their way to the nearside of the angled bed. Sitting slightly propped up, Kaleen smiles up at them. She is extremely weak and pale.

"I'm doin' alright, I guess," she unconvincingly says. Kaleen has stabilized somewhat, no longer in need of the strands of tubes and wires connected to the various medical equipment.

Tez remains seated on the opposite side of Kaleen, still holding onto her hand. Lingering around the opened window behind Tez, Jay, Sonja and Gordon offer their support. Jay looks freshly showered and wears a black Zøø Crüe T-shirt.

"We're about done here, Jon," one of the band's roadies says from across the room. Jon and Rafe casually look across the sterile hospital room. A series of thick cables runs from the opened window to the suspended television set hanging in the corner. "I'm sorry you can't make it, Kaleen."

The roadie makes his way to the nearside of Kaleen and hands her a television remote control. "Channel twenty-eight. The opening band'll start about seven. You're the only one on the *planet* who's gonna watch the concert *live* on TV."

"Thanks," Kaleen says with a smile. Another roadie approaches the window and leans outside. He gives the thumbs-up to the transmitting van parked along the outside of the hospital's first floor.

"Hey, look who made it!" Rafe exclaims. Larry, Zoey, Reggie and Dante enter the room. Zoey is dressed to the hilt in Gothic black, ready to dance the night away. She slides in next to the bed and gives Kaleen a sisterly hug.

"There's she is!" Gio bellows out as he saunters into the room clutching onto a vase filled with two dozen, long stem red roses. He sets them onto the top of the dresser slightly to the side and below the hanging television set.

Gio stands slightly off to the end of Kaleen's bed. She's completely surrounded by all of her closest friends. An awkward silence follows.

"Hey, we better get goin'," Rafe announces. "We don't wanna be late for our own concert."

"Let's go! I'm ready to rock!" Dante eagerly says as he leans over and kisses Kaleen on the forehead.

"You're coming to the show, Dante?" Jon curiously asks. "I thought you'd catch up with us at the after party."

"Yeah, Dante," Rafe chimes in. "I don't know if you'd like our music. It's a lot heavier than the stuff we used to play in school."

"Why wouldn't I like your music?"

"Well... you're black," Jon says as a matter of fact. Rafe looks across Kaleen's bed and shakes his head.

"Yeah... you're black," Rafe states. Everyone around the room nods in agreement.

"You're black, Dante?" Tez asks in a confused tone. The private hospital room falls quiet. Then, the room is filled with uncontrollable laughter. "Got'cha!" Tez smiles, as he points his finger in Dante's direction.

"Oh sure! Real funny!" Dante exclaims, as he makes his way around the opposite side of the bed and playfully wrestles with Tez. "The blind kid's makin' fun of the only *brother* in the room!"

"You all get outta here!" Kaleen says, with a smile and a wave of her hand, shooing them all away. One by one, they all approach Kaleen and gives her a hug or an encouraging pat. There's an odd look on her face, an almost painful expression.

Jon and Rafe are the last two to stumble out of the room. The door slowly closes on its own. Tez remains seated along side of Kaleen's bed. He tenderly squeezes her hand. "We have a few hours before the concert starts. Is there anything I can get you?"

"No, I'm fine," Kaleen says in a whisper. "I'm a little tired. I think I'll take a little nap before the show..."

"Are you sure this is alright, Jon?" Sonja loudly asks. The air is filled with pounding drums, a roaring bass line and a screaming guitar riff. The opening band on stage, most popular in the 1980's, concludes their final song. Cheers and thunderous applauds shakes the rafters as the forward curtains close.

Sonja holds Jay close to her. Backstage is mere chaos. In full costume, T-Bone and Mark bounce up and down, pumping themselves up for the show.

Nearly stripped down, Rafe calmly sits on a stool twirling his drumsticks along his fingers. His legs, torso, arms and shoulders glisten as if he were covered in some kind of oil. His tattooed cheetah spots appear to be exploding from his flesh.

Jon gives Sonja a comforting look. "He'll be fine back here. The guys'll keep an eye on him." Jon nods his head toward the small army of roadies. Standing off to the side, Rick continues to oversee the ongoing musical production. He gives Sonja a wave, acknowledging Jay will be well looked after.

"Hey, Jon." A gruff looking roadie approaches Jon and hands him a pair of laminated V.I.P. passes. Jon takes the passes and loops one of the multicolored lanyards over Jay's neck. Sonja flips the lanyard of her *all access pass* over her head.

"You'll be fine back here," Jon says to Jay.

"Okay guys, we're up!" Rafe says to the rest of the band as he springs to his feet. "Sonja!" A roadie quickly approaches Sonja and takes her by the hand. "Time to go!" The roadie and Sonja disappear from backstage as the opening band appears from the main stage.

"Great show, guys!" Jon says to each of them. Randy, lead vocals and guitarist, Felix, bass player and keyboards then Guy, the band's drummer. They are covered with sweat. Their flashy costumes are drenched.

"We warmed'em up for ya'!" Randy says.

"Knock'em dead!" Felix adds. Guy leads Randy and Felix off to the side of backstage, heading for their dressing rooms along the attached hallway.

Jon drapes his wolf fur over his shoulders and slides his fingers into the elastic securing straps along his fingers. T-Bone adjust this moderately sized horns atop his head as Mark swoops his thick, black mohawk from side to side. All four of the band members adjust their headset microphones in front of their mouths. "Are you two ready for this?" Jon asks.

"Yeah, I'm ready," T-Bone says with a grin.

"Raring to go!" Mark adds.

"Remember, don't *change* until Rafe gives you the cue."

"How are we supposed to know what the cue is, Jon?" Mark asks.

"Oh, *you'll* know!" Rafe says, as he approaches the back curtains. He peers around the corner to see additional roadies scurrying across the main stage. All of the opening band's instruments, cords and gear has been replaced.

The main stage is a replicated jungle with palm trees and simulated boulders. The venue is too small for the band's previously used, acrobatic yellow trampolines. They will just have to make up for the absences of their floor props.

Rafe's towering lime green drum set sits directly in the back middle of the stage. Along opposite sides, massive dark green painted speakers point outward to the over capacity filled theater. Beyond the closed, forward curtain, the nearly eight thousand rock and roll fans begin to chant;

"Zøø Crüe!"

"Zøø Crüe!"

"Zøø Crüe!"

"Zøø Crüe!"

"Hey silly, wake up." The toilet of Kaleen's private bathroom flushes. Tez exits the bathroom and makes his way to the end of Kaleen's bed. "The concert's 'bout to start."

Tez finds his chair next to her bed. He slightly turns his head to the side and upward. The television set hanging up in the corner is slightly dark. The television cameras broadcasting the close circuit concert have nothing to focus onto yet. The bottom of the screen is filled with the main stage's green and orange footlights, glowing at a low level. The enthusiastic crowd continues;

"Zøø Crüe!"

"Zøø Crüe!"

"Zøø Crüe!"

"Zøø Crüe!"

Tez reaches for Kaleen's hand. It's cold and lifeless. Tez turns away from the hanging television set and stares at Kaleen.

"Happy Halloween, Seattle!" Jon yells into his headset microphone from backstage. "It's *great* to be back home!" The audience goes wild with cheers and applauds. With his favorite oddly designed, black and white guitar slung over his shoulder, Jon races onto the stage behind the closed curtain.

Rafe climbs in behind his massive drum set. T-Bone with his bass guitar and Mark with his rhythm guitar, finds their places on opposite sides of the stage. Jon turns and nods toward Rafe, T-Bone and then Mark. They're ready!

"Kaleen, wake up," Tez whispers. "The concert's 'bout to start." Tez hovers over her. Leaning his ear downward, he listens for her breath. There is none. Tez lowers his ear to her chest, he listens for a heartbeat. There are none.

The television hanging in the corner comes to life with exploding green and orange lights. The curtain is hurled open revealing Jon at center stage, T-Bone off to the right and Mark off to the left in front of his black and white, zebra stripped grand piano. Rafe stands behind his enormous drum set twirling his sticks through his fingers.

Jon slams his fingers across the strings of his guitar beginning the intro of the band's theme song. Through careful negotiations, Rick has obtained the rights to the song, *The Zoo*, originally preformed by another popular rock and roll band.

Mark joins in, adding an additional guitar riff to Jon's continuing intro. Behind them, Rafe adds in a growing drum pattern with T-Bone providing a bass line. The orange and green lights explode with the costumed fans screaming. "Kaleen, wake up." From under his dark sunglasses, a tear rolls down Tez's cheek.

Tez leans over and kisses Kaleen tenderly on the lips. He can feel that she has a smile on her face. An odd yet peaceful smile. Tez can feel that her injuries were not the cause of her death. She simply gave up the will to live.

He is overwhelmed with uncontrollable sadness which is quickly replaced by rage. Tez is heartbroken. He storms away from her bedside. Tez frantically searches for the private hospital room's door. He charges out into the hallway, weeping.

Tez collides into the opposite facing wall. He is unfamiliar with his surroundings. Tez searches for any other doorways, for any Braille panels indicating where his is. He slides across the wall, continuing his search.

The hallways are void of nurses and doctors. Tez appears to be alone on this floor. He bumps into a gurney and shoves it away from himself. Tez is distraught and in anguish. He has lost his way. He is seeking an emergency exit or a stairwell. "Tez? What's the matter, dear?"

Kathy reaches out to him. She takes him by the hands and places his palms against her cheeks. "Kathy?" Tez frantically asks.

"Yes, it's me." Kathy clutches onto his hands and draws him in closer. "Where are you going?"

"I was trying to get to the roof."

"The roof?"

"Yes! The roof!" Tez angrily says.

"Alright." Kathy pauses a moment. "Alright. Take my hand and I'll help you." She leads Tez along the brightly lit hallway and halts at the closed elevator door. Kathy presses the button with one hand and continues to hold onto Tez with the other.

"I'm sorry I snapped at you, Kathy. It's just..."

"What happened? Did she..."

"Yes." Tez chokes back. "She's gone..."

"I'm so sorry, dear." The elevator door slides open. Kathy leads Tez inside. They are quite as the elevator takes them up to the top floor.

Tez can feel the cool evening air against his face as Kathy leads him across the rooftop. The sparkling lights of The City surrounds them. She leads Tez to the edge of the rooftop. He raises his head as if he were searching the heavens. "What are you looking for?" Kathy asks in a motherly tone.

Tez looks toward the western sky then towards the east. He slightly turns on his axis and gazes up toward the southern sky then toward the north. He's still searching.

Although Tez suffers from a lack of sight, he can see the nighttime constellations, more of a sense of feeling. "There, that one," Tez says to Kathy as he points up into the sky.

The Beta Aquarii is the brightest star in the Aquarian Constellation. From deep beyond the horizon, a bright shooting star appears and races across the sky.

The shooting star appears to be evading the green and blue planet below. Instead, the shooting star joins the aquatic constellation. The massive collection of stars moves across the sky, maneuvering into position and forms into a familiar outline; a floating mermaid. The stars above seem to be spelling out her name. The name of the most recently arrived celestial being.

~ XIII ~

"I can't see Jay from here!" Sonja shouts into Larry's ear. She slightly shoves her way through the forward mob along the front of the stage. The orange and green footlights are nearly blinding.

"There he is!" Larry announces, as he points his finger. The young man is seen slightly backstage with the laminated *V.I.P* pass dangling from the multicolored lanyard around his neck. Jay bounces his head to the ongoing, upbeat rock and roll tune the headliner band is pumping out across stage.

Rick stands off to the side of Jay, keeping a close watch. Jay is overwhelmed, he has never experienced anything like this before. As Jon leads the rest of the band into the chorus of one of their number one charted songs, Jay raises his fist and hammers it through the air and even begins to mumble through to the lyrics.

Mark rushes across the stage and playfully collides into T-Bone. With his fingers whizzing across his guitar strings, Mark leans into T-Bone's microphone. He and T-Bone belt out the backup lyrics of the song. T-Bone's hands blaze up and down the four thick strings of his bass guitar as Marks races through a furious guitar riff. They are musical warriors.

Jon slightly turns his head and gives Rafe a nod. Quickly looking over toward Mark and T-Bone, they too understand Jon's unsaid direction. The concert's almost over and it's time to wrap things up.

In unison, Zøø Crüe slams down upon their instruments. The large theater is flooded with loud, resonating chords. The orange and green footlights of the stage falls dark just as the curtains draw closed. The crowd goes wild!

Filling the front area directly below center stage, Larry and Sonja thrash their hands through the air. Next to them, Dante and Reggie clap and cheer for their musical friends to return to the stage.

Zoey is still getting used to Gio being back in the family. She does her best, encouraging Gio to coax the band back out for an encore. Gio is less than enthusiastic, yet is slowly loosening up a bit. As a father does, Gordon stands slightly behind his former students, making sure that nothing gets too far out of hand.

The entire theater is a wave of moving bodies and swaying arms. It appears not one soul is out of costume. The legend of The Zøø Crüe has always proceeded them. From the back wall of the auditorium to the front of the stage and filling every seat in between, the costumes become more elaborate and creative.

Loyal to The Zøø Crüe's motif, wolves, cheetahs, bulls and zebras are the most prominent. Tossed into the mass of concertgoers; bears, raccoons, foxes, kangaroos and giraffes. Even a handful of costumed Dalmatians are seen.

Oddly fitting in, a lizard, which became popular due to an auto insurance campaign, waves his reptilian hands through the air. Off to the left side of the theater, a well organized group of fans are seen. Nearly twenty in all, this group of concertgoers are dressed in similar pink and gray rabbit costumes. One big happy family!

In another section of the theater, a group of raging fans are seen. However, quite out of place. The costumed spectators are dressed as their favorite superheroes; Batman, Spiderman, Superman, Catwoman, Thor, The Hulk and even a Wonder Woman or two. They are known as the party crashers.

Consuming the front stage on opposite sides of Gordon, continuing to watch over his brood, the more seductive and sexy costumes are revealed. The tigress and lioness. The dairy cow, the kitty and the bunny. No, the *other* bunny. Then, from behind the stage curtains-

Rafe pounds his worn drumsticks across his deep sounding snare drum. The rhythm is almost military in fashion with more of an edge. Several hard beats are accented within the pattern as it then begins to repeat its self. Over and over.

From the left side of the stage, Mark chimes in with his six string guitar. He accompanies Rafe, repeating the same five chords, up and down along the shiny strings. Rafe kicks in a bass drum pattern as T-Bone begins a low and steady bass guitar riff. The curtains slowly open-

With the orange footlights glowing across his face, Jon stands at center stage with his favorite oddly designed, black and white striped guitar in hand. The soft green spotlight shines down on Rafe along backstage.

Jon casually glances over to Mark then toward T-Bone standing right stage. All four of the musicians have stripped away their onstage garb. There is no wolf head nor fur around Jon's head and shoulders.

Mark's natural mohawk has replaced his black zebra headgear. T-Bone's bighorns are nowhere to be seen. He's even removed the large gold ring from his nose. The three front men wear nearly identical black spandex pants, reflecting off the orange and green footlights.

As for Rafe, his tattooed flesh is only contrasted by his basketball shorts. For the most part, they look normal. Well, normal for a rock and roll band. "You ready, Rafe?" Jon sings.

"A-huh..."

"T-Bone?"

"Yeah..."

"Mark?"

"O-kay..."

"Al-right, fellas!" Jon pauses a brief moment "Let's gooooooooo!" The extended song intro abruptly ends. Jon joins into Mark's five chord riff, up and down along the neck of his black and white guitar. The upbeat tune breaks away into some kind of strange ballroom blitz.

With his guitar, Jon plays the lyrics of the song with Mark and T-Bone providing backup with their instruments. There are no words sung. The fast paced musical interlude continues for several minutes with Jon, Mark and T-Bone bouncing back and forth across the front of the stage.

Along the footlights, the pyrotechnics explode sending clouds of smoke and flames through the air. Jon, T-Bone and Mark step quickly off to the side. The stage falls dark with the exception on the green spotlight focused on Rafe as he begins his drum solo.

Rafe's shoulders begin to narrow. His chest, back, torso and arms are quickly covered with orange fur with black spots. As he continues his monstrous drum solo, his hands mutate into powerful claws, clutching onto the worn drumsticks.

From behind himself, a thick round tail appears from the waistband of his basketball style shorts. The wagging tail is covered with similar orange fur and black spots with a fluffy black tuft at the end.

Rafe's facial features have transformed and has assumed his alter's characteristics. White fur surrounds his mouth and whiskers. Black teardrop fur runs along the sides of his muzzle accenting his piercing orange and black eyes.

The upright cheetah pounds his sticks along the mounted tom-toms then thunders his paws along the peddles of his double-bass drum. He concludes his drum solo yet, keeps a low and constant drum pattern as the green spotlight fades off of him.

Jon steps forward and stands at center stage as the orange spotlight focuses on the creature. His transformation is already completed. The towering upright wolf is covered with dark coarse fur. Shiny and well kempt.

He scrapes his claws across the strings of his black and white guitar creating evil hissing sounds. The wolf quickly moves his forepaws up along the middle section of the neck of the guitar. His claws race across the strings continuing his furious guitar solo.

The wolf's tail seems to be swaying to the constant drum beat in the background. The wolf arches his back and raises his furry head. He howls as he slams down the last chord of his guitar and holds it for several seconds. The wolf steps to the side as the orange spotlight fades.

A purple spotlight shines down on Mark as he steps forward and positions himself along the footlights at the left of the stage. The cheetah continues his low drum pattern as the wolf provides an occasional guitar riff. Mark begins his guitar solo, rivaling the wolf's previous musical efforts.

Mark's ears begin to mutate outward and upward along the sides of his head. These extremities widen and flatten, taking the shape of large bat-like ears covered with light colored, bristly fur. His face begins to mutate outward, taking the shape of a muzzle of a canine.

Although Mark's torso and waist appears to be extending, his legs seem to be shrinking in length. His arms stretch outward becoming longer. This odd, upward appearance seems to slightly off balance the transforming guitar player.

Mark's exposed flesh is quickly covered with light brown fur with black spots in a variety of sizes. His once human mohawk now resembles a small, furry mane along the back of his neck. Mark's fingers and toes have transformed into claws, not those of a feline but those of an odd looking canine.

As the hyena raises his head, he seems to let out a laughing cackle. The wolf bounces his way across the stage and adds a screaming guitar riff.

The hyena and wolf mimic each other for a moment, firing a guitar riff back and forth. With the cheetah accenting the end of the hyena's guitar solo with thundering floor tom-toms, the purple spotlight falls dim.

The low roaring bass guitar solo fills the theater. T-Bone steps forward and stands at right, center stage. A blue spotlight covers him as he strikes his thumb repeatedly along the thick, four strings of the bass guitar, almost a plucking manner.

T-Bone's left hand is a mere blur along the neck of the bass guitar. His fingers fly across the strings as the transformation begins. T-Bone's pinky and ring finger mold together as does his middle and pointer finger. His left thumb retracts inside of his hand creating a nub of sorts.

T-Bone's hands take the shape of hooves, each with two distinctive digits continuing to play the four stringed guitar. His facial features expand outward. At first, taking the shape of a wild pig or a razorback.

His face continues to mutate with two defined pairs of tusks emerging from the sides of his enlarged mouth. The upper set of ivory extends nearly ten inches and is curved at the ends. The smaller second set of tusks are sharper and more dangerous.

Along the extended snout, a smaller pair of gray, fleshy bumps appears directly above the large pair of tusks. Directly below the creature's eyes, a larger set of identical bumps emerge. A thick, dark brown mane, similar to a mule, grows outward between the pair of pig-like ears.

T-Bone's muscular chest is covered with coarse, light colored hair. His flesh gives way to a gray, rough textured hide. Sprouting out from within his black spandex pants, a gray tail with a dark tuft appears.

The warthog pounds his hoof along the strings of his bass guitar. He concludes his solo as he defiantly places one of his hind hooves onto the edge of the stage and footlight.

The stage is flooded with light. The orange, purple and blue spotlights focus and follow the three rocking musicians. Blanketed with the green spotlight, the cheetah increases the volume of his distinctive drum pattern, the introduction of another borrowed musical anthem.

The wolf, hyena and warthog bound along the footlights playing their guitars, encouraging the costumed fans to sing along with their final encore. "*I, wanna rock and roll all night...*"

The wolf leans over the edge of the stage and reaches out his claw toward the festival seating. Among the dancing costumed fans, he quickly takes hold of a panda's forepaw and slightly shakes it. The wolf returns to the hyena and warthog, "*...and party everyday!*"

Directly in front of the stage, the panda stands upright. She raises her clutched, black paws in the air and wildly waves them to the loud, upbeat music. She stands inches from the footlights, surrounded by fellow concertgoers. The panda smiles as she nudges her furry black elbow into the Arian's ribs next to her.

Dante pounds his fist through the air in beat to the rock and roll song. His hooves dance, side to side along the floor. Dante's Pan-like lower appearance blends in with the surrounding costumed fans.

Dante is bare chested but still wears his black leather vest with various patches and insignias. Atop his head, his full set of curved, bighorn sheep antlers. A few of the spectators behind Reggie and Dante are quite annoyed. Their view of the stage is slightly blocked.

Reggie flaps his wings and continues to keep them extended, resembling some kind of Archangel. Reggie has removed his black leather vest, allowing his set of extended condor wings free movement, spanning outward from his upper shoulder blades.

Reggie and Dante knock into each other, dancing to the ongoing upbeat tunc. Reggie slightly bumps into the lioness standing next to him. Keiko lets out a low growl toward Reggie. He is apologetic as he reaches up and scruffs the top of her head.

Continuing to stand upright on her hind legs, Keiko swoops her large paw around and slaps Reggie on the backside. Reggie smiles as he reaches over and gives the lioness a hug from the side.

The wolf lets out a howl as his claws conclude a screaming guitar riff. The wolf bounds to the footlights and edge of the stage and points out toward the nearest group of fans.

Next to Keiko, the tiger roars back at the wolf. The tiger and wolf high-five each other. The wolf bounds from the edge of the stage and rejoins the hyena and the warthog continuing to play their guitars.

Keiko and the tiger slightly glance at each other. She lets out a low growl. The tiger takes his orange and white muzzle and nudges it into the lioness' neck. Her tail wags as she returns the affectionate gesture.

Standing on the opposite sides of Reggie and Dante, the black panther appears quite annoyed. The crashing cymbals and booming of the drums as well as the screaming guitars is too loud for the panther. He looks as if one of the human concert-goers has just stepped on his tail.

The panther is somewhat less than enthusiastic attending the concert. He's just going through the motions. Although he and the tiger have made up their differences, the black panther is just at the concert to show support for the rest of his group of alters.

Trying to get the black panther into more of the spirit of things, the upright komodo dragon reaches up his scaly claws and shakes the large cat by the shoulders.

The large reptile is less attractive than his shapeshifting counterparts with pale tan scales with a hint of green. However, this has always been Gordon's favorite alternative form.

Over the years, this elite group has mastered their gifts. They are able to manipulate their ability to transform. Able to retain their human consciousness and faculties while their outward appearance is quite different.

Although mesmerized by the continuing musical encore, the rock and roll fans near the front of the stage are nothing less than impressed with the elaborate costumes around them; the panda, Keiko and the tiger, the black panther and Komodo dragon, the Arian next to the condor. These costumes must have cost a fortune. Why not? It's Halloween!

From the mayhem on stage, the wolf, hyena and the warthog line up along the left side of the stage. In unison, they violently rock their bodies back and forth to their continuing guitar playing encore. Rafe powerfully slams down on the mounted tom-toms with cymbals ringing as the footlights explode.

Along the front row, the tiger eagerly paws Keiko on her furry shoulder. She seems bewildered for a moment as the tiger motions and points his paw toward the right back area of the stage.

Rick steps out from the drawn curtains. He walks slightly backward as if to be coaxing someone to show themselves. There is no movement for several seconds. Again, Rick motions his hands, "C'mon!"

The tigon is timid at first. He peeks his head around the edge of the drawn curtains. The loud music and flashing lights is a great distraction. Rick smiles as he motions the tigon further out onto the stage.

Jaakko lifts his head several times, sniffing the smoky air. Feeling more confident, the tigon steps forward and strolls along side of Rafe's towering drum set. The cheetah winks at Jaakko as he passes. The crowd goes wild, cheering and whistling for the newly arrived band mascot.

Jaakko paws his way along the blinding footlights of the stage allowing concertgoers to reach up and touch his fur. Occasionally, the tigon leans down and licks a cheek or two. Keiko is very proud as she gives her son a loving scratch under his neck as he passes by her.

The tiger gives Jaakko a fatherly pat on the shoulder with his extended paw. The tigon slightly turns and raises his head toward the audience then lets out an approving roar.

With Jaakko now defiantly standing at center stage facing out toward the fans, the hyena and warthog bound behind him and find their positions at right stage. The wolf remains at left stage as the musicians powerfully strum the last guitar chord and hold it. Rafe's paws are at a mere blur, thundering across his lime green drum set;

The warthog belts out a series of snorts-
The cheetah stands up and lets out a low hiss-
The hyena laughingly cackles-
The wolf arches his back and howls-
The tigon looks out across the audience and roars-
The crowd roars back...

"You did very well tonight, Jay," Gordon says in a fatherly tone. The house is quiet and dimly lit. It's well into the early morning hours. From outside the opened sliding glass door, the soft lapping waves of The Sound roll up onto the shoreline.

Gordon makes his way across his back living room carrying a pair of steaming coffee mugs. He hands the mug of hot chocolate to Jay who sits near the center of the worn couch. Gordon's warm beverage has more of a kick. Along the armrest of the couch, several blankets and a pillow. "Are we ever gonna be normal?"

"Tell me, what's normal?" Gordon takes a sip of his spiked coffee then sits on the loveseat near the end of the couch. He leans over and sets his mug down on the familiar wooden planked coffee table.

"You know..."

"There are a lot of different levels of normality. I think you need to be more specific, Jay."

"Well, what happened tonight."

"The older you get and with more practice, I'll help, you'll be able to control your gift. You'll be able to manipulate the appearance of your outward being while maintaining reason and thought."

"Wow, that was deep," Jay sarcastically replies. "That's *not* what I meant."

"I know what you meant." Gordon takes a swig of his coffee and raises up from the loveseat. A slight and painful expression is briefly seen. His knees aren't what they used to be.

"So, what do you think about mom and Larry?"

"Why would my opinion matter for anything?"

"I know you saw them at the concert. The way they were nudging and cuddling with each other." *Yuk,* Jay seems to be saying without saying it.

"Yeah, I thought you saw that, too."

"So, now what happens? We become one happy family? Am I supposed to call him *Dad* like he's been around all my life?"

Gordon makes his way across the back living room area and approaches a filled bookshelf. He smiles as he tosses a glance toward Dante's framed pro wrestling marquee.

Gordon begins scanning the spines of the rows of books, running his forefinger along each one, searching for the title he is looking for. "I have an extensive collection of philosophers, mathematicians, physiatrists and even several editions of famous movie star and celebrity quotes." Gordon reached up and removes a worn, leather bound book from the shelf.

As he turns and slowly makes his way back toward the loveseat, Gordon opens the book and flips through its soft, parchment pages. He sits and runs his finger along the entry he was searching for. "Therefore, do not worry about tomorrow, for tomorrow will worry about itself. Each day has enough trouble of its own."

Gordon looks over toward Jay who has a slightly puzzled look on his face. The young man ponders the words for several moments. Gordon leans over and hands the book to Jay who closes the book and gazes upon the worn cover; *King James Version*. "I've never seen this book before."

"It's worth looking into," Gordon says before finishing off his spiked coffee. He slightly hobbles around the end of the loveseat, "Don't stay up too late."

"I won't Uncle G," Jay says without looking up. He is focused on the book. Gordon smiles as he makes his way toward the hallway.

"*Uncle G*," Gordon thinks to himself. *"He's never called me that before. I kinda like it.*" Gordon pauses and turns, "Jay..."

"Yeah?" Jay replies, slightly looking up. Gordon pauses a moment before reciting a memorized passage from the worn, leather bound book.

"He who created Heaven and the things that are in it, the earth and the things that are in it and the sea and the things that are in it." Gordon smiles. "That means our kind as well..."

"Larry, can we get outta here?" Sonja loudly asks over the thumping music. "This really isn't my scene." Sonja nearly cowers in the corner of the darkly painted kitchen. Larry stands close to her, looking out beyond the ongoing after party.

Nearly a hundred concertgoers and costumed fans have swarmed their way into Zoey's Gothic dwelling. Bottles of beer, shot glasses and mixed cocktails create a rainbow of colors. There are drinks everywhere.

Larry wraps his arm around Sonja and looks deep into her eyes. He can sense she feels extremely out of place. The eccentric fans of the rock and roll band, the constant thundering music and the continuing movement of the wave of bodies. "Yeah, let's go."

Larry takes Sonja by the hand and weaves their way out of the crowded kitchen into the sprawling living room area. Larry catches a glimpse of Gio off in the corner.

Gio is cornered by two costumed, female concertgoers. One is dressed in a seductive kitty outfit with the other wearing sexy bumblebee black and yellow.

Larry slightly nods at Gio as he continues to lead Sonja through the pulsating crowd. Suddenly from the outside door, three of the band's roadies crash inward. They each carry a circular, old style wash tub filled with ice and a replenishing stock of beer bottles.

Standing against the wall, Mark and T-Bone are surrounded by a group of costumed, female rock and rollers. They appear to laugh at T-Bone's dry wit and Mark's brash sense of humor.

All the way across the room, Dante and Reggie sit at opposite ends of the couch and the dark surfaced coffee table. Sitting likewise next to them, four additional seductively costumed groupies who have crashed the party.

Reggie takes a quarter in hand, carefully aims and throws it to the surface of the table. The quarter bounces, flies through the air and lands in a large glass of beer. The small group laughs as Reggie points to a sexy looking tigress. She takes the glass of beer and pours it down her throat in a matter of seconds.

Larry forces their way through a gathering of concert-goers and nearly topples into Jon. The wall of costumed beauties seems endless. The swarm of seductively dressed women seem uncontrollably drawn to Jon's animal magnetism. "Hey!" Jon smiles as he shouts over the music.

"Hey! We're going to get out of here."

"C'mon, Larry. It's only four-thirty."

"Yeah, I know. It's..."

"It's not like the old days," Rafe interrupts. Rafe and Zoey plow their way through the crowd. Rafe and Larry look at each other. Then, they each curiously look at Sonja and Zoey.

Rafe and Larry smile. Yeah, they get it! "Thanks for comin' guys. Let's not make the next reunion another ten years."

"I'll have my people call your people," Larry says in a jestful tone.

"Sure, Larry. I've heard *that* before," Jon replies. Brief handshakes and hugs are exchanged. There are no farewell tears. Somehow, they know they will soon be together again.

Larry and Sonja trudge through the partying masses, along the wall and back into the kitchen area. Taking a last glimpse of the raging event, Larry and Sonja slip out the door into the early morning hours.

Zoey leans in toward Rafe and whispers into his ear. Due to the loud ongoing music, Rafe could not understand what she said. Zoey tenderly squeezes his hand and gives him *the look*. "*Oh!*" Rafe surprisingly thinks.

Zoey clutches onto Rafe's hand and leads him through the groups of partiers. As they round the corner, Zoey discovers that Mark, T-Bone and an assortment of costumed fans have invaded her bedroom area.

Rows upon rows of empty beer bottles cover the closed lid of her black and lavender lined coffin. The entire room is filled with boisterous people. Shaking her head, Zoey clings onto Rafe's hand and leads him through the crowded room.

Zoey pauses and surveys her desperate situation. Nearly every inch of her home is consumed with bodies. Beyond the kitchen, the outside door slams open with even more costumed fans arriving.

Rafe decides to take charge. He pulls at Zoey's hand, nearly dragging her back through the living room. He reaches up toward the lever of the stereo system as to turn off the loud music. Zoey tenderly reaches up and stops Rafe from doing so. She has a mischievous look on her face.

Zoey leads Rafe along the black painted wall and turns the corner. The closed door seems to be inviting them. Zoey reaches for the knob and quickly opens the door. Rafe and Zoey dart inward and close the door behind themselves.

However, the door does not fully close. It slightly swings open, revealing another area to be conquered by the uninvited guests. From the corner of his eye, Gio sees Rafe and Zoey dismiss themselves from the party. He knows where they're going. They're going upstairs.

The lightly painted side door of Chloe's kitchen opens. Rafe and Zoey burst through and close the door quickly behind. From the basement, they can hear the loud muffled sounds of countless conversations, laughter and the constant thumping of the music.

Chloe's house is dark and lifeless as if no one were home. Zoey leans over and kisses Rafe on the cheek. He smiles and lets the gesture of affection sink in. Rafe turns to Zoey and takes her in his arms. He tenderly kisses her on the lips, not seeming to mind her black lipstick.

Zoey's knees fall weak; her arms tremble. This is the moment she's been waiting for. Zoey's waited years for this chance. Rafe and Zoey embrace. She smiles as she buries her face along the curve of his neck.

Zoey takes Rafe by the hand and shuffles out of the dimly lit kitchen. They are too preoccupied to see the red blinking message light of the telephone.

Zoey and Rafe dart along the narrow hallway and crash into Chloe's bedroom. Rafe kicks his foot, slamming the door closed behind them.

"You have *got* to be kidding me," Chloe mumbles under her breath. She stands at the end of the hallway in sheer disgust. Chloe's shoulders are damp with a towel wrapped around her washed hair. She tightens a matching towel under her arms. She is barely covered.

Chloe tiptoes through the piles of beer bottles and stands at the edge of the living room. Her entire home is thrashed!

The coffee table that stood in front of the matching couch and loveseat has been crushed and lays in shambles on the stained carpet. The couch and loveseat's cushions have been removed and appear scattered across the room.

The morning sun peeks through the windows with the curtains precariously hanging from their bent rods. It looks as if a hurricane had hit the night before.

Chloe cautiously backtracks and enters the kitchen. It is in much worse condition than the living room. The floor is covered with pools of spilled beer and colorful mixed drinks. Dozens of empty pizza boxes blanket the filthy counter tops with half eaten slices everywhere. Empty beer bottles and glasses have been piled up in both of the sinks.

The dining room table is littered with a wide assortment of discarded clothing and costumes. Empty bottles of rum, whiskey and scotch lay about the floor. The inside of Chloe's house appears as if a garbage truck had unloaded its entire payload.

Rafe abruptly wakes up, hearing a terrifying roar from the living room. He sits up in bed and covers himself with one of Chloe's sheets. A painful series of growls echoes into the hallway.

Rafe hears a thunderous crash destroying the dining room table, sending chairs and empty bottles in all directions. The ferocious battle shakes the floor. The sounds of the horrific brawl shifts from the dining room and collides into the living room.

Rafe leaps from Chloe's bed and wraps the sheet around himself. He charges out of the bedroom and races down the hallway. The living room is filled with the sounds of an ongoing war. Ear piercing roars, wild hissing and angry growls.

Rafe stops dead in his tracks. The floor is covered with broken glass, shattered bottles and obliterated furniture. Standing on all fours in the middle of the living room, the panda looks up at him and growls.

Her black and white fur is spotted with smeared blood. A trace of light wounds runs along her white muzzle with traces of blood seeping out of her black nose. The panda seems to be panting and out of breath. Who was she fighting with?

Rafe slowly inches his way forward. She lowers her head and whimpers at him. "Zoey?" He drapes the sheet over his shoulder and tucks it under his arm. With his hands free, Rafe opens his palms and draws closer to the frightened panda. "Zoey, is that you?"

The panda barks at Rafe and begins pacing. He approaches her and tenderly runs his hand along her damp fur between her fluffy black ears. "Over here..."

Rafe leads the panda through the chaotic living room and motions toward one of the cushions of the couch on the floor. The panda pads her way onto the cushion and plops down. She painfully looks up at him. The black patches of fur under her eyes are softened with tears.

The panda raises her head and nestles her muzzle along the curve of Rafe's neck. He reaches over and lovingly wraps his tattooed arms around her neck. The panda lets out a confused bleating sound. "It'll be alright..."

The panda lays her head down in Rafe's lap and stretches out the rest of her body. Her hind legs dangle several feet over the edge of the cushion as the transformation begins.

Her white button tail dissipates and is absorbed into the small of her back directly above her tailbone. The panda's black and white fur begins to quickly retract into her outer skin. The panda's hind quarters shrink in width and begin taking the shape of human legs.

The black fur covering the panda's forepaws is vacuumed inward and mutates into fingers. Rafe loosens the sheet from under his arms and drapes it over the transforming creature.

The panda's large round head reduces in diameter. Her black fluffy ears withdraw and appear to reposition themselves along opposite sides of her head. Her wounded muzzle retracts and begins taking on human facial features.

The girth of the panda continues to transform, shrinking three times the size. All of the black and white fur has vanished. The panda is no more. With her eyes closed, she lays on the cushion covered with the sheet. Rafe runs his fingers through her raven hair. "Zoey?" Rafe quietly asks.

Faint scratches run along her cheeks. Smeared blood runs up and down along her arms. "Chloe?" She remains quiet and still with her head in Rafe's lap. He caresses her forehead and moves a few loose strands of hair away from her damp eyelids. "Chloe, is this you?" She says nothing.

Rafe can feel her breathing intensify. Her chest seems to be slightly heaving up and down. He can feel her entire body becoming ridged. She's tensing up. The raven haired woman is terrified. Then, she begins to uncontrollably weep. Rafe tenderly reaches down and takes her by the shoulders.

She faces him as she continues to sob. The mixture of tears and the blood from her light facial wounds covers her cheeks. Rafe takes a corner of the sheet and wipes her face. "I had to kill them," she finally manages to say. "They were driving me insane. They wouldn't stop arguing with each other." She takes a deep breath, "I had to kill them both..."

"Melissa?" Rafe whispers. "Is this you?"

"Yes," Melissa softly replies. "It's me." She catches her breath as she looks around the destroyed living room. Her weeping has stopped. A strange and confused look fills her eyes as horrific images of her past whirl in front of her-

The house is a raging inferno. Outside, the sounds of a fire engine's siren wails. The front door crashes open with a young firefighter charging inward. Clutching onto his axe, the fireman scans the blazing living room. There is no one.

The flames have consumed the entire second story of the contemporary home. The heat and smoke is quickly inching its way down the staircase and oak banister. The firefighter races forward and darts into the kitchen. The appliances have all been melted away.

The firefighter kicks in the door of the father's den. The air is filled with charring smoke. At first, the firefighter sees nothing but a vacant desk and walls filled with smoldering books. Then in the corner, he sees a frightened, green eyed little girl with matted raven hair and oversized ears.

Melissa Richards sits quietly in her flowered nightgown, clutching onto a damaged framed picture. The firefighter races toward her and scoops her up. He charges back toward the door of the den only to find the flames have reached the lower level of the home.

With little Melissa draped over his shoulder, he turns and dashes back toward the desk. With one hand, the firefighter takes the back of the chair in hand and hurls it through the window. The glass shatters.

The opened window creates a vacuum. Billowing smoke from the rest of the burning home runs like a roaring river into the den and out through the window.

The firefighter clears away the fragments of glass with his axe then crawls through the window. Melissa clings onto his shoulder with one hand and the charred framed picture in the other as they escape the approaching flames-

"I just couldn't handle it, Rafe," Melissa finally says. "What was I supposed to do? I was six..." Rafe quickly raises up from the couch cushion and approaches the hearth and fireplace. He leans over to the floor and retrieves the damaged framed picture.

Rafe plops back down next to Melissa and hands her the charred frame. She is hesitant to look at it. Melissa looks at Rafe with a bewildered look. She seems more confused than ever. "Zoey helped for awhile. She took away the pain. She helped me forget about Mom and Dad."

Melissa slowly turns the framed picture over and gazes upon its charred images. Jonathan and Samantha Richards stand on opposite sides of their beloved daughter. Her family is posing with the colorful and lively amusement park in the background. An athletic looking mother, a strikingly handsome father and a raven haired young girl with piercing green eyes. The family looks quite happy.

The framed picture has suffered some damage due to the chaotic party the night before. The glass has been broken. A single crack runs from the bottom of the frame to the top. The crack appears to split little Melissa in two. "Zoey began to get outta control. She needed some discipline... some order. Chloe took care of that," Melissa says in a near whisper.

Melissa runs her finger down along the crack of the charred picture. The young image of herself appears to be separated down the middle. One side of normality and one side with a darker edge. "Don't you see, Rafe? I had to kill them both."

"Just because they're gone, doesn't mean they're still not a part of you. You'll always have them. Deep inside when you need them."

RING - RING.

RING - RING.

Rafe shuffles across the living room floor, careful not to step into the layers of broken glass and fragments of damaged furniture. As he reaches for the telephone hanging from the kitchen wall, Rafe sees the red blinking message light. "Hello?"

"Hello? Rafe, is that you?" Larry asks from the other end of the receiver.

"Yeah, it's me."

"What are you doing at Chloe's?"

"It's a long story. The party we had last night *kinda* got outta hand..."

"That's all you had to say. That's why we left early."

"So, what's up?"

"I guess Chloe hasn't checked her messages yet."

"No, why?"

"Can I talk to her?"

"Chloe's not here."

"Oh. I called Zoey, too. Can you run downstairs and see if she's up?"

"Zoey's not here, either." Rafe takes a deep breath. "Melissa is here."

"Melissa!?" Larry is completely astonished. "When did *that* happen?"

"Just a few minutes ago. She said she killed them. She said she had to kill'em both."

"I guess she's ready to move past her parents on her own now."

"I guess..."

"Rafe..."

"Yeah?"

"There's no easy way to say this..." Rafe quietly listens to Larry. He lowers his head and runs his palm over his face as he hears the news.

"Yeah, I'll tell her." Rafe hangs up the receiver. He lets out a deep sigh as he tiptoes his way back into the living room.

Melissa has moved from the couch cushion on the floor and stands sideways along the hearth of the fireplace. She tenderly sets the charred, framed picture back in place and gazes upon it. "Tell me what, Rafe?"

"Kaleen didn't make it." Melissa gasps. "Larry said he's taking care of all the arrangements."

"What about Tez?"

"Gio picked him up from the hospital this morning." Rafe and Melissa embrace each other. They are saddened by the loss of a dear friend. Melissa rests her head on Rafe's tattooed shoulder. There's something else in her eyes.

Melissa thinks of Zoey and Chloe and that she has broken their connection. She thinks of her two personas she no longer needs. It will be difficult at first but she feels she's ready to mourn her parents on her own. Melissa thinks of Kaleen. She thinks in a way of herself and her former personalities, collectively as three. "I'm sorry *we* didn't have a chance to say good-bye..."

* * * * *

"Good-morning, Night Crawlers," Tez solemnly says into the suspended microphone. "That's about it for me. I'm gonna send you out with a few commercials. Be right back."

Tez switches off the *on-air* button and flicks a lever. A series of prerecorded commercials begins to fill the dimly lit radio studio.

He's dressed in a black dress shirt with no tie and dark faded jeans. The crush velvet posters of the legendary rock stars look down at Tez as he effortlessly moves his hands across the massive control board.

Along the extended counter to Tez's right, next to a hot pink, oozing lava light, a sealed, funerary urn appears among the shadows. The glass urn has a marbled lavender and purple appearance, like a colorful, psychedelic candy cane.

Tez hears the series of commercials coming to an end. He spins his wheeled chair completely around and swiftly runs his fingertips along the rows of albums and compact disk cases.

Finding the album he is searching for, Tez spins about and slides the round vinyl record out of its cover. His right elbow catches the side of the colorful urn and sends it toppling from the counter to the tile floor. However, there is no shatter.

Tez places the needle of the turntable onto the record and cues up his last song for his shift. "I didn't smell you come in," Tez replies with a slight grin.

"It's good to know I can still be stealthy when I want to be," Gordon says as he tenderly holds Kaleen's urn. The retired professor has cleaned up a bit donning a black turtleneck sweater, dark pressed slacks and spit-shine, black polished shoes.

"Yeah, especially at *your* age." Tez smiles as he holds up his finger toward Gordon. "*Shhhhhhh.*" The series of prerecorded commercials fades to silence. Tez flips the *on-air* button. "Hey, Night Crawlers. Thanks for tuning in. You're listening to one-o-one point three, K-R-W-L. The City's *home* of classic rock-n-roll."

Tez reaches over and turns on the cued turn table. The sounds of eerie wind blowing fills the radio's studio. The wind is accompanied by a low and soft sounding bell or chime. Then, a pipe organ begins a mournful dirge. "I'm off to a *Funeral for a Friend..."*

"Alright, guys. This isn't funny anymore." Melissa stands blindfolded outside of her house facing the closed front door. She wears a black dress, nice looking and not so much Gothic. The thin, dark fabric is perfect for the midmorning's warming sun. Melissa's true self is returning, combining her pair of previous pair of personalities into one.

Along the driveway, neither her older model, black Mercedes nor her psychic pick-up truck and camper are seen. Instead, a more modern, black Mercedes conversion van. Painted on the side;

Madam Melissa
Fortune Telling & Tarot Cards

"Are you ready to go inside?" Jon playfully asks. He stands to one side of her wearing a simple black T-shirt, black jeans and black boots. On the opposite side of Melissa, Rafe is similarly dressed and tenderly holds onto her arm.

Now members of the alternative family, T-Bone and Mark, also in mismatched dark attire, stand slightly behind Jon and Rafe. They appear anxious as if wanting to shove Melissa through the front door. "Here we go!" Rafe announces as he reaches for the brass knob and flings the front door open.

Jon, Rafe, Mark and T-Bone guide Melissa in through the entryway, slightly turns her and pauses between the living room and dining room. Jon reaches up and quickly removes Melissa's blindfold. "It's the least we could do for trashing your house," Jon apologetically says.

Melissa stands there in awe. Her jaw drops open. Melissa's entire house has been repaired, repainted and refurnished. Her residence no longer has two separate identities. One light above and one dark below but one complete and drastically different than before.

In the center of the living room, a zebra print couch with giraffe looking throw pillows. The loveseat is covered with a cheetah design with black and orange striped, tiger throw pillows.

The thick sheets of glass of the coffee table and matching end tables are supported with bamboo stands. Similar bamboo drapes hang off to the sides of the many windows. Lush, potted trees and shrubs fill in the corners, completing the Asian forest environment. Melissa's living room is a reincarnation of her alter's original, mountainous habitat.

Melissa smiles as she continues to soak everything in. Suddenly, she turns and draws her attention to the freshly painted hearth. Melissa feels at lease. Resting on the shelf above the fireplace, the framed, charred picture of her younger self, her mother and father.

Melissa slowly wanders through her freshly decorated living room, touching everything like a child in a toy store. She makes her way toward the hearth and takes the framed picture in hand. "I hope you like it," Jon says from the entryway.

"I love it, guys." Melissa smiles and looks upon the boyish faces of the rock and roll band. Rafe approaches her from the side and tenderly places his hand on her shoulder.

"I hate to be the party-pooper," Rafe says in a low voice. "It's getting late. We have to get goin'..."

"Hello? Can you hear me?" Larry asks loudly into the mounted microphone of his car phone. He's dressed in his usual business suit however in more darker colors.

With Sonja sitting next to him and Jay in the backseat, Larry continues to steer his sports car south along the 99 Highway. From the corner of his eye, he sees The Space Needle passing by from the edge of The City.

Sonja's black dress flutters with the passing wind blowing in through the rolled down passenger window. Despite the circumstances, Jay appears quite content and happy. He's never had a new suit and tie before. "Hello? Are you still there?" Larry asks.

"Yes, Lawrence. I'm here." The feminine voice sounds kind and gentle. Sonja gives Larry a puzzling look.

"*Lawrence*?" Sonja's quiet lips seem to be asking. Larry playfully winks at Sonja then refocuses his attention on the road.

"How's your suite? Do you have everything you need?"

"Yes, it's just fabulous." The feminine voice is slightly distracted with a rustling noise in the background. "Where are you, Lawrence?"

"We're right on schedule. I'm about to turn off to Bell Street Pier now."

"So, the plan's still for six tonight?"

"Yeah, we should be back by six o'clock."

"Talk to you soon. Bye."

"Bye." Larry reaches up and flips off the mounted microphone. He casually glances over toward Sonja. She has a slightly miffed expression on her face. "What?"

"I'll give you one thing, *Lawrence*. You've got brass ones."

"Whatta mean by that?"

"Confirming a rendezvous with a globetrotting girlfriend with me sitting right here."

"It's not like that." Larry fumbles for an explanation. "Well, it is and it isn't."

"Is it a date or not?"

"Yes, it's a date." Larry pauses a moment as a devilish smile rolls across his lips. "Just not for me..."

The luxury yacht cuts across the rolling water of the Pacific Ocean. The sleek, multi leveled ship continues at a moderate speed with no captain at the helm. The autopilot has been engaged for nearly an hour.

The outer decks of the vessel are absent of all life. The standing crew of twenty-five is nowhere to be seen. It's as if the ghost ship was on a rogue mission into the unknown. Along the outer hull on opposite sides of the bow, the vessel's name is seen;

PLAUGUS II
MANCINI PHARMACEUTICALS, INC.

The upper two levels of the ship are mysteriously quiet. Along the top deck, there is no one occupying the jacuzzi or pool with a customized jet stream. Along the stern of the bridge deck below, a circular landing pad and helicopter appears.

From the outer windows and portholes of the owner's deck, there is no movement from inside. The panes of glass are filled with images of the bright afternoon sun, the unusual cloudless sky and the passing surface of the ocean. Then, skimming the surface of the water, just beyond the wake of the yacht, a dorsal fin appears.

The dolphin effortlessly swims along, keeping pace with the luxury vessel. The warm blooded creature lets out a series of clicks, letting the manta ray know his position.

The large manta ray seems to be flying through the ocean, it's watery surroundings part as if clouds among the sky. The dolphin and manta ray continue along the wake of the vessel in a somewhat jetfighter, missing man formation.

The expression of the dolphin is saddened. His large, dark colored eyes seem to be weeping, attempting to carry on without her. "*Come with me*," he thinks to himself. *"Come sail away with me..."*

The manta ray and the dolphin exchange a brief glance with each other. They focus their attention to the churning water of the luxury yacht. For a split second, they see the image of a phantom mermaid swimming along side of them. Kaleen smiles as she futilely reaches out to touch the dolphin.

As the dolphin banks inward to swim toward her, Kaleen vanishes. Her tender touch and loving smile is all that remains in his memory. The warm blooded mammal and his human counterpart will have to find away to go on without her.

Dante's hooves carefully stomp across the wooden planks of the bow of the main deck. He is in his Arian form with his full set of curved, bighorn antlers and lower Pan-like extremities. As if he were cradling a newborn baby, he holds onto Kaleen's colorful urn.

As he approaches the outer railing of the deck, Dante pauses and looks up into the sky. The condor circles several times and lets out a squawk. The condor slows its flapping wings and glides along the surface of the ocean, joining the dolphin and manta ray.

From the aft, sliding glass doors, the four members of the rock and roll band appear. Jon, Rafe, T-Bone and Mark have manipulated their transformation and appear in an upright manner. They have retained their inner human consciousness. However outward, their animalistic features are dominant.

The wolf, the hyena and the warthog approach the railing and look out beyond the sea. The dorsal fin of the dolphin and the extended tail of the manta ray continues to swim through the ocean. The condor glides across the ocean's surface above the pair of aquatic creatures.

From the opened glass sliding doors, the cheetah and the panda appear. The pair of felines are apparently close, drawn affectionately together. They too approach the railing. "Great," Dante mumbles. "You two will have interesting kids."

Walking on all fours, the tiger, lioness and the tigon make their way out onto the deck. The black panther reluctantly follows behind as the small group of felines appear intimidated by the surrounding body of water.

Dante leads the rest of the group down the stairs to the aft, lower deck. The platform is usually accessed for ocean swimming and a landing for scuba diving. He lowers his head a moment, staring blankly at the lavender and purple urn.

The wolf, hyena, cheetah, panda and warthog exchange mournful looks. They respectfully nod at Dante who removes the round lid of the urn.

He looks up and over his shoulder to see the tiger, lioness, tigon and black panther likewise nod at him. Dante carefully steps to the edge of the landing and respectfully pours out Kaleen's ashes into the water;

The felines collectively roar -
The wolf howls -
The hyena cackles -
The warthog snorts -
The panda growls -
The condor high above caws -
As for Dante, he simply lowers his head...

As the manta ray swims along the ocean floor, he passes over an occasional lobster and a scampering crab. The large relative to a shark slows his massive pectoral fins, ceasing his flapping motion.

The flattened fish glides through the water of The Sound, effortlessly floating to the surface. His extended tail begins to shrink in size, shortening in length until disappearing into the grey colored flesh-like lower torso.

The aerodynamic shape of the manta ray continues to mutate and transform, becoming smaller and narrower in size. The grey leathery outer surface transcends to more of a pale texture, more human than not.

From the main body of the manta ray, extremities begin to appear and take shape. Gordon's legs and feet kick through the chilly water. His arms swim in a breaststroke fashion, taking him to the surface.

In his completed human form, Gordon gasps for air as his head floats along the surface of the water like a buoy. He scans the water for any signs of vessels or onlookers. There are none. Off in the distance along the shore, he sees his home and back porch.

The wooded tree line along The Sound is a welcoming sight. The amber colors of the setting sun dance across the sky. It's a little after six o'clock in the evening.

Gordon finds his footing as the water becomes more shallow. Taking a few final strokes through the water, he stands and trudges his way toward the rocky shore. As if he's momentarily confused what species he has become, Gordon shakes the water from his back and shoulders as a wet dog.

It takes a moment for Gordon to readjust his manta ray's aquatic eyesight to his present human form. At first, he squints. Along the back deck of his house, a shadowy image is seen. The outline of the frame is small and feminine in nature. There is something familiar about the petite, dark skinned woman.

Gordon wades through the water, now splashing below his knees. He draws closer and closer to the edge of his back porch. Gordon smiles at her. She has aged very well over the years.

Appearing from the opened sliding glass door, a handsome man appears from the shadows. He has a solid frame and sturdy shoulders. His striking features are a complimented blend of his parents.

The man is several inches taller than his mother. He stands next to her as she turns and slightly waves to Gordon. Looking over the wooden handrailing of the back porch, the man respectfully nods at Gordon as the retired professor continues to approach. The man smiles, "Hello, father..."